Longarm backed up until he was touching the wall, his mind racing to find a way out of this fix without being carved up like a turkey on Thanksgiving. His Winchester stood in a corner, well out of reach even if he'd had the time to chamber a shell. He had nothing with which to protect himself from the arc of the blade when it came at him.

He jumped over to the dressing table just as his adversary prepared to lunge. Longarm grabbed the glass lamp, the only thing within reach, and threw it as hard as he could toward the stranger's face.

The assassin tried to duck—because it was dark he didn't see it coming until it was too late. First the glass globe hit his forehead, shattering, then the coal oil tank broke against his arm and fire erupted in a giant orange ball down the front of his coat and in his scraggly hair.

The stranger staggered back, spreading fire when he did, as oil dripped to the floor. He screamed and pawed at his flaming beard. He wheeled toward the window, his head and chest and legs engulfed in flames and dove through the glass headfirst. He plummeted out into the darkness with a strangled scream and fell to the street below . . .

DON'T MISS THESE
ALL-ACTION WESTERN SERIES
FROM THE BERKLEY PUBLISHING GROUP

THE GUNSMITH by J. R. Roberts

Clint Adams was a legend among lawmen, outlaws, and ladies. They called him . . . the Gunsmith.

LONGARM by Tabor Evans

The popular long-running series about U.S. Deputy Marshal Long—his life, his loves, his fight for justice.

SLOCUM by Jake Logan

Today's longest-running action Western. John Slocum rides a deadly trail of hot blood and cold steel.

BUSHWHACKERS by B. J. Lanagan

An action-packed series by the creators of Longarm! The rousing adventures of the most brutal gang of cutthroats ever assembled—Quantrill's Raiders.

DIAMONDBACK by Guy Brewer

Dex Yancey is Diamondback, a southern gentleman turned con man when his brother cheats him out of the family fortune. Ladies love him. Gamblers hate him. But nobody pulls one over on Dex . . .

WILDGUN by Jack Hanson

Will Barlow's continuing search for his daughter, kidnapped by the Blackfeet Indians who slaughtered the rest of his family.

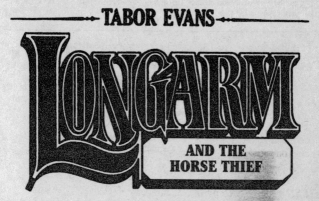

TABOR EVANS

LONGARM

AND THE HORSE THIEF

JOVE BOOKS, NEW YORK

LONGARM AND THE HORSE THIEF

A Jove Book / published by arrangement with
the author

PRINTING HISTORY
Jove edition / April 2001

All rights reserved.
Copyright © 2001 by Penguin Putnam Inc.
This book, or parts thereof, may not be reproduced in
any form without permission.
For information address: The Berkley Publishing Group,
a division of Penguin Putnam Inc.,
375 Hudson Street, New York, New York 10014.

The Penguin Putnam Inc. World Wide Web site address is
http://www.penguinputnam.com

ISBN: 0-515-13046-X

A JOVE BOOK®
Jove Books are published by The Berkley Publishing Group,
a division of Penguin Putnam Inc.,
375 Hudson Street, New York, New York 10014.
JOVE and the "J" design
are trademarks belonging to Penguin Putnam Inc.

PRINTED IN THE UNITED STATES OF AMERICA

10 9 8 7 6 5 4 3 2 1

Chapter 1

Custis Long stared down at the woman. She was half drunk and half naked, only her corset covering the ample charms of her silky body.

"So that's the way you want it?" Longarm asked, a slow smile crossing his face.

"I want it any way you'll give it to me," Georgia replied in a husky voice.

"You speak plain English. I like that in a woman," he said, removing his flat-brim hat.

"Just give it to me now," she said, tracing a fingertip through her crotch. "I'm ready."

"I'm askin' you again. Tell me about Henry Starr."

"I don't want to talk about another man when I'm with you, Custis."

"I just need to know where he is."

"I don't know where he is now. What does it matter? Hand me the bottle of wine."

Longarm took the bottle of burgundy from a washstand beside the bed and gave it to Georgia. "I need to talk to Henry," he said.

Georgia drank a generous gulp of wine. "What do you need to talk to him about?"

"A horse."

"A horse? Henry doesn't own but one or two horses, as far as I know."

"This one was stolen."

"Henry isn't a horse thief. He's shot a few folks now and then, but it was only when he had to. He's a good man, gentle with a lady. He told me he had to shoot a couple of fellas way back last fall. He said it wasn't his fault, that they pulled guns on him."

"I don't care about who he shot," Longarm lied, with a warrant in his coat pocket for Henry Starr's arrest for the murder of Bill Sims. "I'm only interested in getting the horse back to its rightful owner." He stubbed out his cheroot in an ashtray, feeling his erection pulse.

"You damn near sound like a lawman," Georgia said after a second swallow of burgundy.

Longarm showed her his badge.

She raised a brow. "It's just a damn horse," Georgia complained, curling her long legs underneath her. "How come you can't put your mind on me for a while?"

"My mind is on you. I was only asking about Henry Starr and the horse because the barkeep downstairs said you knew him, that you kept company with him."

"Sometimes. When he's in town."

Longarm sleeved out of his coat, hanging it on a wooden peg near the door to Georgia's upstairs room. He unbuckled his gunbelt and hung his Colt .44 over the rear bedpost, still within easy reach.

Georgia smiled. "I can see that swelling inside the right pants leg of your denims. It looks like you've got a really big cock."

2

"I've been told it's adequate," he responded, beginning to unbutton his fly. "Haven't had many complaints about the size of it."

"It looks big," Georgia said, unlacing the top of her corset strings. "I like big cocks. Little cocks, and short cocks, don't satisfy me."

Longarm opened the last brass fastener on his jeans and his stiff member pulsed out, a thick cord of manhood few women he'd known could take easily.

"Will this one do?" he asked, opening the buttons on his bib-front blue shirt.

"My goodness," Georgia sighed, staring at the length and breadth of his engorged prick. "I never dreamed it would be *that* big."

"Tell me where I can find Henry Starr," Longarm said as he shucked off his shirt, remembering his duty as a United States deputy marshal . . . and the things he was forced to do in the line of duty.

"Indian Territory," Georgia whispered, her gaze fixed on his cock.

"Where in Indian Territory?" Longarm asked, sitting on the edge of the bed to take off his boots and pants. "It's a helluva big place."

"On the Cimarron River. I'll tell you how to get there, but you can't tell him that I told you where to find him," Georgia said, reaching for Longarm's throbbing prick.

"I just want to find the horse," Longarm said as his balls began to rise. "Tell me what part of the Cimarron to ride when I go looking for the horse."

Georgia bent over him and put the tip of his cock in her hot wet mouth, ending any chance he had of getting the information he wanted . . . for now.

"It's so big," Georgia mumbled, running her tongue over the glans of his prick.

Longarm decided to wait until he'd satisfied Georgia's urges before he pressed her for more details as to the whereabouts of Henry Starr.

"Please, Custis," she moaned. "Don't make me wait any longer."

"I need a bath first," he said. "I've been on the back of a horse for over a week."

"I don't care," Georgia whimpered. "Just lie down between my legs."

"I still need that bath."

Georgia pushed down her corset and turned to meet him as she came off the bed. She seemed to revel in the way Longarm's eyes roamed over her naked body.

"Like what you see?" she asked playfully.

"I love it. You're a beautiful woman."

Her skin was fair, milky. Her breasts were not overly large, but they were firm, riding high upon her youthful chest. Her pink nipples were hardening under Longarm's stare.

From there his eyes roamed down to her flat belly and to the slight mound between her thighs.

"Nice," he said.

Her legs were just as lovely, long and muscular.

Georgia turned, giving him a long view of her backside as well. As she bent over to pick up her fallen corset, Longarm's pulse began hammering.

He inched forward, his shaft rock-hard.

Georgia threw her corset on the bed. She came into his arms, her breasts flattening against his hairy chest.

"I want you, Custis," she said.

4

"I'm available," he told her gently, holding her in his arms.

His mouth dropped onto hers, and her lips opened without hesitation. She moaned.

Georgia allowed him to plunge his tongue deep into her wet mouth. He pressed one hand into her thick hair, while the other slid down her back to her buttocks so that he could pull them against him.

"That's better," he sighed.

"Not enough," she complained. "Put your hand over one of my breasts."

He obliged her, feeling a twisted nipple with a heat of its own between his fingers.

"Harder," Georgia gasped. "I like a little bit of pain with my lovemaking."

He granted her request, pinching the tip of her rosy nipple until she cried out.

"Better?" he asked before he kissed her again.

"Yes. But I want more."

"I'll do my best," Longarm said. "If I could just get this damn stolen horse off my mind, I could concentrate on what we're doing."

She stroked his cock, staring into his eyes. "Henry isn't a horse thief. He told me he had to shoot a couple of fellas a few years ago, over a card game."

"My friend says Henry stole his horse, a good bay Thoroughbred stud. I've got to talk to Starr about getting that horse back. Where does he stay on the Cimarron?"

"I've never been there. All he told me is that it's near an abandoned army post called Camp Houston. Now please, put your big cock in me."

"I've never been one to refuse a lady's request," Longarm replied, trying to recall where Camp Houston was in

Indian Territory. He knew the territory well. Even though he had a beautiful, naked woman lying on the bed in front of him, he had to try to remember his responsibilities as a U.S. deputy marshal. Making matters worse, she was playing with his prick, begging him to put it inside her.

All in the line of duty, he thought.

"Please don't tell Henry I told you where to find him," Georgia said huskily. "He'll get mad at me. He made me swear I wouldn't tell anybody."

"I won't say a word," Longarm promised, tossing his shirt over the back of a chair. Completely naked now, he lay down beside the woman.

She grabbed his member and started jacking it.

"Put it in," she moaned.

He wrapped his arms around her and planted a deep kiss over her mouth.

"Hurry!" Georgia exclaimed when he drew his lips away from hers.

Longarm's mind was elsewhere for the moment, despite the young lovely lying naked before him.

Years ago he had ridden the Cimarron River country looking for an outlaw named Ned Pike. The region around old Camp Houston and Camp Supply was riddled with deep alabaster caves where a man could hide.

"What's the matter, Custis?" Georgia asked.

"Just thinkin' about a few things."

"Why aren't you thinking about me?" she wondered, with her hand around his stiff cock.

"I am, darlin'." He recalled that a small community by the name of Buffalo sat beside the Cimarron, a refuge for men on the run from the law.

"Why don't you put it in me?" Georgia inquired, stroking his manhood even faster than before.

The alabaster caves along the upper Cimarron would be tough to investigate, he knew. "I am gonna put it in you," he told her. "Just give me a minute. I'm still thinkin' about my friend's stolen horse. You haven't told me much that'll help me find the stud."

"You're the only stud I want to talk about. Lie down between my thighs, Custis, and let me take your mind off the horse."

He glanced down at her pink nipples. "I reckon you could do that, if you put your mind to it."

Georgia smiled. "My mind isn't the only thing I'll use to distract you. Now, lie down."

He could see the rolling hills of northwestern Indian Territory as he stretched out on the mattress beside her. He was dedicated to his job as a deputy marshal, but a man had to have some pleasant diversions once in a while.

"Forget about that damn horse," Georgia murmured in his right ear. "Think about me."

"I am. A horse is just a horse."

She pulled him over onto her with her legs spread wide apart. Her fingers guided the head of his cock into the dewy wetness of her honeypot.

"That's better," she purred.

He was still thinking about the alabaster caves along the upper Cimarron when the head of his prick went between the lips of her hungry mound.

Georgia Sloan had a cave that needed exploring. . . .

Chapter 2

Marshal Billy Vail gave Longarm a stern look. Longarm was seated in the chief marshal's office at the Federal Building on Denver's Colfax Avenue to give his superior the report regarding Henry Starr's whereabouts, information he'd gotten from Georgia Sloan last night.

Longarm had gone through the standard banter with Henry in the outer office. Henry was Vail's assistant and he had no love for Custis Long.

"He's waiting for you," Henry had muttered.

The two men just didn't like each other at all.

Longarm was wearing his usual brown tweed suit, white shirt, and string tie, with black stovepipe boots. A Colt .44 with walnut grips rode in the holster that was canted slightly forward on his hip for a cross-draw. Longarm's flat-brimmed Stetson hat was cocked at a rakish angle on his tangle of brown hair, and the tips of his handlebar mustache were freshly waxed. Strangers thought he dressed like something of a dandy, but he didn't care what others thought about him. He wasn't out to win a popularity contest.

"He's waiting for you," Henry had said in his nasal voice.

"He doesn't mind waiting for me," Longarm told the pasty-faced clerk.

Longarm lit a rum-soaked cheroot and blew the smoke in Henry's direction before he went into Billy's office, slamming the door behind him to further irritate Henry.

Chief Marshal Vail, now plump and pink after a number of years behind a desk, glanced up from a sheaf of papers, pushing his spectacles higher on his nose. " 'Bout time you got here," he said. "We try to keep regular office hours round here, Custis, but I reckon you know that by now, since I've been tellin you the same thing for years."

"I know, Billy," Longarm replied, lowering himself into the old red leather chair that sat in front of Vail's desk. He aimed his cheroot at the banjo clock on the wall of the office. "It's only four o'clock. I've been working on the Henry Starr case and I needed to get all the information I could from a woman by the name of Georgia Sloan. She knows Starr, and she told me where I might find him."

"Is information the only thing you got from her?" Marshal Vail wanted to know.

"Mostly."

"Like hell," Vail snapped. He picked up a piece of paper and put it in front of Longarm. "Read this," he added, reaching into his upper desk drawer for a bottle of brandy and a pair of crystal glasses.

Longarm took the paper and read it, a quote from a newspaper in Fort Smith.

Judge Isaac Parker, known as the "Hanging Judge" for the number of men he'd sent to the gallows, had ordered that Henry Starr be hanged, according to the story Marshal Vail had just given him.

"Starr was defiant," the news report said. "He looked Judge Parker in the eye and said, 'Don't try to stare me down, old Nero. I've looked many a better man than you in the eye. Cut out the rot and save your wind for your next victim. If I am a monster, you are a fiend, for I have put only one man to death, while almost as many men have been slaughtered by your jawbone as Samson slew with the jawbone of that other historic ass. I don't know how you sleep at night.'

"Henry Starr then insisted he didn't get a fair shake when he was arrested in Indian Territory by federal marshals on a stolen horse. He later escaped from the Fort Smith jail, and his whereabouts are unknown at this time. It has been reported that Starr had killed several men in Colorado over a card game, but this has not yet been verified by authorities. More facts will be uncovered."

Longarm glanced up. Marshal Vail was staring holes through him as he handed him a glass of brandy.

"Did you find out where Starr is?" Vail asked.

"I've got a pretty good idea where to look." Longarm took the glass and drained it, holding it forth to request refill.

After a silence, Vail asked, "Will you tell me where the hell that might be, Custis?" He poured another generous glass of brandy for both of them.

"Down in Indian Territory along the upper Cimarron River, near an old abandoned army post called Camp Houston. I know where it is."

"That may be out of our jurisdiction. I'll have to do some checking."

"The murder of Sims and the horse theft took place down in Pueblo," Longarm reminded him. "That's damn sure our jurisdiction and you know it."

"Not many lawmen of any kind in the northwest part of the Indian Nations, if that's where he's hiding," Vail said, a sour expression on his face. "Can you find him?"

"I think so. I know that country pretty well, but it's full of caves where a man could hide damn near forever if he knows what he's doing."

"How long do you figure it will take?"

"I've got no idea. That's empty land. I'll have to do a bit of nosin' around. There's Kiowas and Northern Comanches all over. They ain't too friendly when a white man comes along askin' questions."

"Maybe we should turn this over to the army," Billy wondered out loud.

"The army couldn't find its ass with both hands and you know it," Longarm said. "If you want Henry Starr back in jail, I'd better go after him myself."

Vail sighed. "Seems like a waste of the taxpayers' money to look for just one man."

"Depends on how bad the government wants him."

"He's a killer. That puts him right at the top of our wanted list since he's crossed out of the state. You should know that by now."

"I think I can find him. The woman sounded pretty sure of what she told me."

"Get the supplies you need," Vail said. "I'll have Henry write you a voucher."

Longarm tossed the piece of paper back on top of Marshal Vail's desk.

"Stay in touch with me," Vail said. "Send me a wire now and then."

"I'll leave at first light," Longarm said, standing up before he stuck his cheroot back between his teeth. "I'll keep you posted, Billy."

Vail gave him a sideways grin. "What did the woman look like, this Georgia Sloan?"

"Pretty. About twenty or so."

"I knew it. I've never known you to spend much time with ugly women."

"She knows Henry Starr, Billy. I was only doin' my job the way I figured you wanted me to."

"Like hell!" Vail spat in a good-natured way. "Sleeping with an informant isn't part of your job."

"It was the only way I could get her to talk to me. She wouldn't give me anything I could use until I got her clothes off."

"You're a disgrace to the federal marshals service, Custis. I ought'a suspend you without pay."

"You told me to find Henry Starr. I stayed up all night gettin' information about where to find him."

Vail waved him away. "Get out of here, Custis, before I change my mind. And remember to keep in touch with me while you're down in Indian Territory."

Longarm strolled out on Colfax Avenue, remembering another woman who had given him valuable leads to help solve a case. . . .

• • •

Lady Margaret Wingate had lain facedown on the big, soft four-poster bed and writhed her naked hips back and forth.

"Punish me, Custis," she had said at the time, gasping into the pillow she was clutching in a frenzy. "Now, my darling. Hurry! And don't spare the lash!"

Longarm looked down at the short whip he was holding in his right hand. He was naked, just like Lady Margaret, and the sight of her unadorned blond loveliness wiggling around on the bed had a definite effect on him. His manhood was standing at attention, a long, thick, heavy pole of flesh that was ready, willing, and able to plunge into the pink slit that winked invitingly at him from between her thighs. Warm yellow lamplight reflected off the dewy droplets of moisture that beaded the triangle of fine-spun blond hair adjacent to the cleft of her femininity.

Lady Margaret wasn't interested in the normal sort of romping. It took something else to get her womanly passions fired up.

"Please, Custis," she moaned softly. "Don't make me wait any longer."

With a sigh, Longarm looked from her to the whip and back again. Then he lifted it, poised to strike the first blow across her buttocks.

He now wondered how the hell he got himself into messes like that in the line of duty. How could he make Billy Vail understand that he'd had no choice but to take Georgia to bed in order to get a solid lead on Henry Starr? Or to use a whip on Lady Margaret? None of which look good in an official report.

He had gone above and beyond the call of duty with

Emmaline in the Briarcliff Manor case, and that was one of the strangest assignments he'd ever taken on while wearing a U.S. marshal's badge. Longarm had managed not to gape at Emmaline the second time he saw her, not wanting to look like a damned fool with his tongue hanging out.

"Who the hell would have figured a health retreat showing up in the Colorado mountains?" he asked himself, ambling down a chilly boardwalk along Colfax Avenue, lost in old memories he wished he could forget.

Mineral baths and an Englishman named Sir Alfred Brundage, erecting a health spa in the Trinidad Mountains of Colorado. A U.S. Senator's son, Mark Hanley, and a European from Heidelberg named Dr. Ulrich Ganz.

"What a case that was," he whispered, turning down a side street for his rented rooms.

He had barely been able to save the lives of the Senator's son and the doctor . . . it had taken plenty of hot lead to discourage the men who wanted them dead.

He thought about Georgia. Had she told him the truth about where to find Henry Starr? He was about to make a long ride down to the Cimarron River for nothing if she'd been lying to him about Starr and his hideout.

He couldn't help remembering Emmaline as he headed for his room. There were similarities between her and Georgia.

He'd stared at Emmaline. He couldn't help the reaction. It wasn't every day that a gal who seemed to be the picture of fresh-faced innocence asked him to murder someone for her.

"Oh, dear," she said. "You took me seriously, didn't you?"

15

"You sounded pretty serious," he said.

"It's this dreadful sense of humor of mine. As far back as I can recall, I've enjoyed shocking people."

She placed a hand on his arm, the way Georgia did when they first met, her touch light, almost like that of a bird.

"But I'm telling you the truth," she told him. "A man is following me and I'm certain he means me no good. I'm asking you to help me."

"Let me get this straight," Longarm said. "You talked to me because you think I look like I can handle this gent who's causing you trouble?"

"Well, that certainly helped me make my decision, but you seemed to be the most handsome, interesting man in this railroad car."

"In that case," Longarm said dryly, "I reckon I can help you. Where is this hombre?"

The door at the rear of the car opened, and Emmaline threw a quick glance over her shoulder. Longarm heard her sharply in-drawn breath.

"Here he comes now."

"Are you sure?"

"I'm certain he's been searching the cars for me ever since we left Denver," Emmaline replied.

It had been the beginning of a long adventure for Long-arm, one that almost cost him his life.

He pondered the possibility that meeting Georgia Sloan was about to lead him down the same dangerous pathway in his search for Henry Starr.

Chapter 3

Longarm had been on the trail into Indian Territory for two days, following the Cimarron.

Camp Houston was upriver, more than five miles from the tiny community of Buffalo. Someone had put a torch to parts of the log walls. Longarm could see the charred remains from a distance.

He studied the ruins from the shade of a big red oak tree on a hilltop more than a mile from the fort, until he was satisfied that the place was empty.

He spoke to the old fur trapper he'd met on the trail, Claude Jones. "Appears it's abandoned, like you said." He remained motionless in the saddle, not quite convinced after what Georgia had told him. He would wait for a spell until he felt it was safe to move closer.

"I ain't hardly ever wrong," the old man said.

Clouds scudded across a deep blue sky.

"It ain't very big," the trapper added. "You'd know it if somebody was there . . . you'd see smoke, a horse or a mule, somethin'."

"Can't figure what it's doing way out here in the middle of nowhere," Longarm said.

"It was part of a chain of outposts when the army was tryin' to quiet the Indian troubles. This used to be Kiowa huntin' range."

"I know," Longarm replied. "It was dangerous as hell back then to cross this country."

"Camp Supply is south of here. It was about the same size as Houston."

"I remember it."

"A few folks have settled there at Supply, tryin' to make a town out of it, only the army ain't there no more. Some ranchers run cattle on them prairies. I 'spect that's where you'll find ol' Henry, if he wants to be found. He's a damn Cherokee an' he's smart. He knows where to hide, when to run, an' he don't do no crimes close to where he lives."

"He hides in the caves?" Longarm suggested.

"Most likely. It'd take a man ten years to search every one of them alabaster caverns."

"I don't have that much time."

"Then you'll have to lure him out of his hidin' place some way or another. Won't be easy."

"I'm obliged for what you've shown me. I'll go the rest of the way alone."

Longarm reached in his vest pocket and handed Jones a ten-dollar gold piece.

"That's a helluva lot of money, mister."

"You earned it," Longarm said.

He rode off the hill, leaving the old man and his mule behind as he aimed for the remnants of Camp Houston. A knot of red oaks lay between him and the fort, where he intended to take a bit more time studying things before

18

he rode in. This was the kind of wide-open land where almost anyone could be hiding, and only a fool would make a target of himself where there wasn't any cover.

He crossed the shallow river, only belly-deep on his horse this time of year, and gave the bay time to drink its fill before he rode on.

The land had changed since he'd left the southeastern corner of Colorado, becoming flatter, like the hill country called the Flints up in Kansas, where a man could ride for fifty miles without finding a water hole.

He grinned when he remembered what someone told him about Kansas. There were three kinds of suns in Kansas: the sun in the sky, sunflowers, and sons of bitches.

Henry Starr would fall into the latter category.

For some odd reason, his thoughts drifted back to Emmaline, for she was one of the most beautiful women he'd ever taken to bed. . . .

He had stripped down to his birthday suit while she was in the other room of the mineral bathhouse. Emmaline was taking a bath, and he could hear her splashing in a tub at the spa, enjoying herself.

"Are you ready, Custis?" he heard her ask from the other side of the doorway.

Longarm hesitated. He wasn't sure if he was ready or not, but he had never been plagued with any sort of false modesty in situations like this.

He took a deep breath, swung the door wide open, and stepped out, naked as a jaybird.

Emmaline was in one of the mineral bath pools. The hot water was bubbling and swirling, and it covered her body for the most part, leaving only the upper swells of her breasts bare for him to see.

19

She watched Longarm with an appreciative smile on her face as he strode toward the pool.

"You're quite an impressive specimen of the male animal," she said.

"Much obliged," he replied, not knowing what else to say under the circumstances.

He reached the edge of the pool and stepped down into the murky water, lowering one foot into it rather tentatively. It was hot, all right, but not so hot that he couldn't stand the temperature.

The pool was roughly circular and about fifteen feet in diameter. Steps had been hewn out of the rock, so that Longarm was able to climb easily into the pool. The steps also served as benches, so he lowered himself onto the one where Emmaline was sitting. He was quite a bit taller than she was, so more of his chest stuck out of the water.

Emmaline slid over so that her bare hip was pressed against his.

"Isn't this wonderful?" she asked. "So soothing, like the water just washes away all your troubles."

Longarm had to admit that it felt pretty good. He leaned back, draping one arm along the edge of the pool and the other around Emmaline's shoulders. He closed his eyes for a moment, allowing himself to relax.

Then he stiffened as she moved her hand under the water and closed her fingers around his cock.

His shaft instantly began to harden. Longarm started to turn toward Emmaline, but she stopped him by putting her other hand on his chest.

"No, don't move," she whispered. "Just sit there and let me do this for you."

"Don't hardly seem fair to let you do all the work," said Longarm.

"Don't worry, you'll have plenty of opportunity to reciprocate."

Longarm planned to reciprocate, all right—and more than once if he got the chance.

He closed his eyes again as she began sliding her palm up and down his rigid pole. The minerals in the pool seemed to make it more slippery, so Emmaline's fingers glided with maddening smoothness along Longarm's heated flesh.

She leaned over so her mouth could fasten over his right nipple. She tongued it as it grew hard.

Longarm sat there and luxuriated in the sensations she was creating within him. His shaft throbbed and grew to an arching hardness.

He felt Emmaline shift around, but he didn't open his eyes to see what she was doing. He figured he would find out soon enough.

She straddled him, her fingers skillfully guiding his erection to the slick opening between her thighs. With a teasing slowness that brought a groan from him, she lowered herself onto his cock, sheathing it inside her an inch at a time.

Gradually, Longarm filled her, as he had lovely Georgia in Denver, and a small gasp escaped his lips.

He rode toward the cluster of trees south of Camp Houston with Emmaline still on his mind. And sweet Georgia. But it was time now to be on the lookout for a murderer, and he had to wipe all those pleasant thoughts from his head.

This part of Indian Territory was virtually lawless, and empty. A few ranchers and sodbusters made attempts to

21

settle the land in this panhandle area, but only the hardiest and most determined survived.

Longarm surveyed the fort ruins from a closer vantage point. He saw nothing to cause alarm.

Georgia had given him a location. However, Longarm felt sure Starr would be hiding in the alabaster cave area just south of the ruins.

"This would be too easy to find," he said aloud.

A man with a price on his head wouldn't camp out in the open at a place like this.

Longarm recalled the alabaster caverns. Deep tunnels on both sides of old streambeds and ravines leading down to the river.

Alabaster, Longarm remembered, was a white rock, a form of mineral. Some of it was clear, looking almost like glass in the right light. This was also gypsum country, and a man had to be careful about drinking the water around here. It would give a man one hell of a bellyache, and enough of it would kill a horse or a cow.

A twisting ravine ran off to the southwest. It was choked with brush, the best cover Longarm could find to make his slow approach toward the fort ruins.

He was leaving the tree-studded knob when he drew rein sharply. Three men were riding over the crest of a hill toward Camp Houston.

"Wonder who the hell . . ."

He might have gotten lucky. One of the men could be Henry Starr.

He reined into the ravine to stay off the skyline, his gaze still fixed on the three riders. One was leading a pack mule.

"I'd rather be lucky than good," he said softly to himself, although he didn't believe in luck. Men made their own luck most of the time.

He heard distant voices.

"Stay here, Leon. I seen some tracks a while back. Me an' Jack will check things over. A man can't be too careful round here."

"I'll wait," the man called Leon said, his voice carrying on a gentle breeze so that Longarm had no trouble hearing him from a distance.

"There could still be some goddamn Injuns in this neck of the woods."

"We'll ride in slow from the front an' the back. I don't smell no wood smoke, so I don't figure there's anybody here or we'd smell a campfire."

"Pays to be careful," another said.

Longarm swung down out of his saddle to watch what was going on. The direction of the wind brought him the men's voices loud and clear, and they hadn't noticed him.

All three men had rifles booted to their saddles, but that wasn't enough to make them suspicious in this wild country where a gun was almost a necessity.

"It's all clear, Leon," one man cried. "Don't look like nobody's been here in quite a spell."

The man leading the pack mule urged his horse forward toward the charred ruins of Camp Houston

They won't be with Starr, Longarm thought, but they might know where to find him.

He decided to ride up to the fort after the sun went down, to use darkness as a cover so he wouldn't get his head blown off by a nervous cowboy . . . or an associate of the murderer he was out to find.

Longarm took a pint of whiskey from his saddlebags and settled down behind a clump of brush to wait for darkness. He had plenty of time on his hands.

He wondered about the three cowboys who were making camp at the old fort. If they were from this part of the country they might know Henry Starr, but it would be tricky business getting them to tell him anything about a dangerous outlaw, a killer with a tall reputation.

Sipping whiskey, Longarm waited for the sun to go down. It required patience, finding a wanted man who knew the law was on his trail. Longarm could only hope that the information Georgia Sloan had given him was accurate.

He hobbled his horse in the ravine a few minutes later, and got set to play a waiting game.

"Too risky for a fire," he said, his belly grumbling with hunger. He took a few strips of jerky from his saddlebags and began a meager meal.

Life as a deputy marshal was like this . . . feast and famine, depending upon the circumstances. But getting Henry Starr in irons so he could stand trial for murder made it worth the wait.

Later, as dusk purpled the prairies around him, he lit a cheroot and took the hobbles off his bay. In another hour he could make his way toward the remains of Camp Houston, to find out if any of the three cowboys he'd seen earlier knew where he could find Starr.

Chapter 4

Given time to reflect on a number of things while Long-arm waited for darkness, he sipped whiskey from a vantage point at the crest of the ravine where he could see the fort ruins without showing himself. Sometimes a deputy marshal's job required hours of waiting, and he was used to it by now, although he longed for the comforts of a soft mattress and a feather pillow and a decent meal instead of being stuck out here in a wilderness called Indian Territory.

A campfire had begun to flicker inside the crumbling walls of old Camp Houston as the plains blanketed with nightfall. The breeze that had followed him all day turned colder, causing him to shiver.

The three men who had ridden in with the pack mule were setting up camp for the night. Longarm wondered if they might only be range cowboys drifting toward the next day-wages job. All he had to go on was what Georgia Sloan had told him before he left Denver.

"Billy did this to me," he whispered. "He wanted me

25

out in some goddamn place sleepin' in a bedroll. I'll get even with him one of these days. . . ."

The case involving Lady Margaret Wingate and the castle built by the Englishman down in the Sangre de Cristos had been one of the most difficult and delicate jobs to come across Billy Vail's desk at the time.

Longarm chuckled. After the investigation was wrapped up, he'd gone to Billy's office to give him a report and ask for a few days off to enjoy himself.

Billy had glared across the room at him when Longarm made the suggestion.

The marshal spoke first. "We generally frown on arresting folks and throwing 'em in jail when we know they're innocent, Custis. What makes you think I'd give you any time off for doing something like that?"

Longarm puffed on his cigar and blew out a cloud of thick smoke. "I reckon you're talking about the reverend, aren't you, Billy?"

"He claims you mistreated him something fierce," Billy snapped.

Longarm shrugged. "I figured it was all for a good cause. I had to make Oscar and Jed think they were in the clear so that I could get the evidence I needed against 'em. Of course, not everything worked out exactly the way I hoped it would. This sort of thing happens sometimes."

"But Sir Alfred's safe," said Billy, "and the fellas who were trying to kill him are dead, except for those other two cowboys who took off like a couple of scalded cats when they thought you were coming after them to put them in jail. Right? Tell me I'm right."

"The sheriff down in Trinidad followed their trail for a while, but he said he figured they were still running. Sir

Alfred won't have to worry about them none . . . I can guarantee you that."

Vail made a face, and picked up a pen to scribble something on a paper in front of him. "I suppose that's it then, so get the hell out of here. Take a few days off, but keep me informed as to where you are."

Longarm got out of the chair. "I always try to follow orders, Billy, and you know that." He grinned as he made his way toward the door.

"I'll find a case one of these days, Custis, one that'll keep you from having your way with innocent women and living in a fancy health spa. Just you wait and see. When a tough one comes across my desk, one that'll keep you out in bad weather until your ass freezes off, I'll send you on it."

"I can't wait," Longarm told him.

And now, here he was, crouched on an bleak prairie in the worst part of Indian Territory with nothing but a bottle of whiskey to keep him company.

"You got me this time, Billy," he said under his breath as the sky blackened with night.

Leaving his horse hobbled in the ravine, Longarm started forward in a low crouch to see who was making camp at the fort ruins. One of them might have resembled a man Billy Vail had on a wanted poster in his office, a man who ran guns to the Kiowas by the name of Calvin Dobbs, only Longarm had been too far away to be certain of the man's identity.

He remembered what Billy had said about Dobbs the day the wanted circulars came into the Denver office.

• • •

There was a sheaf of wanted circulars as thick as a man's thumb, and Longarm knew when Billy saw them, he'd be sent off into the wilds of Billy's jurisdiction looking for some of the men listed on the posters.

"Appears there's been some misbehavin' goin' on," Billy said, scowling at the notices. His voice got a certain edge to it when his mind was on business. "You could call it a crime wave, I reckon," he went on. "We've seen some of these names before. Here's Bittercreek Farley again. And Cal Dobbs. I've tangled with him before, when I sent you out to find that girl a couple of years ago when Dobbs was wanted for cattle rustling." Billy grunted. "Dobbs claimed it was his bad eyes, that he couldn't see all those different brands on the beeves. A judge up in Durango offered to buy him some spectacles when he got out of prison, so the same thing wouldn't happen again to honest cattle ranchers."

Longarm got a chuckle out of that. Billy could have a good sense of humor, when he wasn't angry.

Billy continued, thumbing through the posters. "Looks like Dobbs forgot about those eyeglasses. The judge should have hung him."

Longarm watched Billy flip through the notices one at a time.

"Now here's a sorry son of a bitch. Henry Starr. We could have ourselves some real trouble if Starr is in this part of the country. He's a rotten apple. My money says he's down in the Nations, hidin' out with his Cherokee friends. The only time I met the bastard, I did my best to put the fear of God in him, only you can't put the fear of God in a heathen. Starr ain't got no beliefs in nothin', 'cept stealing and killing. What he needs is a hangman's noose around his neck, or a bullet through his heart."

28

"I've got the funny feeling you're going to send me after Starr," Longarm had said.

"Damn right I am," Billy replied, "soon as you can find out where to look for the son of a bitch!"

"I hear there's a soiled dove at one of the cribs off of Colfax who knows him," said Longarm, "but I hadn't heard of him being in town recently."

"Go talk to her. Find out where the son of a bitch is. If he's close by, I want him brought in. Who is this scarlet woman who knows him?"

"Georgia. Georgia Sloan, if I remember right. I can ask around."

"I might have guessed that you'd know every whore in Denver, Custis."

"I've met a few. Also some decent ladies. Hope you'll credit me with that."

"As soon as you meet 'em you defile them. If I could change anything about you, it'd be to teach you how to keep your pants on."

"I'm wearing them now, Billy."

"Thank God for that, or I'd arrest you myself for public exposure of a man's private parts. Now get your ass out of here and find that whore. See if she knows where to look for Henry Starr. I want the son of a bitch in the Denver jail if he's hangin' around here."

Longarm crept toward the remains of Camp Houston with nothing but his Colt .44. If Starr wasn't there with the three men he'd seen earlier, he aimed to ask them some questions and get some straight answers, if they had any information he needed. He wasn't in the mood for bullshit tonight.

Moving upwind so the cowboys' horses wouldn't

catch his scent, he paused when he overheard a conversation going on inside the ruins.

"I say we head up to Kansas."

"How come, Leon?"

"Ain't nearly so many Injuns an' there ain't much law in Kansas."

"The law ain't followin' us. We're free as birds on the wing."

"What the hell do you think, Roy?"

"I ain't so sure 'bout none of this," the man named Roy said.

"You turnin' yellow on us?"

"It's them damn Kiowa renegades that's got me so I can't sleep."

"We ain't seen an Injun in a week, Roy. You've got a bad case of nerves."

"Pass me that bottle of rotgut. It'll help me calm down some."

"How 'bout you, Jack?" the cowboy called Leon asked. "You think we oughta turn north after we cross this damn river an' get our hides from Lone Bear?"

"I sure as hell ain't comfortable in this shithole, like Roy says. Can't hardly sleep. Let's trade these rifles for all the buffalo hides Lone Bear has got, an' then get the hell away from here."

"Kansas suits you?"

"Damn near any place suits me better'n this," Jack said in a tired voice.

"We could lose our hair if this deal don't work right with Lone Bear. A man'd have to be plumb crazy to trust a goddamn Kiowa Injun."

"We'll make a fortune off them hides," Leon said. "There ain't hardly any buffalo left in this country. We

30

can sell 'em for eight dollars apiece to a fur buyer."

"If we live long enough to sell 'em," Roy reminded the other men.

"What the hell's gotten into you, Roy?"

"Could be I'm just gettin' old, but I'm real fond of what little hair I've got. You ever get a close look at a man who's been scalped, Leon?"

"I've seen plenty of 'em. But we ain't gonna get scalped if we promise Lone Bear more rifles an' bullets. Him an' his warriors need 'em."

"I'm nervous about it," Roy replied. "The sumbitch could just take our Winchesters an' kill all three of us. We won't stand a chance against so many redskins if this turns out to be a trick."

"It ain't no trick."

"How the hell can you be so sure?"

"I made the deal myself with Lone Bear a month ago. He needs us if he aims to keep on raidin' ranches. He can't steal no cows without guns an' bullets."

"I never did trust an Injun of no kind," Jack said. "They don't keep their word on nothin'."

"Pass me back that whiskey," Leon said as a sap knot popped in the fire.

"Let's head for Dodge City after we get them buffalo skins," Roy muttered. "Wyatt Earp ain't there no more, or so I hear. I figure we can find us some women there without gettin' our asses throwed in jail."

"Suits me," Leon remarked.

"Count me in too," Jack said. "Now, pass that damn whiskey bottle over here before it runs dry."

Longarm digested what he'd just heard. Looking for a killer like Starr, he'd accidentally run into a bunch of gun

31

traders selling firearms to Kiowa renegades led by an Indian they called Lone Bear.

"Just my luck," Longarm whispered.

There were times, too many of them, where one investigation led to another. He needed to find a telegraph so he could notify Billy.

But with a federal crime being plotted in the remnants of Camp Houston, he had to trail the men with a mule loaded with rifles to the spot where they would be exchanged for buffalo hides. There wasn't time to wire Billy about Longarm's sudden change in plans.

He'd have to go it alone without notifying the Denver office that he was tracking gunrunners and renegade Kiowas. But it was all a part of the job.

Longarm backed away from the fort. It was clear these men intended to spend the night here; thus there was no need to keep an eye on them.

But after dawn, when these galoots headed toward their meeting with Lone Bear and his bunch to provide them with rifles, a U.S. deputy marshal by the name of Custis Parker Long wouldn't be very far behind them.

Chapter 5

Lone Bear, a powerfully built man almost six feet in height, unusually tall for a Kiowa, spoke to the much shorter man wearing denims and a cowboy hat as they watched Camp Houston while astride horses on an inky hilltop near midnight. Five more Kiowa warriors sat quietly on their multicolored Indian ponies just below the knob.

"The white men have come with our rifles," Lone Bear said to Henry Starr. "They have kept their word to us, unlike most white eyes."

"Not yet they haven't," Starr said. "Be careful of a double cross. I know white men. I was raised around them and they can't be trusted."

"We could ride down there now and kill them all," Lone Bear suggested.

"You will need more rifles and bullets, if these men are true to their word."

A doe-eyed Kiowa girl on a pinto pony rode up behind the two men. "There is another white man in the ravine

33

below the river," she said. "He was watching the men in the fort. I saw him again just now."

"The law," Starr said. "Somebody put a lawman on the trail of Leon and his partners. Otherwise, he wouldn't be watching them from hiding."

Lone Bear gave the girl a look. "Are you sure, Tooma? He was watching the fort?"

"Yes. I saw him walk very carefully to a place where he could see the walls. He sat there for a long time, drinking crazy water. Then he went back to his horse and spread out his blankets. He has no fire. He is trying not to be seen by the whites at the fort."

"The law," Starr said again. "I'll slip down there with my knife and kill him. I need four of those rifles for the job we intend to pull at Cache. Like I told you, there's a bank down there that's ripe for the taking . . . no guard, and just one old man who opens the vault. I'm paying you good money for four of those Winchesters and some ammunition. You can have the rest for your braves."

Lone Bear scowled. "We should do nothing to alert the white gun traders that something is wrong. I will send the girl, Tooma, down to this ravine where the white man is camped. She can approach him without causing him alarm. Then, you can kill him."

"I will go," Tooma said, her long black hair hanging in twin braids across her shoulders. She wore a soiled deerskin dress that rode high on her slightly muscular legs when she sat bareback on her pony. She was one of the prettiest girls in the Kiowa tribe, a niece to Lone Bear who had run away from the reservation at Fort Sill in southern Indian Territory when Lone Bear led his renegades off to escape the miserable conditions there. One other woman, Nodemah, had come with them, and she was an experienced warrior.

"It may be dangerous," Lone Bear warned Tooma.

"I will kill him with my knife," she replied.

"I'll be right there close by," Starr promised. "I'll kill the son of a bitch if he tries to hurt you."

"Use no guns," Lone Bear said. "We do not want the white gun traders to suspect anything."

"I'll go alone," Tooma said in a gentle voice, speaking almost perfect English that she'd learned at the Indian school on the reservation. "I can kill him without any help."

"It will be safer if I am there," Starr told her. "We can come up from the caves behind him where my men are waiting. You ride into his camp and say you need some of the white man's money for what is under your dress. If he's any kind of man at all, he'll go for it."

"But I do not want to sleep with him," Tooma protested, looking at Chief Lone Bear.

Starr spoke first. "Don't worry, Tooma. As soon as he gets his pants off, I'll slip up there and cut his throat before he knows what hit him."

"I will send another warrior," Lone Bear said. "Quahip is a good fighter."

"I won't need any damn help, Lone Bear," Starr said. "I can do it alone, with the girl's help. All she has to do is distract him."

"I will send Quahip to watch over her. It is my responsibility, for she is my dead brother's daughter and she has no other family."

"Suit yourself," Starr answered, reining his dun off the top of the hill. He wore white man's clothing and carried a pair of Colt Peacemakers on his hip. "All I care about are those four rifles and some cartridges . . . maybe five or six boxes, so we can take that bank down at Cache. I'll follow the girl and this Quahip, only we damn sure won't need him. I can kill the white bastard all by myself and never make a sound. I'm a Cherokee, in case you've forgotten."

Tooma turned her pinto to follow Starr. Lone Bear motioned to an older warrior on a red roan gelding to go with them as they rode off into the night.

A sixth sense warned Longarm that someone was near. He reached for his Colt Lightning .44 and sat up in his bedroll, blinking sleep from his eyes.

He was almost sure he'd heard a sound, even as deeply as he'd slept.

Longarm looked at his hobbled horse, for a horse's hearing was far keener than a man's. The bay's ears were pricked forward toward the south.

Something's out there, he thought.

Maybe only a wolf or a varmint of some kind, but it paid to be careful. Caution kept a man in his profession alive.

He heard it again, the soft whisper of a horse's hooves moving through tall grass.

"I've got company," he mumbled, tossing his blankets aside to get to his feet quickly.

A black-and-white piebald pinto came slowly up the ravine where he'd made camp. A rider was on its back, but in the dark he couldn't make out any details.

Maybe it's one of those Indians coming to trade for the rifles on that mule at Camp Houston, he thought.

Most Indians would send out a scout or two before they

36

rode into a new place, just to make sure the coast was clear before riding into strange surroundings.

Longarm stepped behind the trunk of a red oak tree to wait for whoever was coming. As far as he could tell, it was just one rider, but he knew there could be a dozen others all around him and he'd be in a fight for his life.

The horse and rider drew closer, only a hundred yards or so from where his bay was hobbled.

In faint light from the stars, the stranger appeared to be an Indian woman. Odd, he reasoned, that she would be alone out here in the middle of the night.

Suddenly, the pinto pony stopped. For a moment there was only silence.

"White man," a soft voice called out.

Longarm glanced around, making sure they were alone before he gave his position away. "I'm right here. What do you want with me?"

"I saw you come. I need money."

"And what do I get for my money," he asked, still wary, watchful.

"You get me. If you want me."

It was a hard proposition to turn down if she was pretty, especially after he'd been on the trail down from Denver for so many days and nights sleeping on hard ground. "Ride closer so I can see what you look like," he told her.

She heeled her pinto toward him.

But Longarm was no stranger to Indian tactics . . . the girl could be a distraction. With his senses keen for the first sign of trouble, he moved away from the tree trunk just enough so the girl could see him in the starlight.

She halted her pony twenty yards away.

"Get down off that horse," Longarm said. "Show me

your hands so I can make sure you're not carrying a gun, or a weapon of some kind."

"I have no weapon," the girl said, sliding easily off the withers of her pony, spreading her palms wide to show she was unarmed.

"Come a little closer," he said.

"Will you shoot me?" she asked.

"I wouldn't want to have to shoot a woman. I hope you won't be the first one to give me a reason."

"I am only looking for money, and some food. My people are hungry on the reservation."

"Are you alone?"

"Yes." She lowered her hands and started walking toward him leading her pinto.

Longarm was still wary. But he could see that the girl was young and pretty.

"What's your name?" he asked when she was less than ten feet away from him.

"Tooma."

"I'm Custis Long," he told her. "It's kinda strange to find a beautiful girl way out here in the middle of nowhere on a night like this."

"I was wondering why you are here," Tooma said, "and why you make no fire."

"Just keepin' an eye on some men camped at the old Camp Houston ruins. I'm lookin' for one man in particular, only he ain't one of them."

"Who are you looking for?" Tooma asked.

"His name doesn't matter. He killed a couple of men up in Colorado."

"Are you a man who wears the star . . . I think it is called a lawman?"

Before Longarm could answer he saw a shadow moving farther down the ravine. He raised his Colt and took careful aim at a man atop a horse. "I thought you said you were alone," he growled.

Tooma lunged toward him, and Longarm saw the glint of a knife blade. He moved quickly behind the red oak trunk, but with his sights set on the horseman he glimpsed in the darkness.

He fired off a quick shot, not certain of his aim. The sound of the gun thundered between the walls of the dry wash. A yelp came from the ravine and the rider toppled off the back of his horse.

At the same instant, Tooma's pony bolted away from the explosion.

"Drop the knife, Tooma," Longarm warned with his pistol in her face.

She stumbled to a halt, but she wouldn't let go of the knife in her fist.

"Don't force me to shoot you," he said, listening to the sounds of two horses running off to the south, wondering if there might be more Indians with Tooma.

Very slowly the Indian girl's shoulders slumped and she let the blade fall to the ground, yet the defiance was there in her eyes.

"Lone Bear will kill you," she spat.

"He can try. Plenty of others have tried before and so far, nobody's been able to get it done, although there've been some close calls."

Then the girl gave herself away when she glanced to the east of Longarm's camp.

"More of your friends out there?" he asked. He cocked his revolver and pointed it straight at Tooma's head. "Lie down on the ground. I'm gonna put cuffs on you before I go looking for your companions. They'll start moving in on me after the gunshot, and I can't have you tryin' to stick a knife in my back while I keep from losing my scalp. And those gun traders heard the shot, so they'll be on the move. Lie down, damn it! Don't force me to put a bullet in you."

Tooma sank to her knees, glaring at him. Longarm walked over to her and picked up her knife.

"That's better, darlin'. Now stay right there while I get a pair of wrist irons out of my saddlebags."

She spat on his pants leg.

"Now, now, sweetheart. No sense in gettin' mad over this until there's a good reason. I won't hurt you if you don't try to hurt me."

"Death to the white eyes!" Tooma said, raising her voice just above a whisper.

With Tooma's knife in his belt, Longarm glanced around him. The sounds made by running horses faded. "I understand why you hate white men," he said. "White men have broken damn near every treaty we ever made with Indian tribes. But I didn't have a damn thing to do with it. Now tell me how many more of your people are out there so I'll know what the odds are against me."

"Find out for yourself!" she snapped. "Your scalp will be hanging from Lone Bear's lodge pole by morning."

"I sure as hell hope not," he answered, moving cautiously to his saddlebags for a pair of handcuffs. "I just got my hair cut up in Denver, an' hadn't planned on having another haircut for a week or two."

Chapter 6

Henry stuck his face into Bill Vail's office. "A marshal by the name of Heck Thomas to see you, sir."

"Send him in," Billy said with a sigh, wondering what had brought his comrade to Denver.

Thomas strode into the office, a barrel-chested man with a handlebar mustache and a stern expression deeply etched into his face. He wore a dark suit and vest, with stovepipe boots in a high state of polish. Underneath his coat he carried a pair of Colt pistols, and he was known for his willingness to use them on lawbreakers.

"Howdy, Billy," he said, offering a calloused hand.

Billy stood up and took the handshake. "Good to see you again, Heck."

"I doubt it," Thomas said, dropping into the red leather chair across Billy's desk. "Seems like nobody's ever happy to see me anymore."

"What brings you?" Billy asked, sitting back down in a hurry.

"Business, as usual."

"I guessed as much."

"Have you got a good deputy available? One you can trust to carry out a tough assignment?"

"Custis Long is off looking for Henry Starr. But he's the man I trust most."

Thomas thumbed back his gray Stetson. "I've heard all about Long and his antics with women. I'd hoped you'd have somebody else."

"Long is good," Billy said. "He gets the job done."

Thomas sighed, resting his hat on his knees. "I intended to look into this affair myself, only Judge Parker left a wire for me at the Denver train station saying he needed me back in Fort Smith at once. I hadn't gotten my valise out of the baggage car before I found out I'm supposed to head back on the next train after I talked to you."

"I can put Custis on the case as soon as he gets back from the Starr investigation. I told him to wire me when he finally located Starr. So far, I haven't heard from him at all."

Thomas stared out an office window overlooking Colfax Avenue for a moment. "We're all running shorthanded. Congress won't give us any more money to hire deputies."

"How well I know," Billy told him.

"Here's the problem," Thomas said, scratching his unshaven chin. "A bunch of redskins have escaped from Fort Sill and they've hit a bunch of ranches just south of the Colorado border."

"How many of 'em?" Billy wondered.

"At least a dozen. Their leader is a Kiowa chief by the name of Lone Bear."

"Any idea where they are now?"

"Headed your way, by the reports. They hit a settlement at Buffalo in Indian Territory, not far from Camp Supply.

They scalped women and children. Ran off with all the livestock. We have to find them. Word is, they're coming across the line to Colorado to pull their raids. Lone Bear was spotted by a stagecoach driver moving north, along the Cimarron. He could wind up in your backyard."

"I'll put Long on it, as soon as I hear from him. Shouldn't be much longer, maybe a day or two."

"He's probably got his pecker buried in some woman, but if that's the best you can do, at least give it a try. Send him down to the border to look for Lone Bear and his bunch. We also got word that an old gunrunner from way back, Calvin Dobbs, is supplying Lone Bear with rifles and ammunition. We need to round this whole bunch up, but it'll be a tough job for just one man. Tell Marshal Long to notify the army at Fort Larned if he finds any of them . . . the gun traders, or those runaway Kiowas. Anything we can use."

"I will. No matter what you've heard about Custis Long, he's a good peace officer."

"The main thing we've gotta do is stop these reservation runaways. Tell Long to use whatever force is necessary. Dobbs has been in and out of prison for a variety of crimes for fifteen years. He's a convicted cow thief, a gun trader, and a whiskey peddler on the reservations."

"I've got a file on Dobbs, Heck. I know all about him and so does Marshal Long."

Thomas nodded. "I've got to catch the next train back to Kansas City and then down to Fort Smith. When Judge Parker says he wants one of his men there, he means it. Put Marshal Long on the case right away. I've got to get back to find out what Judge Parker wants with me."

"I hears he's already hanged nearly seventy men."

"They all needed it. Some of his sentences got overturned by a higher court. A couple of years back, Judge Parker hung six men at the same time. Had the gallows there enlarged so he could string up all six of 'em at once. But they were all convicted killers, so I say it was justice, plain an' simple."

"I read about it in the newspaper," Billy said. "One of them fell through the trapdoor without his head, but his feet were still kickin'."

"I was there. It wasn't a pretty sight, but they all were wanted for murders. They deserved it."

"Must have been one hell of a spectacle, seein' six men die by the rope."

"I've never seen the prison compound so crowded with onlookers, Billy. A couple of kids were out there sellin' lemonade, like it was a damn circus. Nearly a dozen women fainted dead away."

"Judge Parker dishes out stiff justice, Heck."

"I know. I work for him. Big George Maledon is his hangman, an' I'll be damned if he doesn't enjoy his work. He hardly ever says a word to anybody. I'd nearly swear he grins when he sees those trapdoors drop open."

"We handle things a little differently here out of the Denver office."

"You ain't got Judge Isaac Parker looking over your shoulder, or you'd know what I'm up against. Judge Parker believes in fightin' fire with fire."

"I'll get Deputy Long on this search for Lone Bear as soon as I hear from him, Heck. That's all I can promise you. And I'll tell him to keep an eye out for gunrunners."

"Good enough," Thomas said, coming stiffly out of the red chair. "I've got to get my ass back to Fort Smith. A gang calling themselves the Daltons is raising hell just north of Fort Smith. Four or five brothers, according to

44

the wire I got. They hit a train just north of the Kansas line and that puts it in our jurisdiction."

Thomas put his hat back on his head and started for the office door. "Tell Marshal Long to notify the army at Fort Larned if he needs backup. They'll be mostly green recruits, but sometimes numbers can be a help."

Marshal Thomas strode out of the office, slamming the door behind him.

Billy rested his face in his hands.

"This is gonna be one of those days where my indigestion is gonna kill me," he said, climbing out of his chair to walk down to Maude's Cafe for a bowl of stew. And, most likely, a bottle of bellyache remedy afterward.

As he entered the outer office where Henry sat at his desk, Billy found a pretty woman waiting for him.

"Marshal Vail," Henry said. "This lady has been waiting to see you, only I didn't want to interrupt you while Marshal Thomas was in your office."

The woman smiled at him. She wore a low-cut yellow dress with a shawl around her shoulders. "Marshal Vail, could I have a word with you?"

"I was just on my way to lunch, ma'am. Can it wait for an hour?"

"I'd rather talk to you now . . . in private."

"May I ask who you are and what this is about?" Billy asked, with his empty stomach rumbling.

"My name is Georgia Sloan, and it has to do with some things I told your deputy, Custis Long."

Billy sighed heavily. "Please come in my office, Miz Sloan." He remembered the name. Georgia Sloan was the prostitute who supposedly had given Custis information to help him find Henry Starr.

He closed the door behind her. "Please have a seat, Miz

Sloan, an' then tell me what's on your mind."

Georgia settled into the red chair, spreading her skirt over her knees. She smiled again. "Custis wanted to know where to find a man by the name of Henry Starr."

"I know," Billy replied. "Marshal Long is down in Indian Territory looking for him now."

The woman batted her long eyelashes. "There was one thing I didn't tell him," she said. "I like Custis, and I wouldn't want any harm to come to him."

"Go on, Miz Sloan."

"Henry has these outlaw friends who ride with him. They live in some caves near the Cimarron River. They're bad men, murderers. There are four of them, I think, and they plan to rob a bank somewhere. Custis won't stand a chance against so many killers."

Billy took his ink pen out of its inkwell. "Give me their names."

"I'm not sure of their names, Marshal. I heard Henry call one of them Black Jack. I met him once. He wears a black patch over one eye. He's mean to women . . . I know that for sure, and he carries a gun."

"Did you hear any of the other names, Miz Sloan?"

"Not that I recall, but I've been worried about what might happen to Custis if he ran into Henry and the other four. They would surely kill him."

Billy put down his pen. Now he knew that Custis was somewhere in Indian Territory, going up against a dozen Kiowa renegades, some gunrunners, and Henry Starr, who had four more hard cases with him.

"I'm grateful for the information, ma'am."

Chapter 7

"What the hell was that?" Roy cried, scrambling to his feet with his rifle.

"A gunshot," Leon growled, tossing his blankets aside to get his rifle and creep toward the old Camp Houston walls, where a charred spot gave him a view southward. "Ain't you ever heard a damn gunshot before?"

Jack stumbled over his saddle as he was clawing his pistol from its holster. "I heard somebody yell. Some sumbitch just got shot, an' it damn sure wasn't far away from here. What the hell is goin' on? Cal said there wasn't gonna be no trouble on this trade."

"Dobbs spent too many years in jail," Leon said. "Things have changed out here. Douse that fire so whoever's doin' the shootin' can't see our outlines."

"Holy shit," Roy whimpered as he poured handfuls of dirt on their campfire. "You reckon it's them damn Kiowas out to double-cross us?"

"They'd be shootin' at us now if that was the case," Leon told him while he scanned the darkness. "It came from that draw way down yonder . . . I'm nearly sure of it."

"We're gonna get killed over a mule load of rifles," Roy whispered, levering a shell into the firing chamber of his Winchester. "Calvin Dobbs is a lyin' son of a bitch, if you ask me."

"Ain't nobody shootin' at us yet," Jack said, hunkered down near a burned-out log wall that had once protected the fort from Indian attacks.

"Somebody got shot," Roy insisted. "I heard the bastard scream. We could be next."

"It's hard to figure who fired the shot," Leon said. "They wasn't shootin' at us."

"It's just as hard to figure who *got* shot," Jack said. "Who the hell else would be out here?"

"Maybe we oughta saddle up an' make a run for it with these rifles," Roy suggested.

"Not yet," Leon replied. "Let's see what happens next. If it's a bunch of them Kiowas all around us, we ain't gonna get no place anyhow."

"Damn," Jack whispered. "We ain't got no luck of no kind at all."

"Best thing to do is sit tight until we know what the hell's going on," Leon said.

Roy backed away from the burned-out wall. "I'm gonna open another bottle of that whiskey. My nerves is shot all to hell right now."

Leon's palms were damp around the stock of his Winchester. "Bring me one. This is liable to be a long night."

"Or a mighty short one," Roy added, opening one of the packs to remove a bottle of red-eye. "Could be that none of us live to see the sun come up."

"Shut up, Roy," Jack snapped, "an' pass me that jug. My tongue is real dry all of a sudden."

Henry Starr spurred his horse relentlessly until he reached the mouth of the alabaster cave. Bob Weeks was standing guard at the entrance with an old Spencer rifle.

Starr jumped to the ground.

"What's up, Boss?" Weeks asked. "I heard a gun go off someplace."

"Trouble. Most likely some damn law dog who trailed Cal Dobbs' boys to the fort. He killed one of Lone Bear's warriors whilst we were trying to sneak up on the man who was camped in that ravine. One of them Kiowa women said she saw one man down there."

"The law?"

"Could be. An Indian girl from Lone Bear's bunch said she didn't see but one, like I just told you. Ain't you been listening?"

"What the hell would the law be doin' way out here in the Nations?"

Starr gave Weeks a cold stare. "How the hell should I know, Bob? Like I said, maybe they trailed Cal Dobbs' boys up the river."

"Holy shit. I'll unsaddle your horse. Maybe you oughta wake up Black Jack an' Shorty an' Cletus."

"I aim to do just that. Pull my saddle an' bring this horse inside the cavern. I couldn't tell if I was being followed. Too damn dark without no moon."

Starr strode into the inky cave wondering what had gone wrong, who had shot the Kiowa warrior named Quahip. The girl was so far out in front of them he hadn't had time to see what happened to her.

49

He came to a cavern at the end of the tunnel where a small fire burned low.

"Wake up, boys!" he shouted. "We may have some trouble on our hands."

"What the hell kind of trouble?" Cletus Huling asked, sitting up slowly, rubbing his eyes.

"May be the law. I couldn't tell. It was too damn dark to see who it was."

Shorty Russell belched and sat up, tossing aside an empty bottle of whiskey. "Did you say somethin' about the law?" he asked sleepily.

"Could be," Starr answered. "Some son of a bitch shot one of Lone Bear's braves from a ravine south of the fort ruins and I couldn't get a look at him. Whoever the hell it was, he's got real good aim."

Black Jack Ward sat up from his blankets, reaching for his rifle. "Let's saddle our horses an' ride up there to see who it was," he said, adjusting the black eyepatch over his left eye before he pulled on his boots.

"Where's Lone Bear an' his warriors?" Shorty asked, struggling into his boots.

"Camped somewhere north of the river," Starr replied, taking a bottle of whiskey from their packs. "He damn sure had to hear the shot."

Cletus stood up. "I say we let them damn Kiowas handle this if it's the law. All we're after is repeatin' rifles. Let the Injuns find out done the shootin'."

"We need those rifles and ammunition," Starr said, uncorking the bottle of rotgut to take a big swallow. "If we don't show up to claim some of those guns, Lone Bear will take every last one of 'em back into the Nations."

"Did Cal's boys shoot back?" Black Jack wondered, buckling on his gunbelt.

"Only one shot was fired," Starr replied. "It killed this old Kiowa they called Quahip. Right after that, I took off and headed back here. There wasn't any way to tell for sure how many men were in that ravine."

"Let's hope it ain't no big posse after us," Shorty said quietly. "There's reward money out on us. Enough reward money to raise a posse."

Bob Weeks came down the tunnel leading Starr's winded horse with his Spencer balanced in the palm of one hand. "It's all quiet out there, Henry. Ain't heard a sound since you rode up here."

"Saddle a fresh horse for me," Starr snapped. "The rest of you get mounted. We'll ride back north a ways to see what's going on."

"How many of Cal's boys are at the fort?" Black Jack asked as he headed for a line of horses picketed at the back of the cavern.

"Only three," Starr replied. "Leon Graves, Roy, and some tall guy I ain't never seen before."

"Sounds like Jack Trainer," Shorty said. "He runs whiskey an' a few guns in the Nations. He'd work for Cal, if the money was right."

"We won't know until we get there," Starr said, taking another big swallow of whiskey. The bullet that killed Quahip could just as easily have ended *his* life. A dead Kiowa didn't amount to much, but Henry Starr had no plans to meet with an early grave over a few Winchesters and boxes of cartridges. A rich bank down at Cache was asking to be robbed, and he intended to live long enough to get away with the money in that vault, even if it meant taking chances like this.

•   •   •

Longarm came back to the slender tree trunk where he'd left the girl handcuffed. He stood in front of her for a moment before he spoke.

"Tell me who's out there, Tooma. Who was with you when you tried to slip up on me?"

"I will tell you nothing, white man."

"I found the body of an old Indian, a Kiowa by the cut of his hair, at the bottom of this draw. He's the man I shot. I don't want to kill any more of your people unless they don't give me a choice."

"Lone Bear will take your scalp!"

"Maybe. Who else is with him? Do you know the gun traders camped at the fort?"

She showed him a mouthful of teeth when she snarled at him. "Find out for yourself," she spat.

"I'm lookin' for a Cherokee half-breed named Henry Starr. He has a hideout in those caves south of here, according to the information I was given."

Tooma said nothing.

"Have you heard of him? Is he with Lone Bear?"

Longarm holstered his Colt. "Just listen to me, Tooma. I know your people are suffering on the reservations. There isn't a thing I can do about it. My government has a policy toward all Indians, a bad policy."

"My people are starving," she said.

"I understand. And I understand why you and Lone Bear ran away from the reservation. I'm just one man, a U.S. deputy marshal from Denver. If I had my way I'd see to it that all of your people were properly fed."

"All white men speak lies!"

"Not me, whether you believe it or not. I know what it's like to be hungry."

"Lone Bear and his warriors will kill you tonight. We

52

need the guns brought by the Comancheros."

Longarm remembered the names of several Comanchero gun traders from wanted posters in Billy's office. "That means it's probably Calvin Dobbs, Jack Trainer, and a hired gun or two. I have to stop them from giving Lone Bear those rifles. It's my job."

Tooma continued to stare at him. "Your eyes tell me that your words are true, white man."

"I am speaking the truth."

"You are a white eyes."

"I speak the truth when I say I don't want to shoot another Kiowa warrior, like the old man lying dead in the wash. I want this to end. I came here to arrest a Cherokee killer by the name of Henry Starr, and I also intend to arrest those men who brought the rifles to Camp Houston."

Tooma lowered her eyes.

Longarm said, "If I let you go, will you take word to Lone Bear that I want no war with him? But I won't let him get his hands on those guns."

"I will be disgraced in front of my people," she said in a low voice. "I was sent here to kill you."

"You can tell Lone Bear I was a little harder to kill than he figured . . . that I gave you back your life so you could carry my message to him."

She gave him no answer, although she appeared to be thinking about what he said.

"I want Henry Starr, and those men at the fort, along with their guns."

"Lone Bear says we must have rifles to make war on the white men and take their cattle away for our starving children. How is this wrong, if the old ones and children are starving?"

Longarm took a deep breath. "I reckon it isn't wrong, if that's the only way. But I can't ignore my duty. I intend to arrest Henry Starr and those men at the fort. I'll call in the army if I have to."

"I can only tell Lone Bear the words you have spoken to me," she said, still staring at the dark ground near her feet.

"That's good enough for me. Tell Lone Bear to ride away from this place. I won't let him get those guns."

"I will tell him," Tooma whispered.

"I'll take the irons off you, but I hope you'll tell me one more thing . . . is Henry Starr camped close by?"

It took Tooma a moment to reply. "He is camped in the caves where the ravine forks. He is a bad man. Chief Lone Bear does not trust him."

"Thanks, Tooma," Longarm said, reaching into his pants pocket for the handcuff keys. "I'm letting you go. Take my message to Lone Bear. Tell him that I understand why he's on the warpath against white men, but I can't let him get his hands on those rifles at Camp Houston, and I've got to put Henry Starr in jail for the murders he's done. I have no quarrel with the Kiowa tribe. In fact, you're one of the prettiest Kiowa girls I've ever seen. You're a real beauty."

"You think I am pretty?" Tooma asked as he unlocked her handcuffs.

"You're downright beautiful. I only wish we'd met under different circumstances. . . ."

Chapter 8

Longarm tossed the handcuffs near his saddle and gear.
The Kiowa girl rubbed her wrists where the irons had held
her fast to the tree. He hadn't meant to put them on too
tightly, but neither had he been inclined to let her escape.

"Sorry if they were too tight," he said. "I was in something of a hurry."

"You are different," Tooma said. "You are not like the
white men at Fort Sill."

"I'm just doin' my job, Tooma, and I sure don't want
to hurt you. I know about life on the reservations. It's
cruel to starve people like that, but I can't let those rifles
fall into Lone Bear's hands. He'll raid more ranches and
kill more of the people I'm sworn to protect. I have a duty
to protect the white settlers in this area."

"My heart tells me you speak true words, white man,"
she said.

"I am speaking the truth. I'm after a killer. Henry Starr
is wanted by the white man's law for killing people. I
have to find him and put him in jail."

"He is in the cave where the dry stream forks. Lone

Bear does not trust him, but he has money to pay for some of the guns and bullets . . . money my people can use to buy food. The guns we use to take cattle from white ranchers so the Kiowa will not starve. How can this be wrong, if the white soldiers at the fort give us nothing to eat, only bad flour with worms in it and meat that smells like a rotting animal?"

"Stealing cattle is against the white man's laws. I have to make sure they're safe. Where did you learn to speak such good English?" Longarm asked her.

"At the Indian school at Fort Sill. They made us go there every day until we could speak the white man's tongue. Some of the old ones refused to go, and they were put in iron cages to die."

"Seems mighty rough," he said, glancing around them. All was quiet near the fort and to the south. "Was Henry Starr with you when you came to kill me?" he asked, wondering if she would answer him truthfully.

"Yes. He rode away as soon as you shot Quahip."

"I had to shoot him, Tooma, in order to save my own life. I didn't know who was out there."

"I understand," Tooma said, staring up into his eyes. "We were sent to kill you."

Longarm grinned. "I've never had such a pretty lady try to cut me to pieces before. Were you really gonna sell me your body before you cut my throat?"

"No. I am not a . . . *puta*, a woman who sells herself to a man for money."

"You're damn sure a beautiful girl," he said. "I'd have paid you, if you'd come alone. And if you hadn't been carrying that big knife."

"You want me?" Tooma asked, a whispered question.

"Sure. Any man would."

"I trust you, white eyes. I think your heart is good. I will give myself to you, if you want me."

"I'd be a damn fool to turn down an offer like that. Seems like the shooting is over for now. Come over here to my blankets and lie down with me."

"It is cold. Do you want me to take off my dress?"

"I'd like to see what's underneath it. I'll cover you up with a blanket." He reached for her and took her in his arms, wondering if this might be a trick on Tooma's part. She might still try to kill him if he became careless . . . if she could get her hands on a weapon.

"Do you make a kiss like a white man?" she asked, coming against his chest.

He bent down and placed his lips over hers, holding her close. "Does that answer your question?" he said.

"It is forbidden for a Kiowa woman to lie down with a white man," she said softly, placing her slender hands behind his neck, entwining her fingers in his hair.

"Nobody'll ever know, Tooma. It can be our secret. I won't tell if you won't tell."

He reached for one of her firm young breasts and kneaded it between his fingers, although her deerskin garment made it hard for him to find her nipple at first.

"I will lie down with you, white eyes," she murmured, her eyelids closing with pleasure. "I do not know the white man's word for giving you my body."

Longarm took her hand and led her over to his bedroll. He meant to help her undress, but before he could offer any assistance, Tooma wriggled out of her deerskin and settled down on his bedroll, gazing up at him with big, liquid eyes. She was completely naked.

He took off his shirt, then his gunbelt, and unfastened his pants. His cock throbbed upward as he slid his pants down below his knees. He placed his pistol belt close to his bedroll, and his Winchester rifle was not far away in its saddle boot. He continued to wonder if this might be some sort of trick, but when he glanced at his horse, the animal's head was lowered, to show him that it sensed nothing unusual close to his camp.

"Oh!" Tooma exclaimed, staring at his prick. "Are all white men so big?"

Longarm knelt beside her, then took her in his arms and pulled her down on his bedroll. "Some, I reckon. I've never bothered to pay much attention to what other men have between their legs."

Tooma reached for the tip of his manhood tentatively, using only her fingertips while her breathing quickened. Her bare breasts were pressed against Longarm's chest. "I think it is too big to fit inside me," she said. "The young men of my tribe are not so large . . . I watch them from the reeds while they are bathing in the river."

"You've never had a man before?"

"Only one. He was my husband. He was killed, along with my father, by General Crook's soldiers. I was only his wife for two moons."

"Sorry. Don't think about it now."

"My time for grief has passed. It is the way of our people, to mourn the dead for three suns."

Longarm's cock was pulsing with desire as Tooma played with it. "Spread your legs apart," he whispered in her ear. "We'll go about this real slow."

She did as he asked, parting her rounded thighs. Then she began to shiver. "I am cold," she said.

He reached for a blanket as he slid between her legs, covering them both. Her breath smelled sweet, a scent he did not recognize. Her skin was like velvet, but in the back of his mind he still pondered the possibility that Tooma was loyal to Lone Bear and if she got the chance, she would kill him. Never before had he taken such a risk to bed a woman. Most of his conquests had been in hotel rooms, or in a woman's private chambers.

What am I doing? he thought. I'm bedding down with an Indian girl in the middle of a prairie, surrounded by Kiowas and gunrunners and a murderer named Henry Starr. I must be losing my mind.

He placed the head of his prick into the dewy opening of her mound. She was wet and warm.

Tooma wrapped her arms around his shoulders. She shuddered with pleasure when the tip of his cock parted the lips of her honeypot.

"Take it easy, Tooma," he told her. "Give yourself a little time."

"You are so gentle for a white man," she said in a feathery voice.

"Not all white men are like the soldiers at Fort Sill," he replied. Longarm pushed the head of his cock a fraction deeper into her.

Tooma stiffened and let out a tiny groan. "You are too big for me."

"There's no hurry. Relax. It'll feel good in a few more minutes."

"No. You will not fit inside me."

He felt tremors run down her limbs. "Don't be so impatient, darlin'. Give it time."

She tightened her embrace and placed her heels behind his muscular thighs. "I am too small for you and I am sorry for this."

"You give up too soon. Just lie still and let me do the work."

"You will hurt me."

"No, I won't. I promise."

Gradually, a little more of his prick moved into her when he applied a bit of pressure.

"Oh!" Tooma gasped, shaking from head to toe. In spite of the night chill, tiny beads of perspiration formed between her breasts and on her forehead.

His full attention was on the Kiowa girl and the pleasure he hoped they would share, but some inner sense warned him to check his surroundings.

Longarm looked up at the darkness. He saw nothing, but off to the south he heard the faint drum of horses' hooves moving toward them.

"We've got company," he said, rolling off Tooma's flat belly to jerk his Colt from its holster before jumping to his feet with an ear cocked toward the sounds.

Tooma sat up quickly while Longarm was pulling up his pants. "I hear horses," Tooma said.

"So do I, darlin'. What we were about to do will have to wait while I take care of business."

Tooma scrambled to slither back into her dress as the faint sounds became louder. "It comes from the south," Tooma whispered.

"That'll be Henry Starr and some of his men," Longarm said with certainty. "See if you can catch that pinto of yours and get the hell out of here. There's sure liable to be some shooting."

The girl trotted off into the red oak forest flanking the ravine.

"Just my damn luck," Longarm muttered. "I was about to get real well acquainted with an Indian beauty, until some damn hard cases show up."

He put on his shirt and unbooted his rifle, backing into

the trees, waiting. This could be his chance to bring down Henry Starr, and he didn't want to waste an opportunity.

Henry Starr gave his men a silent signal to halt. "Up yonder," he said quietly, jerking a Spencer carbine from a boot below his saddle skirt.

"How far?" Shorty asked.

"Maybe a quarter mile."

"How are we gonna take 'em?" Bob wondered aloud.

"We spread out," Starr replied. "You and Black Jack ride that east rim. Shorty and Cletus ride the west. I'll come up the bottom of the draw."

Shorty sounded worried. "You ain't got no idea how many of them there is?"

"Hell, no," Starr spat. "I just heard the one shot an' that Kiowa was falling off his horse."

"Maybe it's just one feller?" Bob offered.

"I say we don't take no chances," Black Jack said. "We ride up on 'em slow an' careful . . . see how many's up there. That's the only smart way."

"I agree," Starr said. "If you see anyone moving, shoot him dead. We'll find out who he was later."

"I don't like this," Bob said. "Too many trees for 'em to use for cover."

Starr wheeled around in the saddle to speak to Bob. "You wasn't asked if you liked what we're doing, Weeks. We're getting the right guns so we can rob a bank and keep a posse off our trail if they follow us, so just shut the hell up with all your damn worrying."

"Sure thing, Boss."

The five men split up, two pairs riding high on the rim of the ravine, while Starr moved his horse slowly among the stands of red oak.

61

For a few hundred yards all was quiet. Then suddenly a rifle went off from the west side of the ravine.

"I got one of 'em!" Shorty cried. "Knocked him plumb off his pinto horse!"

Starr wondered if Shorty had accidentally shot the Kiowa Indian girl. Lone Bear wouldn't take it lightly if one of his women had been killed by Shorty.

The crack of a rifle answered Shorty's shot.

"I'm hit!" Shorty shrieked as the thump of running hooves echoed through the night.

"Damn," Starr mumbled, readying his Spencer. Someone with good aim was waiting for them farther up the ravine, perhaps more than one.

Black Jack's rifle bellowed. Starr heard the bullet singsong harmlessly between tree trunks in the dry wash.

Starr got down off his horse and tried it off to an oak limb. It was time to do a bit of stalking on foot. Riding into the ravine was too risky now.

Chapter 9

Longarm glimpsed the silhouette of a horse and rider coming along the rim of the ravine. He shouldered his Winchester and fired.

The rider toppled soundlessly off his horse as the sorrel bolted away.

"They shot Bob!" a deep voice cried as another horseman swirled away from the top of the draw, little more than a black shape against a pale night sky.

"Let's get the hell out of here," another voice shouted from the other side of the ravine.

Galloping hoofbeats moved away from Longarm's camp, heading back to the south. He was certain he'd hit two of the men coming up the draw, and he was just as sure that he'd heard someone shout about shooting a rider on a pinto. That could be Tooma, mistaken for an enemy in the dark.

He waited until the sounds of hoofbeats faded to silence before he left the trees where he was hiding. Moving softly on the balls of his feet, he made his way slowly down the bottom of the brush-choked dry wash.

He heard a loose horse wandering somewhere in front of him, and froze behind a clump of brush. There wasn't enough light for him to see anything clearly.

Then, in dim light from the stars, he saw a black-and-white pinto wandering along the eastern slope of the ravine. It was Tooma's pony.

One of them shot her, he thought.

But before he began searching for her to see if her wound was fatal, he had to make sure all the gunmen had pulled out, those he hadn't knocked off their horses with a carefully placed rifle slug.

Inching forward, he moved among the trees. One of the men he'd shot was moaning off to his right, by the sound of it a serious injury that would keep him out of the fight—a wet, gurgling sound like a bullet-torn lung.

Nothing moved across the floor of the ravine. Longarm let himself relax a bit, although years of experience tracking wanted men kept him alert, ready for trouble. Henry Starr was part Indian. He would know how to hide himself, waiting for his prey to make a mistake.

Longarm was also worried that the gunshots would bring Lone Bear and his renegades down to the ravine . . . possibly even the gun traders at the fort. If things went against him, Longarm would be surrounded by deadly enemies.

A dark shadow moved near a clump of trees. Longarm tensed and readied his rifle, for he was certain that what he saw wasn't a product of his imagination.

He knelt down behind a clump of sage. The slender bushes would offer little in the way of protection from a bullet, but they might be enough to keep him hidden from an ambusher's shot in the dark.

Suddenly, a rifle cracked. The wink of a muzzle flash

accompanied the explosion. A bullet sizzled through the bushes where he was hiding, a narrow miss.

Longarm aimed for the fading muzzle flash and fired off a shot, his Winchester slamming into his shoulder with its forty grains of gunpowder. He knew he'd missed the moment he heard the whine of his slug moving down the draw.

He moved quickly to another spot, ejecting the spent cartridge from the Winchester's firing chamber as another round rattled hollowly into place.

An answering shot ran out, a softer sound like a shot from an older-model carbine. The bullet tore through the bushes where he'd been hiding, sending a shower of sage leaves swirling toward the ground.

He's good, Longarm thought. He knew right where to aim for me.

As far as Longarm could tell, there was just one man in front of him, or at least, only one doing any shooting. These were odds Longarm favored . . . man against man, to see who was the best at killing his adversary.

To his left, halfway up the bank of the dry stream, he heard a soft groan, a woman's groan.

"One of them shot Tooma for sure," he muttered softly. By taking her to his bedroll he might have cost her her life, and that notion twisted a knot in his gut. She was hardly more than a girl, too young to die.

He moved behind a tree as quietly as he knew how, filled with welling rage. "Is that you, Starr?" he bellowed into the silence around him.

No one answered.

"I'm gonna kill you, you son of a bitch. You shot the Indian girl, you gutless bastard. Come and get me! Or I'll come and get you!"

More silence. Longarm knew his anger could get him killed unless he used his head. "I'm comin' for you, you half-breed Cherokee bastard! Get ready to die!"

As the last words left his mouth he hunkered over to the base of another red oak. By taunting Henry Starr, he hoped to make him give his position away.

A rifle thundered from a pocket on the west side of the draw. Longarm aimed for the stabbing finger of flame coming from the rifle barrel and fired his .44-40-caliber answer toward the spot.

He heard his slug thud into the side of the ravine, a miss, and he cursed himself silently.

The same rifle bellowed, sending a chunk of molten lead into the tree trunk just above his head.

Longarm's rage was almost out of control. "You missed me, half-breed!" he shouted. "Try again!"

Another loud bang came from the same place, and this time Longarm was ready for it. He fired at almost the same instant, his ears ringing so that he could not tell whether he had a hit or a miss.

Time to move again, he told himself, searching for a thick tree close at hand that would shield him from more bullets. He went into a crouch and made a dash for an oak only a few feet away.

A shot came from a bend in the ravine, the clap of gunpowder resounding off the sides of the dry creek.

"Gotcha," Longarm whispered as he triggered off a shot to the left of the wink of light coming from the gun barrel aimed at him.

"Son of a . . ." a man shrieked.

Longarm stood up, exposing himself, a mistake he would soon regret. Just as he stepped around the tree trunk, a banging noise was accompanied by a sharp pain in his right thigh and he was swept off his feet, slammed on his back by the force of a bullet.

His rifle slipped from his hands. He knew he'd been hit, and reached down to finger his wound. His pants were torn, and blood seeped from a gash in his leg, but it was only a superficial injury, tearing open his flesh, passing through his skin without any damage to the muscle.

"Damn," he hissed, sitting up, reaching for the bandanna around his neck to tie off the flow of blood. His head was spinning, and he required a moment to collect his thoughts and get his bearings.

He tied the bandanna around his thigh, wincing when the pain grew worse, and then quickly drew his Colt. Henry Starr, or whoever had been shooting at him, could be coming for him at any moment.

This wasn't Custis Parker Long's first gunshot wound, but they all seemed bad at the time they occurred. He knew he had to reach cover of some kind.

Fisting his Winchester in one hand, his pistol in the other, he crawled toward the oak tree where he'd been hiding only moments before. In a weakened condition he was easy prey, but he wouldn't go down without a fight.

Moments later, as he lay behind the tree gathering his wits about him, he heard a horse galloping off.

"Maybe that's the end of it . . . for now," Longarm said between clenched teeth, fighting the pain from his flesh wound as the bleeding stopped.

He struggled to his feet, using his Winchester as a crutch, to go back and look for the Kiowa girl.

She was lying on her back in a patch of grass between the oaks when he found her.

"How bad is it, Tooma?" he asked, limping over to her after a careful check of his surroundings.

"My arm," the girl stammered.

"Is the bone broken?"

"I do not know. I cannot move it."

"I'll take a look," he said, dropping painfully to his knees beside her.

"Are they gone?" she asked.

"I think I put a bullet in the last one. Two more should be lying at the edge of the arroyo. I think I got one of them clean, but the other is still makin' noise."

"Where is Henry Starr?" she asked as Longarm felt the top of her forearm, where a bloody hole below her elbow leaked blood onto the grass.

"I've got no idea. One of them stayed long enough to throw some lead at me. He winged me in the leg, but it'll be okay. It's only a nick."

He touched the bone above her wound. "I think it went through, Tooma. I'll help you up and we'll put a bandage around it."

Her face twisted as she sat up slowly.

"It's the best I can do for now, until I can get you to a doctor," he explained.

She looked at him. "Why would you help me, white eyes? I came here to kill you."

"I reckon it's because you need help. And to tell the truth, I don't think you'd have killed me."

"You are wrong," she replied. "Chief Lone Bear told me to kill you. I would do anything for my people."

"Killing me wouldn't have helped your people any."

"We would have the rifles and bullets."

"They won't keep your tribe from starving. You need to talk to the Indian agent at Fort Sill."

"Tatum speaks with a forked tongue. He promises us good meat and flour. We get nothing but worms and beef that makes us sick."

"Something can be done. Now, let me help you up so we can get back to my camp. I've got some whiskey I can pour into your wound that'll help keep it from festering, and some cloth for a bandage."

Tooma allowed him to help her to her feet. She stood there a moment, flexing the fingers on her hand.

"Can you walk?" Longarm asked. "My leg is gonna make it hard for me to help you much."

"I can walk, white eyes."

"Put your good arm around my shoulder. We'll make it, even if the going is slow."

He tied a strip of cloth around her forearm after he poured a splash of whiskey into the bullet hole. Her face registered no signs of pain now.

"That'll stop it from bleeding until I can get you to a doctor."

"A white man's doctor?"

He nodded. "That bullet hole has to be seared with a hot iron and cleaned out."

"I have never been to a white man's doctor. Take me back to Lone Bear. The other woman, Nodemah, will put damp leaves and clay on my arm and I will be well soon. She is very wise in the ways of healing."

"There's another woman with Lone Bear?" Longarm asked.

"Nodemah is a woman warrior. She is a very brave fighter and she knows healing magic."

"Right now you don't need any magic," Longarm told her as he came slowly to his feet. "You need medical treatment, and I aim to see that you get it."

"Why do you help me, white eyes?" she asked as he struggled to lift her off the ground. "I am *una india*. We are enemies."

"I'm not your enemy, Tooma," he told her, limping back to his camp.

"All white men are enemies of the Kiowa," she said. "You took away our land. You put us on the reservation and you starve us and our children."

"I didn't have anything to do with that," Longarm said, making his way carefully to his tethered horse. "That policy was made in Washington."

He was barely able to collect his horse with his game leg. Then he started saddling the bay. "I'll saddle my horse and fetch your paint pony. We're two days away from the closest doctor. I'm gonna give you a sip or two of whiskey. It'll help with the pain."

"I do not need *boisah pah*," she said as he limped off to search the arroyo for her horse.

Chapter 10

Longarm remembered the last time he'd been involved in an attempt to save an Indian girl's life. She was a Comanche, and the circumstances hadn't been much different, except for his involvement with the U.S. Cavalry at Fort Sill. . . .

He piled the troopers' boots on the campfire and stood a moment watching them burn. Then he picked up their pistol belts and tossed them into the dark brush. Remington army-issue rifles were next to be thrown out of sight behind bushes and trees.

In a ravine only a few yards from the solders' campsite he found seven more tethered horses. One at a time, he turned them loose to wander and graze, waving his arms in the air to send them southward, away from the march of the bootless soldiers.

Satisfied that he'd done all he could to keep the troopers afoot, he returned to Senatey, the Comanche girl, while leading the sorrel cavalry horse. She was still unconscious. It would take precious time to fashion a travois with cut poles and his blankets tied between them. By the blood on the front of her dress, he guessed time was running short for the Comanche girl.

He tied the cavalry animal to his saddle horn and then gently lifted Senatey in his arms. In light from the stars he saw her eyelids flutter once. Then she slipped back into unconsciousness as he mounted his horse.

He'd made up his mind, regardless of the girl's wishes. He was taking her to the post doctor, guessing that her injuries were too severe to leave him any other reasonable choice.

Traveling by starlight, he aimed for the fort with the girl nestled against him.

False dawn grayed eastern skies as he rode slowly with Senatey through the fort gates. Dogs barked at his approach. Sentries gave him curious stares when they saw the Comanche woman in his arms, yet they waved him through as if he were a familiar figure at Fort Sill.

He guided his stud to the post hospital, where an orderly half asleep on a wood bench came to his feet, blinking in the haze of pale light.

"What's the post surgeon's name?" Longarm asked, bringing his horse to a halt at the hitch rail.

"Major Green, sir."

Longarm stepped gingerly to the ground with his lovely burden balanced in one arm. "Get him for me. This girl needs medical attention right away."

The orderly blinked. "But she's an Indian. Doc Green don't work on sick Indians."

"He's gonna work on this one."

"Pardon me fer sayin' it, sir, but you ain't no officer

72

an' a civilian ain't gonna tell Doc Green what to do. Besides, he's asleep."

"Then wake him up, soldier, and do it real quick before I lose my temper."

"It's against orders, sir."

"I'm giving you new orders."

"But you ain't a soldier, if you'll pardon me makin' the observation."

"Wake him up anyway," Longarm demanded, carrying Senatey up the hospital steps. "This woman was almost killed by three of your goddamn soldiers, and I assure you Major Thompson will give Doc Green the authority to work on her. Otherwise, I'll be forced to send General George Crook, a personal friend of mine, a telegram about how you and Doc Green and everybody else on this military post refused to help an injured woman."

"Doc ain't gonna like it," the orderly said, but as he said it he turned to leave for a darkened barracks across the parade ground.

"I don't remember asking you if he'd like it, soldier. I said to wake him up and get him over here."

Horace Green bent over Senatey in light from a coal-oil lantern near the bed where Longarm had put her down. Despite what the orderly had said, Major Green had seemed willing enough to examine the girl after what Longarm told him about the nature and cause of her injuries.

"She was kicked in the stomach," Green said, looking closely at a dark purple bruise below her rib cage. "Probably ruptured a few blood vessels, and perhaps even caused some damage to blood vessels in her lungs or her throat. You can see the marks here where someone tried to choke her."

"He gave his name as Sergeant Dave Bandworth."

"Don't recall a soldier by that name here."

"I suspect he lied to me. He and the other two, a couple of privates, ran off when I asked them to bring me a horse to carry her here to see a doctor. But I found them again. Along with a few more who had crushed the skull of another Indian girl after they raped her."

"Crushed her skull?" Green asked, peering over the tops of wire-rimmed eyeglasses.

"Tied her to stakes buried in the ground. Then they raped her and bashed in the top of her head."

Green made a face. "If you can prove that, and if you tell Major Thompson, our post commander, about it, those men will be severely punished."

"I gave 'em a little punishment of my own, Doc. But the army don't need men like them."

"By your Southern drawl I assume you were a Southerner, Marshal Long."

"I was born in the South."

"On either side of that bloody conflict, men who would do this sort of thing to a woman didn't deserve to wear a uniform. And they don't deserve it now. It's a disgrace to every man who serves honorably."

"We see it the same way, Doc."

Green lifted one of Senatey's eyelids. "She's in a deep coma. Probably the result of shock. I'll give her an injection of morphine for her pain and wrap her ribs. For now, that's about all I can do."

"When she wakes up she'll yell like a stuck pig, Doc. She told me she wouldn't go to a white man's doctor."

Green nodded. "These Indians have their own beliefs,

and in particular, the Comanches are the hardest to convince when it comes to medicine. They believe in their shamans and the old ceremonies."

"I'll appreciate anything you can do for her," Longarm said in a quiet voice. "She's too young to die, and when I saw all that blood coming from her mouth, I knew she needed a real doctor to take care of her."

"I'll do as much as I can. Internal injuries can be very hard to diagnose."

"I understand. I'm headed over to see Major Thompson, to give him a report on what happened."

"When she wakes up, if she demands to leave my hospital, there isn't much I can do besides let her go."

"Do as much as you can for her until then, Doc. I'll be back to see how she's doing after I talk to Major Thompson and get a change of clothes."

"Bruce Thompson isn't going to like what you tell him, Mr. Long. I assure you of that. The major is a soldier first and foremost. He won't tolerate that kind of behavior from any of the men in his command."

"I'm glad to hear it," Longarm said, turning to leave the tiny room where Senatey lay. "I would think the Indian agent would be just as upset."

Green gave a humorless chuckle. "Then you don't know Mr. Tatum," he said.

Slocum paused near the door. "What do you mean by that, Doc?"

"George Tatum is about the worst excuse for an Indian agent I've ever run across. He hates all Indians. It's just a nice, comfortable job for him, being Indian agent at Fort Sill. If it were up to him, he'd starve every Indian on this reservation to death."

"I've heard about the beef with worms in it, and the moldy flour."

"It's far worse than that, worse than bad food. I shouldn't be talking about it to a federal marshal, I don't suppose, but if you hang around Fort Sill any length of time, you'll soon see what I mean."

"Conas, one of the Kwahadie chiefs, told me about starving, sick children."

"It runs even deeper. I'd better keep my mouth shut."

"If, like you say, it's more serious than bad food, why does the army tolerate it?"

Green covered Senatey with a thin bedsheet and turned down the lamp. Then he looked at Longarm. "Crooked politics can run deep into the military, Marshal. That's about all I'll say in that regard."

"Does Major Thompson know about it? He doesn't seem like the type to tolerate that sort of thing."

"Knowing about it is one thing. Being able to prove it is quite another."

When Longarm realized the post surgeon did not care to offer any more opinions on the subject, he nodded and left the room.

Crossing the parade ground, he came to the headquarters building, and asked for Major Thompson as the sun rose above the horizon.

"He ain't here, sir," a guard at the door said. "He went out to look for one of his patrols that was late comin' back to the fort. Someone over at the Indian agent's office reported we can expect big troubles from some of the Comanches here. He rode off last night to check into it."

Longarm wheeled for his horse. "Tell the major U.S. Marshal Custis Long asked for him . . . that I need to talk to him about the type of behavior some of his soldiers are guilty of. I'll be at the stable taking care of the horses. Then I'll get a bite to eat and be back here."

"Yessir. I'll tell him. Only, what sort of behavior was you talkin' about that some of his soldiers are guilty of?"

"How does murder sound? Or rape? Killing horses too. Is that enough?"

The private swallowed. "Are you real sure of that, sir? I don't think any soldier from this fort would commit honest-to-goodness murder or nothin' like that."

Longarm nodded. "I saw it for myself, Private. And I intend to inform Major Thompson as soon as possible."

"Them's real serious charges. . . ."

Longarm glared back at the porch, and the soldier who was on guard duty. "You're goddamn right they're serious charges, soldier, and I intend to take 'am all the way to Washington if I have to."

He was bone-weary by the time he got the horses stabled at the livery and returned to the fort. As he climbed the stairs to an upstairs room at the barracks, the soldier in charge signaled to him.

"There's a red-haired female been askin' 'bout you, if you go back an' all, Marshal. Said her name was Annie Mills, an' that you knowed her."

"I know her," he said in a tired voice.

"She wanted me to send our shoeshine boy over to her boardinghouse soon as you got back, so she'd know you was okay."

"No need of that. I'll tell her myself after I get a bit of rest. I've just spent a long night in the saddle and I could use a few hours of shut-eye."

"She give me two bits to send the shine boy, Marshal,

77

so I figure I owe her. She said to send the kid over soon as you got back to Fort Sill."

"I don't suppose it matters," he said, continuing up the stairs.

He was lying in bed naked, almost too tired to move, when a knock came at the door. Longarm sat up quickly and donned a pair of pants, wondering if it could be someone sent by Major Thompson.

When he opened the door, he found Annie standing there.

"I was afraid you'd run out on me," she said, "the way Wade did."

"I'm not the same type of man as your partner. Come on in. I'm so tired I can hardly think straight."

Annie came in and sat on the bed. "Can you tell me what happened?" she asked.

"I found the tracks of the killers just like Major Thompson wanted me to," he began, slumping on the mattress beside her. "I also found two Indian girls, Comanches. One of 'em was dead and the other has serious injuries. I brought her back to the fort to see the doctor. She was unconscious most of the way back."

"What happened to them?" Annie asked, closing the front of her bright yellow dress where too much bosom was revealed in the absence of two buttons.

"Soldiers shot their horses and raped them. They weren't doing anything wrong, just out hunting for wild game. There's gonna be trouble over it."

"Trouble?"

"When I inform Major Thompson it was his soldiers who did it to those women."

"Almost everyone in Cache hates the Indians," she said

78

in a distant voice, gazing out his window. "The worst of the lot is the Indian agent, George Tatum. He shouldn't be in charge of any program having to do with Indians. I've met him a few times."

Longarm's thoughts turned to Tatum. In the back of his mind he had a dark notion, one that he couldn't tell Major Thompson about until he knew more about Fort Sill's Indian agent and the contracts for beef with the government.

And here he was again, with an Indian girl from Fort Sill who had escaped, only to be seriously injured. Longarm knew that the closest doctor would be at the military post at Liberal across the Kansas line, and that was one hell of a long ride from Camp Houston.

The hunt for Henry Starr and the gun traders would have to wait.

Longarm set out for Kansas at dawn, holding the Kiowa girl in the saddle in front of him, leaving his duty behind for the sake of a woman.

Chapter 11

As soon as he returned to the gates at Fort Liberal, he could see a beehive of activity, cavalry troops forming across the parade ground as rapidly as possible, sending up swirls of dust into the winds coming from darkening storm clouds. Earlier, he had taken Tooma to the post surgeon to have her bullet wound treated. It had been a long ride from the ruins of Camp Houston with the girl slumped across the withers of her pony, and he'd needed a few hours of sleep. As soon as they'd arrived at the fort, he'd been told of another Indian raid north of Buffalo in Indian Territory.

"Trouble," he now muttered, guiding his bay past armed sentries at the gates. Word of Lone Bear's raids had already reached the military outpost. Longarm was certain that Lone Bear now had the guns brought to Camp Houston by the Comancheros.

Aiming for the post hospital, Longarm told himself it was none of his concern, that it was army business, despite what he'd told the commanding officer earlier about looking into his suspicions that Indian Agent George Tatum might have a stake in what was going on, a profit motive, since he was starving the Kiowas off the Fort Sill reservation. It was a far-fetched notion, but not without some possibilities. If Indian troubles started in the region around Camp Houston or Fort Supply, it could serve as a distraction from dishonest dealings by an agent of the government who was involved in crooked beef contracts, lining his own pockets at government expense. While it was, admittedly, a stretch of the imagination to think Tatum could be behind the murders of innocent settlers in some way, it was clear the killings and scalpings weren't the work of a typical Plains Indian tribe trying to rid their hunting grounds of white men, leaving the homesteads burned to the ground. Scouting for the army as he had in the past, Longarm knew enough about Indian practices to be wary of government men. Several things simply didn't add up . . . scalped women, log cabins burned to the ground, and Tooma's remark about Henry Starr being involved with Lone Bear.

He tied off the bay in front of the hospital, again noticing the rush of activity inside the fort as more and more soldiers formed on the parade ground. After he inquired as to Tooma's condition, he would ask what all the troop movement was about.

At the far end of a row of empty cots, Longarm saw Major Jones giving a soldier some sort of injection. The doctor looked up as Longarm limped toward the soldier's bed. Custis had stitches in his leg that Dr. Jones had put in the night before to treat his own narrow brush with a bullet.

"Howdy, Major. I thought I'd ask about the Indian girl I brought in."

"She's in that same little room at the back, Marshal Long. I have her heavily sedated. Her bleeding has slowed down to an extent. She hasn't awakened since you left. The morphine is keeping her asleep."

"You reckon she's gonna be okay?"

Jones straightened up with his empty syringe, his brow pinched with thought. "It's not a serious wound. The slug missed her bone, but not by much."

"Gunrunners, and a wanted man by the name of Henry Starr. I intend to inform Colonel Bass about it as soon as he returns."

"He's back. A group of escaped Kiowas have been cornered by squads of troopers somewhere to the south. A patrol reported these were the Indians who murdered those farmers a few days ago near the river."

Longarm frowned. "I suspect they found the raiding party led by Chief Lone Bear. I'd nearly stake my life on it. They're hungry and only looking for food. Might help prevent a war if I told the colonel about it."

"I fear it's already too late for that, according to what I was told. The Indians are fighting back, and apparently very fiercely at that. It's the reason squads are forming now. A request came to the fort for reinforcements."

Longarm shook his head. "It'd be natural for Kiowas to fight back if they were attacked. Trouble is, Colonel Bass has the wrong bunch cornered. He oughta be after Henry Starr and those gun traders."

Jones shrugged. "All I can suggest is that you explain it to our commander, Marshal. Everything will depend on whether or not he believes you. I was told there were already heavy casualties on both sides. We're preparing for a large number of wounded to arrive any moment now. Wagons were sent out to bring them back."

"Sounds like I sure as hell am too late," Longarm said. "If you don't mind, I'd like to look in on the girl. I feel like I owe it to her, on account of what was done to her."

The doctor nodded. "If what you say is true, and I don't

doubt your word at all, those men should be jailed. It disgraces the rest of us who wear these uniforms to have gun smugglers among us who would do anything so brutal to a woman, regardless of her race. I'm sure you know we have some who feel an Indian isn't quite human. It's a sad situation, but I don't have the authority to change official procedures, and no one can effect a change in the minds of certain types of men."

"Those weren't men," Longarm replied angrily, turning for the room where Tooma was being kept. "They were cowards. . . ."

Her eyes were closed and her breathing was slow, irregular, her tiny nostrils flaring. He leaned over her bunk bed to get a better look at the swelling in her arm. It was worse than when he'd seen it in pale moonlight the night before.

"The yellow bastards," he whispered, unconsciously balling his hands into fists.

The sound of his voice awakened her . . . her eyelids fluttered open. For a moment she stared blankly at the hospital ceiling, until she slowly became aware of his presence.

He made the sign for true words. "Just wanted to be sure you're okay," he said gently.

The morphine made her words mushy. "This place . . . is white medicine man lodge."

"I had no choice but to bring you here, Tooma. You had to have medical attention."

"Take me . . . back to my people. Now."

"I can't do that, not until you're a little stronger. You are bleeding. It's serious."

"Take me to Lone Bear. This is a bad . . . place."

Her fear and hatred for white men wouldn't allow her to consider anything else. The morphine was the only thing keeping her from leaving the hospital on her own. "I'll take you to Lone Bear as soon as I can, as soon as you're a little better. Until the bleeding stops, you have to stay here. Moving any more than necessary can start the bleeding again."

"No!" she said, shaking her head on the pillow. "Take me now."

He sat on the edge of her bed, and his actions produced a fearful expression on her face, even though she was too heavily drugged to pull away. "Listen to my words, niece of Chief Lone Bear," he began in halting Kiowa, a guttural tongue he hadn't spoken in years, punctuating everything he tried to say with sign language. "The men who hurt you are bad men. They will be punished. Not all Tosi Tivo are bad. The white doctor here is good . . . he has a good heart," Longarm continued, stumbling over phrases he couldn't recall. "He has medicine that will take your pain away and help stop the bleeding. I know you don't trust the Tosi Tivo, and after what Starr did to you, I cannot blame you for feeling this way. But I'm asking you to trust me. I am a friend of Chief Lone Wolf. I was a friend to old Chief Nocona before he died. I have been welcomed in the villages of the Kotsoteka, the Yamparika, and the Kwahadie of long ago, before your people were forced to live here on the reservation. I speak true words to you when I say the Tosi Tivo medicine man will help you."

"All Tosi Tivo speak with the tongue of a snake," she said heatedly.

"That is not true. There are good Tosi Tivo. I want you to trust me."

She watched him through hooded eyelids, saying nothing, as if she might be considering his request.

He kept pressing her, knowing the outcome might save

85

her life. "When Henry Starr and his outlaws shot you, I brought you here for help. Good medicine, even if it is the white man's medicine."

Again she remained silent, although he detected a softening of the hard look behind her dark chocolate eyes.

"Trust me just this once, Tooma. Let the Tosi Tivo medicine man help you, and then I will take you to Lone Bear. I speak only true words now."

"I am . . . afraid this place," she mumbled in English.

"There's nothing to be afraid of. The Tosi Tivo doctor has a good heart. His medicine will help you."

"Maybeso I stay . . . little time," she answered sleepily.

He knew she was slipping back toward unconsciousness.

"I stay this place . . . for a little time," she told him, her mind wandering, wincing when a stab of pain coursed through her injured arm.

He was silently thankful when her eyes closed again. She was unconscious. He gazed down at her a moment, stricken once more by her rare natural beauty. This woman didn't need lip paint or a fancy dress to catch men's stares. But after what had been done to her, she would only hate white men that much more, and with good reason.

"Sleep, pretty lady," he said softly as he made ready to leave the tiny room. "I'll promise you one thing . . . the sons of bitches who did this to you are gonna answer to me, if the army won't do it. I only gave 'em a little taste of what's in store when I find 'em again."

He strode out of the hospital to find Colonel Bass.

At post headquarters he was informed that Colonel Bass had left with over a hundred cavalrymen for a place called Red Oak Creek, pulling out an hour earlier. A second detachment of cavalrymen was assembling to follow the colonel. An aide to Colonel Bass said the Kiowas pinned down near the creek were about to feel the swift sword of military justice.

Longarm left the building with a sinking feeling in the pit of his stomach. He was certain Lone Bear and his warriors would be killed.

As he was preparing to saddle his bay, he saw a cavalryman ride by, a man who looked a little bit like one of the soldiers he'd encountered at the fort gates when he brought Tooma in. The soldier and another guard had spat on her when he and Tooma rode into the fort.

He stode over and grabbed the cavalryman's reins. "Did you spit on the Indian girl I brought in last night?" he demanded. "I'm a United States marshal and I can have your ass arrested."

"I don't know what you're talkin' about, Marshal," the soldier replied.

Because he wasn't entirely sure, Longarm let go of the reins and stepped back out of the way. "If I was certain you were one of 'em, I'd teach you some manners," he warned. "But just in case you do happen to be one of the men who spat on that Kiowa girl, I give you my solemn promise you'll regret what you did. I intend to take the matter up with Colonel Bass when he gets back, and if that don't work, I'll give you a different kind of justice."

"Are you threatenin' me, mister?"

Longarm gave him a one-sided grin. "It ain't a threat at all, soldier boy. It's a goddamn promise. If you turn out to be one of the yellow bastards who spat on that woman, I'll come looking for you, and the whole goddamn United States Army won't be enough to stop me from teaching you a lesson."

"You talk mighty tough. If I wasn't on duty, gettin'

ready to ride out of here to kill some Injuns, I'd climb down from this horse an' test you."

Longarm's grin only widened. "Any time you feel you're up to it, soldier boy. Any time you've got the nerve."

The trooper urged his horse away to join a formation on the parade grounds, leaving Longarm standing there trying to cool the rage inside him. It was beginning to seem as if the men wearing blue uniforms were the ones who needed a dose of federal justice, not the runaway Kiowas from Fort Sill.

Longarm headed for a tent off the parade ground where he could see men drinking. What he needed now was several stiff shots of whiskey, even a sutler's cheap brand.

A soldier came strolling toward him, staring him in the eye in an unusual way.

"Hey, you!" the man, wearing corporal's stripes, said. "Ain't you the sumbitch who brung in that damn Injun girl?"

Longarm's patience was at an end. He stopped and squared his shoulders. "Let me tell you two things, soldier boy. I'm not any kind of son of a bitch."

"Is that so?" the young cavalryman asked. "You look like a sumbitch to me."

"What I am, soldier boy, is a United States marshal, and if you say one more goddamn word to me, I'll put you in iron and take you to jail."

"You ain't no marshal," the corporal said, slurring his words slightly due to a few extra glasses of whiskey.

Longarm opened his coat to show the soldier his badge. "Now shut up, little boy blue, and go on about your business, or you'll spend the next month in the guardhouse, or worse."

He didn't wait for a reply, walking past the open-mouthed soldier to the sutler's tent.

Chapter 12

Longarm left the sutler's tent at dusk to send a wire from post headquarters at Fort Liberal. He needed to inform Billy of his whereabouts.

As he entered the tiny headquarters building, a sergeant rose up from his chair, giving Longarm a stern look.

"What can I do for you, sir?" he asked.

"I need to send a telegram," Longarm replied.

"This is a military outpost. We don't send wires out for civilians."

Longarm showed the sergeant his badge. "I'm not a civilian, Sergeant. I'm a federal marshal, and this is government business. Show me to the telegraph room, and get me an operator right now."

The soldier's face paled. "Yessir. I'll get Corporal Collins. Sorry, sir."

Corporal Collins held his pencil above a sheet of foolscap as he looked up at Longarm. "What do you want the message to say, Marshal?"

"Send it to United States Marshal Billy Vail at the Federal Building in Denver. Label it top priority."

"I understand, Marshal."

Longarm dictated the message:

US MARSHAL BILLY VAIL STOP FOUND HENRY STARR
AND ASSOCIATES ON CIMARRON RIVER STOP RENE-
GADE KIOWA BAND LED BY LONE BEAR TRADING
FOR REPEATING RIFLES STOP EXCHANGE OF UNPLEAS-
ANTRIES INVOLVING LEAD STOP BROUGHT WOUNDED
WOMAN TO FORT LIBERAL STOP WILL GO BACK AF-
TER STARR AND GUN SMUGGLERS TOMORROW STOP
WILL ASK FOR ARMY ASSISTANCE STOP WILL BE
LEAVING FORT LIBERAL KANSAS IN MORNING STOP
COLONEL BASS NEEDS TO BE INFORMED HERE STOP
US DEPUTY MARSHAL CUSTIS LONG END

"That woman you brought in was an Injun, Marshal,"
the young Corporal said.

"Does that make a difference?"

Collins looked askance. "Seems like it ought to, if
they're the ones causin' all the trouble."

"She needed medical attention, Corporal."

"Should I have the major put her in the guardhouse
when she is well enough to leave the post hospital?"

"No. If she wants to leave, let her go."

"That doesn't seem quite right, Marshal."

"She's my prisoner and those are my orders. If she feels
good enough to leave on her own, she's to be released at
once to return to her people."

"I'll tell the major," Collins said. "But when Colonel
Bass gets back, he ain't gonna be happy about it."

Longarm paused near the telegraph operator's door.
"I'm not in the business of making people happy, Cor-

poral. Let the woman go as soon as she's ready to leave. I'll wire a personal friend of mine, General Crook, if anything else is done. Make sure the Kiowa woman is allowed to leave whenever she's ready. Inform the colonel of my instructions."

"Yessir," Collins said quietly, beginning to tap out Longarm's message on his telegraph key.

Longarm left the headquarters building to stroll across the parade ground, where a flag fluttered in a brisk westerly wind. This was a wilderness outpost where the finer things in life Longarm usually enjoyed were not available at any price. What he needed now was a soft bed.

In the morning he'd head back down to the Cimarron region and resume his search for Henry Starr. But for the time being he needed some shut-eye.

Wandering toward the stable to check on his bay, he was surprised to find a woman in front of one of the stalls, a pretty young redhead with a slim waist and rounded hips, wearing a pale yellow cotton dress with her hair tied in a ponytail.

"Howdy, ma'am," he said, tipping his hat as he went back to the stall where his horse and Tooma's were being fed grain and hay.

"How do you do, sir," the woman replied, and when she faced him, he found that she was pretty in an off-handed way. Plain, but still pretty.

"I'm okay," he replied. "For the shape I'm in, stuck out here in the wilds of Kansas."

"It isn't to my tastes either," she said, smiling a half-hearted smile. "I'm stuck here because of a lame horse. The blacksmith told me it could be a week or two before my buggy horse is ready to travel."

He grinned back at her. "I can't think of a worse place

to be stuck for two weeks," he said. "Nothing here but soldiers and bad whiskey."

"I know," she said. "Out of kindness, I suppose, a Colonel Bass has given me an officer's cabin until my horse is ready to travel again. I don't know what I'll do to pass away the time until I can leave this dreadful place."

Longarm gave her a steady gaze. "Are you traveling alone, ma'am?"

"Unfortunately. My . . . gentleman companion abandoned me at Dodge City. I knew all along he wasn't trustworthy, but I never dreamed he'd rob me and leave me in a place like this."

"Sorry to hear it, ma'am," Longarm said, sauntering over to the stall where she was standing. "I'm Custis Long. I wish there was something I could do."

"I'm Christine Best, Mr. Long, and I appreciate your concern over my welfare. However, I'm afraid there's nothing anyone can do for me. I have almost no money and my buggy horse is lame. I'm a victim of circumstances."

"So am I," Longarm said. "I have to stay in this miserable city of tents tonight. Then I have to head down into Indian Territory tomorrow morning. But perhaps you'd let me buy you a drink at the sutler's?"

"I don't like that place."

"Why is that, Miz Best?"

"It's Miss Best, and it's because all those filthy soldiers keep staring at me."

"You're a downright pretty woman, Miss Best. It's hard to go against natural urges among lonely men."

"It makes me feel uncomfortable."

"Then how about a different solution," Longarm suggested. "I can buy a bottle of their best distilled spirits and we can share it out back, behind the stable, if that makes you feel more comfortable."

"I might agree to that," she said, a slight flush creeping up her cheeks.

"Then I'll go buy a bottle of their best brandy, or wine, or whiskey. Whatever they have. If you're still here when I get back, I'll know you intend to share it with me. If not, I'll drink it myself and go to bed."

"You sound like an honorable man, Mr. Long."

"I am, Miss Best. All I'm interested in is some pleasant company and someone to share a bottle with me before I turn in for the night."

"I'll be here when you get back," she said, leaning against the stall door. "I'm a pretty good judge of character and I think you're an honorable man."

"You are indeed a good judge of character, Miss Best," he said, tipping his hat again.

"Call me Christine," she told him.

"Only if you'll call me Custis," he replied, backing away to head for the sutler's.

He retuned with a bottle of cheap corn whiskey, the best to be had at the fort, only to find the stable empty.

"I'll drink this myself," he said, turning for the entrance into the horse barn.

Suddenly, he heard a muffled scream behind the stable. He was sure it was a woman's voice.

Longarm ran toward the sound, tossing the bottle into a mound of hay, running past the light cast by a lantern hanging from the stable doors, racing headlong into a dark corral behind the barn.

"Stop it, mister!" the woman cried.

He saw Christine being held against the side of the

93

clapboard shed by a uniformed soldier. Longarm drew his Colt and thumbed back the hammer.

"Let her go, soldier boy, or I'll blow a hole through you big enough for my fist."

The soldier glanced over his shoulder, still pinning the woman against the barn. "Get the hell away from here, mister, or I'll have you put in the guardhouse."

"Not likely," Longarm said with a calm belying his rising anger. "I'm a United States marshal, and I can have you sent back to Washington to face a court-martial. Then there's the possibility of additional federal charges."

"You ain't no goddamn federal marshal!" the soldier snapped.

Longarm opened his coat to show the soldier his badge. "I am. And I've got a gun aimed at you. Back away from the woman or you'll be bleeding like a bucket with a hole in it. I swear I'll shoot you if you don't let her go."

The uniformed man released his grip on Christine's arms and took a step backward. "I was only meanin' to have a little fun," he said.

"Have your fun someplace else, soldier. Now get the hell out of here before I report you to Colonel Bass as soon as he gets back."

"Sure thing, mister." He started up the alleyway between the stalls of the livery.

Christine buried her face in her hands as if she were crying now.

Longarm stepped over to her. "It's okay. He won't be giving you any more problems."

She stared into his eyes. "Are you really a United States marshal?" she asked.

"Some of the time, when I'm on duty. Tonight, I'm

94

only gonna drink a bottle of whiskey with a pretty lady and forget about my official duties."

The woman shivered. "I was scared. When I tried to scream he put his hand over my mouth."

"He won't bother you again. You have my word on it. Let's get that bottle. It'll do your nerves some good."

"I could use a drink now," she said, drying her eyes with her hands.

He took her arm and led her into the stable.

"He came up behind me," Christine said. "I didn't hear him."

"Forget about it," Longarm said, picking up the bottle. "No harm was done that I can see."

She wiped her cheeks again. "Why is it that a woman alone is always a victim of unwanted attention?"

"This is the West. There aren't many women out here," he explained. "Men get lonely for a woman's company, and when they see a woman unescorted . . ."

"I know," Christine said.

Longarm pulled the cork from the bottle with his teeth and offered it to her. "They didn't have any glasses they'd part with."

"I'll manage," she replied, tipping the bottle back for a swallow.

"Your hands are shaking, Christine," he observed, taking the bottle for himself.

"I was scared. I was sure that soldier meant to have his way with me."

"You're safe now," Longarm told her, pouring flavored corn whiskey down his throat.

She smiled. "I've never met a United States marshal before."

"I'm just a man doin' a job, pretty lady."

"Do you really think I'm pretty?"

"Wouldn't have said it if I didn't mean it."

Christine took the bottle again and drank thirstily. "Not many men tell me that anymore. I'm twenty-eight years old, and most men prefer younger women."

"I like a woman with experience," Longarm said.

"Experience? Do you mean experience with a man in bed?"

"I reckon that's what I meant. No offense intended."

"None was taken, Custis. I was merely surprised by what you said."

"A woman who knows how to please a man is hard to find."

Her eyes sparkled . . . they were a shade of green. "I know how to please a man," she said.

He gazed down at her. "If you don't have any other plans for the evening, I'd count myself a lucky man if you showed me how."

Christine smiled. "Follow me to my cabin, Custis. I'll do my very best to convince you that I can make you happy."

"That's an invitation you don't have to offer me twice," he said, giving her his arm. "Just show me the way."

Chapter 13

When he began taking off her corset, he found the bind-
ings tight, too restrictive to allow his fingers room to
work, and he had trouble with knots on laces across the
front after placing her blouse across a straight-backed
chair at one side of the bed. Christine moaned, her face
illuminated by pale moonlight from the window.

"You must promise me you'll stop if I tell you to," she
mumbled under the strong influence of whiskey, her
words slightly mushy. He'd had to help her into the vacant
officer's quarters, steadying her with an arm around her
waist while she giggled over her poor balance when she
lost her footing.

Longarm unfastened the knot and pulled strings off the
hooks holding her undergarment in place. "I promise not
to make any inappropriate advances. Don't you think this
is appropriate?"

"I invited you here." She giggled softly.

"I am a gentleman. I'll show you just how gentle I can
be under any circumstances, if that's what you want."

"Your . . . cock is so big. I can feel it against my leg

when you rub against me. It's so big, I'm sure it will hurt. Please don't hurt me."

"I promise I'll be gentle, just a little bit at a time until you tell me to stop."

"And what if I don't ask you to stop?" Christine giggled again.

He pushed the corset down, across her hips, past her knees, until the garment fell at the foot of the single cot occupying the small room. "Then I won't stop," he promised.

Her breathing became faster when his hand moved gently over the mound of soft hair at the tops of her thighs. "It feels so good when . . . you touch me, Custis. But I want you to stop. We only met a few minutes ago."

"How long do a man and woman have to know each other?" he asked, taking her hand, placing it so her fingers curled around the thickness of his shaft where it strained against his underwear.

A moan, a mixture of pleasure and fear, escaped her lips. "I'm quite certain you'll think I'm a cheap woman," she said in a husky voice, slowly stroking his member. "My mother wouldn't approve. I couldn't tell her about *this*."

He cupped one creamy breast with a palm and gently rolled her nipple between his thumb and forefinger. She gasped, and a tiny shudder coursed down the length of her body. "Oh, Custis," she whispered. "Take off your underwear so I can feel the skin of your cock with my fingertips."

He obliged her while lying on his side, tossing his underwear to the floor. Her hand encircled his prick, and when it did, she let out another gasp. "I've never seen . . . I've never felt one so big! Even if I were to decide to let you make love to me, this wouldn't work . . . I just know it wouldn't."

He grinned. "I'd never be one to push you to such a decision, Christine, but let me assure you that if you did decide to make love to me, I'll put it in very gently—not all of it, you understand." He pinched her rosy nipple a little harder, and suddenly her spine arched off the mattress.

"It's too big around to go in at all," she groaned, fingers measuring his circumference almost unconsciously while she kept pumping up and down on his cock. "I'm afraid it will tear me in half. I won't let you hurt me that way, but I do wish there was something we could do. . . ." She trembled, and fell back on the bed with a sigh, still jacking his prick, moaning, moving her head from side to side on the pillow with her eyes tightly closed.

Longarm put a finger between the moist lips of her cunt and gently entered her, feeling her slick wetness and the fever in her loins. He was sure he could work his cock into her if he did it slowly, without too much pressure right at first.

Involuntarily, she began hunching against his finger as tiny spasms gripped her thighs. "Please, Custis," she whimpered. "You must think of something. I feel like I'm about to explode."

He withdrew his wet finger and moved carefully between her legs, placing the tip of his cock against her mound.

"No, Custis!" she cried, grinding her pelvis up and down as she held firmly to his cock with her fingers. "It's much too large."

With only the slightest pressure he pushed his prick between the lips of her cunt, and now, as she thrust herself against it, he saw a tear glisten on her cheek.

"I want it," she whispered, "but there isn't room. You have the biggest prick . . . too large for a girl like me. I'm not all that experienced, you see."

Ever so slowly he pressed his member slightly deeper,

until it would go no further, meeting resistance. And still, Christine ground her tight opening back and forth, making a wet, sucking sound when the tip of his prick went in and out.

"You must stop," she gasped, releasing her grip on his cock to encircle his buttocks with both hands, clawing fiercely into his skin with her fingernails, pulling him closer, deeper.

The irony did not escape him, her protests and her hunger for his prick, asking him to stop while she drew him closer to her, gyrating her hips, thrusting forward with her wet cunt, at the same time she told him to halt his advances.

"Just a little more," he said into her ear, scenting the sweet smell of her red hair and her lilac perfume.

"No. Please, no," she hissed, clenching her teeth, yet with an ever-increasing tempo to her pelvic thrusts, again voicing a wish for him to stop while her body seemed to be demanding more of his prick. "You said you would stop if I asked you to."

"I'll do it gently," he replied, pushing harder, feeling the muscles in her mound relax, opening a fraction more to accept his cock.

"That . . . feels . . . good," she breathed, "but you simply must stop. You're hurting me."

"You said it felt good."

"It does. It hurts, and it feels good. I don't understand how. Oh, please stop before you hurt me any more."

Longarm had known for years he would never be able to understand women. "There's such a thing as hurting in a good way?" he asked, pumping gently, more deeply, into her opening. Slippery sounds accompanied their every move, and the heat from her cunt was like a fire now.

"Yes. I mean . . . no." Her fingernails dug deeper into

his buttocks. Tiny beads of sweat formed on her brow and in the cleft between her breasts.

His erection was throbbing, and the warm wetness around it caused his balls to rise, spreading a warmth of their own down his thighs, across his abdomen. He could smell her sweet musk, and the tremors in her limbs only added to his excitement—he pushed deeper inside her, and suddenly her body went rigid underneath him.

"Now," she sighed, hammering against his shaft in spite of a lingering trace of resistance where the walls of her hungry cunt held him back. "Please stop now."

He closed his mind to her feeble protests, and thrust a half inch more of thick cock into her.

"Oh, Custis . . . no more. I can't take any more."

The bed began to rock, bedsprings squeaking, and the headboard tapped the wall of the cabin with every stroke, and he was sure that any second now, his testicles would explode.

Her breathing came in short bursts, and soft sounds arose in her throat. "Please stop, Custis."

Her skin had grown so clammy, he found he was barely able to stay on top of her, the friction between their bodies creating more sweat, matting the thick hair on his chest. Her breasts swayed with every stroke, rotating against his ribs like giant mounds of quivering egg custard.

Without warning her cunt opened, and despite his promise to be gentle with her, he buried his member inside her almost all the way to the hilt.

Christine screamed, clawing his buttocks until he felt blood run down his sides—she arched her spine, shaking violently, as the echo of her scream became a wail, then a softer groan that Longarm hoped wouldn't be heard by soldiers outside. And all the while she continued to thrust against the base of his shaft with powerful lunges, hammering against him, his balls slapping the crack between her hips as he pounded his cock into her slit more rapidly.

She slammed her groin into him several more times, and then her entire body went rigid. She wailed, digging her heels into his calves, rising off the bed with him on top of her in spite of his weight.

As she reached her climax, his testicles spewed forth a stream of jism, and the feeling of ecstasy was so intense, he let out a groan, driving his cock into her at tremendous speed and with the full force of the muscles in his hips.

"Oh, dear!" she shouted, cords of muscle standing out in her neck, her arms clasped around him with surprising strength for a slender girl.

She collapsed on sweat-soaked bedsheets, panting, completely out of breath. Her head lolled to one side on the pillow, and for a time she was motionless, her limbs falling limply on the mattress.

He spent the rest of his jism in her as gently as he could, and then halted the thrusting motion of his cock, finding he was also short of breath. Resting on his elbows so she could breathe, he looked down at her in moonlight from a window.

"You're really some special kind of woman," he said. "I never felt anything quite like this."

Her eyes fluttered open. She stared at him a moment. "You bastard," she said softly. "You promised me you would stop if I asked you to. After all, you're a U.S. marshal."

"I meant to stop, only you felt so good ... it felt so good being inside you that I couldn't help myself."

A slow smile crossed her face. "I knew you were a liar

the minute I set eyes on you. Men who lie to women have a certain look about them."

"I'm sorry if I disappointed you."

Her smile changed to a mock scowl. "You hurt me. Your cock was too big and you used it anyway."

"Like I said, I just couldn't help it. And you didn't say a man has to be perfect, did you? Sometimes people are overcome by emotion. It's a human characteristic. I'm only a man, and if a beautiful woman winds up in my bed, I can't always control some of my urges."

"You lied to me." She said it playfully, not with reproach in her voice.

"I simply forgot in a moment of passion what I said. I hope you won't hold it against me."

She stirred underneath him, and the movement brought a smile to her lips. The muscles in her thighs quivered. She kissed him hard across the mouth, and he sensed her hunger was about to come alive again.

Very gently, he moved his prick inside her, pulling back as if he meant to withdraw. She reached for him to hold him where he was.

"Don't leave yet," she whispered. "I like the way it feels now, when your cock isn't so hard."

"I hadn't planned on leaving, my darling. Just a change in my position, is all."

Her groin tensed, and he could feel a tightening around his prick.

"I want more," she said huskily, "only please don't put it in me so deeply."

He began slow strokes in and out, and now the wet, sucking sounds were louder than before with her juices mingling with his jism.

"Like that," she sighed, closing her eyes, wrapping her arms around his back.

His slow pumping aroused her further, and her limbs began to tremble again.

"Not too deep," she groaned, wincing slightly as if the pain had also reawakened within her downy mound.

Longarm continued his shallow strokes, feeling his member thicken again, and at the same time her cunt opened slightly to allow him deeper penetration.

"Faster," she whispered in his ear, increasing the pressure of her embrace as her fingernails dug into his back. Again the bed began to squeak as their passion mounted.

"Faster," Christine cried, gasping, curling her legs around his to hold him in a viselike grip.

He felt a pulse in his cock. Her cunt was so slippery and wet that despite his second promise not to drive his prick into her too deeply, he found himself almost out of control. When she bowed her back off the mattress, seeking more of him, he obliged her and sent his prick all the way to the hilt.

"Oh, yes!" Christine exclaimed, clawing his back fiercely. "Do it harder . . . faster."

He let go of all his reserve and began hammering his cock into her, feeling the lips of her cunt stretch to accept him. Her juices flowed down his balls, warm and slick.

"Now!" she cried, rocking against him with so much force, he had to cling to each corner of the mattress to stay atop her, seeking a purchase in the bedsheet with his toes.

"Yes! Yes! Yes!" she screamed, her body turning to iron beneath him when a second climax overwhelmed her.

His balls erupted a few moments later, and it seemed to him that the room was spinning . . . or was it the bed?

Chapter 14

He looked in on Tooma at the post hospital after he saddled his horse. Eastern skies pinked with dawn. Christine had been asleep when he slipped quietly out of the officer's cabin to set out for Cimarron country. She had been wild, fun, a chance meeting that had turned into something more. However, he couldn't get involved in her problems now. He had a murderer to track down and a gang of gun traders to bring to justice, if he could find them.

An orderly, dozing in his chair near the front door, sat up when Longarm came in.

"How's the Kiowa girl?" he asked.

"She don't hardly say a word, 'cept that she wants to get the hell out of here."

"I need to talk to her, if she's awake."

"Who the hell are you, mister? This a United States Army hospital."

"And I'm a United States marshal," Longarm said, showing his badge. "I brought the Kiowa woman here for medical treatment and I damn sure intend to talk to her."

"Sorry, sir," the orderly said, coming to his feet. "She's in that little private room at the back. I'll turn up the lanterns so you can see your way down the hall. Didn't mean no disrespect, sir."

"I'll find my own way," Longarm said, strolling toward the rear of a narrow building lined with cots. He noticed that only a few of the beds were occupied. This was a peaceful time for the army, with most of the warlike Indian tribes settled on reservations.

He came to a small room, a ten-foot square, and peered inside. Early light from a window revealed the Kiowa girl's features and that her eyes were open, staring at him. A thick gauze bandage was tied around her damaged arm.

"Are you feeling okay, Tooma?"

"I want to go back to my people."

"It might not be a good idea right now."

"Why?"

"Soldier patrols are out looking for Lone Bear. It would be best if you went back to the reservation as soon as you can travel. Your pinto pony is at the cavalry stable . . . it's being cared for and well fed."

"I have to go back to Lone Bear. Our people are starving on the reservation."

"I'll see what I can do about that," Longarm promised, "but first I have to find Henry Starr and those gun smugglers. It's my job."

"I can ride now," Tooma said, sitting up slowly, cradling her injured arm against her chest.

"Give it a day or two. The doctor here will make sure your wound doesn't fester."

"I do not know that word. . . ."

"He'll make sure it doesn't swell. If gangrene sets in, you could lose your arm."

"I do not understand these words."

Longarm took a deep breath, wondering how to explain the risks to her. "You'll have to trust me on this. You need to wait a day or so, just to be sure."

"I do not like this place. Even the white medicine man looks at me with hard eyes. He does not like the Kiowa. He is like all white men."

"He'll take care of your wound."

"I want to go with you, white star man. You are . . . different and I am not afraid of you."

"You shouldn't get out of bed so soon," Longarm said as he leaned against the door frame.

"I go with you," Tooma told him, tossing a thin blanket aside to swing her feet to the floor, where a pair of worn deerskin boots lay beneath the bed.

"It'll be too dangerous, Tooma."

"I go. I follow you."

The last thing he needed now was an Indian girl tagging along.

She pulled on her boots gingerly, using her good arm, then stood up. "I am ready to go," she said.

Longarm's shoulders slumped. "I'll take you as far as the river, the Cimarron, but from there on I'm going after Starr alone."

"I can show you the cave where he makes camp," she said as she came toward him.

"It'll be too risky. Starr will have a guard or two posted and there could be some shooting."

She walked past him out of the room without saying a word, aiming for the front door of the post hospital.

"What should I tell Major Green?" the orderly asked as they made ready to walk outside.

"Just tell him the Indian girl is with U.S. Marshal Custis

Long, and that I'll assume responsiblity for her." He hesitated. "I could use a bottle of laudanum for her pain, if you've got one handy."

"There's some in the medicine cabinet. Don't reckon it'll hurt if I give you one."

"I'll pay for it, if that's a requirement."

"Ain't likely, sir, seein' as you're a federal marshal an' all."

Moments later the sleepy-eyed orderly brought Longarm a small purple bottle.

"Tell Dr. Green I'm obliged, and that if I owe anything he can send a voucher to the chief marshal's office in Denver."

"Don't suppose there'll be no need for that," the orderly said as Longarm led Tooma out of the hospital and the sun crept above the horizon.

Traveling southeast, they soon crossed the line into Indian Territory, aiming for the tiny settlement called Beaver on the Beaver River. For the first few miles Tooma said nothing, clinging to the back of her pony.

"Does that arm hurt?" Longarm asked.

"No. It is nothing." She stared straight ahead at the open prairie and remained silent.

"I've got the painkilling medicine in my saddlebags if you need it."

"No. I only need to return to Lone Bear."

"It's here if you want it," he said, deciding against further attempts at conversation.

They came to the Beaver River. Tooma seemed uneasy now, and Longarm couldn't understand why.

"Is something wrong, Tooma?"

"Men are watching us."

Longarm gave the horizon and surrounding hills a careful examination. "I don't see anyone. Are they your people?"

"No. If the Kiowa watched us, no one would see them."

"Could it be Henry Starr?"

"I do not know. I only see them twice. Two men, watching us from the south."

Longarm unbooted his Winchester rifle and jacked a load into the firing chamber. "Let 'em come. I'll be ready for them if they do."

She looked at him. "What is it like to be a star man? You are a big chief among your people?"

"I represent the law. When my people or anybody else in this part of the country breaks the law, it's my job to put them in jail."

"The iron cages," Tooma said softly, looking away. "So many of my people have been put in the iron cages."

"I can't explain it so you'll understand, Tooma, but some men have to be put away where they can't harm anyone else. Even some of your people."

"It seems wrong. Cages are for animals."

"Murderers like Henry Starr aren't much more than animals. They kill people who can't defend themselves."

"It is your work to kill them?" she asked.

He nodded once. "If they won't go to jail when I ask 'em to, I've got no choice but to kill them."

"It seems strange, this white man's law."

"It's meant to protect folks who don't carry guns or believe in killing to get what they want. Somebody has to come along to take their side in things."

"A Kiowa who is too weak to fight will die. It is the way of our people."

"White folks see things a little differently. That's why they've got men like me."

"You are a brave warrior, star man."

"Why don't you call me Custis."

"Cus-tis," she said, trying to pronounce it the way he did. Then she smiled.

"Have you ever been in battle with the Kiowa?" she asked.

He recalled an incident years ago when Billy Vail took a Kiowa bullet during a powerful snowstorm in the eastern part of Colorado, back when Billy still rode the wild country during the Indian troubles.

"Yeah. I've had my share of fights with the Kiowa," he said. "Your people are tough. Clever. Hard to shoot unless we know what we're doing."

"I do not understand."

"The chief marshal out of Denver took a Kiowa bullet several years ago."

"Did he die?"

"Nope. We made it through, but it was one of the toughest assignments we ever had. A chief by the name of Lone Wolf had led a band of warriors north, to our jurisdiction."

"Chief Lone Wolf was the bravest chief in all the history of our people."

"He was tough, I'll give him that, and he knew how to fight in open country," Longarm agreed.

Tooma looked at the horizon. "The men who were watching us are gone. Tell me about your fight with Lone Wolf, and then I will tell you about the caves made of glass."

"Seems like a fair trade," he said.

Chapter 15

"Here's how I remember it," Longarm began, thinking back to the time when he and Billy Vail rode together. "We were down at the border where Indian Territory and Colorado meet. It was snowing like crazy. We'd been in a fight for our lives, and Billy had taken a bullet.

"All at once all six ponies were moving in different directions, bounding away at full speed with riders clinging to their backs. I saw an Indian with a lone eagle feather tied into his hair swing a rifle to his shoulder as he urged his pony across the creek. Before I could bring my sights to bear on him, a shot cracked. A ball of lead struck the tree where I was standing, a sound that made me flinch involuntarily. Bark chips flew a foot higher than my head, as limbs on either side quivered with the bullet's impact.

"Snow on the ends of branches dropped to the ground with a soft plop I was scarcely able to hear, because of thudding pony hooves. Snowflakes kicked up by speeding ponies swirled, dancing on the wind like ghostly apparitions, until they fell back to earth. I was tempted to fire at poor targets, although I resisted those urges, waiting for a shot that wouldn't miss. But due to my hesitation, in a matter of seconds all six warriors were well out of range, racing back down the creek banks on both sides, their ponies' manes and tails flying in the wind.

"My mouth was suddenly bone dry. I watched the Indians gallop away into spits of windblown snow farther downstream. I tried to slow my breathing and my heart. Only one shot had been fired, and none of the warriors had shown much inclination to continue our brief encounter with more shooting.

" 'Maybe they won't come back,' " I said softly, peering into a veil of white to see if they were doubling back, or splitting up to flank me.

"I understood the weakness of my present position immediately when I glanced both ways across the wash. They could easily have me in a cross fire by riding along the top of the draw, shooting down at will, using the rim for cover if they came for me on foot later on. I had to get up on top, on the ledge above the cave. It was the only spot I could find where I'd have a view of every possible angle of attack.

"After a final look downstream, I took off running for all I was worth to climb the bank above our camp, stumbling through one deep drift after another. My lungs got so full of icy air, it was painful to take a breath. I reached the bottom of the incline in record time and started up, slipping and sliding, struggling for a purchase in loose snow while wearing slick-bottomed leather boots not made for climbing.

"I glanced over at Billy. He was where I'd left him, lying on his side near the fire, unconscious. There wasn't time to pull him away to the back of the cave, where he was less likely to be hit by a stray bullet.

"I made the top and looked along the rim, and saw a pair of Indians galloping toward me through falling snow. I dropped to one knee and held my Winchester steady. I could hear the thump of hooves growing louder. I fixed my gun sights on one of the Indians and a second later, I drew the hammer back. I was gasping for air and it was hard to steady the muzzle.

"Billy had warned me not to start shooting until we knew who these Indians were, but a shot had already been fired at me and as far as I was concerned, I knew enough to be satisfied they meant to kill us.

" 'A little closer,' " I whispered, shivering, trying to catch my breath. Even the best marksman would have trouble hitting me from the back of a moving horse when it was snowing so heavily. I waited until I knew I couldn't miss.

"I squeezed the trigger. That .44-caliber Winchester packs a hell of a kick, and when the cartridge exploded it rocked me back, while the sound was like thunder in my right ear. Yellow flame spat from the barrel. The roar of the shot echoed from the far side of the wash.

"For an instant I thought I'd missed, until my target fell back across the rump of his speeding pony. His legs went up, and he rolled like a ball off the rear of his horse with his robe fluttering around him. He appeared to float in midair for a moment before he fell, toppling into a snowbank, sending a cloud of white flakes away from the spot where he landed. His dark pony shied, bolting off to the left without its rider in an all-out run.

"I was levering another shell into the chamber when I heard a shout, a yipping cry like Indians sometimes make when they enter into a fight. Far to my right, across the draw, a gun roared in the distance. I could hear a slug whistle overhead, high and too wide to the left.

"I turned my sights on the second warrior, guessing he'd make a swing in another direction rather than continuing straight at me. But I guessed wrong. He was pounding his heels into his pony's ribs as hard as he could, yelling at the top of his lungs. I saw a muzzle flash, and heard the crack of a rifle. Ducking as low as I could, I held my gun steady.

"He was almost on top of me before I fired, because he stayed down near his pony's neck and I didn't want to shoot an animal if I could help it. My finger nudged the trigger when the Indian was barely twenty yards away. My rifle slammed into my shoulder so hard I felt it all the way to my toes, and the noise left me momentarily deaf as a stone.

"I saw the Indian's head jerk backward. In the same instant his pony swerved. He went off one side of his horse so quickly, I would have sworn he'd vanished altogether until I saw him land, skittering across the snow, twisting this way and that with arms and legs windmilling. He slid to a halt where snow drifted deep, and sort of bunched up, his knees under his chin. He lay there a moment while I was chambering another round before his legs fell flat.

"I noticed then he had a single braid of hair, making him a Kiowa. Billy would be glad to know we weren't facing Comanches, if he ever woke up long enough to realize we were in a fight.

"A shot from across the creek sent me diving flat on my belly with my face buried in snowflakes. When I rolled over on my side, I saw an Indian on foot, standing in front of his pony with his rifle smoking. I swung the Winchester to my shoulder, resting on an elbow, trying to see through spits of snow that were making it hard to be sure what I was aiming at. I blinked snow from my eyes, but before I could clear them, the warrior was aboard his horse at a dead run away from there.

" 'Damn it,' " I hissed, clenching my teeth to keep them from chattering. I watched that Indian disappear into the storm with a thankful feeling. He'd had a perfect shot at me, and I'd been so careless I hadn't even noticed him before he got off a shot. I knew I couldn't count on being so lucky again.

"It was then I realized how out in the open I was, lying on my belly at the top of the creek. If any one of them got a good shot at me, I'd be an easy target.

"I crawled backward, inching through powdery snow, feeling a wet, chilly sensation down my chest where snow had gotten inside my shirt, melting with the heat of my body. Now I could hear the wind moaning overhead, and feel gooseflesh pimpling my skin. If I was forced to stay up there very long, I'd freeze. But where else could I find a vantage point where I could protect our camp and our horses?

"Looking around, I discovered I had no other choice but to hold my present position as long as I could. As I was taking stock of my situation, a gun banged to my left. When I heard the noise, I couldn't be sure of its direction, and like a fool I'd been taken completely by surprise.

"I flipped over to find where the shot came from, clutching my Winchester close to my chest. The bullet had gone so high I didn't hear it. However, the sound was close, too close for me to relax and get my wits together.

"I made a turn on my belly and shouldered the rifle,

sweeping its muzzle back and forth, searching for anything I couldn't be sure of that looked like it could be a target. I saw a riderless pony plunging into a snowdrift north of the draw, trailing its jaw-rein. In a few seconds it went out of sight into sheets of snowflakes, leaving me without a clue as to where the shot had come from. For what seemed like an eternity I remained frozen there, looking across the tiny metal sight at the end of my rifle with nothing to shoot at.

"A movement on the far side caught my attention. An Indian rode brazenly along the western edge of the creek, out in plain sight like he wanted to draw my fire. I was ready to oblige him just then, until something moved on my side of the stream.

"A galloping pony appeared through the whirling snowflakes, and for a moment I was sure the little horse ran loose without a rider. Until I saw a darker shape clinging to the sorrel's high withers, a Kiowa with a rifle.

"There was no time to get ready for a clean shot—I had only a second or two to aim and fire. I held the Winchester's stock to my shoulder as tightly as I could, and brushed the trigger with a finger enclosed by a half-frozen red mitten.

"The blast drove me backward. When the shell went off, my toes weren't dug in to keep me from moving. I slid back as a puff of smoke billowed from the muzzle, and in spite of myself I closed my eyes when the sound was so loud, it felt like it threatened to break something inside my right ear.

"I'd missed. I knew it the minute I fired. Working the lever as fast as I could, I readied another shell, and at the very same instant, a chilling scream came from the Indian bearing down on me. I saw him working a bolt on a single-action carbine, and I suppose the fact that he had an older weapon must have spared my life—he took too long getting ready to shoot, just long enough for me to fire first.

"My Winchester belched flame. The Indian was so near, I could see a tuft of brown fur torn from his buffalo robe where the slug went through his shoulder.

He yelled, twisting on the withers of his charging pony to reach for his shoulder wound, at the same time tossing his carbine in the air. That's when his mount stumbled over some object hidden beneath deep snow. It went crashing on its chest, legs flailing, making a grunting sound as it fell.

"The Kiowa was tossed forward through the air, kicking his feet helplessly as though he meant to run as soon as he hit the ground. He was coming straight at me, propelled toward me by his pony's fall, so close I could see the wild expression on his face and even the whites of his eyes. There was no time to eject my spent cartridge and chamber another—I scrambled to my knees and swung my rifle like a club as he was falling on top of me.

"The barrel struck bone midway through my swing. I heard a snapping noise and felt the shock of the blow clear down to my shoulders when I hit him across his skull. The angle of his dive changed suddenly when I knocked him to my left with every ounce of strength I had. He tumbled to the snowbank with blood squirting from his head, groaning, landing disjointedly the way a man does when he's out cold. Blood was spreading around him so fast it colored the snow crimson, like someone spilled a bucket of red paint.

"I gathered my wits while I rocked back on my haunches to get another cartridge chambered, looking around me as the empty shell went spinning away into the snow. The sorrel pony struggled to its feet, and snorted once before it whirled and galloped off into the storm.

"Before I could collect myself from such a close encounter, a shot rang out across the wash. The whine of lead screamed above me, forcing me to dive down on my belly again. I caught a brief glimpse of a buckskin pony racing through a curtain of snowflakes before a gust of windswept snow moved in front of my eyes, temporarily blinding me. It looked like the Indian was aimed for our camp as hard as he could ride.

"I crawled to the rim as rapidly as possible with my rifle in both hands, bringing it to my shoulder the minute I had a view of the streambed. The mounted warrior urged his buckskin across one last drift at the bottom of the slope, forcing it to run where no horse could without floundering. Deep snow was slowing the pony just enough for me to draw a bead on its rider.

"My arms were trembling when I pulled the trigger. The sharp report of my Winchester popped, a noise like snapping timber. At almost the same time, a fraction of a second before I fired, that buckskin sank to its knees in the drift. My bullet kicked up a big cloud of white on the slope behind the Indian's head, a wide miss, way off its mark.

"I chambered again quickly while the buckskin got to its feet and shook itself. The warrior clinging to its back attempted to fire up at me. His rifle roared an instant before mine.

"I felt a breath of air whisper past my right cheek. My gun exploded, kicking, ramming the butt plate against me. I blinked and shook my head.

"Down below, the robed figure atop the buckskin slid

118

off one side of his pony as the little horse was dashing toward our cave at full speed. I saw him fall into the snow, losing his rifle. It had been a difficult shot, but I'd made it.

"The Kiowa rolled a few times before he came to a halt with his arms and legs landing loose. I couldn't tell where I'd hit him from that distance. He was out of the fight for now, and that was what mattered.

"My spare ammunition was back at camp. I'd downed four Indians, leaving two more who might still be looking for more fight.

"I came to my knees quickly and cleared my coattail out of the way to get at my pistol. As I was getting up, I thought I heard a sound behind me, a quiet footfall in the snow.

"I wheeled around, jerking my Colt free, when I saw a dark shape in the snow. I cocked my gun and prepared to fire, when something made me stop."

"What made you stop?" Tooma asked.

"I was looking at an Indian, a Kiowa warrior, with blood all over the front of his deerskin shirt. He was staggering toward me."

"You did not kill him?"

"No. I found I couldn't shoot him."

"Why, Star Man Custis?"

"He didn't have a gun. He was carrying a crude iron hatchet in his fist. He was so weakened by loss of blood, he could scarcely move his feet."

"But he was your enemy."

"It didn't seem that way then. He was just a man, fighting for what he believed in, even though he was dying. I couldn't pull the trigger."

"What happened to him?"

"He was only a few yards away from me when he sank to his knees in the snow. He'd gone as far as he could."

"What did you do?"

"I had to get back to Billy because there were two more Kiowas running loose. I couldn't let them get to Billy, so I hurried back to the ledge."

"You are a brave warrior," Tooma said.

"I didn't feel all that brave back then. I felt real lucky to be alive."

"I do not understand a man like you," she said in a faraway voice, staring at the prairie.

"Why's that?"

"You could have killed the warrior. You did not. This is not the way of our people."

"He was too weak to fight me. What was the point in shooting him?"

"He was your enemy."

"Not then, not with a wound as bad as his. He was just a man who was bleeding to death. The battle between us was already over."

"I will never understand white men," she said, guiding her pony over a shallow depression.

Longarm chuckled, reaching into his saddlebags for a pint of the sutler's bad whiskey. "Not much to understand really. We're just trying to live peacefully out here. I know the white man has taken away your hunting lands, but I had nothing to do with it. I'm only enforcing the white man's laws. It's what I get paid to do. . . ."

Chapter 16

"What happened to your star man friend, the one you called Billy?" Tooma asked as they sent their horses across the shallow Beaver River under a clear morning sky.

"I spent a long night worrying, and listening to Billy cough in the wee hours before dawn," said Longarm. "I dozed from time to time, although I never really slept soundly, thinking about the possibility more Kiowas would come back to have their revenge for the warriors I shot. Every now and then I'd look out at a lump in the snow where one dead Kiowa lay, and the sight of it made me all the more jittery. On the good side of things, it was snowing less when a streak of gray brightened the eastern horizon. However, my brief celebration was over the minute I could see down that draw well enough to recognize forty or fifty Indians riding slowly toward our camp.

"I scrambled to my feet holding my rifle. My heart began to thump. 'Wake up, Billy!, I cried, edging over near the pallet where Billy lay, never once taking my eyes from that fierce-looking party of Kiowas moving along both sides of the creek, until I was close enough to reach down and shake Billy's shoulder. 'Better open up your eyes if you can,' I added quickly as a sinking feeling got started in the pit of my stomach. There were so many Indians, I knew we could never stand them off.

"Billy stirred underneath his blankets. 'What did you say, Custis?' he mumbled sleepily, rubbing his eyes.

" 'I said you'd better sit up. There's at least fifty Indians out there.' I was only guessing at the number.

"Billy sat up quickly, focusing on what he saw riding toward us in dawn's pale light. He coughed once, and spat a mouthful out in the snow. 'Hand me my rifle,' he said softly. 'An' whatever you do, don't fire a shot unless I tell you to.' He put on his hat, and came slowly to his feet, as I was handing him his Winchester.

" 'There's too many of them,' " I said.

"Billy tugged the brim of his hat low over his eyes. 'It's a comfort to know you can count, Custis,' he said. He buttoned his coat and turned to me. 'The one ridin' the piebald roan stud is Lone Wolf. It's gonna take some fancy talkin' to get us out of this.'

"He made it sound like I was to blame. 'I had to shoot back yesterday or they'd have killed us both and taken our horses,' I said. 'I didn't see no other way out."

"Billy didn't offer an opinion, watching Kiowas ride closer to our cave. I paid attention to the one he'd identified as Lone Wolf, riding a colorful roan pinto stallion. Shrouded in his buffalo robe, he made a fearsome sight. He carried a rifle with an eagle feather tied to the stock, resting it across his pony's withers. His face was as hard-looking as nearly any Indian I'd ever seen, with the possible exception being Quannah Parker. Quannah's pale eyes gave him the meanest expression, but Lone Wolf had his own fierce look, fixing us with a cold stare as he rode in front of his warriors.

"They came toward us like they knew we didn't have a chance against them, appearing real confident, unafraid of our repeating rifles. I was cold before I saw them, but right then I felt a chill all the way down my spine.

"Billy walked away from our camp, balancing his Winchester in the palm of his left hand. His stride was a little unsteady as he crossed all that snow, and I knew it was because he'd been so sick he hadn't eaten right for a spell. But he still managed to carry himself like he had pride, walking straight out to face a half a hundred armed Indians without showing any visible signs of fear. I had to hand it to him. If he knew we were gonna die, he damn sure didn't let on to those Kiowas.

"He stopped about thirty yards from the cave and raised his right hand, making sign talk while Lone Wolf and his bunch kept coming toward us. I watched Lone Wolf real close to see if he answered back with a sign. He didn't, and that convinced me all the more that me and Billy were in the last fight of our lives, as soon as the shooting started.

"Lone Wolf rode his pinto right up to Billy, with warriors on either side of him. When Lone Wolf stopped, so did the others.

"Billy said something, words I didn't understand. When he was speaking Comanche or Kiowa, it sounded more like grunting than making words, most of the time. He told me once that Comanche and Kiowa are nearly the same language, and that the two tribes were almost kin. I listened as close as I could, waiting for Lone Wolf to answer.

" 'Pe-she-pah Mah-e-yah,' " Lone Wolf said, and then

he pointed right at me, staring like he would kill me any second now. Then he uttered another string of words, spitting them out so rapidly they all came at once.

"Billy looked over his shoulder. 'Come here, Mr. Custis. Be real sure you don't act scared or go for a gun. No matter what he says or does, just stand still an' don't act like you're the least bit afraid of him.'

"My heart quit beating entirely for a second or two. 'You want me to come out there?'

"The look on Billy's face told me it was a dumb question. I'd heard him right the first time. I took a big breath and started walking toward Billy and the Indians, wondering if these might be the last steps I ever took. I kept my rifle pointed down at the ground, but my eyes were on Lone Wolf. If I could, I aimed to see if I could stare him down.

"The closer I got, the more it appeared that Lone Wolf was in a killing mood. He watched me without a trace of expression on his face, but his dark eyes said enough, a mouthful. He gave me one of the meanest stares I've ever seen, until I was standing to the left of Billy with my feet spread slightly apart.

"Billy spoke to me first. 'He wanted to get a good look at you up close, Custis. Just stand there till he satisfies himself about you. Don't look off, an' whatever you do, don't make any kind of move with a gun. He's curious about you. The two boys who rode back to the village told Lone Wolf you had a pair of red hands. It's those damn mittens you brought along. They also said you were a brave warrior, that you fought with a lot of courage. He wants to see if you're really all that brave-lookin'. If we're lucky, all he'll do is look. Those boy warriors who traded lead with you yesterday were young, out on a huntin' trip, when they smelled our smoke. When they saw you an' those damn red mittens, they figured you were somethin' evil from the spirit world.'

"I didn't dare look down at my hands after what Billy told me. 'He'll know they're only mittens, won't he?'

"Billy lowered his voice. 'I'm hopin' he won't ask.'

" 'Pe-she-pah Mah-e-yah,' " Lone Wolf said, and it sure didn't sound friendly. He was giving me the eye so hard, I felt near naked. I sensed the other Kiowas were listening real close, but I never stopped looking up at Lone Wolf.

" 'He's given you a Kiowa name,' " Billy went on, 'and a while ago he asked how you got that cut on your face. He's callin' you Red Hands, on account of those mittens. So far so good, Deputy Long.'

"I spoke to Billy without looking at him. 'I suppose you could tell him I didn't have no choice in that fight with his hunters.'

" 'I don't intend to tell him a damn thing he doesn't want to know,' Billy answered. 'He knows he can kill us any time he takes the notion. Showin' we ain't afraid is the smartest thing we can do. Kiowas are like Northern Comanches when it comes to courage. They understand that sometimes, when it's all a man has.'

"Lone Wolf spoke to a warrior seated on a sorrel pony beside him. He said just a few words, then made a circular motion with his right hand. When he looked at me again, he closed his fist over his heart.

"I didn't know what to do. I waited for Billy to tell me what Lone Wolf meant. Some of the Indians on either side of us turned their ponies away.

" 'He made the sign for a brave heart in battle,' Billy

told me. I wasn't sure I understood. Before I could ask, Billy spoke again.

" 'He's payin' you about the highest compliment an Indian can pay a white man. It also means he won't take our hair today. He knows your hands ain't really red, that they're just some bit of clothing a white man wears. The warriors who came yesterday were young an' they'd never seen anything like 'em before. Lone Wolf is gonna punish the other two for startin' a fight before they had his permission. Those you killed have already been punished. He asked to take back their bodies so their families can hold a burial ceremony. We're free to ride on any time we want.'

"I was looking up at Lone Wolf while Billy was talking, and an idea occurred to me. 'How about if I offered to give him these mittens as a way of showing we're friendly? That we didn't mean no harm when his warriors rode up and started shooting at us.'

" 'He'd be a fool to take 'em, ugly as they are.'

"I put my rifle down in the snow and pulled off my red wool mittens, then held them out to Lone Wolf. 'Tell him we're making him a present out of these,' I said, although I figured the Kiowa chief already knew what I was doing.

"Lone Wolf looked to Billy for an explanation, not making any move to take what I was offering him. Billy said a few words and made a looping motion with his hands.

"I saw the chief's gaze return to the mittens. He grunted, and urged his stallion forward until he could reach down to take them. He looked me in the eye right after that, and said something. For some reason I wasn't afraid of being that close to him now.

"Lone Wolf wheeled his pinto away and rode off into

the snow with warriors following close behind. Several Kiowas had begun to load the stiffened corpses of the warriors lying near our cave onto the back of a pony.

As I was bending down to pick up my rifle, Billy made what he thought was a joke.

" 'He'll be the only Indian in all of creation wearin' a pair of bright red mittens. Serves you right for wearin' those damn things. They nearly caused us to get scalped.'

"I noticed how Billy was still a little shaky on his feet, and I said, 'Maybe you oughta go back and lie down, Billy. It looks like you've still got a touch of fever.'

"He turned to me and snapped, 'When I need a nursemaid you'll be the first to know. Let's get saddled. If we ride hard we can make Camp Supply in a day or two, if we ain't completely lost.' He staggered across a deep drift with his rifle slung over his shoulder, like he was sure he could walk all the way to Camp Supply if he had to. I watched him go a few feet farther until he began to cough, sinking slowly to his knees. He dropped his Winchester to grip his sides, coughing so loudly it startled a few of the Kiowas close by.

"I ran up to him and held his shoulder. 'Let me help you to the fire, Billy. Maybe it ain't such a good idea to saddle up just yet.'

"Pride wouldn't let him admit he couldn't ride. He spat a mouthful of clotted spittle into the snow and shook his head. 'Saddle the damn horses, Custis,' he said, wheezing between breaths. 'I can lie on that drag you made as easy as I can lie on frozen ground.'

" 'But it's still snowing, and the snow's mighty deep. Our horses will have a time of it plowing through.'

"When Billy looked up at me, then I knew I'd argued one time too many. 'It's wintertime,' he said evenly, bit-ing down around each word. 'It could snow from now till spring. The longer we stay here, the less chance we've got of findin' those boys who raided the ranches. Word'll get to 'em and they'll hightail it out west someplace where we'll never find 'em. I haven't gone through all this misery to let 'em get away. Help me up an' then put me on the travois, even if you have to tie me there. The last thing I need from you is a bunch of coddling.'

" 'I was only saying how you're still sick.'

" 'I sure as hell ain't gonna get no better layin' here. Now help me up an' get those animals ready to travel.'

" 'I'll make us some coffee while I'm at it,' I said, avoiding the way he stared at me. I glanced up at the sky. It wasn't snowing quite so hard now. I took Billy's arm and helped him climb to his feet, picking up his rifle afterward when I saw he could stand on his own.

"As we were walking toward the fire, I noticed several Indians up on the rim above our cave, loading frozen bodies on the backs of horses. I didn't want to remember that Kiowa I'd shot at close range, but I couldn't help it when I saw them hoisting him over a pony's rump. If I could, I wanted to forget the entire affair quickly.

"I helped Billy to his blankets, and put snow in our coffeepot along with a few beans. When it was nestled in the coals, I went over to our horses to begin saddling. I sure wasn't looking for more days' riding through that north wind, but Billy wasn't hearing of anything else.

"I led our animals out to eat snow when the last Kiowas rode off to the east with their dead. Billy was coughing every now and then, sipping whiskey to quiet his cough. Above the rim, wind whipped snowflakes into the air like millions of tiny feathers, carrying them off. We were in for another rough ride, and I had no choice but to make the best of it.

"The last thing I did was tie the travois poles to my bay's saddle horn, fixing a blanket between them with ropes. I tested it myself before I went to the fire to fill my belly with coffee for the day's ride.

"That was when I noticed Billy had passed out again."

"Lone Wolf could have killed you, only two men," Tooma said.

"Believe me," Longarm told her, thinking about it, "I've never been able to forget about it. He let us live, and I'm not sure I'll ever understand why he did."

"Because you were a brave warrior," Tooma told him. "The Kiowa know when a man has no fear in his heart."

Longarm wondered if she could be right, although he'd been scared to death at the time.

Chapter 17

Before noon, Longarm saw a cavalry patrol on the horizon, moving toward them at an easy trot.

"Time for you to head south," he told Tooma. "This bunch of soldiers won't take a kind attitude toward an Indian woman, not a Kiowa. See if you can find Lone Bear. Tell him I'm after Henry Starr and the men who intended to trade him those rifles. Get going, before they get a good look at you."

"You are a gentle man, Custis Star Man. I will tell Lone Bear your words."

"Just get going," he said. "Maybe we'll meet again at the caves. Here's the bottle of painkilling medicine. Drink a swallow or two if your arm starts to hurt."

Tooma took the lavender bottle and swung her pony away to the south, striking a gallop.

Longarm rode toward the cavalry troop.

"I'm Captain Lawrence," the commanding officer said, giving Longarm a cautious look.

"I'm U.S. Deputy Marshal Custis Long," he replied,

flipping his coat open to show his badge. "Have you seen any sign of a half-breed Cherokee named Henry Starr? Or three men with a mule who might have a load of rifles? I have warrants for their arrest."

"We've been looking for Starr," the captain said. "We met a traveling drummer from St. Louis who was robbed by Starr and two other men. He died from a gunshot wound, but not before he told us that he heard one of them say they were headed for Dodge City until things quieted down."

Longarm gazed north, in the direction of Dodge. "I'll be headed into Kansas, it seems," he said. "Thanks for the information, Captain."

"Who was that Indian we saw with you?" the captain asked while he watched the southern hills.

"Just an Indian guide, a peaceful one. Now, if you'll excuse me, Captain, I'll be heading up to Dodge. It's at least a day's ride from here."

He rode off with the sun directly overhead, riding toward one of the toughest towns on the Western frontier.

Longarm heard a noise. When he opened his eyes, that hotel room in Dodge City was so dark that he couldn't see his hand in front of his face. He'd been so sound asleep after the long ride across the southern part of Kansas that he hadn't moved since he lay down on the bed after a hot bath and a shave.

He lay there listening for the sound to come again, but everything was quiet out in the hall—even downstairs in the bar, where a piano had been playing before he went to sleep. It being the slow season in Dodge, the hotel was almost empty and the bar had only had a couple of patrons when he came upstairs after he took his bath, after asking if anyone had seen Henry Starr in town. No one could remember seeing an Indian half-breed riding in.

As a precaution Longarm now sat up and took his revolver from a small washstand beside the bed, cocking an ear toward the door leading into the hallway. Gradually, as his eyes adjusted to bad light, he could see shadows on the floor cast by a sliver of moon, spilling through a window beside the bed. He didn't have any idea what time it was, only that it must be late because things were so quiet.

He decided, after a bit, that he was hearing things, maybe in some sort of dream. That room was so warm and the bed so comfortable, he'd been asleep minutes after he lay down. He couldn't even be sure of the kind of sound he'd heard, only that it woke him from a deep sleep.

He got up, tiptoed over to a tiny dressing table, and struck a match to an oil lamp, turning the wick down so low it was only a pinpoint of light burning inside the globe, just enough to let him see where he was going as he got back under the covers.

He lay back on a soft feather pillow with his gun resting on the mattress beside him. He figured so much had happened over the past few days that he'd gotten too jumpy, expecting more trouble.

"Won't be no Indians on the prowl in Dodge City," he whispered to himself, closing his eyes, feeling mighty snug and warm in clean long underwear under a pile of quilts.

Before he drifted off to sleep again he felt a little bit of nervousness, thinking about meeting up with Henry Starr and whoever rode with him. He'd have to handle it on his own if he found them in Dodge, considering the local law.

He bolted straight up in bed when he heard something rattle in the lock on his door. He'd hardly gotten his eyes open when someone burst into the room, a blacker shape among black shadows, only this one was moving, rushing toward him.

Half asleep, Longarm dove off the mattress when that dark blur became the silhouette of a man lunging for his bed with a knife in his hands—the biggest bowie knife Longarm had ever seen, gleaming in moonlight from the window as it swept downward toward his pillow.

Longarm rolled to the floor, scrambling away from the bed almost before he landed, watching that knife being stabbed into the place where he'd had his head only a half second before. As he jumped up, he got his first look at the man wielding the knife, a stocky, muscular man with long shaggy hair hanging to his shoulders.

Goose feathers flew away from the pillow—Longarm heard a ripping noise, then a grunt when the shaggy owlhoot saw he'd missed. Longarm barely got his feet under him before the intruder whirled, crouching down as though he meant to spring over the mattress, brandishing his knife, drawing circles in the air with it.

"Who are you?" Longarm cried, backing away. He'd left his gun on the bed when he jumped off so quickly. The owlhoot had Longarm cornered against the wall of the room with no place to run.

The stranger spat out, *"Pendejo!"*

Longarm backed up until he was touching the wall, his mind racing to find a way out of this fix without being carved up like a turkey on Thanksgiving.

The man started around the foot of the bed, and Longarm knew he'd run out of time. His Winchester stood in a corner, well out of reach, even if he'd had the time to chamber a shell. He had nothing with which to protect himself from the arc of the blade when it came at him.

He jumped over to the dressing table just as his adversary bunched his muscles for a lunge. Longarm grabbed the glass lamp, the only thing within reach, and threw it as hard as he could toward the stranger's face.

The assassin tried to duck—because it was dark he didn't see it coming until it was too late. First the glass globe hit his forehead, shattering, but it was what happened next that he wasn't expecting, and neither was Longarm.

The lamp's glass coal-oil tank broke against the owlhoot's arm when he tried to shield his face and eyes, and then fire erupted like a giant orange ball down the front of his coat and in his scraggly hair.

He straightened up and shrieked for all he was worth, at the same time dropping his knife to paw at the fire sizzling in his scalp and coat. Burning oil spilled on the floor around him, licking up his legs, catching his pants on fire.

Longarm drew back when that ball of flame ignited, nearly blind in its sudden bright glare. Then his head cleared and he leapt over to the mattress, grabbing his gun in one hand, a heavy quilt in the other.

Longarm threw the quilt at the man, trying to smother the flames while keeping the gun aimed at his chest. "Smother it!" he shouted as a terrible smell filled his nose, burning hair and clothing, maybe a bit of flesh. The whole room would go up in flames unless he got the fire out.

The stranger staggered back, spreading fire when he did, as more oil dripped to the floor. He screamed again, knocking the quilt away to paw at his flaming beard. Longarm saw his eyes rounding with pain and fear. The stranger wheeled toward the window, his head and chest and legs engulfed in flames illuminating the room as brightly as if it were daytime.

What he did next had to be a result of fear. He ran to the window and dove through the glass pane headfirst, smashing it to pieces—he had to know it was a second-floor room since he'd come upstairs to knife his target. He plummeted out into the darkness with a strangled scream caught in his throat, and fell down to the street below.

Longarm heard him thump when he landed, but right then was so busy gathering more quilts to put out flames dancing all over the floor that he scarcely noticed when the assassin fell.

The edge of the mattress burst into flame. Longarm's bare feet got so hot he yelped like a scalded puppy. Then he started to scream as loud as he could, "Fire! Fire! Somebody help me!" He pounded the floor with one quilt, tossing his Colt aside to grab another cover so he could smother flames with both hands. For a few seconds the fire got the best of him, until at last he got all of those puddles of oil burning on the floor put out.

He started beating the mattress as hard as he could, using both quilts to suffocate flaming bedsheets. In a moment the last bit of fire was snuffed, leaving only sparks here and there, and a room full of smoke so thick he could hardly see a thing. That was when he heard boots running down the hall, and voices shouting back and forth. He was completely out of breath by the time two men got there carrying lanterns.

"What happened?" an older man asked, peering in at all the smoke.

Longarm was standing there holding two smoldering quilts, and it didn't seem like events needed an explanation. "The room caught fire," he gasped. "Some gent busted into my room and tried to cut me up with a knife . . . it's lying over there on the floor. He went out that window yonder. Somebody run fetch the sheriff while I get dressed. His hair and clothes were on fire when he jumped, and he's gotta be burnt pretty bad. I'm a U.S. deputy marshal, and I aim to arrest him for attempted murder."

"Who was he?" another man asked, standing out in the hallway looking over the other's shoulder. "An' how did this fire get started?"

Longarm didn't give all the details. "A lamp broke. I'll tell the sheriff all about it soon as he gets here. Leave one of those lanterns so I can see to get dressed. I reckon a bucket of water tossed on this bed wouldn't be such a bad idea, 'cause there's a few sparks still burning."

One of the men took off at a trot while the other handed Longarm his lantern. The lawman limped over to the dressing table on scorched feet to put on his denims and boots.

"Who woulda been tryin' to kill a U.S. marshal?" the old man asked again, walking into the room to stomp on a piece of bedsheet glowing red on the floor, then gazing out the broken windowpane for a moment. "The sumbitch had to be crazy to jump so far. Every bone he's got is liable to be broke." He went over and stuck his head out the window. "Don't see nobody down there," he added.

Longarm got dressed in a hurry, strapping on his gun before he put on his coat and hat. "He won't get far," he promised, taking his Winchester along. "Keep an eye on that bed until somebody gets here with a bucket of water. I'll see to that big bastard who tried to carve me up."

The man went over to the nightstand for a pitcher he'd forgotten about, taking it over to the mattress. "This'll help some till Jesse gits back with a pail." He poured water on a smoking pile of sheets and stood back, wrinkling his nose.

Longarm left the room at a brisk walk, moving down a darkened hall as fast as he could without being able to see. His mind was on the owlhoot who'd tried to kill him. He wondered who he was. Why would a robber pick his room to make his play? Some of it didn't make any sense.

On his way downstairs he remembered the killer called him "pendejo" in Cherokee. Longarm started to put things together all of a sudden, if he was guessing right. "That was Starr," he whispered, shaking his head in disbelief when he got to the bottom of the staircase. "He found out where I was in town and tried to kill me."

Longarm ran over to the hotel's front door and unlocked it, seeing as the lobby was dark. When he rushed out on the front porch he drew his gun, expecting to find Starr out in the darkness, with broken leg bones, lying directly under his window. But when he got there, to his surprise he didn't see anyone.

He walked over to the spot right below the busted windowpane with his breath coming from his nose and mouth in frosty curls. There was only an impression in the ground where somebody had landed, and then a set of footprints leading away toward the cow pens beside the railroad tracks. Somehow, possibly because the ground was soft enough to break his fall, Starr had gotten away.

It took a minute for things to sink in as Longarm stood there with his pistol.

He looked toward the stockyards south of Dodge. Starr was probably there now with burns on his face and body, trying to find a way to give Longarm the slip.

"How the hell did he know I was here?" he asked himself out loud.

There was just one answer. The only person in Dodge City who knew where he was staying was the county sheriff. Longarm had made a courtesy call when he got to town. But was he ready to believe the sheriff was in cahoots with men like Henry Starr and his gang?

A commotion in the hotel kept him from making up his mind what to do right then. A man wearing a night-shirt came outside with a lantern. Longarm recognized him as the hotel clerk who'd rented him the upstairs room.

"What's all the ruckus about?" the clerk demanded. "I'd nearly swear I heard a window break an' then some-body yellin' about a fire. My wife claims she can smell smoke. . . ."

"A man broke into my room and tried to kill me," Longarm said. "A lantern got smashed, but the fire's out now. He dove through my window, only I can't find him. Yonder's his tracks, heading for the cattle pens."

"You right sure the fire's out?" he asked, turning quickly to go back inside.

"A couple of men showed up. One's gone to fetch a bucket of water from out back. Another gent is up there keeping an eye out for sparks. When the sheriff shows up, tell him what happened."

The clerk was on his way inside, his mind clearly on another matter upstairs. "I'll tell him," he said, disappearing through his front door. Before he closed it he said,

"By the way, there was a feller askin' fer you earlier tonight. I told him you was already retired for the evenin'."

"What did he look like?" Longarm asked.

"An Injun. Short feller. He stunk worse'n high heaven. Needed a bath worst I ever smelled." At that, he closed the door.

Longarm decided to go after Starr, with a fresh trail to follow.

He took off at a trot down a deeply rutted road packed with mud, levering a cartridge into the firing chamber of his rifle. It was a clear night with stars overhead and a piece of moon showing him the way. He was still troubled, thinking Starr could only have learned where he was from the local sheriff. There was no other way to explain how Starr had known where to ask for him.

Chapter 18

Longarm followed faint tracks in the mud until he lost them in the dark on the south side of the railroad tracks. He gave up and turned back for the hotel. Henry Starr had escaped him for now, but the hunt was far from over.

Shoulders slumped, he trudged back toward his hotel room, wondering about Tooma. For some reason the Kiowa girl captured his imagination, and that night in the draw below the Cimarron he'd almost enjoyed a few moments of her charms. She reminded him of another Indian beauty he'd met a few years back, when conditions at Fort Sill were at their worst.

Longarm wondered how the army and Indian agents could allow the starvation of a proud race of people who only wanted to keep the lands they believed were theirs. The Comanches and Kiowas had been lords of the southern plains for years, and until the white man came to rob them of their birthright, there'd been no trouble between races. Longarm supposed he had a soft spot in his heart for the Indians, as unpopular as it seemed.

He recalled that other Indian girl, a Comanche, and the

difficulties he'd faced when he was a green deputy marshal. It had happened so long ago he'd almost forgotten about it, until he met Tooma. . . .

When he saw her for the first time he was on his way to Fort Sill in the company of a cavalry patrol under the command of an officer too young to realize the dangers. With forty troopers moving in a slow column behind him, Captain Boyd Carter had no idea the men riding wiry little ponies crossing a hilltop in front of them were the most feared of all plains tribes, the Kwahadie Comanche. Longarm recognized them at once by the twin braids of black hair hanging down their backs, and the pairs of eagle feathers each had tied so that they fell carelessly across a shoulder.

"Indians!" Captain Carter exclaimed, reaching for his pistol clumsily, jerking his horse to a halt.

"I wouldn't do that if I were you, Cap'n," Longarm warned as the Indians rode down a grassy slope at a walk toward the cavalry patrol. "Those aren't just Indians. They're Kwahadies. I'm sure they don't mean us any harm, or we'd already be in the fight of our lives. They're lettin' us see them, so they don't want trouble."

Carter sounded angry. "What the hell is a Kwahadie?" he asked tersely, although he left his gun in its holster.

Longarm sat his horse with his hands resting in plain sight on his saddle horn, making it clear to the Indians he had peaceful intentions. "A Kwahadie is a Comanche, Cap'n, the worst of the five bands when it comes to fighting and torture, but by the look of 'em we're in luck today. This isn't a war party. They've got a few women with 'em." He noticed one girl in particular in a deerskin dress with the fringed bottom of her skirt riding high on

142

her slender legs clamped to her pony's sides. She had long black hair framing an oval face with broad cheekbones. She rode with four other women behind the Comanche men.

"If they're Comanches, they are off the reservation illegally, Marshal Long, and my orders are to see to it that all Comanche and Kiowa Indians remain inside the boundaries. I intend to tell them this . . . at gunpoint, if necessary."

"Aiming a gun at this bunch would be a mistake," Longarm said as he swept the hills, making a quick count of warriors. "We're badly outnumbered and the Kwahadie men are carrying rifles. Your soldiers won't stand a chance against them. You told me on the way up from Fort Sill your men are raw recruits. Soldiers who don't know how to fight Comanches won't last very long. If it was up to me, I'd see what they want before I started a fight we can't win."

"You appear to have too much respect for these heathens, Marshal. They are nothing more than half-naked savages who have a few single-shot rifles. We have repeaters, the latest Winchester issue."

"Your boys won't hardly get the chance to use 'em," Longarm said, wishing he'd ridden alone into Indian Territory instead of seeking a bit of company in empty land . . . the company he'd sought was on the verge of getting him killed if Captain Carter ordered his men to draw their rifles. Unless someone had fought against the Kwahadies, it was hard to understand why one particular tribe had such a menacing reputation. "They may be half-naked, like you say, and their guns won't be as good as the ones your men are carrying. But I promise you they'll kill every man in your company before it's over if you give the order to fire at this band. I'm no coward, but I'm sure as hell not gonna hang around to see how it comes out. I'm bettin' this chestnut stud of mine can outrun those ponies. I damn sure ain't gonna help you fight Kwahadies. If you're foolish enough to try it, you'll do it on your own."

Carter gave him a cold stare. "Are you calling me a fool?" he asked.

"Only if you start shooting at these Indians, Cap'n. Then I'm gonna call you worse than a fool, only you won't hear me say it because you'll be lying somewhere in all this grass with your belly slit open, your eyelids cut off so your eyeballs will boil in the sun, and your scalp will be tied to the stock of one of those old rifles. You'll still be alive for a few hours, but you won't hear much besides your own screaming. I've heard of a few men the Kwahadies sliced up who lived for two or three days."

Carter, a pink-faced youth of twenty-five or so with a close-cropped headful of red hair, gave the Indians a closer look after what Longarm said. "I suppose we can find out what they want before I order them back to the reservation."

"There's another mistake you're making," Longarm said with his eye on the Indian woman. "Kwahadies don't follow orders. If I was you, I'd ask 'em real nice to go back where they belong, unless they've got a good reason for being here."

"This is army business, Marshal," Carter snapped. "I won't let you tell me how to do my job."

Longarm shrugged. "I was only trying to keep you and your men alive, Cap'n. But if you're of a mind to die today, then by all means give those Kwahadies a good dose of army business. I won't be here to see to burying you and your troopers. Forty graves is too much digging for a man who ain't inclined to use a shovel in the first place. Let the buzzards pick your bones. Tonight, the coyotes and wolves will clean up what's left, and by tomorrow, there won't hardly be any sign of what happened here. Maybe a few bloodstains on the grass."

The young captain swallowed, still watching the Indians as he too counted them. "There are only fifty or so," he said, but with less conviction now. "With repeating rifles I say we stand a good chance of defeating them. I won't take any guff from a savage, no matter what variety they may be. If they won't go back to the reservation peacefully, I'll order my men to draw and shoot to kill."

Despite the seriousness of their situation, Longarm chuckled softly. "You may get that order out of your mouth, but getting it accomplished is gonna be a little tougher. Before your men can get their rifles out, half of 'em will have bullet holes in their fancy new uniforms. The other half of your troopers will last a little longer . . . maybe long enough to fire one shot before a few Kwahadie marksmen cut them down. Of course, I told you I won't be here to see it. I'll hear it from a distance, from the other side of those hills yonder, 'cause I'm gonna ask this stud for all the speed he's got. Like you told me just now, this is army business and I'm not a soldier. No sense in me hanging around to get killed if it's none of my business."

A thick-chested warrior riding at the front of the Indians gave the sign for peace. Captain Carter sat motionless with a puzzled look on his face.

"He gave you the sign for peace, Cap'n," Longarm said.

"I don't understand Indian sign language. I'll speak to him instead."

"He won't understand English."

"Then how shall I tell him to ride back to the reservation?"

"I don't reckon you will, not in words they understand. If you want, and if you'll promise there won't be any shooting, I'll translate for you."

"Do you speak Comanche, Marshal Long?"

"Some. Sign language is universal among Plains tribes. It's how they communicate with other tribes when they don't speak the same tongue. I'll have to use a little of both," he said as the Comanches rode closer, within a hundred yards of the front of the column.

Longarm gave the sign for peace, and the sign for "I speak true words." Then his gaze wandered to the girl again. She had a beaded necklace hanging between the swells of two large breasts straining the front of her dress, hard nipples making tiny peaks where they swayed back and forth with the gait of her gray pony mare.

The Comanches halted, spreading out to form a ragged line blocking the soldiers' path. Then their leader began using more sign talk, watching Longarm carefully each time he used another series of movements with his hands.

"He says his people are hungry, Cap'n. The meat they gave 'em at Fort Sill had worms in it and it made the children sick. They decided to go hunting for deer or the last of the buffalo, the ones white hide hunters haven't killed. He says the women and children are starving. They have nothing to eat."

Carter turned to Longarm. "The meat rations had worms?" he asked.

"That's what he told me, and he signed for true words.

You are new out here, Cap'n Carter. You and your green troopers are about to find out just how bad the army treats reservation Indians. It's enough to make you sick. The older ones starve themselves so the children can eat because the Indian agent won't give them enough food for everybody. The old people make this sacrifice so the children won't die."

"I don't believe it," Carter said, although he was looking at the rib bones showing on most of the warriors. "They do look a little on the skinny side, however."

Longarm took a deep breath, passing another glance across the beautiful Comanche maiden. "If you want my advice, and if you have any compassion for starving kids and women, you'll let 'em hunt for whatever they can find. Nearly all the buffalo are gone these days, but Kwahadies are good hunters. They'll find a few deer and go back to the reservation with the meat so their people won't starve."

"Colonel Warren wired us our orders when we got off the train in Fort Smith, that if we ran into any Indians on the way up to Fort Sill, we'd order them back or kill them."

Longarm heard less resolve in Carter's voice now. "You're the one who has to live with your conscience, Cap'n. When you see conditions at Fort Sill, you'll understand. A bunch of crooks got the beef contracts at the fort . . . I've been there half a dozen times and I've seen it before. Most of the beef is too rotten to eat, and what flour they get is moldy. It's a damn shame to treat human beings the way these people are treated, and once you see it for yourself, you'll be glad you didn't start a fight with this bunch. Let 'em go. All they're doing is what any man would do if his children were hungry."

"I suppose you are right," Carter replied, chewing his lower lip. "You can tell them about those two old buffalo bulls we saw back at the river. I won't order them back to the reservation, after what you've told me, only I want you to ask them to give me their word they'll come back when they've found something to eat."

Longarm began giving sign talk to the Comanche leader, every now and then taking a quick look at the girl. She was staring at him, and he thought there was a suggestion of a smile on her face a few times.

When he'd done the best he could to convey Captain Carter's message, he signed for an end to their talk.

The Comanche closed his fist over his heart.

"He's saying thanks, that he is glad you have a pure heart so his people won't die of hunger." As Longarm spoke, his eyes wandered again to the young woman briefly.

"Did they promise to come back to the reservation?" Carter asked.

Longarm knew the Indians would go back on their own, but to satisfy the captain he said, "They sure did."

Suddenly the Comanche leader gave Longarm several quick motions with his hands, inclining his head toward the girl.

Longarm signed that he understood. He had just been warned that the girl was the daughter of a Kwahadie chief and she was another man's property.

"Suvate," he said, a Comanche word with several meanings, including an agreement that something was over, in this case referring to the way he was looking at the girl. Yet Longarm found himself wishing for a way to get to know her, to speak with her alone. She was one of the most beautiful, shapely Indian maidens he'd ever

seen, and his lustful side struggled with his better judgment.

"Column forward!" Captain Carter cried, signaling his men to move on.

Longarm forced his eyes away from the girl and rode off with the column, pushing the pretty Comanche from his mind.

Tooma was every bit as pretty, he now told himself as he neared the hotel. He hoped she'd made it back to her people.

At dawn, when footprints would be easier to follow, Longarm meant to track Henry Starr down. Pretty Indian girls would have to wait until he had some time away from his work.

Chapter 19

Longarm was given another room at the Long Branch Hotel, and the fire was officially declared "of no consequence" by the Dodge City fire chief.

He put his belongings just inside the door, locked it, got undressed, and was fast asleep in a matter of minutes. At sunrise he would again take up the trail of Henry Starr and his accomplices, but for the time being he was exhausted. A sign across the road from the Long Branch above a tiny cafe promised "a cowman's breakfast." He intended to partake of the offering at first light.

A mound of scrambled eggs, fried potatoes, biscuits, and orange marmalade lay before him after his third cup of coffee, the Arbuckle's brand of coffee he was accustomed to. But as he was digging into his meal, a man with a star pinned to his vest sauntered through the door. He sported a waxed handlebar mustache and a recent blacking on his stovepipe boots. He had an arrogant look about him as he surveyed the customers scattered around the room.

He came straight toward Longarm's table with a stern look on his face.

"Are you Custis Long?" the peace officer asked, hooking his thumbs in his gunbelt.

"I am," Longarm replied. "What can I do for you?"

"I'm City Marshal Masterson. I understand you caused a ruckus at the Long Branch Hotel last night."

"A ruckus?" Longarm asked.

"That's what I was told."

"No ruckus, Marshal," Longarm said. "A man wanted by the law tried to kill me in my hotel room last night. He changed his mind and jumped out my second-story window. I wasn't able to find him in the dark."

"Get up from the table, Mr. Long," Masterson said. "I'm taking you to jail until you pay for the damages to the hotel room."

Longarm dropped his fork beside his plate, then gave the city marshal a steady gaze. "No . . . that isn't the way we're gonna do this," he said evenly. "You're going to turn around and walk back outside. You're disturbing my breakfast. It's getting cold."

Masterson opened his split-tail frock coat, revealing a .45-caliber Remington pistol holstered at his waist. "Maybe you don't hear so good," the city marshal said. "I told you to get up from that table. I'm taking you to jail."

Longarm came to his feet slowly, staring Masterson in the eye. "You're the one who doesn't hear so good, Marshal," he said coldly. "You're interrupting my breakfast. If anybody goes to jail, it'll be you."

"Is that so?" Masterson said, a mock grin crinkling the skin around his eyes and mouth. "Apparently, you're an ignorant man who knows nothing about the law."

Longarm pulled the lapel of his coat away to show the city marshal his badge. "I'm United States Deputy Marshal Custis Long. I know a great deal about the law, about jurisdiction, and who has authority in legal matters when a federal crime is committed. I can lock you up in your own jail and have you sent to a federal prison for interfering with the lawful duties of a federal officer."

Masterson's eyes were glued to Longarm's badge. "I didn't know," he stammered.

"Well, now you do. So get the hell out of here while I eat these eggs or you'll be under arrest. The incident at the Long Branch last night was an attempt on my life by a half-breed Cherokee named Henry Starr. I have a warrant for his arrest and I intend to find him."

"Nobody told me," Masterson said, aware that other patrons of the eatery were listening.

"Now I have, so get the hell away from my table and go on about your city business."

"Sorry, Marshal," Masterson said, lifting his hands in an apology. "You enjoy those eggs and biscuits. The food is really good here."

Masterson turned on his heel and strode for the door as fast as he could walk. As he was going out, a few snickers could be heard in the cafe.

Longarm sat back down to finish eating, reminding himself that there was nothing worse than pinning a badge on a man who used it to bully people when he thought he could get away with it.

He put his mind back on Henry Starr. The man who had gone out his hotel room window would have burns, and possibly more serious injuries from a second-story jump to freedom. Unless Starr, or whoever he was, had pulled out

153

of Dodge last night, he should be easy to spot . . . even in a crowd.

The first place to look was at the local doctors' offices. Severe burns, or a broken leg bone, would require medical treatment.

He buttered a biscuit and forked eggs into his mouth as a chubby waitress brought him more coffee.

"I'll get you for this, Billy," he said under his breath after the waitress left his table.

He longed for a good meal in a fine restaurant, maybe one of the better places in New Orleans, Baton Rouge, or San Francisco.

He resigned himself to his present circumstances, continuing to eat his breakfast, allowing his mind to drift back to more pleasant circumstances.

There had been that time in New Orleans at the Hotel Rue Royale, and a Cajun beauty named Angeline. . . .

Chapter 20

The Grand Hotel Rue Royale in New Orleans suited his tastes. A tile bath at the end of a second-floor hallway offered cast-iron tubs filled with hot water and scented soap while he rested and smoked a rum-soaked cheroot, sipping brandy from a bottle he'd had sent up from the bar downstairs. Mosquito bites covered his face and hands, and when he rented his room the hotel clerk had given him a suspicious look until she saw the gleam of his money. His pants and boots smelled too much like swamp water when he strode into the lobby, after putting his horse and buggy in a livery down the street. His carriage had gotten stuck in a bayou near the outskirts of New Orleans, and the mosquitoes had almost eaten him alive until he got the buggy wheels free of the mud.

A mulatto girl now brought him more buckets of hot water from time to time. Her skin was so fair it resembled the yellow butter Longarm's mother used to churn when he was a boy, and her eyes were a deep shade of green. She wouldn't look at his nakedness when she entered the bath, her eyes averted while she slowly poured more steaming water into his tub.

"What's your name?" he asked on her third trip upstairs with buckets.

She batted long eyelashes. "Angeline," she replied, even more embarrassed that he'd spoken to her so directly.

"It's a pretty name. French, isn't it?"

"I've got some French blood, my mammy says. Most everybody in Louisiana do got some in 'em. Folks call us quadroons."

"My name's Custis."

"Very pleased to meet you," she said with a polite bow.

"You look young. I'd guess sixteen."

"I'm older," she answered. "Almost twenty."

She was wearing a shapeless, faded cotton dress that had lost its color from too many washings.

"I couldn't see your figure, I reckon, and that's why I guessed wrong. That dress you're wearing hides a woman's shape and I couldn't tell you were older."

"I haven't got many dresses," she said. "We're poor folks an' dresses are expensive. My mammy made this one for me a long time ago."

He looked more closely at the swell of her bosom. "A real pretty lady shouldn't hide her charms. Men like to look at the figure of an attractive woman now and then."

Her smile was one of deeper embarrassment. "You say the sweetest things, makin' me feel pretty even if this ol' dress covers me up. Thank you, sir, for sayin' it."

"How much does a dress cost in New Orleans? A really nice dress?"

"More money'n there is in the whole world, maybe much as ten or fifteen whole dollars. A piece of a bolt of cloth don't cost all that much. A dollar or two."

"A young man who wants a beautiful woman would pay ten or fifteen dollars to buy you a dress, wouldn't he?"

She shook her head. "No, sir. The menfolks I know is all as poor as church mice, like we are."

He stirred in the soapy water, leaning his head back against the tub to further admire her beauty. "Silk stockings too. You need a pair of silk stockings to go with a new dress."

She put down her buckets. "Those things are jus' dreams for a poor girl," she said. "Silk stockings are for rich folks."

He chuckled over her continuing bashfulness. "A woman's real beauty lies underneath. It's not what she's wearing, but what she's covering up with dresses and stockings that catches a man's eye."

Angeline giggled. "You're makin' my face feel hot. Wish you wouldn't say all them things."

"I'm only being honest, Angeline. Underneath that dress is a beautiful lady, only no one will ever know what's under there unless you take it off or wear dresses that show your figure to its fullest."

"Can't afford no new dress," she said, looking down at the floor.

"You seem very bashful, and yet you have no reason to be. I know a pretty woman when I see one. You should learn to take a compliment when it's sincere."

"Nobody ever says that kind of thing to me," she told him, unable to look him in the eye.

He blew smoke toward the ceiling. "I'm saying it now. And I mean every word of it. You're very pretty. A woman with a full figure should show it off to her best

157

advantage by wearing clothes flattering her shape. I'm quite sure that underneath your homemade dress there's a striking figure."

She smoothed the front of her skirt. "You're jus' sayin' that, hopin' I'll show you."

Longarm glanced at his pocket watch on a dressing table next to the tub. It was past two o'clock in the morning. "I'd call it an honor to catch a glimpse of such a beautiful woman without her clothes, but I wouldn't expect you to do it unless you wanted to."

"I do believe you're jus' funnin' with me," she said as a trace of color rose in her cheeks.

He stubbed out his cigar in a nearby ashtray and stood up slowly, water and soap suds dripping down his hairy chest, his pubic hair, his prick and balls. "I'm not playing games with you, Angeline," he told her gently. "I think you are a remarkably beautiful woman."

At first, she looked away quickly, until her eyes strayed back to his cock briefly. "You sure are . . . big, Mr. Custis. I don't b'lieve I ever did see one so big as that. Course, I ain't seen all that many either."

He reached for a towel and stepped out of the tub, standing very close to her as he dried himself off. "Some women say it feels good inside 'em." He patted his balls and prick dry very carefully. All the while, Angeline was staring down at his thickening member—it was her stare, and what it foretold, that gave rise to a slow swelling in his cock.

"Looks like it would hurt," she said, her voice barely above a whisper.

"Like anything else, from a bullwhip to a gun, it depends on how it's used. Why don't you come down the hall to my room and I'll show you how it can be used very gently. We can share the rest of this bottle of brandy."

She took a half step backward, still watching his cock with a look of fascination. "I might get in trouble with Mr. Cartier if I did that," she replied.

"It's after two. Nobody's gonna want any bathwater brought up at this hour."

"Maybe he's done gone to bed by now," Angeline said, with a glance over her shoulder at the bathhouse door. "I s'pose I could go down real quiet an' see." Her gaze returned to his prick. "It ain't very ladylike to say so, but I sure would like to know what . . . that thing feels like inside me."

"I'm in Room Twenty-five down the hall," he said, letting his towel fall to the floor. "I'll leave the door unlocked so you can come in whenever you wish."

"I hadn't oughta," she told him. "It'd be wrong to jus' be jumpin' in a bed with a strange man I don't hardly know at all."

"No one but the two of us will ever have to know," he said, giving her a one-sided grin.

"I'll go down an' see if Mr. Cartier is asleep, if he's done hung up the Closed sign in the front door."

He watched Angeline hurry out of the bath with her buckets as he gathered up his clothes. "Damned if these Louisiana women aren't all pretty," he muttered, tiptoeing down a carpeted hall to reach his room with the bottle of brandy clenched in his left fist.

He heard a gentle tapping on his door as he lay naked with his face to an open window, enjoying the cooler air of night.

"Come in," he said softly, lowering the wick on an oil

lamp on a bedside table so that the room was almost totally dark.

Angeline came in and closed the door behind her. She saw him reposed on the four-poster bed with his heavy cock resting against his thigh.

She crossed over to the bed and stared down at his prick for a moment. "Lordy, but that thing do look large," she whispered.

He grinned, propping his head up on both feather pillows. "Now you can take off that dress so I can see how right I was about your figure."

"It'd be better if you turned out the lamp," she protested in a quiet voice.

"But then it would be too dark for me to see if I was right about things," he responded. "Don't be so bashful. You have no reason to be ashamed of what you look like without any clothes."

She began unbuttoning her top buttons, stepping out of her worn sandals while she continued to open the front of her dress. "Don't pay me no mind if I act a little nervous," she said. "I never did do this before, not with a man I jus' met about an hour ago."

"I'll help you get rid of your nervousness," he said. "Come over here and I'll help relax you."

Angeline wriggled out of her dress. It fell around her ankles, revealing she was completely naked underneath. She had bulbous breasts the size of ripe melons, a creamy color in the half dark accented by dark red nipples. A tiny mound of curled pubic hair grew at the tops of her thighs.

"Come here," he whispered throatily, just as his prick began to rise, becoming engorged with blood at the sight of Angeline's magnificent body.

She took a few tentative steps toward the mattress, until he reached for her hand.

"Touch this," he said, wrapping her thin fingers around his stiffening cock. "You see? It won't bite you."

She giggled softly, then bent down to give it a closer inspection. She stroked his shaft gently a few times, until she let out a deep sigh and opened her mouth.

She took the head of his cock between her lips, only the tip at first, running her tongue over it, licking his foreskin and the underside of his glans.

He let out a helpless moan, feeling warmth spread through his groin, beginning in his balls.

Angeline started making sucking sounds as her head bobbed up and down, her mouth taking his cock deeper and deeper with each thrust. His hip muscles tightened with the ecstasy of an intensifying pleasure. His testicles rose higher.

He watched the sway of her breasts as the tempo of her head movements increased. Reaching for one dark nipple, he squeezed it between his thumb and forefinger, rolling it back and forth until it grew hard, twisted.

"Oh that feels good, Angeline," he groaned. It felt as if his balls were about to explode. His prick throbbed, sending a wave of sensation all the way to his toes each time her tongue passed over his glans.

She gripped the base of his shaft, and he noticed her hand trembling with desire. The sucking sounds she made grew louder and louder.

"Climb on top of me," he said with a sigh. "I can't take much more of this or I'll bust wide open."

She took his cock from her mouth and knelt on the edge of the bed, swinging one beautiful curved thigh over him. Placing her hairy mound over the tip of his prick, she pulled the lips of her cunt apart and lowered herself onto a few inches of his shaft until she felt too much resistance.

"It's too tight," she gasped, panting now, making very short thrusts downward until she could go no further.

"Give it time," he whispered, gripping her slender waist with both palms, rocking gently upward to meet her thrusts.

"It jus' ain't gonna go," she said, thrusting faster, yet allowing his cock to go no deeper. Beads of sweat formed on her brow and between her heavy breasts, glistening in light from the lamp.

"It'll go in a moment or two," he told her, rising a bit higher inside her wet cunt despite a very tight fit. "Give me time to help you relax. Let yourself go. . . ."

"I want it inside me real bad," she moaned, her eyes closed as though she was in pain, or in the throes of passion so intense it forced her to continue in spite of the hurt.

His balls were about to burst from her warmth and the damp slickness surrounding his cock. While he didn't want to cause her any real pain, he found he was helpless to control his deepening thrusts.

She was panting so hard now he could hear her breath whispering through her nostrils and lips.

"Deeper!" she cried suddenly as she started hammering her pelvis down on his shaft with tremendous force, the noise from her wetness like that of a water-soaked fireplace bellows.

He rose upward powerfully, feeling her cunt resist his deep penetration. She pushed herself down further, taking all of it inside her.

"Oh, dear!" she cried as the tip of his member reached

into the deepest recesses of her cunt, pounding against places that had never been touched before, seeking a trigger point that would send her over the edge.

"I can't hold back any longer," Longarm panted as he shot jism into her. He felt her begin to contract around his member, and knew that she had reached her pinnacle with him. The rhythmic contractions were slowing, milking him for all he was worth, and he felt she was going to drain him of all that he had, the tightness of her causing him sweet pain as she collapsed on his chest in one final cry of passion.

As their breathing slowed, Longarm could tell she was still aroused.

"Custis, you're still hard," she murmured. "Didn't you get enough?"

The stiffness inside her prompted her to start grinding her pelvis against him again. He could feel the throbbing of her mound around his member and the rising of his balls to meet the demand her cunt was placing on him to fire his jism again. He rolled her over on her back and plunged himself inside her, holding back not one inch of his substantial length.

"Yes! Go deeper, give me more of it. Fill me up with it."

Longarm guessed she would be sore in the morning, but he could no longer contain himself. When the milking started again he knew he was a goner. He shot his second load of seed inside her as her nails clawed at his back. Her legs wrapped around his waist, locking him to her body, imprisoned in her cunt.

"You're one hell of a woman, Angeline," he whispered in her ear.

•   •   •

He brought himself back to the present as he downed his fourth cup of coffee. As far as he knew there were no four-poster beds in Dodge City, nor were there any pretty mulatto women like Angeline.

Instead, he was on the trail of a Cherokee murderer named Henry Starr.

"I swear I'm gonna get you for this, Billy," he said as he pushed back his chair. It was light enough now to look for the tracks of the man who'd jumped out his hotel window with his hair and clothing in flames.

Chapter 21

Below the broken window of his upstairs room at the Long Branch, in an alley running between the hotel and a dry goods store, he found what he was looking for: a set of boot prints in the mud heading toward empty cattle corrals lining the railroad tracks passing through Dodge City.

Longarm followed the prints until they came to the iron rails, where he lost them completely.

He's smart, Longarm thought.

The man who attacked him last night with the bowie knife had run between the rails, stepping on thick wooden cross-ties to hide any traces of his passing.

An older cowboy riding a high-withered blue roan gelding rode toward him. The wrangler stopped his horse a few yards away.

"Lookin' fer somethin', mister?"

"Footprints. A man attacked me in my hotel room at the Long Branch last night. He jumped out a second-story window with his clothes on fire. He'd probably be limping."

"I seen him," the old man said, glancing east. "Real late last night, it was. He had real long hair. Kinda stocky. I'm a night watchman fer the railroad an' I was just about to head fer home."

"Which way did he go?" Longarm asked.

"East. He run between these here tracks till he met up with two other fellers. His shirt was smokin', like he'd set it on fire on purpose. I smelt him afore I seen him. My horse give off a big snort, an' that's when I seen him runnin' along these rails."

"He joined up with two other men?"

The cowboy nodded. "Sure did. They was holdin' this spare horse, like they was supposed to wait fer him. He got mounted an' they took off to the south. The way he was walkin', he acted like his right foot was hurt real bad. Nearly didn't make it to his horse."

Longarm gazed at the brightening prairies to the south, in the direction of Indian Territory. Starr and his partners were likely headed back to the Cimarron, to the cave Tooma had told Longarm about.

"Much obliged," he said, turning toward the livery where he had stabled his horse.

"There was one more thing," the drover said.

"What's that?" Longarm asked.

"I ain't no judge of such things, mister, but he looked to me like he was an Injun. He was real thick through the body, an' he wasn't much more'n five feet tall, if I was to take an educated guess. He was an ugly son of a bitch. His head looked like a burnt pumpkin. Can't recall ever layin' eyes on a man ugly as him."

"Henry Starr," Longarm mumbled. "I wonder how he knew I was here."

"Couldn't quite hear what you said, mister," the cowboy remarked.

"Nothing important, only now I think I know for sure who the man was."

Longarm hurried off toward the livery stable to saddle his horse. He was tired of this bleak country, tired of attempts on his life, and he meant to do something about it.

He picked up the trail of three horses southwest of Dodge, and set in behind them. By the length of their hoofprints the horses were being pushed hard.

As he rode into a late morning sun, he wondered how Starr had known where he was staying . . . the local county sheriff, a man by the name of Coggins, was the only man who knew that Longarm was in town yesterday and why. He'd checked in with the sheriff right after he rode into Dodge, since a county official might know more about the comings and goings of strangers than the city marshal, the man who'd interrupted his breakfast.

Miles of empty land stretched before him. He urged his bay to a ground-eating trot, intent upon his quarry.

It satisfied him some that whoever had come into his room last night bore the scars from their encounter . . . a lame right foot and burns. When Longarm found him, and his accomplices, he meant to give them something else to think about.

Suddenly, on the crest of a grassy knoll after he crossed the line into Indian Territory, he saw a lone Indian on a black-and-white pinto pony.

He reined to a halt.

The Indian raised a bandaged forearm with the sign for peace.

"Tooma," he whispered.

He rode toward her at a walk, pondering the chances that Lone Bear and his warriors could be on the other side of the hilltop. But something inside him said that Tooma would not betray him, or lead him into a trap.

He rode up to her, and with the wind blowing her hair over her shoulders, she looked prettier than ever.

"How's the arm?" he asked.

She ignored his question, pointing south. "The men you look for are going to the cave," she said.

"What about the gun traders?" he asked.

Tooma looked down at the ground. "Lone Bear killed them all. They would not give us the rifles. They fired guns at us, and Chief Lone Bear ordered an attack on the old fort. All are dead."

"And Lone Bear has the guns and ammunition," Longarm said quietly.

"Yes."

"Will he kill any more white men?"

"I do not know. I am not a chief."

"Too bad," Longarm told her. "The army is out looking for him now."

"We have seen them. They do not know where to look," Tooma replied.

Longarm took a look at the southern horizon for a moment or two. "It's my job to stop gunrunning to the Indians. But right now, the only men I'm interested in are Henry Starr and the two men who ride with him."

"They go to the cave. Follow me and I will show you where they make camp."

"Where is Lone Bear and the rest of your people?"

"Hunting. There are only a few buffalo. They hunt for antelope and deer . . . any meat the children and old ones can eat without becoming sick."

"Show me where to find this cave," Longarm said. "For now, I'm gonna act like I don't know about the rifles and bullets so your people can hunt."

Tooma swung her pony off the knob and took off at a trot in the direction of the Cimarron. Longarm rode up beside her, still stricken by her unusual beauty.

He found himself torn by emotions. Lone Bear and his warriors were looking for food, even though they'd broken the law by leaving the reservation. There were times when it seemed best to ignore a few regulations.

Off in the distance he could see the faint green line of the river winding its way across the plains. Just below the Cimarron he expected to find Henry Starr and two of his henchmen; however, odds of three to one didn't bother him all that much. What he needed most of all was to find some sort of advantage.

They came to the river. Tooma stopped her pony to look up and down the river. "All is safe," she said, heeling her pinto into the shallows.

Longarm wondered how she knew . . . how she seemed so certain that no one was watching them.

The crossing was shallow this time of year. On the far side of the river, he found the hoofprints of three horses. "Looks like you were right," he said.

She gave him a thin smile. "White men do not learn these things," she told him, urging her pony back to a trot.

She led him in a southeasterly direction. He noticed that the bandage around her arm was encrusted with dried blood, but she seemed to be able to use the arm without pain.

It occurred to him how strange his present circumstances were. He was after a savage killer, a mindless beast who thought nothing of killing, the infamous Henry Starr. And his guide to the hideout where Starr avoided the long arm of the law was an Indian beauty, a Kiowa girl who had set out to betray Longarm first.

"Things sure do have a downright unusual way of turning around," he muttered.

Chapter 22

They rode to the ravine where Longarm had made camp when he first spotted the fort ruins. Tooma halted her pony and pointed to a winding arroyo surrounded by low hills well south of the ravine. The minor wound in Longarm's thigh was healing fast, and he felt no real pain from it.

"There," she said. "Turn to the setting sun. Be careful, for they will have someone watching."

"I'll flank the arroyo from the hills," he said. "If they have a guard posted, he'll be up high enough to see in all directions."

"There are three now," Tooma told him. "One of our warriors saw them come back early this morning. The man named Henry Starr is sick. He had a hard time sitting on his horse when Powahcut saw him."

"He had a little accident with a fire," Longarm said, "and he jumped out a window of my hotel room in Dodge. Someone had to have told him I was there."

Tooma scowled. "Lone Bear tells of a bad star man in your place called Dodge. I do not know his name. He helps other bad men sell whiskey to our people, and some of the other tribes."

"It has to be the county sheriff," Longarm said. "I'll pay him a visit after I get Starr and his men in irons."

"Go carefully," Tooma said quietly.

He grinned at her. "I always do." He leaned out of the saddle and kissed her lightly on the lips. "One more white man's kiss, and thanks for showing me the way here."

She blushed and lowered her head. "Will you come back here, Custis Star Man?"

"It kinda depends. If I can, I will."

He tipped his hat to her and rode off toward the hills north of the arroyo, wondering what it might have been like to make love to an Indian beauty like Tooma.

Keeping to the red oaks lining both sides of the arroyo, he rode carefully, stopping often to survey his surroundings. This was easy country to be bushwhacked in. An ambush could come from almost anywhere.

His horse warned him of someone's presence long before he saw a man slumped against the base of a tree . . . the bay bowed its neck and let out a soft snort.

"Easy, boy," he said, stepping down from the saddle to tie off his horse.

He tied the bay to an oak limb and began creeping forward on the balls of his feet, his Winchester in one hand, his pistol in the other. He made slow progress to keep from being heard until he was less than thirty yards away from a seated cowboy with a black eyepatch over one eye. The man appeared to be dozing, even though it was the middle of the afternoon.

"Catching a nap, stranger?" he asked, drawing a bead on the man's chest.

172

The one-eyed man jerked, glancing in the direction of Longarm's voice. His hand fell near his holstered pistol as he got to his feet.

"Who the hell are you?"

"United States Marshal Custis Long. I'm looking for a wanted man by the name of Henry Starr."

"Never heard of him," the man said, squaring himself, still making no move toward his gun.

"I doubt it," Longarm replied, "but maybe you'll recognize him by his description. He came to my hotel room in Dodge City last night and tried to light a cigar. Funny thing, but his shirt caught on fire. He jumped out a second-story window to get clear of the flames. Does any of this help with your recollections?"

"How'd you slip up on me so quiet?"

"I've got a pair of wings underneath this coat. Now take that six-shooter out with two fingers and drop it on the ground. Otherwise, I'm gonna kill you."

"You ain't got no call to do that. I ain't broke no laws of no kind."

"Maybe," Longarm replied. "We're about to find out if you're telling the truth."

"How's that?"

"There's a cave down in that dry wash. If Henry Starr is in it, I'm taking you to jail. If it's empty, I'll take my handcuffs off you and let you take the rest of your snooze."

"You ain't gonna put no cuffs on me," the man snarled as he tensed the muscles in his shoulders.

"Suits me, One-eye. I'll just shoot you, and that way I won't have to worry about where I put the keys to those irons in my saddlebags."

173

"You're bluffin'. Besides that, a real lawman can't just shoot a feller down in cold blood."

"I'll tell the judge you reached for your gun," Longarm said, losing patience. "It'll be my word against yours, and you'll be dead so the judge won't hear your testimony."

"Henry an' Shorty will kill you deader'n pig shit when they hear the shot."

"I thought you said you didn't know Henry Starr."

The cowboy's jaw went hard. Then he clawed for his gun without saying another word.

Longarm shot him in the breastbone with his Colt. The man staggered back a few steps and crumpled to the ground on his back, with the echo of the gunshot still ringing through the red oak forest.

Longarm ran back toward his horse. If Starr and someone called Shorty were close by, they would be coming toward the explosion of his gun any moment now.

He untied his horse and led it quickly into a dense stand of trees, where he tied it off.

Longarm knew the killing had just started, and he didn't aim to be one of the victims.

A man wearing a flat-brim hat, with his arm in a sling, crept along the bottom of the dry wash . . . Longarm remembered shooting two of the men who'd slipped up on his camp that night.

It would have been an easy shot to drop the stalker with one bullet, yet duty required that he give the man a chance to surrender.

"Drop the gun!" he called from the base of a live oak. "I have you covered."

A rifle came up in the cowboy's hands and it was kill or be killed. Longarm took the logical option.

He fired at the man's good arm, the thunder of his Winchester bellowing up and down the dry streambed.

"Shit!" the cowboy yelled, spinning around on one foot, flinging his rifle in the air before he fell to his knees in the dirt. He grabbed his left shoulder and moaned, then sank over on his face.

"One more . . . Mr. Henry Starr," Longarm whispered.

He started cautiously down the side of the arroyo, jacking another shell into the firing chamber of his rifle, being very sure of where he placed each foot to make as little noise as possible.

He knew Starr would have trouble moving around with a bad limb after his jump from the hotel window. And if his burns were severe enough, he might also be at another disadvantage.

But caution had kept Custis Long alive in a dangerous profession. Thus he entered the dry wash slowly, searching for the mouth of a cave nearby.

Henry Starr heard both gunshots clearly. He was lying on a pile of old blankets and buffalo robes with his Walker Colt in his fist. An old Spencer rifle lay beside him.

His swollen ankle was wrapped in strips of deerskin and he'd been drinking whiskey, both to ease the pain in his foot and to quiet the agony of the burns across his face and chest. His hair hung in scorched ringlets down his neck and back. Bloody scabs had formed on his forehead and cheeks and neck, and on his arms and hands.

"The bastard," he croaked, wondering if this lawman could have killed both Black Jack and Shorty.

He glanced across the embers of a dying fire to the horses tied to picket ropes at the back of the cavern. He wasn't sure he could manage to saddle a horse and climb aboard it on his own, and even if he did, this tin-star lawman could be waiting for him as soon as he left the safety of the cave.

If only I could have killed him last night, Henry thought.

He knew he should have used a gun instead of making the attempt on the lawman with a knife.

Starr struggled up on one elbow, watching the mouth of the cavern. He checked the loads in his Walker and waited, even though he was having some trouble seeing things clearly due to the burns around his eyes . . . and his eyeballs were watering. He'd been afraid he might be going blind.

Chapter 23

Longarm saw the faint glow of a fire inside the tunnel, and he stopped in his tracks.

Starr will be there, he thought.

Tooma had told him there were only three men, and he'd taken two of them out of the fight.

Hunkered down, clutching his pistol in one hand and his rifle in the other, he crept forward. Somewhere deeper in the cave, a horse snorted softly, sensing his approach.

He came to the opening of the tunnel and stopped. Beyond the mouth of the opening he could see the glow of a dying campfire, shadows dancing on rock walls.

He had his adversary cornered. A sardonic grin twisted the corners of Longarm's mouth.

He holstered his pistol and knelt down to pick up a rock, a piece of pink alabaster half the size of his fist.

"We'll see how jumpy Starr is," he whispered, remembering the attempt on his life at the Long Branch Hotel.

He hurled the rock into the cavern so that it ricocheted off a wall.

Three thundering explosions erupted from inside the

cave. Bullets whined off the tunnel walls, making a curious singsong noise. Longarm was still hidden around the side of the opening, out of harm's way.

After the fading echoes of the gunshots stopped, Longarm spoke. "Ain't but one way out of here, Henry. You toss down your guns and come out with iron around your wrists. Otherwise I'm gonna kill you."

"To hell with you!" an angry voice shouted. "Black Jack an' Shorty will get you from behind."

"They're both dead," Longarm replied evenly. "Shorty, if he's the one with his arm in a sling, might still be alive, but the son of a bitch with the black eyepatch is on his way to heaven or hell . . . I suspect the latter is his destination. The fella named Shorty has bullet holes in both arms."

"I'd sooner be dead than in prison," Starr snapped, his voice like the growl of an angry lion.

"I can arrange either one," Longarm told him. "You fire one more shot at me and you'll be attending your own funeral. If you give up now, you get to tell your side to a judge and a jury. It seems like the smartest way, judging the shape you're in. You had a little fire in your hair last night, and if I remember right, some of your clothes was on fire. That long hair of yours made a pretty sight when you dove out my window. Must still hurt mighty bad. I can take you to a doctor before I lock you up in jail."

"You can kiss my ass, lawman."

"It don't seem likely. I'm between you and the only way out of here. You'll have to kill me to get away, and I can promise you I'm a hard man to kill."

"Those Kiowas will help me, when they hear the bullets."

"They've already cleared out. They killed Leon, Jack,

and Roy. Got all the rifles and cartridges and now they're headed back toward Fort Sill. I'm afraid it's just you and me, Henry, when it comes down to settling this."

"You'll never take me alive," Starr shouted.

"It don't make a damn bit of difference to me either way, Henry. As a United States marshal I can't collect the reward that's out on you, so to tell the truth, I'd just as soon bring you in tied over the back of your horse. I won't be worried about you trying to escape."

"You rotten bastard."

"Maybe I am. But to me, you're just a hunk of rotten meat worth the same, dead or alive. You can toss down that gun and come out where I can see you, or I'll start sending bullets into this cave as fast as I can shoot."

"You can't do that," Starr snarled. "You're sworn to uphold the law."

"That's what I'll be doing, Henry. And it'll be your word against mine as to how it happened, only you won't be alive to give your testimony."

"I shoulda killed you with a gun when I had the chance in your hotel room."

"You thought a knife would be quieter, so you could get away clean. Just another mistake you made."

"Come and get me, Long. I ain't gonna go quiet."

"Suits the hell outta me." As Longarm said it, he crept around to look into the tunnel, and a man lying on a blanket next to a rock-encircled fire stared back at him.

Longarm jerked out his Colt and sent a bullet into Henry Starr's upper chest. The blast sent five horses jerking back on their picket ropes.

Starr was slammed on his back, groaning, his gun falling beside him. His feet began to twitch as Longarm walked toward him with his gun leveled.

"Not very smart, Henry," Longarm said. "You let me distract you with a few words."

"I'm shot!" Starr groaned.

Longarm looked down at the half-breed's badly burned face and neck. "I hardly ever miss, Henry," he said.

"Get me to a doctor."

Longarm holstered his Lightning .44. "I could do that, or I could let you lie there and bleed to death."

Starr's trembling right hand came up to feel his wound. "You can't do that. You're a lawman."

"Sometimes," Longarm replied. "Then there's other times when I'm just a man who enjoys seeing a sorry son of a bitch bleed to death."

"Damn, this hurts," Starr said. "You gotta get me to a doc real quick."

The horses at the back of the cave settled after the noise of the guns ended. "I'm gonna hurry as fast as I can, Henry, only I've got this bullet wound in my leg and it makes me slower than usual. But you can count on me to do everything I can for a man who tried to murder me in my hotel room up at Dodge. That's just the kind of feller I am."

He saddled three horses, one for Black Jack Ward's body, a second horse for the gunman called Shorty, the last for a badly wounded Henry Starr. Shorty was dead by the time Longarm found him. Starr was the last of the three outlaws still alive.

Longarm tied the two corpses to their saddles and put handcuffs on Henry Starr, after he fashioned a bandage around the bullet hole in Starr's upper right shoulder. Starr was still conscious as Longarm led the string of horses toward Fort Liberal across the Kansas line.

Once, as he was about to cross the Cimarron, he thought he saw two Indians on a bluff to the east. He stopped long enough to stare at them. One was riding a black-and-white pinto pony.

"Tooma," he said as the pair rode off the crest of the rise out of sight.

He urged his horse into the shallows, remembering the rare beauty of the Kiowa girl. In most ways they were enemies, but for a short time they had become friends. Longarm knew it would be a long time before he forgot her.

He aimed for Fort Liberal to turn his prisoner over to the army, and to arrange for having the two unlucky gunmen buried. All three had had the misfortune of crossing Custis Long, and two of them had paid for it with their lives.

He glanced over at Henry Starr, his face a mass of scar tissue and scabbed-over burns. On this particular assignment Longarm had encountered one of the ugliest creatures he'd ever seen, and one of the most beautiful women in his memory.

He gave Starr a grin that did not reach his eyes. "You're an ugly son of a bitch, Henry. This part of the world will be a prettier place when you're behind bars. . . ."

Chapter 24

He sat in Billy Vail's office smoking a rum-soaked cheroot, flicking ashes on the floor. It had taken Longarm a
week to get back to Denver.

"Why did you do this to me, Billy?"

"Do what?" Billy asked, frowning.

"Why did you send me down to Indian Territory? I
haven't had a decent meal since I left."

"You're a U.S. deputy marshal, Custis. You take whatever assignments I give you."

"I slept on hard ground for three weeks. I got a bullet
in my leg."

"It comes with the job."

"You could have handed this one to the army."

"The army would never have found Henry Starr and
you know it."

"You wanted to teach me a lesson, Billy. You wanted
me to appreciate a feather pillow and a good tick mattress."

"You've gotten a little soft, Custis. Not long ago I sent
you down to that health spa with the hot mineral baths.

You ate good food and lived like a king at Briarcliff Manor. It was time you got back to the basics of law enforcement."

"I know the basics," Longarm said. "In case you've forgotten, I've been at this for a number of years."

Billy shrugged off his remark. "I got a wire confirmation that Starr is in jail at Fort Smith. Judge Parker intends to hang him."

"We'll all be better off."

"Starr claims you shot him while he was unarmed, trying to give himself up."

"He's a liar," Longarm said.

"I don't suppose there were any witnesses."

"None. Two dead men who were with him. Both of 'em tried to kill me."

Billy nodded. "Not that it matters. Starr is headed for the gallows. The one thing I managed to do was to keep you away from women for a while."

Longarm thought back to a few pleasurable nights while he was after Starr, and also to the Kiowa girl. "You're right about that, Billy. Wasn't anything out there but wide-open prairies and a few stars over my head."

"I've got a case for you," Billy said.

"You can tell me about it tomorrow, Billy. Right now I need a bath and a woman."

"You'll never change, will you, Custis?"

"I hadn't planned on making any sudden changes."

"Be back in my office tomorrow morning at ten so I can go over the case with you."

"I may be a little late," Longarm told him, standing up with his cigar.

"And why is that?" Billy asked.

"Depends."

"Depends on what?" Billy wanted to know.

"On whether or not I find a lady who wants to spend a little time with me."

Billy shook his head as Longarm started for the door.

Watch for

LONGARM AND THE LADY BANDIT

270th novel in the exciting LONGARM series
from Jove

Coming in May!

Explore the exciting Old West with one of the men who made it wild!

__LONGARM AND THE NEVADA NYMPHS #240   0-515-12411-7/$4.99
__LONGARM AND THE COLORADO COUNTERFEITER #241
                                     0-515-12437-0/$4.99
__LONGARM GIANT #18: LONGARM AND THE DANISH DAMES
                                     0-515-12435-4/$5.50
__LONGARM AND THE RED-LIGHT LADIES #242   0-515-12450-8/$4.99
__LONGARM AND THE KANSAS JAILBIRD #243   0-515-12468-0/$4.99
__LONGARM AND THE DEVIL'S SISTER #244   0-515-12485-0/$4.99
__LONGARM AND THE VANISHING VIRGIN #245   0-515-12511-3/$4.99
__LONGARM AND THE CURSED CORPSE #246   0-515-12519-9/$4.99
__LONGARM AND THE LADY FROM TOMBSTONE #247
                                     0-515-12533-4/$4.99
__LONGARM AND THE WRONGED WOMAN #248   0-515-12556-3/$4.99
__LONGARM AND THE SHEEP WAR #249   0-515-12572-5/$4.99
__LONGARM AND THE CHAIN GANG WOMEN #250   0-515-12614-4/$4.99
__LONGARM AND THE DIARY OF MADAME VELVET #251
                                     0-515-12660-8/$4.99
__LONGARM AND THE FOUR CORNERS GANG #252   0-515-12687-X/$4.99
__LONGARM IN THE VALLEY OF SIN #253   0-515-12707-8/$4.99
__LONGARM AND THE REDHEAD'S RANSOM #254   0-515-12734-5/$4.99
__LONGARM AND THE MUSTANG MAIDEN #255   0-515-12755-8/$4.99
__LONGARM AND THE DYNAMITE DAMSEL #256   0-515-12770-1/$4.99
__LONGARM AND THE NEVADA BELLY DANCER #257 0-515-12790-6/$4.99
__LONGARM AND THE PISTOLERO PRINCESS #258 0-515-12808-2/$4.99

Prices slightly higher in Canada

Payable by Visa, MC or AMEX only ($10.00 min.), No cash, checks or COD. Shipping & handling:
US/Can. $2.75 for one book, $1.00 for each add'l book; Int'l $5.00 for one book, $1.00 for each
add'l. Call (800) 788-6262 or (201) 933-9292, fax (201) 896-8569 or mail your orders to:

Penguin Putnam Inc.	Bill my: ☐ Visa ☐ MasterCard ☐ Amex _____(expires)
P.O. Box 12289, Dept. B	Card# _____
Newark, NJ 07101-5289	Signature _____
Please allow 4-6 weeks for delivery.	
Foreign and Canadian delivery 6-8 weeks.	

Bill to:

Name _____

Address _____ City _____

State/ZIP _____ Daytime Phone # _____

Ship to:

Name _____ Book Total $ _____

Address _____ Applicable Sales Tax $ _____

City _____ Postage & Handling $ _____

State/ZIP _____ Total Amount Due $ _____

This offer subject to change without notice.   Ad # 201 (8/00)

DISCARDED

"What do you want of me, Nico?"

Samantha gave an involuntary shudder as she spoke.

"Everything," Nico answered. "Your heart, your body and the promise of a son."

He seemed to be reaching out to her, as if he wanted to break her or turn her into his own creation. "B-but I know nothing about you," she whispered.

"You know you belong to me, Samantha, for such things are decided for us," he said somberly.

This was crazy, medieval, unreal. Samantha started trembling violently, like someone who'd stepped across a forbidden threshold only to discover too late that a great door had thundered shut behind her.

This man was a stranger to her, a man from another world whose life was littered with tragedies. Yet, something locked them together like an invisible chain....

MARGARET WAY

is also the author of these

Harlequin Romances

and these

Harlequin Presents

A Season
for Change

by

MARGARET WAY

Harlequin Books

TORONTO • LONDON • LOS ANGELES • AMSTERDAM
SYDNEY • HAMBURG • PARIS • STOCKHOLM • ATHENS • TOKYO

Original hardcover edition published in 1981
by Mills & Boon Limited

ISBN 0-373-02448-7

Harlequin edition published December 1981

CHAPTER ONE

OF course they arrived without an appointment and the patients that were left, Mr Fenton and old Mrs Pettigrew, looked up in open-mouthed astonishment and immediately made a place for them to sit down.

The Medici have descended, Samantha thought sardonically, trying to stifle her own violent interest. The Martinellis had only been in Bramston six or seven months, but already they had made an impact to a degree hitherto undreamed-of. The father as a business man of the most tycoonish kind; the daughter as an incipient femme fatale and from all accounts a surprisingly good hostess for her father.

Not that he looked like anyone's father, Samantha thought dryly, staring at *that* profile. More like Lorenzo the Magnificent. Apart from the fact that he was still in his thirties and arrestingly handsome, he looked and moved like a man who had never been caged. Poor old Mrs Pettigrew's face was a study.

'Good afternoon,' he acknowledged the old people with the merest flash of a brilliant smile, infinitely sexy and sophisticated, shepherded his beautiful daughter to a chair, then turned on Samantha with what seemed to her a sizzling hauteur.

'Ah, Miss Harrington!' The voice and the accent were intensely attractive, but the heavy-lidded black eyes perceived her lack of fellowship.

'Mr Martinelli.' Samantha responded like an opponent in a duel.

'I wonder if your father would be good enough to see Antonia *now*,' he stressed exquisitely. 'She has suffered a bad faint.'

'I'm sorry.' For once Samantha was without her usual sympathy. Antonia had probably worn herself out partying or dieting, or both.

'You don't mind, do you?' He turned back to the avid old people, giving them a smile of such severe charm that Mrs Pettigrew piped up eagerly:

'We're in no hurry, I'm sure!'

'Go ahead!' Mr Fenton seconded, when he would have fought anyone else to the death. 'Old people have all the time in the world.'

'*Grazie.* I so appreciate it.'

Win 'em all! Samantha thought, and pushed up from her chair. Inside the consulting room she carefully closed the door and leaned against it, genuinely unnerved.

'How many, Sam?' Luke Harrington looked up from writing a progress report to ask.

'Just two, so I thought, but the Martinellis have arrived.'

'On purpose or by chance?'

'Antonia has had a faint.' She rolled her eyes.

'Let's see her, then.' Luke Harrington muttered something else and stood up. 'Show her in, Sam, there's a good girl.'

'Don't you want me to stay?' Samantha asked playfully, but her father never even heard her, very much the doctor.

In the reception room she smiled at the sick or bored girl, give or take an expression. 'Would you go in, please, Miss Martinelli?'

Grazies from the father, none from the daughter. She swept past Samantha with only a little raising of her winged black brows.

Cheery little thing, Samantha thought.

'That's a beatiful girl you've got there,' Mrs Pettigrew told Martinelli.

Martinelli smiled his total agreement, came across to the old lady and sat down. 'You will allow me to drive you home, *signora*?'

Eighty-four-year-old Mrs Pettigrew blushed like a young girl. 'I'm sure I'll be taking you out of your way.'

In any case *I* usually drive her, Samantha thought wryly, but said nothing to spoil the old lady's chances.

'Come, you know that is no bother,' Martinelli insisted.

'I don't suppose you could take me home as well?' Mr Fenton asked the question. 'I'm tired.'

'The heat, no?' Martinelli turned his lean, powerful body towards the frail old man. 'It will be my pleasure.'

Mr Fenton's habitually testy expression turned angelic, and Samantha wished she could clap. For the next fifteen minutes the old people plied the *magnifico* with questions which he parried graciously and without a blink, but never, to Samantha's mind, really answered.

She, meanwhile, was forced into taking refuge behind a show of efficiency, although in reality hanging on his every word. Once or twice she tried to check herself, but failed. After all, the Martinellis, so handsome and foreign appealed to the imagination. It had even been thought in the early days that the luscious Antonia was his child bride, but when one really looked at them, the resemblance was unmistakable. Obviously he had been married very young, if indeed such a ceremony had taken place. There had been no talk from either of them of a mother or a wife. But then such a thing would spoil his image. He looked alarmingly proper.

Samantha glanced up with particular care, only to find the brilliant black gaze on her. He was reading her thoughts, she was sure of it, when his were a brick wall. Her flawless skin coloured and just when she was hoping something would distract his attention, there was the murmur of voices, and her father, preceded by a somewhat chastened Antonia, came through the connecting door.

'Ah, Doctor!' Martinelli got to his feet, a tall man well over six feet.

'How are you, Mr Martinelli?' Luke Harrington put out his hand, showing his rare, sweet smile.

'Concerned about my daughter.' The black eyes transferred themselves to the daughter's adored face.

'Nothing much wrong with her,' Luke Harrington reassured him. 'She's simply not been eating enough.'

Martinelli looked astounded. 'In a house of plenty?' He threw up his splendid head.

'I must *diet*, Nico!' Antonia said plaintively, her voice lacking the beauty and resonance of her father's. 'I do not wish to spoil the line of my clothes.'

'*Dio!* I had no idea!' He let his disapproval show and Samantha thought she wouldn't like to see his anger close up.

'It's common enough among young girls,' Luke Harrington said soothingly. 'I've given Antonia a diet sheet which will allow her to keep her slim figure and still get the proper nutrition.'

'Staying thin isn't easy, except for *you*, Nico,' said Antonia with a kind of seething jealousy. 'I haven't got the height.'

'Enough!' Martinelli's dark face tautened to dark golden skin over chiselled bones. 'Leave this to me, doctor.'

'Perhaps I might see Antonia again in a month's time?' the doctor asked mildly.

'Certainly.' Martinelli agreed. 'I think that would be wise.'

'Please, Nico, I'll listen!' begged Antonia in a wavering voice.

She wasn't terrified or even scared, but Samantha realised Martinelli was a man to be obeyed.

'I'm very grateful to you, doctor,' he said smoothly. 'I assure you Antonia will heed your warning.'

I certainly hope so, Samantha thought faintly.

Luke Harrington was silent for perhaps thirty seconds, then he said in his clipped, pleasant tone, 'In a social vein, you might care to visit us at Malabar at the weekend for drinks or perhaps dinner, if you have the time? I've been so busy myself with all the spring allergies it would be nice and relaxing if you and Antonia could pay us a call.'

'How kind!' Martinelli's formal style suited him perfectly. 'We have, in fact, been planning to ask you to our home, but I am too busy for so much of the time.'

'Then shall we say Saturday evening?' Luke smiled. 'Come before sunset. I'm sure you'll enjoy our garden. Won't they, Sam?' Luke turned his greying head to include his daughter.

Samantha immediately saw herself showing Martinelli winningly around the grounds. 'If you like gardens,' she smiled.

'And who does not?' Martinelli sounded very foreign indeed. 'I am looking forward to it.'

Antonia, Samantha noticed, was still looking stifled, but she could of course, Samantha thought fairly, still be feeling ill. No matter, she was a beauty with lustrous hair and eyes and skin, and if there was just a hint of a would-be voluptuous figure it was hard to believe any male would object.

By the time office hours were finally over, Samantha was near cracking point. 'Did you *have* to ask them?' she remonstrated with her father.

'Why ever not?' Luke Harrington laid down his glasses. 'They've been here for months.'

Imperturbable, Samantha fiddled with a folder. 'They're unsettling kind of people, don't you think?'

'Yes, I suppose they are,' Luke returned to his notes. 'Young Antonia was going the right way to develop anorexia nervosa.'

'Really?' Samantha stared.

'That's what I've got here,' her father answered wryly. 'Young girls simply don't realise the consequences of their actions. However, I feel that's all cleared up. Mr Martinelli appears to be a man to get results.'

'Placated at all costs,' Samantha remarked dryly. 'Anyway, Mamma will be pleased.'

And so she was. Charlotte Harrington received the news with a flush of pleasure. 'I must say, Luke, it's about time. They've been settled here for months.'

'It takes time to get to know people,' he returned soothingly. 'In any case, it's all arranged.'

'Bingo!' said Samantha.

'You'll have to ask Eliot,' Charlotte told her daughter frowningly, never understanding her daughter's sense of humour.

'Certainly,' Samantha smiled. 'Don't go overboard with the menu, though. Dad's put Antonia on a diet.'

'Show me,' Charlotte demanded. 'I believe I can plan around it.'

'I'm sure you will, my dear.' Luke came up to his wife and kissed her gently on the cheek. 'You love company, don't you?'

'I need it, Luke,' Charlotte said tersely. 'Far more than you and Samantha. Two of a kind. She'll never catch a husband if she doesn't smarten herself up.'

Luke's face was a mixture of astonishment and laughter. 'You see, Sam, you're on the shelf!'

'It's no joke, Luke.' Charlotte said earnestly. 'Samantha is twenty-four. High time she was married. Eliot is a dear boy and very fond of her, but she keeps putting it off.'

'Marriage is a serious step,' Samantha protested.

'Yes, indeed.' Charlotte shivered in the golden warmth. She had married Luke because she thought him the best man in the world and indeed she still thought so, without finding happiness. With Luke's brilliance he could have been a leading consultant in a big city, instead he had chosen to bury himself in a country town. 'It might be an idea if you get yourself a new dress,' she told her daughter a shade tartly. 'From what I've seen of Antonia Martinelli, she'll show you up.'

But Luke dismissed this with a quick smile and a shake of his head. 'Not to worry, darling,' he put an arm around his daughter. 'You've got your grandmother's wonderful bones. She was beautiful at eighty.'

'There you go, Luke!' Charlotte complained. 'You refuse to help me. You've taken Samantha's part since she was a baby. Instead of making herself attractive and getting out, she's always preferred to stay at home with you.'

'So I have!' Samantha looked at her father with a teasing light in her eye. 'I love my parents and I love my home. Why are you always trying to push me out, Mamma?'

'It's for your own good!' Charlotte seemed disinclined to smile. 'When you finally decide you'll marry Eliot, he'll probably have found someone else.'

Samantha mentioned this to Eliot when she saw him the following night.

'As if I ever could!' Eliot extended his hand across the table in the little restaurant and took Samantha's in his own. 'I've been intending to marry you since we were five years old. But your mother's got a point. When are you going to name the day?'

'I ought to.' She laughed a little, wondering why she always felt so apprehensive. She and Eliot had grown up together, gone to the same primary school, shared the same interests.

'Mother and I were just talking this morning about you,' Eliot confided. 'She doesn't think we should waste any more time. I mean, I have a future—better than I ever expected now Miller & Harland have taken me into the firm. You'll make a wonderful solicitor's wife, always so calm and in control. Truly your father's daughter.'

'If so, I'm all right!' She smiled at him, her clear green eyes revealing her feelings for her father.

'You know, I've always felt a bit sorry for Charlotte,' he said objectively. 'You and your father are so close.'

'Why not?' Her beautifully cut mouth curved.

'I'm serious, darling. You don't see your mother as you should. She's still a young woman and a good-looking one at that. I daresay it helps to be a Harrington and mistress of one of the most beautiful old houses in the district, but I've always thought she hungered for another way of life.'

'What is that you're drinking?' Samantha countered, feeling a stir of unease.

'Ah, yes,' Eliot murmured. 'You don't want to think about it and I'm sure I don't want to intrude. It just often seemed to me that your mother isn't a happy woman though she covers it extremely well.'

Samantha couldn't get to sleep that night for wondering if Eliot was right. In all the years she had never known her parents to have a serious argument. Her father was such a civilised man, a man who was dedicated to his life's work. At times it preoccupied him and he was at everyone's beck and call, but could this make her mother unhappy? She was always so concerned for him, telling him he should rest and relax more, but by that, Charlotte meant having friends over, whereas Samantha and her father spent their happiest moments working in the garden. To be sure, Charlotte and Luke were completely unalike, but they had a good marriage, surely?

Saturday came and Malabar had never looked more beautiful. Samantha sat on the lawn with Lucy, her golden labrador, curled up at her feet. Looking back at the house she felt a thrill of pride. Harringtons had lived there for close on a hundred years, putting down roots. Malabar was a splendid old Queensland colonial with deep shaded verandahs, high-set on brick piers with octagonal dome-covered bays at either end of the front elevation. Her great-grandfather had seen such bays in a mansion in the State capital and immediately had his architect incorporate corner pavilions in the design for his own house.

Samantha loved her home dearly. Between her father, herself and dear old George who had always worked for them, their garden was considered to be one of the finest in the tropical North. Now in late October, the superb ornamentals had burst into flower, making a brilliant display. Poincianas ablaze with colour lined the sweeping drive and there were jacarandas and leopards and tulip trees, bauhinias, casuarinas, the magnificent Flame of the Forest, magnolia, fifteen different types of frangipani, masses of palm, lush creepers, glossy lilies and grasses, the orchids they were well known for, white and yellow ginger, hibiscus galore; a controlled jungle with a hundred different favourite spots. She had been immersed in gardening since her earliest childhood when Grandma Harrington, the one she had taken after, had been alive.

Extraordinarily, her mother had no skill as a gardener and though she took great pleasure in showing visitors around the extensive grounds, she had no interest whatever in making things grow. The magic existed only for Samantha and her father, and it began with what Grandma Harrington had called 'having green hands'.

She was standing in her slip wondering what to put on, when her mother came into her room. 'I say, you *do* look nice!' Samantha's glance went back to her mother's small, trim figure. In her late forties, Charlotte Harrington was still a very pretty woman with dark curling hair and dark eyes. Now she was wearing a two-piece outfit in yellow silk and her eyes were bright with excitement.

'Oh, do hurry, dear. They could arrive at any time.'

'What shall I put on?'

Charlotte gave a nervy frown. 'There's never been any pleasure in telling you what to wear. When you were a little girl and I wanted to put you in a party frock you wanted to wear shorts. You were such a pretty child too, but so unfeminine!'

'I robbed you of a lot of pleasure, didn't I, Mamma?' Samantha said wryly. 'You should have had a dark-haired, dark-eyed little doll.'

'Don't worry about that now.' Charlotte went to the window and looked out. 'How could you dally on a day like this? It's absolutely *you*, Samantha.'

'Hey now!' Samantha tried to defend herself. 'Didn't I do the vacuuming and the polishing and arranging the flowers?'

'Eliot is usually here,' said Charlotte, ignoring that. 'You'd better get something over your head, and I wish you'd get your hair out of that old maid's bun. You really should get it permed.'

'*Permed?*' Samantha gave an outraged squeal. 'I've got good hair.'

'There's no style to it.' Charlotte went to the huge red cedar wardrobe and inspected Samantha's dresses. 'Not *one* garment I admire!'

'What about the white?' Tall, long-limbed, Samantha crossed the polished floor to stand beside her mother's diminutive figure.

'It's so *plain*. Nothing to it. Nothing at all!'

'That's me, darling, plain. But what you're missing is that it's got cut and line.'

'Oh, put it on!' Charlotte snapped. 'Sometimes your lack of interest in your appearance gets me down.'

I mustn't feel hurt, Samantha told herself after her mother had gone. It was very trying for Charlotte having a daughter who didn't share her interests. But perming her hair, *never*! It was long and thick and shining with health, and so cool in its chignon for the tropical heat.

Samantha pulled the white dress over her head and paused before the mirror. What she saw was a tall, slender young woman whom her father in his tender moods called his white swan. Mamma had no use for swans. What she had really wanted was a replica of herself, a dainty little creature who was always ready to go shopping.

By the time she walked through to the drawing room, Eliot had arrived, and the pleasure in his eyes made her heart lift in response.

'You look lovely and cool!'

'I'm glad you think so.' She smiled up at him and he bent and kissed her cheek. 'Your mother seems delighted to have the Martinellis over.'

'Well, they're very pleasing to the eye.'

'You can say that again!' Eliot turned his head and looked through the french doors across the verandah and beyond. 'Every time I see them I have to resist the urge to stare.'

'Ah, there you are, Eliot!' Luke Harrington had joined them, his handsome, rather serious face relaxing into a smile.

'How are you, sir?' Eliot took the older man's outstretched hand. He very much admired Samantha's father, as did everyone in the town.

Luke asked after Eliot's mother, who was a widow, and as they stood there talking, a red Ferrari swept up the drive.

'They're here!' said Samantha, trying to inject a little enthusiasm.

'Where's your mother?' Luke walked through to the entrance hall where he was joined by his wife.

Afterwards Samantha was to remember the expression on Eliot's face when he was introduced to Antonia. It was dazzlement, a brush with the unknown and exotic, but Antonia was unruffled, used to admiration from an early age.

To her surprise, her father and Nico Martinelli achieved harmony at once, stopping to admire the huge terracotta pots that housed this or that showy plant, each pot decorated in traditional Spanish or Italian design.

'I imagine, doctor, you are something of a botanical scholar?' The splendid dark head lifted to look around the blossoming landscape.

'Never so meticulous as my mother,' Luke Harrington countered with a smile. 'She was English, you know, and as a young bride still very much under the influence of English and French ideas about landscape, so you can imagine how strange all the extraordinary richness of the tropical plant life seemed to her.'

'I'm sure it didn't take her long to explore,' Martinelli said pleasantly. The sunlight struck across his face and his head, hair so black the brilliant sun could not touch it with brown, bone structure that had been reproduced for centuries in sculpture and art. It was fantastic any man could be so startlingly, sternly beautiful.

Arrested, Samantha stood there, feeling an irrational fear of the man. Indeed, it cost her a deliberate effort not to run away. Yet her mother and father were smiling, transformed, her father speaking contentedly about the old days and how the garden at Malabar had been Grandma Harrington's special pride.

'Sometimes I think you find her here?' Nico Martinelli said perceptively to his host.

'Oh, I do!' Luke Harrington bent with a sigh to loose a stray weed. 'I was intensely devoted to my mother. She was a wonderful woman. Samantha resembles her greatly both in looks and character, and she shares all the Harringtons' great love of a garden.'

Now the black eyes moved to Samantha's face, disturbing her in a way she decided she didn't like. In fact, she wanted to shut her eyes. In all her life she had never been so aware of another human being, or so frightened. But of what?

In the delicious cool of the verandah, they sipped at drinks, Charlotte chatting happily, showing a marked pleasure in her visitors' company. Not that Antonia was any great asset, Samantha thought. She sat back rather detached, her spectacularly beautiful dress ruffled around her, her good looks excessive and to Samantha's mind rather sullen. Some other face was there besides the father's. Two faces—one like a medieval *magnifico*, the other more theatrical and modern. With a flash of excitement, as vivid as a bird in flight, she wondered what kind of woman could hold Martinelli. He had such a tempered, high-mettled look about him, and underneath the fastidiousness and the razor-sharp intelligence an ancient sensuality. It was there in the eyes and in the mouth.

'Will you come to my party?' Antonia was asking her, a husky, accented voice.

'I beg your pardon.' Samantha turned her blonde head. 'I was daydreaming for a moment. I'd love to come.'

'You must wear something special,' Antonia gave her a languid smile. 'I can hardly bear it when no one dresses up.'

'So it's formal?' Eliot moved his chair out slightly so he could have a better view of Antonia's petite figure.

'Oh, very much so.' Martinelli's chiselled mouth sketched a faint grimace. 'My daughter cares a great deal about clothes.'

'And she wears them beautifully,' Charlotte said admiringly, earning herself one of Antonia's languid smiles.

'I sometimes think to myself I shall found an exclusive salon,' Antonia confided. 'Something featuring exquisite clothes. I have a flair for colour and balance, what you might call a superb eye.'

Samantha couldn't help glancing at Nico Martinelli and he gave her a faint smile in return.

'The market is here,' Charlotte said encouragingly. 'There's plenty of money in the North and I'm sure your looks and personality would enhance such a venture.'

'There you are, Nico!' Antonia cried triumphantly. 'Mrs Harrington agrees with me.'

'You have had no experience, *cara*.' Unexpectedly he stooped to pat Lucy, who was dozing at Samantha's feet. 'It takes more than youthful enthusiasm to run a successful business.'

'But as your daughter, surely——?' Eliot too appeared to be on Antonia's side.

'Antonia has not inherited my business sense,' Martinelli told the younger man smoothly, 'though I've no doubt she could persuade clients to buy clothes. Women love dressing up, no?'

'Not Samantha,' Charlotte said dryly, making her daughter sound very sensible and dull.

'Probably she doesn't have to bother,' Martinelli replied with only the briefest glance over Samantha's slender figure.

'I agree,' Luke Harrington said quietly, a little saddened by his wife's insensitivity towards her daughter. 'Before the light fails shall we look over the garden?'

'I'd like that.' Martinelli stood up immediately, lifting back Samantha's chair. 'I believe, Miss Harrington, you help your father a good deal?'

'*Samantha*, please.' She wondered why she said it when she didn't want him to call her by her name at all.

'Samantha,' he repeated, trying it out on his foreign tongue.

Most of the time they all stayed together touring the extremely beautiful, well designed garden. Luke was in his element pointing out this or that spectacular plant or shrub. The natural planting showed a strong English influence, but very different plants thrived there than in an English garden. There was even a touch of Italy in the fountains and sculptures, and Nico Martinelli began to talk very knowledgeably about the famous gardens of Europe, many of which had inspired the doctor on his visits.

Antonia and Eliot appeared to have slowed up, Antonia no doubt hampered by her high heels. In the garden's Japanese tea-house they came to a halt, Eliot waving tranquilly, and Charlotte, who really didn't want to go any farther, excused herself saying she must see to the dinner.

'I'll come with you, my dear.' Luke took his wife by the elbow. 'Samantha can take over our role. She's extremely good at it.'

'So, Samantha,' Nico Martinelli gazed down at Samantha's blonde head rather sardonically. 'Lead on.'

The intimate atmosphere of the garden soon blocked them off. They might have been lost in a tropical paradise.

'Water is a very important element in the garden, is it not?' he said, still in that dry tone. They were standing near the large pond, its dark green surface covered with aquatic plants and gorgeous tropical waterlilies in shades of white, gold, pink and the magnificent blue lotus.

Samantha tried to remember when she had ever felt so uncomfortable in her life. The rich fragrance of the waterlilies reached them and as she stepped forward a little precipitately she nearly slipped on some loose gravel.

'Allow me.' He caught her arm firmly and though she was ashamed of herself afterwards she tautened and almost but not quite pulled away.

'You don't like me, do you, Samantha?' He sur-

he looked and sounded as strained as she was, his fingers stirring across her hair.

'You see,' he looked down into her face, 'I have released you.'

Black magic, of course. He had the air of a sorcerer. 'I expect we should be getting back.'

'Of course.' It was obvious he had noticed her desperation. 'Don't touch your hair.'

'Oh, I *must*!' She was positively shaking.

'I think you fear your own beauty.' He took her elbow as the path narrowed.

'Hardly.' She would rather have been anywhere but with him.

'Then why do you play it down like a shy little girl?'

'I think that's probably wise.'

'Then you have agreed with me, *piccola*, I'm afraid. You don't want your own or anyone else's feelings to get out of control.'

'I'm a very calm person,' she said.

'You think so?' He lowered his eyes until they rested on the pulse beating away frantically in her neck.

'One can't always be, I suppose.'

'You have had very little experience.' It wasn't a question, but a brutal opinion. No, she had never reached an emotional peak. Her childhood hero had been Eliot. She couldn't remember a time when she hadn't been cheered by his presence. He had kissed her many times, made light love to her; now in a few moments she had been forced to accept a judgment of herself.

So be it! She was cool and calm and frightened of turbulent emotion. So were a lot of people. The less she had to do with Signor Martinelli, the better. A man like that was capable of upturning one's whole world.

All the same, he was a splendid guest, drawing each of them out in turn with the only exception of Samantha. She stayed very quiet, a little dismayed and puzzled at how readily her father had accepted this man. Luke Harrington wasn't a man given to quick, easy friendships, yet from the very moment Nico Martinelli had arrived the two men had established an extraordinary harmony.

Antonia too had lost her sullen look, her black head tilted back a little to answer Eliot's well chosen questions. Eliot had the knack for conversation without ever descending to the banal, and Martinelli had discovered in him a latent wit that he had never bothered to polish and put to frequent use. All in all, Samantha considered, Nico Martinelli had a first-class technique. It even occurred to her that he could win Eliot to any one of his own business ventures. A promising young solicitor could always be found a place in the firm.

'I'm sure I can't remember when I enjoyed myself more!' said Luke as they began to walk back towards the house. They had all seen the Martinellis off after what seemed on the face of it to be a highly successful evening.

'I'd like to see a good deal more of them.' Charlotte looked happy and relaxed. 'They really have everything, don't they?'

'I suspect he's ruthlessly ambitious,' Samantha said.

'He perturbs you does he, darling?' Luke kissed his daughter's hair.

'I can't think why he left his own country.'

'At least you didn't *ask* him!' Charlotte said tartly. 'We have a good many Italians in this country and are proud of them.'

'It seems to me a man like that wouldn't readily abandon a stately home, and whatever else he is, he looks as if he came from one.'

'I agree,' said Eliot, a man who could recognise true class. 'On the other hand, his family could have become impoverished. It does happen.'

'Backgrounds interest me,' said Samantha. 'For all the talk tonight he revealed nothing of his former life. It's human nature to talk.'

'I suggest we all wait until he's ready to confide in us,' Luke said mildly.

'There are all sides to people's characters,' Samantha pointed out, earning from her mother a cross look.

'I think they're charming, absolutely charming. Antonia is the most beautiful girl I've ever seen in my life.'

'A real stunner!' Eliot seconded. 'I wouldn't have missed this evening for worlds.'

Twenty minutes later, after coffee and some further discussion of their guests, Samantha and Eliot walked a little way down the drive to Eliot's car. It *was* Eliot in a way, conservative, safe and reliable, but that evening Eliot seemed stirred up.

'Sit in with me for a while, Sam?' he begged her.

'For a few minutes.' She, too, was feeling scarcely herself.

'You were rather quiet tonight.' Belatedly he recognised the fact.

'I expect I was.' She settled into the passenger sea. 'I'm rather uncertain about the Martinellis.'

'But they're such attractive people!' Eliot reached over and held her hand. 'I mean, he's faultless—manner, looks, the power of his mind.'

'A little too much of everything,' Samantha said very quietly.

'Don't, darling.' His hand tightened over hers. 'It's only because he's so ... *continental*, he seems strange. I felt that too, at first, but it's simply the difference between the new world and the old. He's in our country now and doing extremely well. I sometimes feel we don't even know business. Mr Martinelli will no doubt finish up a multi-millionaire, if he isn't one already.'

'And what was Antonia's appeal?' she asked lightly, not even questioning her lack of jealousy.

'She's very vivacious, isn't she?'

'She is when she begins to talk,' Samantha remarked dryly.

'She really should open that shop, you know,' Eliot said seriously. 'I can see her becoming a great success.'

'Possibly.' Samantha leant her head back. 'Didn't it strike you that she's a man's woman?'

'Are there any others?' Eliot gave a satisfied laugh.

'Some find the time to befriend their own sex. Antonia scarcely looked at me, or Mamma, but Mamma, of course, was helplessly smitten.'

'Oh, let's forget them!' Eliot cried, feeling his

mood begin to change. 'Kiss me, Sam.' He put his arm around her and gripped hard.

The face that she turned up to him was almost blind. The light pressure of his mouth deepened and moved by her stillness which he took for acquiescence he dropped his free hand over her breast.

'Sam—darling.' His breath came warm and clean into her mouth.

It was an astonishment to find she didn't want him, neither the gentle sweetness of his mouth or the imploring caress.

'Marry me, Sam.' He raised his brown head little. '*Please*, Sam. I've waited long enough.'

Feeling as she did then, she couldn't bear to say yes. Neither could she bring herself to hurt him in any way. Maybe she was frigid and only half knew it.

Because she hadn't answered, a little fiercely he took her mouth again. It even seemed like despair.

'Crumbs, Sam,' he told her. 'You only offer me crumbs.'

'What is it you want?' In an instant there was tension between them.

'I want to love you,' he said in a pained voice. 'I want to make love to you—not betray you but marry you. I've always wanted to marry you. In fact, I've never looked at anyone else. Maybe too you're the kind of girl who can only respond in marriage. You're twenty-four, Sam, and I know and you know you're still a virgin.'

'You sound as if it's a sin!'

'It's a little unnatural when I long for you.'

'Let me think, Eliot.' She made a swift movement and kissed his cheek. She had to face it. Was she really frightened of marriage? She had loved Eliot all her life.

'A woman like Antonia Martinelli wouldn't keep her man away,' he pointed out bitterly. 'She looks as if she's got passion to spare!'

'I think you're right!' Samantha had recovered enough to smile. 'I'm in two minds whether to go to her party.'

'Well then, *I'm* going,' Eliot pushed his disordered hair away from his forehead. 'Is it possible, Sam, you don't really love me?'

'Of course I do!' she said helplessly, convinced it was true.

'I don't know.' He sighed deeply. 'Mother doesn't think you do.'

'Goodness, do you discuss it?' Samantha looked at him with distaste on her face.

'Of course we do!' Eliot's nice, curvy mouth straightened. 'You mightn't tell everything to *your* mother, but I do mine.'

'I'm sorry!' Samantha apologised. 'I know you're very close.'

'Mother thinks the world of you,' Eliot told her, visibly upset. 'I want you to know that.'

'I do.' Samantha shook her blonde head. 'Don't let's argue, Eliot. It's unbearable.'

'Oh, darling, then just let's be quiet and kiss me. Properly this time. If you let yourself go, it will happen.'

In spite of Eliot's evident emotion, Samantha never for a moment lost control. It was Eliot who trembled, kissing her again and again.

'We belong together, Sam,' he whispered, at last releasing her with an effort. 'We always have.'

CHAPTER TWO

LESS than a fortnight later, a few days before Antonia's birthday party, Eliot rang to invite Samantha to his home for dinner.

'I've a bit of news,' he told her over the phone.

'Aren't you going to tell me?' Eliot's voice sounded excited.

'It might be best if we discuss it when you get here. Mother thinks so.'

'All right, then. What time?' She asked the question because one simply didn't call on Mrs Nicolson before the appointed time.

Eliot named the hour and Samantha walked through from the hall to the kitchen to tell her mother.

'Eliot wants me to go over.' She looked at her mother with almost a note of apology in her voice. Charlotte, too, was acutely fussy about meals and meal times and being told.

'A bit late notice, isn't it?' Charlotte said shortly. 'I've already prepared the vegetables.'

'Sorry.' Samantha hesitated, then picked up a strawberry. 'He told me he had some news, something he wants us all to discuss.'

'Really?' Charlotte sounded as though she didn't care. 'It's really been one long struggle trying to get you to the altar. Perhaps Dorothy is going to put her foot down.'

'I've always thought she didn't really want me as a daughter-in-law.'

'Perhaps she doesn't,' Charlotte returned, having thought the same herself. 'I would advise you not to live with her whatever happens.'

'I think that's what Eliot expects of his bride,' Samantha observed wryly. 'How could the average girl cope with such perfection? I even understand why Mr Nicolson went so early.'

'To tell you the truth, she always struck me as a wonderful housewife,' Charlotte said firmly. 'In fact I take my hat off to her.'

'Having everything *exactly* in its place, can be a vice,' Samantha countered dryly. 'She doesn't relax for an instant, on the go from morning till night. Before one has scarcely finished one's steak, the plate is whisked away and washed. No lingering over dinner. Straight into the washing-up, but before that's done, the dining table has to be rubbed over with a polishing cloth and reset with the candelabra and the ruby glass épergne, just so. There's no such thing as rotating, or shifting the furniture about. She has everything in the house exactly as it suits her, and it will very likely remain that way until the day she dies.'

'Sometimes Samantha you can be very unkind,' said Charlotte with her face cold. 'We all have our little foibles.'

'Some more remarkable than others!' Samantha sighed. 'I don't mean to be unkind, I'm just stating facts. Perfectionists can be very irritating to live with.'

'That's true!' Charlotte said shortly, and never gave any reason for the slight bitterness of her reply.

On the dot of seven, Samantha arrived at the Nicolsons' front door.

'How are you, dear?' Mrs Nicolson greeted Samantha pleasantly, taking a quick glance at her dress.

'Fine, thank you, Mrs Nicolson—and you?' Samantha moved into the hallway, pretending not to notice the lightning assessment. Another of Mrs Nicolson's foibles was to have exactly the right dress for every occasion. Dining with a friend during the week demanded a little silk with a single string of pearls, or then again, a very good cotton.

'I admit I haven't been myself lately,' Mrs Nicolson was saying in her soft, consciously ladylike voice. 'One begins to wind down a little when one is past forty—the relentless passage of time.'

'The house looks as immaculate as ever,' Samantha hazarded, keeping the sardonic glint out of her eyes. She couldn't remember exactly when, but Eliot had told her his mother was fifty.

'Well, yes.' Mrs Nicolson lapsed into a slight smile. 'I try to keep everything nice for Eliot. After all, in time, this house will be his.'

'Where is he, by the way?' Samantha asked.

'Sit down, dear.' Mrs Nicolson indicated an armchair, the back and sides of which she kept covered with protectors, something Samantha personally detested. 'He's taking a phone call in the study. It's gone on rather a long time.' There was an undertone of excitement in that quiet tone that Samantha found intriguing.

'And how are you affected by his news?' Samantha crossed her lovely slim legs sedately at the ankles, watching Mrs Nicolson's pale gaze travel to her shoes.

'Actually, we're waiting for your opinion, Samantha. As you and Eliot are to be married, it's important we all agree on his choice of a career.'

'Career?' Samantha queried, surprised.

'Of course, he hasn't told you. . . . Don't worry, dear. He'll be here in a moment.'

And so he was. Eliot, looking very neat and boyish and well behaved, trod quietly into the room.

'Sam, how splendid you've arrived!' he came to her, bent over and kissed her cheek. 'Guess who I've just been talking to?'

'Would you care for a sherry before dinner?' Mrs Nicolson inserted, just to add to the breathless challenge.

'Thank you.' Samantha didn't really care for sherry, but it was part of a long-standing ritual. 'Well, tell me!' She looked up at Eliot, after his mother had gone.

'Martinelli!' Eliot announced with the air of a magician effortlessly conjuring up a miracle. 'Did I make you jump?'

'No,' Samantha answered a little flatly. 'Business is booming and he's offered you a place in his organisation.'

'I've never seen anything like it, Sam,' Eliot shook his head. 'You're psychic!'

'Call it common sense.'

'You don't sound pleased?' Eliot sat down in the armchair opposite her and leaned forward. 'He's

offered me a great deal more money than I'm getting now and the promise of swift promotion if I
shape up the way he wants.'

'I hope you're not going to take it,' said Samantha, and Eliot almost wailed.

'Be sensible, Sam. You always are!'

'Surely there are more considerations than
making money?' Samantha protested. 'Miller &
Harland is a very respected firm. You have a career
with them. I thought it was what you always
wanted.'

'And so I did!' Eliot looked quite agitated. 'But
I'd be crazy to pass up a chance like this! Let's face
it, Sam, we're all working for money.'

'You're not greedy, Eliot.' She looked at him
searchingly, because of her deep affection for him,
trying to think what was best. For *him*, not herself.
There was nothing high-pressure about Eliot, no
great driving power, though he had an excellent
legal brain. 'I can appreciate why Mr Martinelli
might want you, but I can't see why you might
want him.'

'He's going to be a power in the North, Sam!' He
knelt down in front of her, speaking urgently. 'I've
seen him a few times since that evening at Malabar
and each time I find him more compelling, more
dynamic. He has wonderful plans, plans that will
benefit us all. Don't think I haven't searched
my soul, Sam, and each time I've thought about
you.'

'About me too, I hope!' Mrs Nicolson had come
back into the living room, speaking with an unaccustomed sharpness.

'Of course, Mother.' Eliot struggled to his feet to take the silver tray from his mother. 'That goes without saying.'

'You're not pleased, Samantha?' Mrs Nicolson asked with a tight, challenging smile.

'Are you?'

Mrs Nicolson sat down in her favourite chair and accepted a sherry from her son. 'I'm quite unable to decide. If only my dear husband were alive! We've never been gambling people, and such a decision would change Eliot's life.'

'Let's hope for the better!' said Eliot, and his voice held a forceful note contrary to his nature.

Martinelli's influence already. Samantha sipped her sherry in silence. 'What *is* it exactly he wants you to do?' she asked finally.

'Train for a top executive position. My Law degree will be a tremendous help—in fact he told me it was a deciding factor. I can be of invaluable help within the companies. Naturally I can't speak about his plans, they were told to me in confidence, but I can tell you they're big. Why, a man like that could revolutionise the North, change the lives of all of us who live here. We *need* men like Martinelli,' Eliot announced, his face flushed.

'But what about the pace?' Samantha asked quietly. 'Some men are destroyed by pressure. You're a gentle, sensitive person, Eliot. Not every man can dream dangerous dreams.'

'I'm sharp enough, Sam, you know that. A good lawyer. I can't hide all my life. Martinelli has offered me the chance at a little bit of power. I can accomplish a lot of good.'

'And what if he goes broke?' Samantha felt forced into asking the question. 'Will Miller & Harland have you back?'

'Can you foresee him going broke?' Eliot asked excitedly, his light blue eyes on fire. 'Why are you talking like this, Sam? You've met Martinelli. Is he a man to fail?'

'All I know is,' Samantha said doggedly, 'he's a complete stranger to us all.'

'And his dealings are unquestionably above board. I can tell you that from my sources. Apart from the fact that he's not one of us, he's held in very high regard by the business community. Some are jealous, of course. That's inevitable.'

'Have you any idea of his real wealth?' Mrs Nicolson asked worriedly. 'I must admit I share Samantha's apprehensions. You're so settled, dear, with Miller & Harland. Both of the senior partners have known you all your life. Indeed they acted for your father and they, of course, hold my will. Mr Martinelli may well have great plans, but what if they fail?'

In her heart Samantha thought they wouldn't, but in actuality she was frightened for Eliot. And herself. Their lives had been so pleasant and in a way sheltered now they were faced with an enormous, threatening take-over. To be in Nico Martinelli's power!

They went in to dinner, but Samantha found she had all but lost her appetite. True to form, Mrs Nicolson ceremoniously whipped dishes away, and as she only served very delicate helpings Samantha made some impact on a totally unmemorable meal. Mrs Nicolson prided herself on being a 'good, plain cook', which meant everything was astonishingly without flavour.

Eliot, now, was used to it and he passed up nothing. Not one mouthful, including a very sickly pudding Mrs Nicolson informed Samantha he had adored since he was a boy.

'Life has taught me that people prefer simple, well prepared food,' she announced with a good deal of private satisfaction. 'Spare me haute cuisine!'

As far as Samantha was concerned it was a case of give me haute cuisine every time. Even a little salt stirred in would have helped.

Before it was time to go home—again Samantha remembered Mrs Nicolson liked her living room cleared around ten-thirty—the subject of a marriage date was broached.

'So here you are, both twenty-four, and I'm waiting for a grandchild.' Mrs Nicolson complained.

'Set the date, Sam!' Eliot begged her softly. 'We've always known we'd get married.'

Samantha now had to ask herself, why not? Certainly she had never conceived a passion for anyone else.

'Why do you hesitate, Samantha?' Mrs Nicolson asked almost angrily.

'I care very deeply for Eliot, but we must be quite sure.'

'You know he has always loved you?' In Mrs Nicolson's pale eyes there was a flicker of hostility.

'Never looked at anyone else from his boyhood?'

And I get the feeling you never have quite approved, Samantha thought. Her thoughts raced and jumped and shockingly she thought of Nico Martinelli. There would be no half measures with him, her head insisted, even her blood. No peace and calm, only a fiery passion, if one dared. It struck her as very odd that she should be thinking of him in that way, but then it occurred to her that she didn't know herself very well.

You are such a child!

Was that right?

'Sam, what's the matter? You're a million miles way!' Eliot's voice sounded almost panicky.

'It's such a hot evening!' Samantha smiled, rising. 'Whatever makes you happy, Eliot, makes me happy, but I think we should wait and see what significance Signor Martinelli is going to have in our life.'

'With you behind me, Sam, I can handle anything,' Eliot said touchingly.

'I'm sure we're both very proud of you just as you are.' Mrs Nicolson rose to her full five feet two, bringing the rather shattering evening to a close.

The next morning before work, Samantha decided to speak to her father.

'Something bothering you, darling?' he asked her before she had actually opened her mouth. 'You're very quiet.'

'You like Eliot, Don't you?' She sat on the side of the desk staring down into her father's calm, distinguished face.

'Who could not like Eliot?' he answered, patiently waiting for more.

'Why is it I can't bring myself to set the date for our wedding?' Samantha's green eyes looked distressed.

'I guess, darling, you don't love him,' Luke Harrington said finally.

'But, Daddy, I *do*!' She hadn't called him Daddy for years.

'I know you're very fond of him,' Luke smiled. 'After all, you grew up together. You're compatible in many ways, but I've always had the feeling that when love comes to you it will be shattering.'

'So why do you say that?' Samantha demanded, deeply surprised.

'You're made for the peaks, Sam, not the quiet satisfactions. You're like me.'

She couldn't seem to stop staring, searching her father's fine eyes. 'Did you love someone like that?' she asked with suspended breath.

'A long time ago when I was very young.'

'And what happened?' They both knew he had spoken of someone else but Mamma.

'She married someone else. It was agony.'

'She didn't love you?' She looked at her father again. He was still a very handsome man.

'Oh, yes.' There was an echo of strong feeling in his voice. 'But her father didn't want her to marry me and her father won.'

'What a terrible story!' Samantha actually felt her father's young pain.

'Not so bad!' He took a deep breath and smiled at her. 'I have your mother and you.'

'But who *is* she?'

'*Was* she.' Her father got up and crossed to a cabinet. 'She died, and why she died made me work long and hard. Her illness wasn't serious and her death could have been prevented. I thought I would never find happiness again, but I did. I've lived to prevent suffering.'

'You're a fine doctor,' Samantha said. 'The best.'

'Your mother always wanted me to have a brilliant career, a fashionable practice.' Luke drew a long breath and released it wearily. 'But I've always wanted to be where I'm needed. I belong here.'

'The whole town is sure of that!' Samantha said swiftly. 'I think you can claim a brilliant career, Dad. Probably the best career in the world.'

'Marie Flannery,' he said, and withdrew a file from the cabinet. 'She's dying.'

'Oh, *no*!' Samantha forgot her own little problems.

'Leukaemia, nothing less.' Luke shook his head grimly. 'I just wonder how I'm going to tell that poor man. Marie is wonderful, beautiful and brave, but poor old Jim is going to break.'

'You don't think. . . .

'No.' Luke looked into his daughter's saddened eyes. 'It's exactly what I feared.'

So the subject of Eliot was temporarily dropped. There were so many life-and-death issues about Samantha's every day that she felt quite foolish dramatising anything in her own life. There was no hope for Marie Flannery, thirty-five years old, but Samantha thanked God for her own perfect health.

If what her father said was true and she didn't really love Eliot, she had to set him free.

It was an upsetting week. Jim Flannery had to be told, though Marie had recognised her own doom and accepted it with astonishing bravery. The Rodgers baby was brought in with convulsions, the young mother almost terrified out of her wits.

'I am going to lose her!' she had shouted over and over, agitating the waiting patients until, with his lips tight, Luke had had to give her a calming shot. The baby, he told her, would be all right. The convulsion was caused by the high fever, the fever the result of ignoring a cold. The baby was admitted to hospital with a chest infection, and because the mother was so distraught Samantha rode with her in the ambulance.

By Saturday she felt too depleted for Antonia's party.

'You *have* to go!' Charlotte said firmly. 'You can't take all the suffering in the world on your own shoulders. So Mr Conway had a stroke and poor little Marie Flannery has to die? Who can be indifferent, but you can't let it get you down. I told Luke at the beginning you weren't tough enough to deal with suffering.'

'I wouldn't call Dad tough, would you?' Samantha asked quietly.

'You know what I mean, Samantha,' her mother returned shortly. 'Your father is in many ways an aloof man. He holds back.'

'That's just his way of dealing with suffering,' Samantha explained. 'Every doctor has to develop his own ethic. Some develop a black humour, others a high wall of reserve, Dad is always very gentle and caring, one pace removed. He has to be, but he's never aloof. He's always *there*.'

'I wish he were here now!' Charlotte sighed in exasperation. 'You're going to go to the party tonight. You have a new dress and Eliot told me himself how much he's looking forward to it.'

'All right, Mamma,' Samantha said quietly.

'And no need to sound so noble. If you ask me Eliot was rather smitten with Antonia, and who could blame him? Your attitude to Eliot is all wrong. You think he's always going to be there at your beck and call, but you could be wrong.'

If there was a warning there Samantha scarcely heard it, forcing herself into a lighter frame of mind. The garden was her refuge, so she went there spending a couple of hours in what she and her father called the 'secret garden', surrounded by brick walls on three sides and approached through a brick archway over which an allamanda in a delicate rose-violet climbed rampantly. Here her father found relief from the pressure of his work, and here too in the course of the afternoon did she make the decision to tell Eliot she couldn't marry him.

'You're looking lovely, Samantha!' her mother told her with great approval when she was finally dressed for the evening. 'Why you don't look like this all the time, I'll never know!'

'A little too much for the patients, don't you think?' Samantha turned back to the mirror and smiled. A far more glamorous creature confronted her than she saw there every day, a make-believe self—enormous green eyes, delicate bones, hair that fell over her shoulder in a golden slide. Suddenly, starkly, she realised why she had left her hair loose, and the blood beat hotly under her high cheekbones.

'Wow!' exclaimed Eliot when he saw her. He had always thought Sam very beautiful but underplayed. Now, he saw, when she made the slightest effort she was dazzling. He loved her dress too, long and clinging and ultra-feminine, showing an alluringly slender body and matching those green, suddenly lorelei eyes. 'You'll knock 'em rotten, in that outfit,' he told her.

'Antonia too?' she asked him, lowering her heavy, darkened lashes.

'You look like an angel!' he said rapturously, thinking how much he was going to kiss her on the way home.

'And Antonia is a little devil.'

'I wish I had her problem,' Charlotte said dryly. 'I really do.'

Because her father was working hard on a report for a medical journal Samantha went to his study to show him how she looked.

'*Celestial*, darling!' he beamed, leaning back in his chair.

Samantha floated a little, happily, showing him how the beautiful chiffon skirt swirled.

'Have you considered you might put the beauteous Miss Martinelli's chiselled nose slightly out of joint?'

'Shall I take it off?' she smiled.

'It's so unfair,' Luke's mouth twitched dryly. He had his own opinion of Miss Antonia Martinelli. 'And what moved you to wear your hair loose?'

'Never mind.' Samantha stopped twirling.

'It wasn't Eliot.' Luke regarded his daughter narrow-eyed. 'Walk carefully, my darling.'

'Have I ever done anything else?' She rushed to him, bent over his shoulder and kissed his cheek.

'To tell you the truth, I just think you've been marking time!'

CHAPTER THREE

THE property Nico Martinelli had acquired had been hacked from the jungle by one of the early pioneering families and worked originally as a sugar cane plantation. The homestead still stood, surrounded by the wide Queensland verandahs, screened by latticed timber with its many french doors opening out on to the gleaming timber floor.

'Wonderful old property, isn't it?' Eliot remarked. 'He bought the fields, the lot!'

'It must have cost him plenty,' Samantha observed. 'The setting is superb.'

'Surely it's supposed to have a ghost?' Eliot harked back to the old rumour.

'Exorcised by the parish priest.' Samantha felt her body warmed by excitement. 'I can't think the old house will suit him. It's nearly falling down.'

'Don't worry, he's building!' Eliot told her. 'A palazzo, no less.'

'And what about the old house?' Samantha asked almost wrathfully. 'He's not going to pull it down?'

'Didn't you just say it was *falling* down?' Eliot laughed at her agitation.

'Even so,' Samantha said more mildly, 'it's a part of us, part of the history of the North. It would be a crime to pull it down when he has the money to restore it.'

'And that, my darling, is what he intends to do,' Eliot passed on the information triumphantly. 'It's going to be re-sited and turned into an art gallery.'

'Good heavens!' Samantha was startled. 'You're very much in the know.'

'Actually Antonia told me.' Eliot nosed the car in under a magnificent poinciana. 'She's very knowledgeable about art.'

'No one told *me*,' said Samantha.

Antonia's eyes, when they fell on Samantha, betrayed a certain animosity, but no one could have wished for a warmer greeting.

'You look very stylish too, Eliot,' she told him, giving him an altogether different look from the one she gave Samantha.

Why, she's attracted to him! Samantha thought, amazed. Dear and funny and nice as Eliot undoubtedly was, she hadn't thought he would appeal to the exotic Antonia. Tonight she blazed in almost a ball gown—Saint Laurent, she told someone later.

All the premier young people of the district were there, all of whom were known to Eliot and Samantha. It was a young people's party exclusively (Antonia's wishes), but Samantha felt extraordinarily restless until her eyes alighted on her host.

My God, she thought. *My God!*

When he moved towards her across the intervening space she couldn't speak, swept by a cross-current of sensation, fear and a painful pleasure. He was so incredibly handsome—though handsome didn't say it. The bright colour in her cheeks faded and her beautiful skin paled.

'Good evening, Samantha.' He took her hand and surprised her by lifting it briefly to his mouth.

She had to bite on her inner cheek, though he must have felt the tremble in her hand. She had never heard her own name sound so melodious— much, much too disturbing.

'May I tell you how beautiful you look?'

'Thank you.' She had to blink her lashes to break the spell. 'This is the first time I've ever been here,' she told him, her voice a little too quick and excited.

'Then you must allow me to show you around.'

'Please . . . I didn't mean. . . .'

'Come, Samantha, you are safe with me.'

He was mocking her gently, of course. She knew that. He knew she was twenty-four, without sophistication, experience.

'Eliot may have told you my plans.' He glanced down at her with his brilliant black eyes.

'To work for you, or this house?'

'Both,' he said as their eyes met. 'You don't wish for him to come into my organisation, Samantha?'

They were surrounded by laughter, music, blossoming lights, but she only saw him. 'Did he tell you that?'

'Yes.' The beautifully cut mouth twisted into a faint grimace. 'You think if you marry him you will live happily ever after?'

'And you, Mr Martinelli, what do you think?'

'I think you don't belong.' His voice was very deep and foreign. Black velvet.

Abruptly she moved ahead of him, aching with a

kind of anger. 'Did you know this house was once visited by a ghost?'

'Ghosts do not perturb me.' He took her elbow and drew her into the library. It was smaller than the other large reception rooms and deserted. The lights shimmered softly and Samantha could see the flash of the gold lettering on the rows of books.

'I am going to be building a new house,' he told her, watching her stand uncertainly under the central chandelier.

'Eliot mentioned it just now in the car.' Her heart was beating so erratically she almost put her hand to her breast to calm it.

'The plans are here.' He moved nearer and her fingers clenched into her palms.

'You have a superb site.' She was checking her agitation, looking downwards so her eyes would reveal nothing of the flame inside.

'Are you as nervous, Samantha, as you sound?'

'Worse,' she said, and smiled.

'That is better.' He suddenly put his hand beneath her chin and lifted it so that he could see her eyes. 'I don't want to terrify you.'

She had no time to change her expression and it told him many things—her youth, her sensitivity, her acute awareness of him. 'I'm not usually such a frail creature,' she apologised.

'I don't think so either.' His black eyes seemed to have deepened and darkened, brilliant yet completely unfathomable. 'The people who live here tell me how wonderful you are, so cool and calm and competent. I have seen this myself.'

'What else would one expect of a doctor's daughter?' Her attempt at lightness was rewarded, for he dropped his hand.

'And you are intensely devoted to him, are you not?'

'I adore him.' Samantha spoke the simple truth.

'Which makes it all the harder for your Eliot,' he replied.

'In what way?' Her green eyes suddenly flashed. 'I want you to tell me.'

He smiled at her, a charming, remote smile. 'The man you marry, little one, you must greatly respect. You won't be able to settle for less, neither will you be able to find a man just like your father.'

'I've never thought of that at all.'

'Possibly not.' He unrolled the plans of his new house and set them down on the magnificent, richly carved desk. 'Come here, Samantha.'

She seemed to hesitate as though he had said something unpardonable to her.

'I only mention this, because I think you don't know yourself. *Yet.*'

'Eliot is my dearest friend.'

'So?' He glanced up and a thrill like electricity ran through her.

'So I can't think you know anything about me, the way I feel.'

'You should be honest, little one,' he said dryly, 'and not comfort yourself with nonsense. You are not so difficult for me to read.'

'And you are not as *sympatico* as you could be.' A little defiantly she came around the desk to join him, looking down at the top sheet of the plans. 'So you intend to stay in this part of the world?'

'You wish to question my motives?'

That did seem to be true, but she marvelled at his effrontery. 'I expect it's only human to wonder.'

'About *what*?'

She refused to look up at him, standing so lean and dangerous by her side. 'Please don't make me say things I don't want to. I'm not usually impertinent or prying.'

'Yet you want to know what has happened to bring me here? You want to know if I am a man of honour? You want to know if it is safe to deliver your *dearest friend* into my hands?'

Samantha felt so pent-up, she was startled, and her lovely face flushed with embarrassment. 'If I'm wondering about Eliot,' she evaded, 'it's because I want to help him in every way.'

'Yet he has begged you to marry him and you do not?'

'How do you know that?' She lifted her head, her green eyes glittering.

'He has told me.'

'*Eliot* did?' She spoke out her anger and disbelief.

'So, it is not a disgrace to confide. He is a very honest and likeable young man. Not president of a company material, perhaps, but with the intelligence and determination to do well for himself. Such men I can use.'

'And how do you guarantee them job satisfaction?' she demanded. 'Eliot is very contented where he is.'

'*Is* he?' He looked down on her in his arrogance. 'You should ask yourself, Samantha, is he?'

'Surely you're not telling me he's been shutting me out?'

'It might be better for him if you had,' he answered gravely. 'For you're not going to marry him, are you?'

'I think I shall!' she said with astonishing perversity.

'No.' He shook his raven head. 'Though you look very fragile and sensitive, there's an indomitable character in you that I have marked. The grandmother, no?'

She felt giddy from his very presence. 'I don't feel very indomitable with you.' I don't think I can handle you at all, she thought helplessly.

'But please don't run away.' His voice was very beautiful and accented on her ear. 'I want you to see my house.'

'I'd like to,' she murmured, half mesmerised. 'I'm sure it's going to be very, very imposing. Perhaps recapturing another era.' Gleaming white, Italianate. . . .

'*Al contrario,*' he said a little curtly, 'a new house for a new country.'

'You wish to forget the past?' she asked him, amazed at her own temerity.

'I suppose you are right, but it is impossible. The past remains.'

Samantha was shaken by his grimness, his appearance so handsome and foreign it seemed almost sinister. He seemed a long way off as if he stood listening to the sounds of the past.

She turned away, unrolling the edge of the plans and holding them with her hand.

'You are looking at it the wrong way, *piccola*.'

'It looks just as pleasing upside down. . . .' the rest of it was lost in her throat, for his hand closed over her own.

For a touch to push her to such limits, when it was plain he was amused and helping her out! All her normal coolness, self-control, was nowhere in sight. If she turned slightly, she could turn herself into his arms, only every instinct of self-preservation warned her.

'Give it to me,' he said, with unexpected gentleness.

What it was to be so adult, so responsible, so self-assured!

'As a matter of fact, you're right!' He smiled at her, careless and serene, a male beauty built into every clean bone. 'It *does* look better upside down.'

'Of course you're starting out with a perfect setting!' She said the words almost to herself, dreamily. 'A beautiful big house presided over by a mountain.'

'This is a very beautiful part of the world. Astonishingly beautiful.' His black eyes rested on her downbent blonde head and her flushed cheeks. 'My brief to the architect was perfectly clear-cut. I want a practical house—a big one but with a relaxed ambience, white throughout, a white marble floor with the colour taken up with the furnishings, the paintings, pieces of sculpture. Every room will have a view and the swimming pool looks towards a rock cascade.'

'A tropical house!' The way he spoke brought the plans to life.

'But of course, little one. This is not the Veneto.'

'Where you were born?' She lifted her eyes to his, perplexed at her own longing to know.

'Undoubtedly I *know* it. As you are so curious I will tell you that I grew up in a villa that was built in the second half of the seventeenth century. It was destroyed by flood in the greatest chain of tragedies in my life.'

'I'm sorry.' If she wished to uncover the truth, she never expected this. His face looked full of mystery, the bone structure immemorial. A patrician he was, but there seemed no way he would talk about it.

'I believe you are.' His eyes were veiled by his emphatic black lashes. 'How would you plan my garden, Samantha, if you could go about it?'

'Are you really asking me?' She was surprised.

'It would please me to hear what you have to say!' He looked straight into her face in the most disconcerting way. She had been trained to deal with all kinds of people, so it was shocking to find confusion so strong in her.

'Well. . . .' I must, she thought, sound sensible. 'You have so much ground and the extraordinary richness of our plant life, I think you could have the most ravishing landscape. You have the mountain, for one thing, to crown it all, the view of the lagoon. . . . I'd ring it with calla lilies and the waterlilies bloom there all the year long. If it were my garden, I'd want all the wonderful open vistas, things that aren't possible at Malabar. Our garden was designed differently, gardens within gardens, but as you have so much land I'd hardly bother taming it at all, seemingly very natural. It would be a Herculean task to start a formal garden here, allées and hedges and arches, and so unnecessary when the land has a grandeur of its own. Dad and I have always loved this place and recognised its enormous potential, but of course, while the old ladies were alive it almost went back to jungle. What I *would* do,' she said with a lovely seriousness, 'is bridge the lagoon. You'll have to make it a crooked bridge so your resident ghost can't travel over it.'

'Surely that is a Chinese idea?' he smiled at her.

'Your ghost is or was Chinese,' she told him. 'A young girl. She was bought—and I mean *bought*—by the first owner of this house. Apparently after a year or so she disappeared, and rumour had it she drowned herself in the lagoon.'

'I am used to ghosts,' he said lightly. 'I have lived with them all my life.'

'You mentioned the Villa Taranto to my father the other day,' she said seriously.

'One of the most famous gardens in Italy and the life's work of a Scotsman, Captain Neil McEachern. It is very much the English style with many beautiful flowers and natural settings.'

'Why don't *you* think of a network of waterways? Not all at once, of course, but a continuing plan. Then again, as you're using columns on the terrace, why not have a columned walkway covered in time with one of our luxuriant flowering vines? There's a young landscape artist here I'd like you to talk to. He's brilliant and a great devotee of Roberto Burle Marx. Our North is prodigiously lush, like Brazil, and I see your garden as that kind of landscape.'

'And what is this paragon's name?' He took her delicate white hand and held it gently.

'Robert too—Robert Hughes. He often comes over and has long discussions with my father. Gardeners are forever making new friends.'

'So they are.' He looked down at their joined hands, her skin very pale against his dark olive tan. In that instant she felt irretrievably lost, then there was a small commotion and Antonia's husky voice uplifted in surprise.

'So what are you doing, Nico? Everyone is asking.'

Without the slightest haste, he released Samantha's hand. 'Really, *cara*? You can't manage?'

'I'm surprised, that's all.' Antonia's black eyes were all over her father's face. 'Please come back to my party.'

'Your father has been showing me the plans for your new house,' Samantha told the younger girl, allowing a smile to shape her mouth.

'*Si*, Italian style,' Antonia returned a little shortly. 'It will be the finest house in this part of the world.'

'*Italian* style,' Samantha couldn't resist saying gently. Some of the cattle barons owned mansions.

The rest of the evening passed in a whirl. The food was sumptuous and everyone seemed to be having a particularly good time. Most of the girls had steady boy-friends, but it was apparent that they were utterly dazzled by Nico Martinelli.

'God, isn't he *fantastic*!' A friend of Samantha's threw her arm around Samantha's shoulder and hissed in her ear. 'I can't stand to see a man like that go to waste! One of us will have to marry him.'

Samantha sipped her cold drink, then another, and kept carefully off the subject of their host. If she looked at him and she wanted to, she felt odd inside, but obviously he was upsetting quite a few, and knowing this restored a little of her balance.

Antonia was simply brilliant as the centre of attention, disregarding anything she had heard about Samantha and Eliot, urging him to dance, laughing merrily at whatever it was he said to her. Something about Eliot pleased her and she kept him willingly, and sometimes unwillingly, by her side.

'Hey!' the same girl friend squeezed Samantha's arm. 'She's making a play for your feller!'

Samantha, sinking on silky cushions, didn't care. If Eliot really wanted to get away, he could.

Gillian, her girl friend, walked away looking puzzled. Everyone in Bramston knew that Samantha and Eliot had been inseparable for years, yet the luscious Antonia seemed to be throwing herself at Eliot with Samantha's approval. It didn't make sense.

Before they all left, plans were made for a barbecue-swimming party the following weekend.

'Golly, he must be as rich as Croesus!' Eliot remarked. 'Antonia was telling me all about the house. The pool is going to be three times the size of the one they've got now. It'll be like swimming out to sea.'

'She seemed to like *you*,' Samantha remarked.

'I find it hard to know why,' Eliot answered modestly. 'Unless she was trying to upset you.'

'Surely not?' Samantha turned her large, luminous eyes Eliot's way.

'As gorgeous as she looked, she was second best to you,' he told her.

'Naturally *you* would say that!' Samantha said affectionately.

'Let me finish.' Eliot's blue eyes were serious. 'I think she's jealous of you. Nothing she said—I just sensed it. Then you were a long time talking to her father. Antonia is a very possessive sort of person, and I think she's always come first.'

Despite her decision to tell Eliot she couldn't marry him, Samantha found he didn't even give her the chance. The excitement and gaiety of the evening had spread through him and he kissed her with so much love, even passion that Samantha's tender heart shrank from causing him pain. Long ago she had given him the gift of love and the trustful acceptance that one day they would marry, now, because of an encounter with a handsome, compelling man, she had a glimpse of a self she had never seen. How could she discard the things of a lifetime, memories, promises, commitments, and go in search of an impossible dream? And it *was* a dream, a piece of girlish infatuation she couldn't face. Nearly everyone at some time of their life committed such a folly.

She found her father still up and ready to go out. 'Mrs Larkin,' he told her. 'One of the children has become ill.'

'Can't it wait until morning?' A glance at the grandfather clock confirmed that it was after one o'clock.

'She's had enough to bear,' said Luke, looking around for his car keys. 'I can't leave her alone with a sick child.'

'I'll come with you,' Samantha offered. 'I'm wide awake and we can have a sleep-in in the morning. Maybe!' she added wryly. Her father never refused a home visit.

'Thanks, darling,' keys in hand, Luke picked up his bag, 'but you'd better stay here. You never know what the child's got.'

'You're a good man, my father.' Samantha went with him to the door, resting her head for a moment on her father's shoulder. 'I'm very proud of you, you know that?'

'I know,' Luke said quietly, feeling the wonderful warmth of his daughter's love. 'We've been very lucky in each other.'

For long terrible months after, Samantha wished she had gone with her father, for as he was driving towards Mrs Larkin and her sick child, a panel van, rocking on its wheels, hurtled out of the lonely night, skidded out of control and ploughed into the doctor's car, with the destruction of three lives.

When the police arrived, deeply distressed, for the doctor had been universally loved and admired, Samantha had only one lucid thought.

It *can't* be! It's not *right*! She said it over and over through a gasping throat while her mother gripped on to a chair and held it for dear life. Young lunatics, filled with drink or drugs, might expect a violent death, but not a man who had accomplished so much good; a man who had lived to heal.

The grief was unbearable, the shock and the desolation. Samantha had no recollection of the weeks that passed. But people were very kind, overwhelmingly kind. In a way, the whole community had suffered a disaster. The two young men who had been killed had been established as drifters, sometime members of a 'hippy' community many miles north, but the doctor had been one of their own.

The sense of loss prevailed, even when Luke Harrington's practice was taken over by a very capable younger man, who realised he had a difficult fight ahead of him to measure up to his predecessor.

Though Samantha had never even registered it at the time, one man, almost a stranger, had taken over all the formalities. Niccolo Martinelli had come to Charlotte and offered his support, and Charlotte, carried away with a sense of inadequacy and grief, had accepted his strength with gratitude and relief. Even the fact that he was a stranger made it easier, for all of their old friends were rendered almost helpless by sheer shock. No one could accept it, not on the day of the funeral and for many months after. Such was the stuff of Luke Richard Harrington.

'We'll have to do something about the house.' Charlotte turned to her daughter one day as Samantha sat aimlessly on the verandah. Even the garden had failed her, the beauty and the pain, her father's bent figure.

'What did you say, Mamma?' Samantha suddenly recalled her mother's voice.

'I might as well talk to myself!' Charlotte eased herself into a chair, tearfully. 'We've got to face this, Samantha, your father has *gone*.'

'Never from my heart.' Samantha looked up at the radiant sky.

'I wonder if you would grieve as much for me?' Without intention bitterness crept into Charlotte's voice. 'I have to sell the house, Samantha.'

'Oh, my God!' Samantha knew suddenly and certainly that her mother meant it.

'I know your father expected it to be passed to you, but I intend to live a long time, and it won't be here. Sometimes our tragedies offer escape. Had your father lived I would never have thought for a life of my own, but recently I've been persuaded I'm entitled to one.'

'By whom?' Samantha stared at her mother, oppressed with dread.

'Does it matter?' Charlotte asked. 'Does it really matter to you?'

'I love you, Mamma,' Samantha said gravely. 'Have you forgotten?'

Charlotte let that pass in silence. 'Bruce Armstrong has asked me to marry him,' she said loudly.

'Am I going crazy?' Samantha asked, her beautiful eyes widening.

'This isn't India!' Charlotte cried emotionally. 'I don't have to be sacrificed on the pyre. Your father has gone, but I'm still here.'

Samantha nodded dumbly, unable to speak.

'Look at me, Samantha!' Charlotte pulled her daughter around roughly. Samantha's eyes looked dazed and she had lost so much weight she was just skin and a handful of slender bones. 'You must stop thinking about your father and think of *us*!'

'He's only been gone a few months!'

At her daughter's tone, Charlotte stopped short.

Her shoulders hunched and she burst into tears. 'Don't look at me like that. I've done all I can for you, but you've always shut me out. You were always Luke's girl. Bruce has explained to me that I must come first now. Don't look back.'

'Bruce Armstrong,' Samantha said with blank eyes and a empty voice. 'Bruce Armstrong after Dad. I can't believe it.'

'Then you've come a cropper!' Charlotte blew her nose soundly. 'You've never recognised what I think and feel. I'm a pretty woman, Samantha, if I have to say so myself. A *pretty* woman, do you understand? I want love, a man. I want to feel wanted and secure.'

'And you haven't?' Samantha's voice was like the wind whispering through dry grass.

'Don't make me say things we'll both regret!' Charlotte checked herself with a visible effort. 'I know you've ignored Bruce's presence all these weeks, but he's come to mean a lot to me.'

'Good God!' Samantha stared out across the velvety lawn. In the distant brightness one of her father's favourite trees was flowering, but there was no sign of him on the path.

'Please, Samantha, help me,' Charlotte appealed. 'We've come this far together. I believe I love Bruce—not in the way I loved your father but in a different, easier way. Sometimes your father was too much—too much to live up to. I want some fun in my life. When I sell the house Bruce and I are going to travel. We'll have no one to think of but ourselves. It will be wonderful!'

'Travel if you must, Mamma,' said Samantha, 'but don't sell the house. You know it was always intended for me, and after me, my children.'

'You expect too much, Samantha,' Charlotte said harshly. 'I will *not* be tied to this house. No matter what your father thought or believed would happen, I am left alive to decide. Your father had very little besides this house and it will fetch, I've been told, a good deal of money. In any case, if you really think about it, we won't be able to afford it. It takes a good deal of money to maintain. Something always has to be done. And there's the garden! You've lost all interest in it, except to sit looking into space, and even poor old George has lost all direction. You'll thank me in time.'

'Never!' Samantha's voice drowned her mother's defensive tone. 'I will *never* thank you. This house was built by a Harrington for all the Harringtons that came after. It has a feel about it—*family*. The garden has been our family joy. You could never sell this house if Grandma were alive. She would never let you.'

'And I was never good enough for her precious son!' Charlotte said in a tone of indescribable, mournful resentment. 'Never a day went by that I wasn't made to feel it.'

'She was kindness itself to you!' Samantha stared at her mother disbelievingly.

'That was just one of her ladylike tricks,' Charlotte insisted. 'She lived for her son—and you. I never had her respect. It's as simple as that. Sometimes when you speak I hear the old lady. I see a lot of her in you.'

'And we both cared for you, Mamma,' Samantha said gravely. 'It's just that our kind of caring doesn't seem to appeal to you.'

Charlotte shrugged and stood up, her smooth-skinned, round face hardening. 'As soon as I can fix it, the house goes on the market.'

'I'll speak to Eliot,' said Samantha. 'He'll know if you can do it.'

'Your father made his will when you were a baby,' Charlotte said briskly, in reality fighting down tears. 'He never got around to changing it or protecting your interests more fully. You see, he believed too much in family. Like you.'

When Samantha rang for Eliot that evening, his mother answered the phone.

'I'm sorry, dear, he isn't in,' Mrs Nicolson murmured in her soft voice, implying without words that her son didn't need Samantha's permission to go out.

'That's all right, I'll speak to him tomorrow. Thank you, Mrs Nicolson.'

'For all I know he may not be in his office tomorrow,' Mrs Nicolson supplied. 'He's really doing very well since he joined Mr Martinelli. *Very* well!' she added, which was to say Samantha had been paying very little attention to her son or his career.

But Eliot was in his office when Samantha called on him the very next day.

'*Sam!*' he stood up and came round his desk, taking her two hands in his own. 'How are you?' The blue eyes searched her face.

'I need your advice, Eliot.'

'Anything!' He led her to a chair, thinking he would have to cancel an appointment. These days he was very busy, disposing of piles of work. 'Just let me speak to my secretary for a moment.'

Because she was so preoccupied Samantha hadn't taken note of the change in Eliot. He was looking and dressing very much better, his manner brisk and alert. In actual fact the change was striking to anyone interested enough to mark it, but where once Samantha would have remarked at once, today she was frantically upset.

Eliot came back into the room and took his place behind the desk. 'What is it, Sam?'

'I've been awake all night,' she told him, though he knew it from her shadowed eyes. 'My mother wants to sell Malabar. Not only that, she told me she intends to remarry—Bruce Armstrong.'

'*What?*' Eliot's voice wobbled.

'Bruce Armstrong,' Samantha repeated, concentrating on her fingernails.

'Well, I guess he's not a bad guy!' Eliot said encouragingly, wondering privately how that rather flashy real estate agent could compare with the doctor.

'I can't handle it, Eliot,' Samantha said tragically.

'Darling!' She could still make his heart turn over, though she had been living all these months in almost total seclusion.

'*Can* she do it?' she asked him, her green eyes swallowing her delicately boned face.

'You've read your father's will?'

'No.' Samantha drew a deep sigh. 'I had no interest in wills. Whatever my father had was for us, Mamma and me.'

'Your mother would have spoken to her solicitor,' Eliot pointed out. 'Ted Harland, isn't it?'

'Yes,' Samantha sounded hopeless, even to herself. 'How could she do it to me, Eliot?'

'I told you, darling,' Eliot stood up and came round to her, 'your mother has never been a happy woman. Mother only said to me the other day that she thought Charlotte would remarry. She's still a young woman, very nice-looking, with a second chance at making something of her life. I didn't think it would be someone like Armstrong—but then again it makes sense. He's one of those gregarious, party-loving chaps, and your mother really sparkles in company.'

'My father has been dead four months,' Samantha said in an intolerably shocked voice. 'I cannot credit it. Not that my mother could be thinking about marriage; the sort of man she has chosen, and in the end, most terribly, that she would be willing to surrender up our home.'

'You're forgetting, Sam, it's worth a good deal of money,' Eliot pointed out gently. 'Your mother has a good many years left and it's obvious she wants to spend some.'

'They intend to travel.'

'Well then!' Eliot gave a deep, unhappy sigh. 'You can't tell me you don't benefit at all?'

'Half of everything will be mine. Half of nothing,' Samantha said in a shuddering voice.

'Leave this to me to check out,' said Eliot carefully. 'I can probably talk to Ted. They weren't all that happy when I left them, but we're still on speaking terms.'

'Thank you, Eliot,' Samantha went to stand up, and because she looked so lost and ethereal Eliot gave in to his deepest feelings and took her into his arms.

'Poor little girl. Poor little girl!' His hand shook a little at her grief and his own. He too had lost a friend and his grief was genuine enough, God knew.

'I can't cry, Eliot. I've no tears!'

And all the worse for you, he thought, tightening his arms. Always sweetly slender, now there was nothing of her. He bent his smooth brown head and kissed her hair.

'Sam!'

Neither of them marked the opening of the door, nor the presence of two people, until a woman's voice flared its anger.

'So she approaches you again. Shows her hand!'

'Toni!' Eliot dropped his hands, but he didn't back away.

'Yes, Toni, indeed.' Antonia Martinelli swept into the room, her black eyes brilliant with outrage and betrayal. 'As soon as my back is turned, you go back to her!'

'Antonia!' Frowningly Nico Martinelli put his hand on his daughter's arm, saying a dozen words to her in Italian, but his meaning was apparent: *Be quiet!*

'But, *Nico*!'

He didn't raise his voice above the normal, but

his glance struck his daughter's face. 'I will *not* speak again.'

Silenced, Antonia sank into an armchair, in the grip of a powerful anger. It was unthinkable, *unthinkable* that Eliot should go back to *her*.

'You can do one thing for me, Eliot, as a great favour. Take Antonia out for coffee,' Nico Martinelli said curtly.

'Yes, sir.' Eliot gave Samantha a beseeching glance, but she wasn't even looking in his direction. Her enormous green eyes were fastened on Nico Martinelli, her beautiful face white and strained.

'Please, little one, sit down,' he said gently.

'I must go.'

'*No.*' He gestured, briefly, swiftly, to Eliot to be gone.

'I'll contact you tomorrow, Sam.' Eliot stopped beside her.

'No matter.' She looked a little strange.

'Let us *go*!' Antonia cried with sudden passion, and gripped Eliot by the arm.

Partly out of sorrow, partly out of a profound sense of futility, Eliot allowed himself to be borne away. Sam didn't really need him. She never did.

The door closed behind them and Samantha put a trembling hand to her temple. 'Have I lost everything in the world?' she muttered.

'In your heart you know you have not.'

'My father, Eliot. . . .' she went on.

'You were fond of him only.'

'My home,' she continued as though he hadn't even spoken.

'What *is* this?' He stretched out his hands and
caught her slender arms. 'I cannot bear to see you so
unhappy.'

'No, you're a cruel man!' She looked at him in
profound fright.

'Do not speak so foolishly. You have no reason to
say that.'

'All the reason in the world!' Now tears blinded
her so that his dark face was seen through a mist.
'You know you took Eliot from me. You, then Antonia, with *your* full knowledge and support. Don't
trouble to deny it.'

'But you made it so,' he told her. 'Eliot is no fool.
Marriage between you would have been a folly.'

'Eliot was my friend, my dearest friend.'

'He is going to marry Antonia.'

At once Samantha was overcome by a weakness
so intense it was almost a faint. 'Damn you,' she
whispered. '*Damn* you!'

'Because your world has gone awry?' Quite obviously he forgave her, for somehow she was in his
arms with his mouth just touching her ear. It gave
her a feeling of inevitability, protection, so that her
body of its own accord began to yield. 'The light
will return to your life, little one. You won't lose
your way, you are strong.'

'No, I'm not strong at all.' She lifted her face in
an unbreathing stillness, searching his eyes, trying,
failing, to understand why they were here together.
Then he bent his head, pinning her face like a but-
terfly to his hand, taking her mouth.

It was so extraordinary she wanted to cry, allowing herself to be folded into his arms. His strength made her feel insubstantial, like someone in a dream, but it wasn't only comfort he was offering her but the weight of magic and passion.

He could, with his dominant strength, never let her go, and she had no power of her own.

'*Samantha.*'

Her eyes were tightly closed, but her mouth and her slender, yielding body in that moment were irretrievably his, to be taken while she stood rapt and trembling under the influence of a desperate hunger.

They stayed together, his mouth taking hers, until her trembling became too much.

'Please . . . *please* help me. I don't know what to do!' Her voice was the softest whisper, very young and bewildered.

'Would you let me look after you?' he said slowly, at last.

'What is it? I don't understand.'

'You have. Long before now.' His face had an authority that shocked her, like someone who expected always to have what he wanted. 'Samantha, look at me.'

'*Please!*' She jerked her head away, fighting out of the spell he had placed on her. 'Don't you see I'm not responsible?'

'In my arms you were perfectly happy.'

'If you'll just tell me what you want of me?' She gave an involuntary little shudder because without warning he had cupped her head again, holding her face still.

'Everything,' he said in his beautifully inflected

voice. 'You, your heart and your mind and your body and the promise of a son.'

'You can't command me.' Her voice shook.

'But of course I can't.' His black eyes were impenetrable. 'You will tell me yourself.'

Samantha couldn't have removed herself from his arms even if she had wanted to. Not only his body but his mind seemed to be reaching out for her as if he wanted to break her or turn her into his own creation.

'I know nothing about you,' she whispered.

'You know you belong to me.'

'How?' This was crazy, medieval, with time and reality dimmed and blurred.

'Such things are decided in a moment of time,' he said sombrely. 'You are frightened, not well. I will take you home.'

What home? she thought wildly. She was trembling violently like someone who had stepped across a forbidden threshold only to discover too late that a great door had thundered shut behind her. This man was a stranger to her, a man from another world, a man whose life on his own admission was littered with tragedies, yet something locked them together like an invisible chain. She couldn't rationalise, or find control. It was so.

CHAPTER FOUR

CHARLOTTE watched them arrive. She was deeply offended with her daughter, but never for a moment did it show. She rose from her chair on the verandah and came down to the bottom of the stairs to greet them.

'Nico!' she exclaimed.

Nico? Samantha thought. It came from nowhere, the realisation that whole months had dropped out of her life. Grief had turned her into an amnesiac, and she looked at Nico Martinelli with sudden perception. He was a clever man, very clever and sophisticated, and he was taking over all their lives. It wasn't her imagination.

Charlotte was smiling up at him, offering him her hand, the breeze blowing through her short dark curls. She looked very pretty and youthful, with no part in Samantha's deep confusion.

'Each time I see you, you look younger!'

A more worldly woman would have taken the compliment in her stride, but Charlotte blushed sweetly and glanced into her daughter's face.

'Just when one thinks one's world has come to an end, a door opens!'

'How fortunate you are, Mamma, to feel that way,' Samantha said simply.

'Oh, come, darling,' Charlotte's happy expression

changed. 'It's been very hard,' she told Nico.

'Yes.' He glanced down at Samantha by his side, her head tilted and averted like a statue.

Charlotte sighed and blinked rapidly. 'You are coming in, aren't you, Nico?' she asked eagerly.

'Perhaps for a little while.'

'I know you've been able to advise me from time to time and I hope you'll be able to help me now.'

'You'll both excuse me, won't you?' Samantha didn't hesitate at all.

'No, Samantha, we won't!' A deep and bitter anger surfaced in Charlotte's eyes and was gone.

'Well, how is it I can help you?' Nico put a calming hand on Samantha's arm.

Charlotte shook her head. 'All I've ever had from Samantha is opposition. Maybe I just thought she'd grow out of it, but these past months have been hell.'

'Perhaps we should all sit down,' Nico suggested, and his voice sounded sombre.

Charlotte led the way, speaking with a kind of swift desperation. 'It's about the house, Nico.'

'Tell me.' He waited until the women had sat down, then he sat down himself.

'You believe I mean everything for the best, don't you?' Charlotte appealed to him.

'You wish to sell Malabar, is that so?' He glanced away from Charlotte to Samantha's bent head.

'I've lived here a long time.' There was a bright flush on Charlotte's cheeks. 'People will think I'm empty and shallow, but Nico, I've fallen in love again.'

Nico Martinelli wasn't at all startled. 'I have heard,' he said, marking Samantha's brokenhearted expression.

'I love Bruce,' Charlotte said, and her eyes filled with tears. 'Is it so terrible to want some life of my own?'

'Of course not,' he shrugged. 'Please don't upset yourself, Charlotte.'

'It's difficult with Samantha sitting there looking so tragic.'

'Might it be better if I go away?' Samantha offered, lifting her head.

'You've buried yourself here at Malabar for months!' Charlotte accused her.

'We each handle our own grief,' said Nico as Samantha looked at him with huge eyes. 'You are sure of this love, Charlotte?'

'Oh, God, I don't know!' Charlotte suddenly stood up and threw out her arms in a theatrical gesture, that was nevertheless genuine. 'It's Samantha who makes me afraid. When I'm with Bruce, I'm sure. We're two of a kind, content to be with one another—nothing demanding, but fun and *easy*. God, so easy. That's the great thing about Bruce.'

'And you wish to go away for a while?' Nico asked.

'Exactly.' Charlotte drew a long, audible breath. 'There's a big world to see and time is running out fast.'

'I see.' He dipped his raven head. 'So Malabar was left to you?'

'To *me*, yes,' Charlotte insisted, not looking at her

daughter. 'Of course it was always intended that the house should eventually go to Samantha, but with Luke gone we can no longer consider it.'

'So you wish to sell?'

'Yes,' Charlotte replied violently, shaken by some expression on that handsome chiselled face. Some suggestion of what? Distaste? It didn't seem possible.

'Then in that case, I am willing to make you an offer.'

'*You?*' said Samantha in a terrible voice. She looked at him not with anger or aversion but an advancing horror. 'You have a house of your own. How could you want Malabar?'

'Be still.'

'*No!*' She flew for him then with an abandonment so out of character Charlotte gasped aloud in shock and dismay.

'*Samantha!*'

But Samantha was past hearing. If he was hurting her to control her she didn't feel it. Hopelessness and grief rioted in her mind, the hateful memory of rapture. She could hear her own ragged breathing, Nico's beautiful hated voice in her ear. She had never felt violent in her life, yet now she was struggling like someone demented, wanting to pound him with her fists, her hair fallen loose, swirling between them in a golden cloud, her heart pounding, her ears roaring. It wasn't love at first sight, it was hate! He was ruthless, absolutely ruthless, and he had only one purpose, to take over the whole town.

'Please, Samantha,' Charlotte was crying in a broken voice. 'Oh, what's to become of her!'

Furiously Samantha fought being held impotent. She shut her teeth and raged: 'Let me go! Do you hear! Let me go. I *hate* you!'

No, *no*, a voice protested within her. She only meant to show him he couldn't do this to her—take her life, take her home. Such things didn't happen.

Nico felt her check in her passionate rage, and at that very moment he swept her off her feet.

'Where is her room Charlotte? Show me.'

'Oh, through here!' Charlotte leapt to obey. Never in her life had Samantha acted so wildly, so unpredictably, her green eyes glowing with strange lights.

In Samantha's bedroom, Nico lowered her to the bed and she turned away and pressed her face into the pillow.

'She's always so *sensible*!' Charlotte wailed.

'She has also been through a great deal.' Nico's deep voice answered her. 'You have brandy in the house, Charlotte? Just a little.'

'Of course.' Charlotte flew away with a desire to help. In a moment she was back again, glass in hand.

'Come, Samantha.' Nico put his hand on the girl's trembling shoulder.

She turned quietly, all the fire seemingly gone out of her. 'I'm sorry, so very sorry.'

'Samantha, *darling*!' Charlotte wailed.

'Might we not all have a cup of coffee . . . tea, whatever?' Nico suggested, glancing back at Charlotte's small, distressed figure.

'Certainly—I'll make it.' Charlotte smiled at him

through a mist of tears. 'Samantha drives herself, you know. Luke was that way.'

'So, *piccola*, you know how to suffer.' Charlotte had gone and Nico lifted Samantha very gently. 'Come, drink this. I am concerned for you.'

'Are you?' She looked at him with untrusting eyes. 'Everything gone. My father, Eliot, and in the end, my home.'

'Everything that gave you happiness.' He looked down into her lovely, strained face. 'But in every life, Samantha, is the season for change. Your memories are precious and I think, for you, rare, but after all, you cannot live in the past. That is only for the very old or those who are alone. Life is a celebration!'

'*No*.' She gave a deep sigh of grief.

'It *is*. Would I lie to you?'

'I'm sure you would.' She was very pale.

'Drink this.'

Her hand trembled as she held the glass and he covered her fingers with his own, lean and warm and so very strong. 'How is it you see me as such a terrible character?'

She swallowed the spirit as though it was poison, then she shook her head. 'Something about you tells me you're capable of anything.'

'Such a curious reaction, and all in your imagination.' He sat down on the side of the bed, seeing how her heavy lashes made spikes on her pale cheeks.

'I can't sleep any more,' she said pathetically. 'No more happy dreams.'

'You need someone to sleep with you, *cara*.' In an instant the sensuality had returned.

'Probably, I'm twenty-four,' she said bitterly.

'And, I believe, a virgin.'

'Did Eliot tell you that too?' she exclaimed in a sudden rage.

'You know we would never speak of any such thing. However, I know a little about women. I see your face and your mouth and your eyes. I have kissed you, held you in my arms. Moreover, I am the one and only man you will ever know.'

'For God's sake!' The colour flew under her porcelain skin, and her green eyes looked threatened.

'You will learn to love me.' He lifted her hand and carried it to her mouth. 'You do a little now.'

'Oh, *no*, Signor Martinelli!' she gasped.

'*Nico*.' He said it in a way completely Italian, his black eyes like polished jets.

Charlotte came in hastily, her pretty face flustered, her dark hair faintly dishevelled. 'Bruce is here,' she announced.

'See, Bruce is here,' Samantha told Nico. 'It's no longer my home.'

'Oh, *please*, Samantha,' Charlotte begged her. 'He's so kind and nice and sweet.'

'Jovial, I'd call it!' Samantha felt the fiery liquid in her veins.

'Charlotte, can you give us a few minutes, please?' Nico asked persuasively.

'Indeed I can!' Charlotte took heart. 'Samantha can't condemn me because I want a fresh start at life.'

'Please go away, Mamma,' Samantha sighed. 'Have your fresh start, have the house, Bruce Armstrong, everything, but don't ask for my blessing.

You don't need it. I would never do to you what you're doing to me.'

'This is a pretty situation!' Charlotte exclaimed, stricken.

'I'm truly afraid it is.' Samantha started to laugh. 'Run along now. Don't keep Brucie waiting.'

'Enough! Compose yourself, Samantha.' Nico's toone halted her.

'Don't think for one moment I could live my life Italian style,' she told him, when Charlotte had gone.

'You mean you are afraid of being dominated?' His brilliant eyes mocked her.

'Whatever my fears I'm going to get over them.' Her tender mouth firmed and the delicate bones took on a tauter, stronger cast. 'What's happening to me now seems intolerable because I've been sheltered, and foolishly I thought my dream world would go on. . . .'

'So you are going to dedicate yourself to what?' He took her hands and held them, the thumb caressing the palm.

Shockingly it filled her blood with heat, a sudden turbulence after long months of icy calm. 'Why *me*?' she asked him slowly, turning her blonde head on the pillow. 'You could have any woman you want.'

'An aspect of my character is that I am one-track.' His black eyes were confident. 'I decided I would have you the first time we met.'

'I can't accept that.' She rose from the bed, swaying a little.

'It's unusual, I will admit.' He too stood up, with

the careless grace that was bred in him. 'Forgive me.'

'I think I never will.' She laughed shortly. 'Shall we go out while you arrange with Mamma to buy our house?'

'You demand perfection, don't you, little one?' he said, watching her with searching eyes. 'I ask you now to have a little charity for your mother. She is not like you. Hers is another way.'

She laughed at that too, an unhappy sound. 'Don't worry, *Nico*,' she mimicked his accent, 'I'll behave. But my thoughts are my own, if you don't mind.'

'Walk softly with me, *piccola*.' His black eyes sparkled and he suddenly took hold of her shoulders.

For a minute they stared into each other's eyes. 'You've a devil in you, haven't you?' she challenged him.

'Then don't try to shake hands with him.' His velvet voice was a little harsh, even menacing.

'Maybe I will!' Her temper was rising to meet his own. 'If I work at it very hard, I might discover who you really are.'

'At your peril.' He said it very softly, but a dangerous light flickered in his dark eyes. His hands dropped to her narrow hips and he began to draw her body hard against his. 'I want to make love to you, Samantha,' he said with immense deliberation. 'I want you struggling against me, then after . . . you will follow wherever I wish to take you.'

Samantha's reaction was so violent it was almost a terror. 'So you fascinate me,' she said jaggedly.

'It's not love.'

'You think I am constantly pursuing *love*?' he asked angrily. 'I have never known it, but I desire you a great deal. You are mine. So please remember.'

She wasn't even conscious of walking with him to the living room, staring a little blindly, first at her mother, then at Bruce Armstrong. Their expressions matched—pleading, defensive, even a touch guilty.

'How are you, Mr Armstrong,' Samantha said like an automaton.

'Oh, please—*Bruce*.' He came forward, hand outstretched, a good-looking man in a somewhat florid style. Samantha was forced into physical contact and he shook her hand as though the slightest pressure would fracture all her bones. 'Especially as we're going to be family.'

She couldn't help it, she winced. Family, my God! she thought.

'I don't think you know Mr Martinelli,' Charlotte intervened hurriedly, introducing the two men.

'A great pleasure to meet you, sir!' Bruce Armstrong spoke with his habitual affability. 'Wonderful things you're doing for our town.'

'Tell us,' Samantha said bluntly, but Bruce Armstrong only smiled at her as though she had said something naughty.

'I'm only sorry I couldn't get your people to sign one of my contracts.'

'Your price was too high,' Nico explained smoothly, with at the same time an alarming directness. 'You should not have been surprised.'

It was easily seen that Charlotte was agitated. She moved closer to Bruce Armstrong and fixed her eyes on his face. 'Nico was wonderfully kind to me after . . . after. . . .'

'Your *husband* died.' Samantha said with an aloofness and regality Nico had often shown.

Bruce Armstrong slipped his arm around Charlotte's waist and his florid cheeks burned with colour. 'You're not respectful enough to your mother, young lady!'

'Evidently neither of you are respectful to the dead.'

'*Samantha!*' It wasn't Charlotte or Bruce Armstrong who spoke, but Nico, who moved back towards Samantha and laid his hand firmly on her shoulder. 'Do let us all be civilised.'

'Sure!' Bruce Armstrong shrugged his leonine head, while Charlotte sighed deeply, over and over. 'I know how Samantha feels, but I sincerely love her mother. She turned to me in a time of stress, now we have a valuable relationship. I swear I'll do everything in my power to make her happy.'

Nico regarded the older man gravely. 'Charlotte has told me she wishes to sell this house.'

'Well, we can't live here!' Bruce Armstrong's black brows tangled together. 'Charlotte wants to forget. . . .'

'Her past,' Samantha supplied again, visibly trembling beneath Nico's calming hand.

'Her pain, I was going to say, Samantha,' Bruce said quietly. 'We all understand that you adored your father. I thought the world of him myself. But now he's gone.'

'Long live the king!' Samantha said in despair.

No one made any reply to this and for a moment there was silence in the lovely, mellow room, each of them thinking of Luke Harrington, how things had been.

'I am prepared to make Charlotte an offer for this house I hope she will accept,' Nico said finally.

'Why, that's splendid!' Bruce shook himself out of his momentary depression. 'May I ask what sort of figure you had in mind?'

'Does it have to meet with your approval?' Samantha asked.

'It's customary, girlie,' Bruce returned a little harshly.

'Not at all!' Nico showed no sign of anger except a sharpening of the aristocratic features. 'It might perhaps be better, Charlotte, if I spoke to you and Samantha alone. You see, I wish to protect Samantha's position.'

'But Samantha and I will benefit equally,' Charlotte pressed her hands together. 'Be assured, Nico, that's how I want it.'

'Of course, Charlotte.' Nico's voice was entirely without emotion. 'The property is beautiful and, without a doubt, valuable. Many people would wish to buy it, but I hope you will allow me first option.'

'You see, everybody,' Samantha announced quietly, 'Mr Martinelli makes plans. People aren't important. He isn't like the rest of us.' Every delicate bone in her face seemed to stand out tautly, her green eyes so brilliant they glittered like gems.

'I am really not.' Nico glanced only briefly at Samantha. 'Most people aren't so determined.'

'Ruthless,' Samantha corrected, shaken to the heart.

'My poor little girl, you need a holiday.' Charlotte sat down beside Samantha and tried to put an arm around her.

'I'm quite all right, Mamma.' Samantha's voice was strong and steady. 'I expect I'll have a lovely long holiday when you sell the house.'

Charlotte saw defeat and the end of an era. She was taking away from Samantha the only thing she had left, but a sense of self-importance held her to her course. For the first time in her life she wanted control of her own money. Bruce was reasonably well off, but if they were going to do things in style she needed her share of everything. Hadn't she worked for it for nearly thirty years? Samantha was young, and anyway she was going to marry Eliot. The money would be more than enough for a modest house.

Less than a week later, Malabar changed hands with the occupancy until the end of the month when Charlotte announced that she and Bruce Armstrong would be married quietly.

'I'm not coming, Mamma,' Samantha told her mother almost indifferently.

'Do I understand you correctly?' Charlotte stood in the doorway of her daughter's bedroom, her expression that of a woman who had been offered a mortal insult.

'You do,' Samantha said calmly. 'I wish you

happiness, but I don't want to see you married to Mr Armstrong.'

'For God's sake call him Bruce!' Charlotte cried out, enraged. 'He's well aware you don't like him, but by the same token he thinks you're a very selfish, self-centred girl. Your father spoilt you deplorably.'

'Perhaps he did spoil me for other men.' Samantha gazed at and through her mother. 'Have you forgotten what a fine man he was? Compare him with your Bruce.'

'At least Bruce is *human*!' Charlotte burst out, driven. 'He isn't so very far above me in every way that he shuts me out.'

'Do you mind terribly if we don't talk about Dad?' Samantha looped her long hair into its familiar coil. 'If you're sure, Mamma, that you're going to be happy, go ahead, but I can't find it in my heart to celebrate.'

'You never wanted me anyway,' Charlotte shook her head angrily. 'You'll live to regret your decision, Samantha. Life teaches us a lot of things.'

'And in the meantime you can't waste a single day.'

The whole town, in fact, was shocked at the series of events. The older people and Luke Harrington's ex-patients were affronted by Charlotte's hasty re-marriage. It was this that finally decided Samantha to change her mind. Love wasn't destroyed in a day and she really did love her mother. She owed her a measure of protection and support, for people were already condemning Charlotte for her actions. By boycotting the wedding Samantha would only be adding to the town's censure, so she found herself telling her mother she would go.

'I *knew* you would. I never gave up hope!' Charlotte's dark eyes filled with ready tears. 'My Samantha always had a tender heart.'

Samantha smiled through her distress, seeing how immensely pleased and excited her mother was. 'Be happy, Mamma,' she spoke almost in a whisper, while Charlotte on a sudden wave of lightheartedness began planning Samantha's dress.

'What about a very pale green, like springtime? Something very soft and filmly. I'm wearing that beautiful jacaranda blue and I'm determined Antonia Martinelli is not going to surpass either of us.'

Of course Samantha knew they had been invited, but she hadn't laid eyes on Antonia for weeks and Nico only briefly over negotiations for the house. What he intended to do with it he had not even troubled to disclose, but his own splendid residence was nearing completion.

If Charlotte had hoped the sun would shine on her brilliantly, it poured the day of the wedding, a tropical deluge that turned the world to silver and a wavering green.

It was a civil ceremony that Charlotte had first thought of holding in the garden of Malabar, but discarded after one look at Samantha's incredulous face and later organised at the most beautiful reception house in the town. As it had lately been taken over by Martinelli Enterprises Samantha considered bitterly whether Nico had the same plans for Malabar. It was very big for a private home, so probably it was that.

Bruce Armstrong, married, divorced, was unaccountably nervous, making his responses in only half his normal voice.

'Heaven weeps!' Samantha thought, overcome by a sense of total unreality. Was this really her mother getting married again? Could she possibly love this big, gruff stranger?

It seemed she did, for Charlotte was radiant, her voice confident, already assuming the upper hand with her new husband.

'My God!' Eliot came up to Samantha when the kissing and being kissed was over. 'Who would ever have believed it?'

'If you want to know,' she said soberly, 'I'll believe anything.'

Something in her voice, the black humour and severity, broke his heart.

'You never loved me, Sam,' he sighed.

'Kindly don't make excuses.' Gently she removed his hand.

'Darling, you *didn't*.' She looked exquisite with her heartbreaking face and her green dress.

'That's beside the point,' she said, sounding more like her old self. 'You may be sure, my old friend, you're going to have a very jealous wife. She's looking this way now and her eyebrows have disappeared.'

'She's really very sweet!' Eliot rasped, gingerly turning his head.

'I shall be very surprised if I see you again,' Samantha couldn't resist driving her point home. 'What we all should have done in the first place was ignore the Martinellis.'

'Don't blame me,' said Eliot. 'You didn't want me. *She* does.'

'Just think of it,' said Samantha. 'All your life!'

'Oh, *Sam!*' Eliot put his hand on Samantha's arm again.

'Now you've done it.' For some extraordinary reason she lifted her blonde head and smiled at him brilliantly. 'Your little Antonia is about to join us.'

'Weren't you getting me some champagne?' Antonia accused Eliot with a flash of her black eyes.

'Forgive me, darling. I was just having a word with Sam here.'

'So I see.' Antonia was unimpressed.

'Never apologise,' Samantha said to Eliot in a wry aside. 'You'll keep on doing it all your life.'

'Please, Eliot,' Antonia said sharply. 'I'm thirsty.'

'What about you, Sam?' Eliot asked gallantly.

'Oh, I think I'm allowed a little party drink.' Little demons of pain were hammering inside Samantha's head.

'Your mother looks lovely,' Antonia told Samantha when Eliot had gone.

'She does.' Across the room Samantha could see her mother's radiant small figure.

'So why can't you be happy for her?' Antonia asked attackingly.

'Stick around and you'll find out.'

'I don't think I like you!' Antonia looked vehemently into Samantha's green eyes.

'No wonder!'

'What does that mean?' Antonia stared at the older girl incredulously.

'You mean your father hasn't found the time to tell you the great news?'

Antonia shook her head with its curls and deep waves. 'I think something is disturbing your mind.'

'I'm sure it is!' Samantha agreed wryly, looking into the beautiful, slightly bewildered face. 'Tell me something, Antonia. As Eliot's nice sensible ex-girl-friend, I want to know, do you really love him?'

'*Madly!*' said Antonia in an impassioned tone. 'My emotions are never simple.'

'It must run in the family,' Samantha said musingly and with no trace of a smile.

Antonia sighed, not understanding. 'Do not try to take Eliot back again,' she said intensely and with a flicker of fear. 'You cannot have him. His mother has told me what occurred between you, but it wasn't passion. You were friends, all peace and tranquillity,' she laughed a little, her dark eyes bright and excited. 'Now that has changed. With me, Eliot is ardent. Sometimes he calls me his pocket Venus.'

'You *are* a little plumper!' Samantha surveyed the younger girl's lovely rounded figure dispassionately.

'I know how to go out and get my man!' Antonia retaliated swiftly, shaking back her heavy, glossy hair.

'Be careful with him,' said Samantha, very simply, very seriously, and took leave of the younger girl without another word.

Fifteen minutes later, the newlyweds left and

Samantha stood forlornly in the driveway thinking she had taken leave of her youth for ever. Her mother had looked happy and glowing, committed to a new live with a man whose personality was so far removed from her father's that she couldn't seem to accept this marriage at all. The rain had started to come on again, obscuring the few brilliant stars, and someone took her by the arm and drew her back on to the shelter of the deeply overhung verandah.

'You look as if your world has collapsed around you,' Nico said to her gently, but with a flickering mockery. His hands were on her shoulders, holding her back against him, and she remained there, captive, too far gone to move.

Now the whole world was wrapped in the profoundly sensual rain, the lantern lit grounds a tossing, scented, drenched Garden of Eden, a beautiful and threatening world. A wave of giddiness passed over Samantha and she felt his hands tighten, his long fingers pressing into her bare skin.

'My poor little orphan!'

'And *you* are going to show me the way?' In another moment, she thought helplessly, I'll be crying. Actually crying, with this man to dry my tears.

'It only needs time.' He turned her around towards him and looked down into her face. 'I do not expect you to adjust to me at once.'

'Why didn't someone prepare me at the beginning?' she said strangely, her blonde head thrown back and her green eyes fastened on him with complete absorption. She knew now he was the most compelling force in her life.

'But, Samantha, you instinctively knew.'

'So why am I afraid?'

'I think,' he said quietly, 'to give yourself. This is partly because you have a deep reserve and partly because you are innately passionate.'

Her cheeks flamed with colour and her eyes went brilliant. 'You seem to see something in me others do not. Eliot would tell you I'm very cool and controlled.'

He lifted his hand and touched her cheek caressingly. 'You will only permit one man to love you.' He spoke meditatively, his black eyes rather sombre. 'Come, the rain is over for the moment, I want to take you home.'

In the car she seemed tired, drained of all will, her shining blonde head resting back against the midnight blue upholstery.

'Your daughter seemed outraged that we left together,' she commented.

'She has too much of a possessive streak,' he said smoothly. 'In time she will learn to control it.'

'As you have had to?' She turned her head a little to look at his strong, patrician profile.

'But of course!'

'So many secrets!' she said with constraint. 'You never speak of your wife.'

'What is it you wish me to tell you?' His velvet voice was sardonic.

'Were you very happy? Did you love her? How did she die? *Did* she die?'

'She was killed in a hunting accident more than four years ago.'

'I'm sorry.' She was dismayed by the starkness of his tone. 'Life is very cruel.'

'Merciless at times. I have tried to make up to my daughter for her grief.'

'She must have been very beautiful,' Samantha said compassionately.

'I see her in Antonia.'

'Yes.' Samantha bit her lip. She too caught glimpses of that other face. 'Is it because of this you left your own country?'

'I wished to rid myself of memories, yes.'

'I think I have a headache,' she said plaintively.

'It is because you are very tired. You will sleep well tonight, I promise you.'

When she first saw the house, she drew in her breath. 'But how beautiful!'

'There are many things I have left to you.'

'But why, Nico?' She couldn't yet acknowledge the chain that bound them.

'Are you not interested in furnishing your own home?'

'My home is Malabar,' she said rigidly.

'Then I will give it to you as a wedding present.' They had pulled in to the massive, four-door garage and he didn't protest as she opened the car door swiftly and got out. There was a desperate hunger within her, she knew that, just as she knew she was unwilling to let it out.

When she went to walk through the front door, Nico lifted her like a long tradition, but it didn't lighten her mood. Somehow she saw herself as a victim of his plans, and it disturbed her deeply. He had had a wife whom he had loved, a woman he had lost in tragic circumstances—a calamity that had marked him and driven him away from his own country, his own people.

'What is wrong?' he asked, looking into her widened eyes.

'I'm trying to seize on some sense of reality.'

'Because things are moving too fast?'

'They would always move fast with you.'

'Leaving you no time to run away.' Very gently her lowered her to her feet, but held her linked to him with his arm around her waist. 'Let me show you *our* home.'

It would have been dangerous then to try some escape, though she felt with a terrible intensity that she *would* live there. If only he would treat her with tenderness, not command. But the house, she saw with faint apprehension, was superb; a bold, sensuous house with wonderful possibilities.

'The basic furniture is here,' Nico told her, 'but you can add and alter as much as you like.'

'You might allow me a will of my own!' she said severely.

'I think what you really want is for me to make love to you. You are feeling so insecure.'

'Am I?' She gave a guarded little laugh, but her fingers clenched themselves together in a betraying gesture. 'I'm afraid of you, Nico Martinelli.'

'And you know why.'

She was aware of nothing very clearly except that

he came to her, cupping her face in his two hands. 'I feel a little afraid of you, too. Why are you so fair, so beautiful? An angel after one has lived so long in the dark.'

She couldn't answer him and her eyelashes fell.

'*Samantha.*' His voice had altered, moved into another sphere.

She opened her mouth in wonderment, trembling, instantly aroused, then her breath catching in her throat as he put his mouth over hers. Such incredible intimacy, so perfect it had to be a fantasy.

They seemed to stay that way for a long time until the dissolving sensation spread so completely through her body, she couldn't stand, and he started to lift her again.

'Please, Nico. We *must* stop.'

'You *can?*' He held her high against his shoulder. 'God forgive me, I can't.'

Samantha felt distraught and excited out of her mind, wanting what was happening but afraid to give in to it.

It's too easy . . . too easy for him to take me, she thought.

At the top of the stairs she threw her arms around his neck, pleading. 'You *can't* do what I don't want.'

'But you do. Very much.'

She shook her hair back violently. 'Don't start telling me my *feelings!*'

'Not right now,' he said. 'In a minute.'

A pool of light emphasised the bed, a brilliant piece of modern furniture with the Italian flair. Nico didn't even pull back the luxuriously textured covering but laid her upon it, standing back to look at her as though she were a golden ornament he could begin to move around.

'*Please*, Nico,' she whispered before the flame of longing got too strong for her.

'I will do nothing to alarm you.' Still looking at her, he pulled out of his raw silk jacket and flung it over a chair, a little violence in his graceful movements. 'I just want you to stay with me.'

'For how long?' She looked excessively frail and helpless, her silver-green dress shades lighter than her luminous, searching eyes.

'Kiss me,' he said quietly, drawing her into his arms. 'Cling to me.'

'Because you're going to marry me?'

'Because I wish it.' He lifted both her arms and put them around his neck.

The melancholy in her beautiful eyes deepened, making her, if anything, even more desirable. 'What I have is a fever.'

'You don't know yourself.'

'Shameless creature!' She looked up into his black eyes. 'Don't laugh. I mean it.'

'And why are you so shameless?' His hand moved over her bare shoulder, brushed her breast.

'That's obvious, isn't it?'

'You are very shy, very modest.' He bent his dark head, drinking in her fragrance. 'Remember when you showed me over your garden?'

'Yes.' She was taking in quick little breaths.

'I wanted to tell you then how beautiful I found you.'

'What else did you think?' She turned her head away, the light gleaming on her pearly skin. 'That my whole world would come to an end within a few short months.'

'Don't say that!' he silenced her urgently, pressing his fingers across her tender mouth. 'Try to see for a minute that you have known grief . . . no, be quiet, *piccola*,' he pinned her slender body with sudden force. 'The fact is that you are very young with a great expectation of happiness. Don't you see how it will be?'

'I daren't trust,' she said sadly, and the tears welled into her eyes.

'So I'll make you.' He urged her fragile body right into his arms, overwhelming her with his nearness. Now his hands were on her, and his mouth, and she felt as though no one had ever touched her skin in her life, nothing even vaguely so erotic.

When he began to free her from her dress, like a baby, her desire had grown much larger than her fear, so even as she lay half naked in his arms, she still couldn't find her voice; frantically excited when his hands claimed her breasts, the tips of his fingers caressing so she was half crazed with the pleasure.

There didn't seem to be an adequate word for what was happening to her, and Nico wouldn't tell her, for he had lapsed into a liquid Italian, torturing her with whispered words, words she couldn't understand when she desperately needed to come to terms with her own sensuality, her direct responses to this overpowering rapture. He had cast a spell on her as old as time and she gave herself up to it almost unwillingly.

Why did a woman's body have to be so closed yet so vulnerable; burning, yearning, to be violated, ravished? Why was a man's hand so delicately cruel, the deepest intimacy a woman would ever know? His touch was inducing a delirium. Wasn't it enough for him to declare her his, without sealing her fate? In the midst of a vast passion, Samantha began to think.

Man the exploiter, woman the exploited. Could it ever really be otherwise?

'What is it, Samantha?' he asked in a low voice— a deeply intuitive man, dangerous and subtle.

But she wasn't truly *Samantha* to him, but woman; white skin and fluid limbs, her hair floating around them in a golden cloud, bright strands even fixed to his heated, polished skin.

'I want you to free me,' she said, when she could find her voice.

'You speak like a coward.' His eyes gave the illusion of being unfathomable, brilliant yet infinite. 'Do you think because you give yourself to me that makes you my slave?'

'I know I've lived all my life with restraint.'

'A vestal virgin.' He considered her lovely face and her milky white breasts. 'Who taught you to despise passion?'

'But how *can* I?' She turned her head away with a shuddering sigh. 'All my secrets, *me*, you're taking away. It's like being dispossessed.'

'And that, my swan, is how it is supposed to be.' He answered her with mockery, kissing her tremulous mouth. 'You can converse with yourself to your heart's content. You can marvel at the hand of fate, but you will never get away.'

'I will tonight.' Her green eyes begged of him a breathing space.

'So,' his heavy lashes veiled his eyes. 'I will even allow you the time that you need, but you were meant for me from the time you were born.'

Even in the turmoil of her thoughts, Samantha knew no oppression. She thought too of the way he had called her his swan. How could be possibly have known? Yet it had touched her deeply, healing a great wound.

Without even knowing why, almost without her own will, she turned to him and laid her shining blonde head against his breast. It was a gesture that spoke of a compulsive need for comfort.

She felt his lips on her hair, strong arms cradling her like a lost child, but still he spoke in Italian.

'I don't understand,' she said with an anguished sweetness. 'Why do you speak to me in Italian?'

'So, little one, secrets all round.'

Her head flew up to look at him, but although he was smiling, as usual, she could not read his thoughts.

CHAPTER FIVE

WHEN Antonia heard that her father intended to remarry, her shock was mixed with a more complex jealousy. When she further heard that Nico planned on returning Samantha's old family home to her, she went up like a Roman candle.

'But I thought it was for *me*!' She, who had always had what she wanted, was pale with rage. 'A wedding gift, a home for Eliot and me!'

'What gave you that idea?' Samantha stared at the younger girl, confused. It was a Saturday morning and here she was in the middle of a blazing row.

'Why else would Nico have bought it?' Antonia's impassioned eyes swept over Samantha's slender figure. She had been working in the garden and she wore cotton slacks and a T-shirt printed with strawberries. There was a streak of dirt on the side of her nose where she had swiped at a mosquito and Antonia fixed her eyes on it as though it offended her mightily. 'I tell you originally Nico intended this house for me. I am going to be an important hostess. I have great plans both for myself and for Eliot. He shall be my father's right-hand man.'

'Surely that's rather difficult to foretell?' Samantha got up off her knees and sighed. 'Eliot's no dynamo!'

'And how would you know?' Antonia stood back as Lucy, Samantha's golden labrador, ambled up to say hello. 'When did you ever pause to look at him?'

Samantha checked the impulse to tell Antonia off. 'I grew up with him,' she offered mildly. 'I've known him all my life.'

'Not at all!' Antonia's extraordinary looks conferred on her an imperious, self-assured look for all her youth. 'You never knew, for instance, that Eliot is ambitious. With you he would have been a dull old solicitor all his life. With me he will work to show his true potential.'

'Does he know about it?' Samantha asked, seeing Eliot sitting bolt upright night after night ploughing through reams of Martinelli business.

'Do not make fun of me!' Antonia's dark eyes glimmered. Not her father's eyes, either in shape or setting, but their liquid brilliance was the same. 'You who pretend to be so cold and innocent!'

'I've always done the best I can.' It seemed like a very high price to have Antonia for a daughter-in-law.

'God knows *that*!' It was said with such vehemence that Samantha was taken back. Even gentle, affectionate Lucy gave a muffled growl. 'You surely can't think my father loves you?'

'I really don't see it as your problem!' Samantha removed a few blades of grass that clung to her slacks. 'Surely it would be better, Antonia, if we could be friends.'

'The trouble is,' said Antonia, 'I don't *like* you. In no way could you take the place of my mother. She was a great lady, a Petrangeli, my father's cousin.'

Samantha, who had so recently been shown grief and loss, tried to be kind. 'Please don't think, Antonia, I would even try to take your mother's place.'

'You couldn't!' Antonia said scornfully, twisting her sensuous mouth. 'My mother was a great beauty. She spoke several languages, as does my father. They loved one another from childhood. It was all arranged. She was glorious and I adored her.'

'I'm sorry, Antonia,' Samantha said gently, seeing the tears that sprang into Antonia's lustrous eyes.

But Antonia didn't want pity, much less Samantha's. 'Of course what it is—he wants a son. What are women, after all?'

'I'm inclined to think God's finest creation,' Samantha observed mildly, though she was starting to feel thoroughly churned up.

'Don't tell me it did not occur to you?' Antonia fixed her eyes on Samantha's grave face. 'You are young, intelligent, good-looking in a way I do not admire, my father has assured himself you would be suitable.'

'It's not only me you don't like, Antonia,' Samantha said slowly. 'You would see any other woman in your father's life as a usurper.'

'As soon as he has what he wants from you, you will be *nothing*!' Antonia promised.

Hours later Samantha felt she had made her decision, or the decision had been made for her. What she felt for Nico was some kind of obsession, a quirk of fate that put her temporarily under his spell, but what were his real motives for marrying her? For years he had lived with a woman he adored, a woman who had given him everything except the great gift of a son. Nico himself had told her what he expected of her, but as she loved children in wanting a family they spoke the same language. Mentally she went over his list, her heart turning over as she remembered the sound of his voice. . . .

Everything, he had said. *Your heart and your mind and your body and the promise of a son.*

One expected almost that he loved her, but deep down she knew he didn't. She was simply a part of an elaborate plan.

George was still working in the water garden when she went down to speak to him, and because he was going very deaf she had to raise her voice far above the normal.

'George?' He didn't hear under his wide-brimmed straw hat, so she knelt down beside him and touched him on the shoulder. 'George, dear.'

'Hello there!' he greeted her the same way as he had done since she was a baby. 'It's amazing the weeds that have popped up.'

'I don't know what I'd do without you, George.'

George was touched and saddened and tried not to show it. 'Ah, Manthy,' he said, and shook his head.

'I'm so grateful you've still got a job. You love the garden.'

'Ay, I do.' George looked beyond the pond as though he expected to see his old friend coming through the archway. 'I doubt I'll ever love another one the same way again. In a way, Malabar has been my life, a kind of home. I've always looked on you Harringtons as family.'

'And we've loved you too, George.' Samantha kept her hand on the old man's shoulder, feeling it trembling. George had been desolated at her father's death, only now finding some peace again tending the beloved garden.

'To think your mother went off and left you!' George was visibly becoming agitated.

'It's all right, George.' Samantha continued to pat the bony shoulder. 'We couldn't condemn her to an empty life. She's happy now.'

'Bah!' George made an explosive sound of disgust. 'Sellin' this house. Why, the old lady would have turned in her grave.'

The thought of Nico's intentions only brought back Samantha's problems. 'I have to get away for a few days, George,' she confessed. 'More, probably a couple of weeks.'

'What's wrong, lass?' George knew Samantha's every expression.

'I have to think.'

'Of course.' Though George didn't know the extent of Samantha's involvement with Nico Martinelli, he knew Mr Martinelli was seeing to Samantha's every need. More, he had assured George of continuing work in the environment he loved. A gentleman, was Mr Martinelli, George had decided. 'What about Lucy?' he spoke aloud Samantha's worry.

'Could you look after her for me, George? I couldn't bear to put her in a boarding kennel. She'd fret and I can't take her with me.'

'She'll be happy with me.' George sounded pleased. 'It's a bit lonely these days without your dad.'

Close to tears, Samantha positively had to control her feelings. 'Thanks, George,' she said gently. 'I'll leave you the money to feed her. *Yes*,' she said, when the old man shook his head, 'and I'll let you know when I'm coming . . . back.' She could no longer say home.

George's faded blue eyes clouded, yet he could see Samantha's father clearly in his mind. 'There are many people in this town who deplore what your mother has done. If she wanted to start off again like a young girl, she should have left you your home. It was your dad's wish. Harringtons have been here for more than a hundred years.'

'Other people lose their homes,' Samantha said gravely. 'We must be just. My mother needed her share of the money and it was mostly all in the house.'

'I don't know how you endure it,' said George, staring sightlessly before him. 'But then you're a brave girl.' He made an involuntary movement of pain and Samantha stood up, then helped the old man to his feet.

'Let's have a cup of tea,' she said soothingly. 'Will you ever forget the afternoon teas Grandma Harrington used to make?'

The following day she flew to the State capital and

a few days after that hired a car to take her to the south coast resort area known as the Gold Coast. Millions of people passed through the Gold Coast annually, drawn by twenty miles of the most beautiful beaches, some said, in all the world. The surf had always attracted Samantha, the glorious blue Pacific and the ritual of bathing and sunning had always had a calming, relaxing effect.

Bypassing the more glittering places on the pleasure strip, she rented a little timber house that nevertheless led right out on to the beach, and there she stayed for more than a week in sight and sound of the glistening, crystal-clear ocean, hearing its dull roar as she fell off to sleep and then again in the morning with seagulls wheeling outside her picture window.

It was peace of a kind, but it couldn't last.

As she lay one afternoon in the shelter of a big sand dune, a shadow passed across her body, then someone dropped down beside her.

She knew before she even opened her eyes, her heart hammering in precognition.

'*Nico!*' she exclaimed in a repressed voice, temporarily unable to lift her body from the sand.

'What, no explanations, no apologies?' The black eyes burned in the handsome dark face.

'I intended to write to you.'

'When?' He lifted his black brows in wonder. 'You have been gone more than a week.'

'And I don't think I've had a single moment's peace.' Now she lifted herself and her hair fell over her shoulder in a silver-gilt slide.

He laughed in his throat, a sound without

humour. 'Your deepest instinct seems to be to run from me.'

'I was only trying to think,' she said painfully, conscious of the familiar heat that licked along her veins.

'I did not think you were so——'

'Immature?' She still couldn't seem to look at him.

'You could put it that way, Samantha.'

'Whatever way you like.' She drew her lovely, sun-gilded legs to one side. 'Why have you come?'

'I believe I've already told you,' he said, somewhat acidly, 'to get what belongs to me.'

'Naturally I have no say.'

Too swiftly he said, '*No*. You want to be . . . what is the word? . . . mastered.'

'I assure you I do *not*!' She half rose from the sand, but he caught her so she fell back.

'You're lovesick, are you not?' He pinned her half beneath him with his powerful male body, looking at her face, then her shoulders and the swell of her breasts.

'Oh, go away!' she moaned, turning her face aside. 'Go away and leave me alone.'

'I want you, Samantha.' He held her more tightly. 'We belong together.'

'Oh, I'm easy,' she said, still moaning, 'you only have to hold me.'

Nico muttered something in his own tongue, something harsh and not gentle, and in the next instant took possession of her mouth. She had dreamed of him often, dreamed he had made love to her. Now he was doing so—violently, a punishment for daring to cause him an instant's bother.

'*Please*, Nico,' she whispered before his mouth came down on hers again. '*Please*. Someone might come along.'

'Are you frightened?' His hand closed over her wildly beating heart. 'You should be.'

It seemed easier to close her eyes than meet his brilliant accusing gaze, then she felt herself gathered up and he was carrying her from the beach, across the timber decking and into the cool, silent house.

All of it was unreal. She wondered in a deep panic if she was still in a dream.

'And now, little one, you are going to discover the truth about yourself.'

He almost threw her on to the soft, downy double bed, moving backwards to close the door.

'You're fanatical, Nico!' she accused him.

'About you, yes.' His beautiful voice sounded bitter. 'Even so, I am not callous. I could not have left you without a word.'

'I told you, I had to think.'

'I see.' He came back relentlessly towards her. 'You have had time to think, now prepare to feel.' His face looked dangerous, starkly autocratic.

'I could scream,' she said urgently.

'I hope you do.'

'Why are you so angry?' She shuddered as he came to her and put a hand beneath her hair.

'Not angry,' he said, sounding very foreign. 'Something a bit stronger than that.'

'I thought I was doing the right thing.' In spite of

her resolve, she was trembling, trying to placate him.

'I am trying to make allowances.' His hand reached for the catch on her tiny bra top.

'Please, Nico. Please stop!'

'I want to see you,' he said.

Samantha didn't answer, feeling the tremendous pressure building up in her too.

'Do you want to scream. *Do* you?' he demanded.

With his eyes on her she found herself arching her body and he drew her to him and put his mouth to her breast.

'*Nico!*' She speared her fingers through his thickly waving hair, stimulated in an instant, revelling in the knowledge that he found her body beautiful.

'You haven't yet asked me to forgive you.' He let his hands move over the satiny smoothness of her skin.

'I love the way you kiss me.'

'I know that.' He brought her down on the bed. 'I asked you a serious question. You are going to marry me, yet you ran away.'

'You're such a definite person, aren't you?' She looked at his strong, sensuous mouth.

'So you tell yourself will it matter when we're married?'

'I think I love you, Nico,' she whispered. 'I don't want you to hurt me.'

'Hurt *you*, of all people?' His dark face was tense with passion. 'I ache for you!'

His words invited chaos, a wild yearning in the flesh. Just having him beside her was like being enveloped in a consuming fire.

'I've been dreaming you made love to me,' she was urged into telling him, exciting him so violently he crushed her beneath him, imprisoning her with his body, his hands slipping under her, lifting her closer, activating a desperate sexual hunger and the far more dangerous emotion that had visited her—love.

What was happening was inevitable, something to be desired above all things. Yet as she feared, he was far more in command of himself, halting to stare at her enfolded within his arms.

'We must think of the possibility of a child.'

'Isn't that what you want?' She regarded him gravely out of her beautiful green eyes.

'You must want it too.' He put his hand over her delicate breast. 'And then I think, not yet. How could I live with myself if I forced you into something you are not ready for?'

'You can't deny you are forcing me into marriage.'

'I *will* have you,' he said with a look of gentle triumph. 'I am only asking to protect you now. Could I make you pregnant, Samantha?'

'Yes.' The word came out on a fluttering sigh.

'Then we cannot take the risk.' He groaned and lay back against the pillow and she swam out of her fevered state, raised herself up on her elbows and stared at him.

'I never imagined you'd care,' she said curiously.

'Thank you.' His beautiful mouth twitched sardonically, his humour covering a driving male need. 'I always end up doing the right thing.' He lifted his hand and ran it down the length of her silky, sun-silvered hair. 'You must know how I feel.'

Ah, yes! Sweet Antonia had told her.

Samantha lowered her lashes, hiding her expression, gazing musingly at his striking face, the faultless bone structure, the fine olive skin, tanned by the tropical sun to the deepest, darkest gold.

Our child could have such skin . . . such bones . . . black eyes fringed with the thickest lashes, she thought. A deep shudder ran the length of her body. Nico's silk shirt he had discarded to feel his skin against hers, and the beauty of that tautly fleshed torso almost made her cry. There was a small scar on the powerful rib cage and she wanted to put her mouth to it, but did not permit herself the intimacy. In truth she was still fascinated and frightened by her own helpless enslavement.

'Have you satisfied yourself there are no hoofs and horns?' he asked dryly, interrupting her staring.

'I never thought you were the devil!' Her green eyes flew to his.

'I think so. Often enough.' His hands slid over her shoulders to cup her breasts, lifting them gently, so the pleasure was so boundless she couldn't encompass it.

'Nico, *don't!*' The plea was involuntary, her heart racing.

'It is your punishment for running away.' There was a trace of severity in the taut, handsome face.

Punishment? *Rapture.*

'Well?' The caressing hands grew even more possessive and she tilted her head back and closed her eyes.

'Nico, *Nico*,' she whispered shakily, stricken with a surge of passion that promised to devour her.

'Tell me you are my woman.' He pulled her down on him hungrily.

'You already know.'

'*Tell* me.' He turned her over on her back, then bent to kiss her trembling mouth.

'You've always read what's in my mind.' She was crying.

'And I hardly dare touch you!' Nico gave a great shuddering sigh and pushed himself away, his black eyes moving all over the very ordinary little room. 'This is not what I intend for you anyway. Get up, Samantha, and help me get your things together. We are going home.'

CHAPTER SIX

The night before Antonia and Eliot were to be married, Samantha had a phone call. It was Mrs Nicolson, and her voice sounded so tight and strained Samantha had difficulty piecing the words together. Finally she had to come right out and ask:

'What *is* it, Mrs Nicolson? What's the matter?'

Again a few choking words that left Samantha all at sea.

'Shall I come over?'

The answer was an uncompromising *yes*. No stumbles that time.

Twenty minutes later, Mrs Nicolson let Samantha in the front door, her faded, pretty face puffy from crying, her eyes so chilly it was like snow falling.

'It's Eliot,' she said baldly. 'He's told me he simply can't get married tomorrow.'

'Bridal jitters,' Samantha observed.

'More likely he's gone mad! All I can say, Samantha,' Mrs Nicolson said to Samantha's slender back, 'is it's *your* fault.'

Samantha was quite shaken. 'How is that?'

'You've never let him go.' There were tears in Mrs Nicolson's button eyes.

'What rot!' Samantha walked through the house to Eliot's spartan bedroom and banged on the door.

'Come on, Eliot. What's this all about?'

'He won't find it easy to throw Antonia aside,' Mrs Nicolson muttered fearfully.

'She threw herself at *him*,' Samantha couldn't help saying. 'Hurry up, Eliot. We're waiting!' she called.

The door openly slowly and Eliot emerged looking rumpled and grim and very unemotional. 'Hi, Sam.' A scornful glance at his mother.

Through force of habit, Samantha went to him like a sister, gripping him around the waist. 'What's the matter?'

'I'm not getting married tomorrow. There'll be no wedding.'

'A bit late, isn't it, to make your decision?'

'I'd tear out my hair if it would help.'

'Let's sit down.' Samantha led him gently into the living room and Mrs Nicolson followed like a member of a wake.

'I can't do it, Sam, and that's that!' Eliot put his hand to his throat as if he was choking.

'It's just nerves, dear.' Samantha took hold of his other hand.

'Or brain damage,' Mrs Nicolson said caustically. 'Why, we couldn't live here any more if Eliot acted so dishonourably.'

'So what?' said Eliot, suddenly angry. 'You're not thinking of me but yourself.'

'I wouldn't care to leave Antonia in the lurch,' Samantha said wryly. Tears might be good enough for some women, but not Antonia. She would be livid with rage.

'It's not so much Antonia but Nico,' Eliot con-fided. 'I can't take the pace, Sam. I'll never shape up.'

'But damn it, Nico knows that quite well.'

'Does he?' Eliot returned somewhat petulantly. 'Have you been discussing me?'

'You should have more early nights,' Mrs Nicol-son said fretfully. 'Then you could cope better. Antonia is a dear girl, but very few people would match her energy.'

Samantha sat quietly trying to figure the whole thing out. 'You want to marry Antonia, but you're not sure if you can handle her ambitions?'

'You've an advance on Mother, Sam, that's for sure.'

'But my boy has a lot to offer!' Mrs Nicolson looked at Samantha as though she had implied that Eliot had a limited potential.

'Shouldn't you have discussed this with An-tonia?' Samantha looked at Eliot's haggard, boyish face.

'I tried to, but she wouldn't listen.'

'You didn't try hard enough,' Samantha said with the straightforwardness of a lifetime friend. 'Can you imagine what Antonia is thinking tonight?'

'Going to bed with me, probably,' Eliot said candidly, then apologised to his mother. 'Sorry, Mother.'

'Marriage is a sacrament,' Mrs Nicolson said soberly because it was all she could think of at that moment. 'You know you can't possibly do this, son. It would create such a stir!'

'I'd die if someone left me at the altar,' Samantha

confided, watching Mrs Nicolson straighten doilies even now. 'And for a girl of Antonia's pride! Surely, Eliot, you love her?'

'What's love?' he asked morbidly. 'It goes as quickly as it comes.'

'I think you want to see her.'

'*No!*' Eliot and his mother shrieked as one.

'No, Sam,' Eliot said more quietly. 'The truth is I've examined my soul too late. I suppose I'll have to go through with it.'

'Oh, God, this is serious!' Mrs Nicolson wheeled around the room in her distress. 'Fancy offering an insult to Mr Martinelli!'

'Oh, yes, let's consider Nico, by all means,' Eliot said bitterly. 'He pinched my girl—just swept her off her feet.'

'And so we get to the heart of it,' Mrs Nicolson crumpled like an old, old woman. 'You've been a bad influence on Eliot, all the way.'

'Notice that about mothers?' Eliot threw out his arms to the world at large. 'They'll blame everyone else but their own offspring.'

'This is a terrible situation!' Samantha sighed gloomily. 'How could you have let it go so far?'

'Do you love him, Sam?' Eliot closed his fingers around Samantha's arm.

'Never mind about that!' Mrs Nicolson cried.

'Yes, Eliot.' Samantha looked full into Eliot's serious eyes, revealing her feelings in a flash. These days she looked radiant, a dream, the most beautiful blonde in the world. His heart shook with joy and fear for her and underneath a deep, jagged jealousy. 'Antonia, I'm coming!' he called suddenly.

'Oh, dearest!' His mother jumped up and hugged him ecstatically.

'I'm coming, Antonia!' he shouted again. 'None but the brave deserve the fair.'

'Why, what's the matter with him?' Mrs Nicolson stammered, looking back at Samantha.

'I told you—bridal jitters.'

Mrs Nicolson laughed happily.

The wedding proved a brilliant spectacle for the local people, the bride's beauty matched only by her wonderful self-confidence.

'Poor old Eliot looks a bit peaked,' Samantha's long-time friend Gillian gave her a sharp nudge.

'Please God they'll be happy!'

'He's supposed to be, today.' Gillian's expression was both humorous and aghast.

'It's a big thing getting married,' Samantha pointed out.

'I believe so,' Gillian sighed. 'I wish to God someone would ask me.'

'Don't underestimate Simon,' Samantha looked at her and smiled.

'I did I think.' Gillian looked around her. 'I'd better go and grasp him. By the way, who's that incredibly snooty-looking woman?'

'Antonia's aunt.'

'Gosh!' For a moment they both sighed.

'They're not exactly ugly, are they?'

Both girls had singled out for their attention a very handsome Italian lady on the bright side of forty who was gazing around her as though she considered herself on a much higher plane than the wedding guests who swarmed around her.

'Look,' said Gillian. 'Mr Martinelli has joined her.'

It should have been very ordinary, yet it seemed suddenly oppressive. The lady smiled and the haughty face took on a melting look.

'She's a bit like Sophia Loren, isn't she?' Gillian ventured. 'Only much more supercilious. Is that the right word?'

'It'll do.' Samantha still felt that strange dismay. She had been introduced to the Contessa Torrelli only that morning and she hadn't needed any of her intuitive faculties to recognise the fact that the Contessa found her completely unimportant, even primitive. Maybe the word had gone around that she only spoke English when Antonia and her aunt had carried on in a mixture of Italian and French.

'Frankly, darling,' Gillian observed sagely, 'she's looking at your Nico not quite like ... family. They're a fairly erotic race aren't they, Italians?'

The rest of the evening was equally unreassuring, for the Contessa clung to her brother-in-law's side.

'Drink up, dear girl!' Eliot, despite strong disapproval from his bride, fought his way across the crowded room to his dearest childhood friend.

'Thank you.' Samantha held up her champagne glass, greatly fearing Eliot's voice was slurred.

'Well, I did it, Sam.'

'You did.' It struck her that they both sounded fatalistic.

Thirty or more feet away Antonia stopped smiling long enough to give them both a look of concentrated rage.

'Should you not return to your bride?' Samantha tried not to sound so melancholy.

'Never mind.' Eliot assumed a masterful look. 'It's occurred to me that I should start out as I mean to go on.'

'After all, women like the dominant male.'

'You certainly do,' Eliot returned broodingly. 'Where did we go wrong, you and I?'

'You're just having one of your moods,' Samantha told him briskly. 'Antonia is ravishing and you've got a very bright future.'

'The fatal mistake is to marry an ambitious woman,' Eliot sighed heavily.

'It's all your own fault. Anyway, you love her. You know you do.'

'It's possible,' said Eliot, 'to love two women at the same time.' He took a good gulp of his drink and observed, 'A very patronising woman, the aunt. I'm sure had we been in Italy she would have shown me the door.'

'You probably wouldn't be very comfortable in a palazzo,' Samantha pointed out.

'If you ask me,' Eliot said rather testily, 'she's out to make trouble.'

It was one thing for Samantha to think so herself and another to have Eliot's blunt warning hanging in the air.

'Do you really believe she's come all this way for Antonia's wedding?' he went on.

'That's what she said.' Samantha stared up at him in confusion.

'It just so happens, lovey, I've got my antennae out. I'd worry about that lady if I were you. If you haven't gathered yet that she dotes on her brother-in-law, you should.'

Samantha took a deep, difficult breath and said nothing. She knew very little at all about the Contessa at this stage except that Antonia had specially sent for her. That was understandable, of course. Antonia would want someone of her own family and in Antonia's face could be seen a good deal of the aunt. Despite Samantha's determined efforts she was finding it very difficult to like Antonia; there seemed little of Nico in her except the burning energy. No humour or tolerance or the beautiful, graceful manners. Her only saving grace so far as Samantha could see was that she loved her father deeply and only showed him her good side. In maturity, Samantha thought, unless she underwent a personality change or life taught her a few lessons, she would make a ruthless enemy. She had the makings of one now.

With his easy assurance Nico excused himself from a laughing group and came across to join Samantha and Eliot, considering both their faces with his penetrating black gaze.

'So quiet, both of you?'

'It takes time to sink in that I'm married.' The looseness of Eliot's tongue indicated that he had over-indulged.

'Antonia is suffering no such confusion,' Nico said smoothly. 'She looks very beautiful, does she not?'

'I've never seen anyone more beautiful,' Samantha said humbly. Unless it's *you*.

Beside them Eliot's face had softened magically. 'I still can't fathom what she sees in me.'

'You have a good deal to commend you,' Nico said kindly, knowing full well that Eliot was fussed about his work, 'though I suspect Antonia's feelings are a good deal romantic.'

'I think I'll go to her,' said Eliot.

'Yes, you must.' Nico smiled at him. 'I'll take care of Samantha.'

'Cheers!' Eliot finished what was left of his drink, put the glass down on the small table behind him and strode off.

'Well, of course he still loves you,' Nico said.

'It's not like that at all.' Samantha shook her gleaming head.

'God knows I told Antonia, but she would have him.'

'Did you?' Samantha looked up at him, dazed. 'I thought you approved of Eliot?'

'Antonia approved of Eliot,' he corrected dryly. 'She spoke to me about him at every opportunity, begged me to give him a job. You may be sure she wanted him right from the beginning; a kind of compulsion. One of the few characteristics she shares with me.'

'But you knew he was *my* friend.'

'Of course. But then I saw how innocent you were. Far more important, I saw you didn't love him at all. Your feelings were merely affection, the feelings one reserves for a dear friend—never a lover.' He looked deeply into Samantha's eyes, watching them widen in a kind of affront.

'If you'd never come here I would have married Eliot,' she said faintly.

'Then you've been extraordinarily fortunate.' He

took her arm and drew her out into the cool night air. 'Destiny brought me here, to you. In the same way it carried my daughter towards Eliot. Given half a chance they will be happy. Antonia fully intends to make her marriage work.'

'Then she should know Eliot is not a man in the mould of her father. He's dreamy, in a way.'

'He would do better to get his head out of the clouds,' Nico returned rather curtly, 'and better for you to chase a few of his dreams out of the door.'

'Meaning what?' Even in the soft lighting it was possible to see her eyes flash.

'It is not really a subject for a wedding,' he said dryly. 'You understand the psychology of the thing, Samantha. You must remove yourself from your childhood friend many paces. He cannot run to you with his problems, talk over every little thing. He has a wife now, a young woman, it has to be said, with a possessive nature. They will be living here when they return in two months' time, by which time you will be *my* wife. Gossip flourishes every-where, but I have found, like everything else, it blossoms hectically in the tropics. There will be no gossip, only two very happy young wives.'

'Do you tell everyone what to do?' Her own con-fused feelings were stirring up a perverse anger.

'Don't be public, *piccola*.' He turned her out of the light. 'There is plenty of time for us to talk later.'

'With the Contessa around?'

'I had no idea,' he said coolly, 'she was coming. Antonia planned it as a surprise.'

'That strikes me as very strange,' observed Sa-mantha.

'In my lifetime, little one, I have seen the most astounding things. No matter, she is here.'

'For how long?'

'Did you think I would worry a guest immediately about a departure date?'

'I'll ask her just in case you forget,' Samantha said tartly. 'After all, you *are* my prospective husband.'

'Don't panic,' he said quietly. 'We will entertain Rena for a short time, then she will go back to her own world.'

'Your world too, Nico. How could you have left it?' She didn't know it, but she had one small fist locked in tension.

'I made up my mind in a minute,' he said with a little flare of arrogance. 'I do not regret it. Come, you are becoming disturbed.' He took her hand and smoothed out the pale, slender fingers, his fingers across Samantha's palm trailing tingles of sensation. 'It seems to me you are trying to stir up a quarrel.'

'*No!*' Suddenly she reproached herself bitterly. 'Forgive me, Nico.' She bent her slender neck, looking down, a child confessing a misdemeanour, and instantly he put his hands on her waist, drawing her close to him.

'If only we were alone!'

Always the sound of his voice turned her heart over.

'I love you, Nico.' There, she had said it quite openly.

'You are such a wicked girl!' His voice seemed to deepen with a real passion. 'You plan exactly when to tell me such a thing.'

Samantha had a great craving to have him kiss her, but there were people all around them and though his fingers were crushing her side she could only lift her head and look deeply into his eyes. 'I'll be glad to tell you again when everyone has gone.'

Neither of them observed that someone was walking towards them, intruding into what was palpably a special world.

'Nico!' The Contessa's tone suggested treason that he had deserted her.

'Ah, Rena,' he turned casually, still keeping a hand at Samantha's waist.

'I have come to tell you Antonia is leaving.'

'Eliot too, I hope.'

'Of course.' The Contessa smiled faintly, her eyes on Samantha; the beautifully coiffured blonde head, diamond earrings that Nico had given her and surely a dress from a collection, so exquisite was the cut and style and the flower-printed fabric.

The glance, Samantha thought, was curiously familiar, and far more fraught with womanly rapport. The Contessa conveyed perfectly what she wished to say, while Antonia was forced into adding on a few harsh words.

It was quite impossible to feel crushed with Nico's hand at her waist, though the Contessa's dark eyes flashed down in extravagant disapproval. With all he had been born to how could Nico look at such a nothing! The sooner he packed up and went back to Italy the better. The Contessa didn't concern herself with the very many of her own countrymen and women who had been invited to the glittering function.

In her haste not to throw the bridal bouquet Samantha's way, Antonia nearly stumbled, and as she threw out her hands in faint alarm, the exquisitely wrought creation landed quietly against Samantha's breast. From the flash in the Contessa's almond eyes Samantha wondered briefly if it was going to be wrenched away, but then the bridal couple were in the car and everyone was giving them a noisy farewell—perhaps too noisy for the Contessa, for she moved off instantly.

As always a few guests remained when everyone else had had the sense to withdraw, and the Contessa didn't seem in the least inclined to take to her bed. She had taken off her magnificent ensemble and replaced it with a hostess gown of such splendid nonchalance it was difficult to take one's eyes off her. She was really a fantastic-looking creature, dazzlingly handsome more than beautiful, for her features were too strong and, in the hostess gown with its deeply plunging neckline, monumentally sexy.

Only Nico seemed impervious to her glamour, or he had become used to it over a very long time and knew how to cover up better. Many times she addressed a remark to him in Italian, a husky little aside, while her long-fingered hand heavily emblazoned with jewels trailed insinuatingly down his jacketed arm. Together they presented quite a spectacle; two extremely handsome examples of a notoriously handsome race.

Finally Samantha knew she had to go home. Or rather, the Contessa looked so much at home with Nico, she wanted to go some place else.

'But I'll come with you!' the Contessa rose to her feet, so the few remaining guests mustered themselves instantly to leave. 'The breath of fresh air!'

Another woman might have thought she hadn't the right to intrude, but the Contessa's self-confidence was daunting and much, much more. She took the front seat in the car and for an instant Nico looked at her as though her actions were quite beyond him, then he put Samantha gently in the back seat, his chiselled mouth firm as though he was smothering the desire to laugh or fight back.

When they arrived at Malabar the Contessa shook her regal head incredulously. 'You mean this is your home?'

Was, Samantha went to say, but Nico forestalled her.

'A splendid example of colonial architecture and ideal for the tropics. North Queensland, Rena, you may not know, is the most successful tropical settlement in the world by people of European descent. I hope you will be able to stay with us long enough to see its many beauties and enormous potential. The Great Barrier Reef just off the coast is one of the great natural wonders of the world. I have never seen better seascapes in my life.'

'Then you must take me!' the Contessa exclaimed. 'Surely Antonia told me this property belongs to you, Nico?' She stared at him sharply.

'I am giving it back to Samantha to do as she likes with it. She has a great feeling for her family home.'

'But how is it that she sold it?'

Evidently the Contessa didn't know everything or

Antonia had not had the time to tell her.

'I had no choice.' Samantha interrupted, forcing the Contessa to acknowledge her presence. 'My mother decided on a new life and of course we divided things equally.'

The Contessa gave the overwhelming impression that she wasn't listening attentively. She looked towards Nico and addressed a remark to him in Italian.

Perhaps, Samantha thought, it's time to take a crash course. Italian in twenty lessons. It would be worth it to know what dear Rena was saying.

Thinking it might be carrying things too far, the Contessa stayed in the car as Nico escorted Samantha to her door.

'Well, I shall have to do without a goodnight kiss, shan't I?' Samantha said cautiously.

Nico looked down at her very briefly, then with his hands around her narrow waist brought her right into his arms. 'I am not going away without one.'

Before Samantha could make another comment he lowered his head and kissed her with a deep pressure, the frightening delight it gave her shutting out everything; the Contessa, considerations, the rest of the world.

When at last he set her free, the magic was in her face, the excitement, the exultation, the way it was unbearable to let him go.

'Goodnight, little one,' he said gently. She made a funny little sound of yearning and he tipped up her chin. 'Now that we have sorted everyone else out, there is just you and I. I'll ring you in the morning. I expect we shall have to take Rena out for the day.'

'Well, that's easily managed.' Samantha tried to

sound interested. 'There are dozens of beautiful spots.'

He raised her hand to his mouth and kissed it. 'I am having made for you a ring—deep, deep emerald and brilliant diamonds. You are committed to me for good.'

In the car, the interior light came on; the Contessa, no doubt impatient for her bed. 'Take care!' Samantha said softly and so portentously that he laughed.

'When you go inside, look at yourself in the mirror.'

She gave him a little sceptical glance. 'Just between the two of us, I don't think I'd rate a glance beside the Contessa.'

Nico had moved down a step, now he looked back at her as though testing her sincerity. 'Could you really believe that?'

'Yes.' Her green eyes widened.

'Then I'm afraid you're excessively modest. Among Italians a woman knows her own beauty, and you are very beautiful. More so, probably, in maturity.' He gave her one of his severe glances. 'Go in now and lock the door. I am virtually in a state of anxiety until I have you every minute under my eyes.'

Safely in her bedroom, Samantha went to the mirror and subjected herself to an intense scrutiny. She did look rather lovely; excitement-touched face, wide luminous eyes. Of course it was a very beautiful dress and she had had her hair done specially. Was she too modest? Nico didn't seem to like it. She put a hand up and touched her hair, seeing how it was silvered all around the temples. Even now, she could scarcely believe he loved her, but one thing was certain: she loved him!

CHAPTER SEVEN

For a week they entertained the Contessa non-stop, which for Samantha was very trying indeed. Now and again she found herself in the front seat of the car, a piece of diplomacy on Nico's part when he was quick-footed enough to smoothly tuck Rena into the back seat, but for the most part Samantha chose to give the older woman what she considered her due.

Each day Rena stunned them with her elegance and Samantha had to check the impulse to ask her how she did it. Never a raven black hair was out of place, never a make-up that looked less than perfect even in the tropical heat. The magnificent olive skin remained matt and though they travelled many hundreds of miles in different directions the spectacularly beautiful clothes remained creaseless.

'Where I would really like to go,' she told Nico with one of her elaborate hand motions, 'is to this Barrier Reef you spoke of.'

'Of course it can be arranged,' Nico answered her suavely. 'Where would you like to stay? One of the more sophisticated islands or a true cay?'

'*Caro!*' she glanced at him meltingly and smiled. 'Sophisticated, of course.'

In the back seat Samantha tried to remember the exact roll of the Contessa's r's. *Caro.* She said it silently, engaged a good bit of the time now in mastering another language. *Nico. Caro.* Clearly she would never be able to trill it off like the Contessa. When she caught sight of herself in the rear vision mirror, she was frowning.

It was on one of the occasions when Nico couldn't possibly avoid business that Samantha and the Contessa finally came to grips.

And here it comes! Samantha thought, as they sat together in the long golden afternoon.

'Not a word yet from Antonia!' Rena announced, yawning so deeply that for a moment Samantha thought it would strangle her.

And only a few postcards from Mother, Samantha thought, but spared the Contessa any boring talk of her family.

'I hope I am not mistaken,' Rena went on, 'but I think that young man is not good enough for her.'

'I've known him all my life.' Samantha lifted her blonde head with a kind of resolution.

'There have been so many mistakes in the past—' The Contessa sighed voluptuously and fixed Samantha with her brilliant black eyes. 'God forgive me, even you and Nico. Why, Samantha?'

'I'm sorry, I'm not following you,' Samantha said quickly, following very fast indeed.

'It is not like Nico to be so impetuous!' the Contessa contemplated Samantha's vulnerable young face. 'Please, I don't want to make you unhappy, I only wonder why you do this. I *must* understand!'

'That Nico wants to marry me? Is that what you can't understand?'

'Not only me, *cara*,' Rena put her shapely, be-ringed hand to the splendid column of her throat. 'You see, Antonia has spoken to me of her feelings. She wrote to me as soon as her father told her his plans.'

'People don't usually marry to accommodate their families,' Samantha pointed out from experience.

'But they do marry for a variety of reasons,' the Contessa retorted with a good deal of derision and scorn. 'I am completely at a loss to understand Nico. He could have anyone.'

'He chose me,' Samantha said clearly.

'And you do not ask yourself *why*?' the Contessa demanded with restless impatience. 'Oh, you have looks, a certain wit, but forgive me, Nico must re-member my sister. She was glorious!'

'Nico tells me he recalls her in Antonia's face.' Samantha stared away towards the mountain.

'We might have been twins!' said Rena, almost harshly. 'There was only eighteen months between us. I remember what people used to say when they saw us together.'

'You must feel her loss deeply,' Samantha mur-mured, feeling some natural sympathy.

'It almost destroyed Nico!' the Contessa said with even more violence. 'I shall tell you he adored her. He would not allow her to escape him for one minute. It was only I he could turn to when his heart was broken—a little more and more each day.'

'You care for him, don't you?' Samantha said.

'A little more than that, *cara*.' The Contessa smiled at her contemptuously. 'As I see it, it is you who could ruin Nico's life. This country is big, very beautiful, I grant you, but can't you see Nico is a Venetian? A man of a different world. This house he has built may seem to you very extraordinary, but it is nothing compared to what he is used to. Where are the art and the architecture, the splendours of his past?'

The comparisons were unsettling in the extreme. 'He seems happy enough,' Samantha sighed.

'He is in retreat!' the Contessa exclaimed forcefully. 'He tried to kill himself in those first terrible days. . . .' she paused and a wave of colour beat under her flawless skin.

'I don't believe that!' Samantha said flatly. 'A man like that, no matter how much he loved, would still be aware of his responsibility to himself, to this family, to life. Life is a celebration—he told me so himself.'

'I think you don't know Nico at all!' The Contessa leaned towards Samantha, holding her with her burning dark eyes. 'Perhaps it is even dangerous for you to come to know him. He has always taken what he wanted, refused advice, nevertheless I cannot allow him to make this decision. You have trapped him, with your youth and your long blond hair.'

'Such men are not trapped.' Samantha rose to her feet, staring down at the Contessa with all her concentration. 'They do the trapping.'

'That's not all!' The Contessa stood up as well, so

daunting in her physical presence that Samantha moved back. 'I don't expect Nico to give up his business here immediately. He has always been brilliant, an exact duplicate of his father, but without him our own fortunes are falling apart. You know, of course, that Nico and I are cousins, and I want him back where he belongs.'

'Antonia too?' Samantha looked into the ruthless eyes.

'I will have nothing of the husband!' The Contessa threw up her hands. 'I am prepared to make you a reasonable offer to go out of Nico's life.'

'Such as?' Samantha raised her eyebrows and began to shake with pent-up rage.

The Contessa shrugged as though that was the first intelligent remark Samantha had made. 'You see this bracelet?' she extended her arm. 'It is a masterpiece of antiquity and consequently very valuable. It is yours.'

'Surely there's something to match it,' Samantha's voice trembled. 'Isn't there a necklace, pendant earrings?'

'Don't be stupid!' the Contessa's voice sharpened. 'This piece alone would fetch fifty thousand dollars.'

'Surely dirt cheap!' Samantha could hardly speak for emotion.

'All right, the necklace,' the Contessa's black brows drew together. 'You are very grasping. One could not imagine it to look at you.'

'And you must be crazy to take me seriously!' Samantha cried angrily. 'I love Nico!'

The Contessa turned blazing eyes upon her. 'Who

are you?' she growled. 'Who *are* you to imagine such dreams? Nico is not for you. Your own head warns you. What have you to offer after all? A girl's body. He wants you to have his child. What then? You're mad if you think he loves you. He simply wants a son, someone to survive him.'

'Then you may be sure I'll provide him with one!' Samantha retorted with unaccustomed fire.

Too late she saw the malevolence in the Contessa's eyes. The older woman moved towards her, speaking almost inaudibly in Italian, then she lifted her hand and hit Samantha across her flushed cheek.

'How *dare* you threaten me!' she cried violently, a woman who never let anyone or anything stand in her way. Again another word in Italian that had to be an insult.

'I think you must be neurotic,' Samantha said coldly. 'I'm not someone you can tell what and what not to do. Neither am I someone you can intimidate. I only wish you would act like the aristocrat you are supposed to be.'

It was too much for a woman used to deference all her life. The Contessa wheeled away with a face black as thunder, leaving Samantha to the deserted terrace.

How difficult it was all going to be!

She had been expected to dine with them, but she left a message with Nico's housekeeper, a very pleasant and amiable Italian lady who with her husband looked after the household, that she had a bad headache and would rest quietly at home.

Apparently Nico was not a man to accept an idle message, for as Samantha was drying her hair he presented himself at the front door.

'You mentioned a headache?' he said coolly, 'you don't, I'm afraid, look as though you have one.'

'Come in.' Samantha held the door open, hating the fact that she was caught in a simple robe with her hair flying from the hair dryer.

'I rather guess,' he said, 'it is because you are bored.'

'Ah well,' Samantha decided to get in a dig, 'the Contessa is fairly wearing for a simple country girl.'

'Don't be ridiculous,' he said curtly. 'Simple you are not.'

'I wish I could explain.' Samantha stared at his brilliant, faintly menacing eyes.

'I wish you would at least *try* to,' he said a little flatly. 'I have the feeling you will never confide in me.'

'I have a feeling,' Samantha said wryly, 'that this is all a dream.'

He shrugged exasperatedly, looking so darkly, impatiently male that Samantha was almost driven into the submissiveness she thought he was expecting.

'Rena tells me you have been extremely unkind to her.' He stood there with his hand on the back of a chair, taking in her slender, graceful figure, the carelessly knotted green robe.

'What a liar!' she said dryly, thrusting her long hair away from her face.

'Are you going to tell me?'

Not with that arrogant head and flaring nostrils, she thought defiantly, turning her head away.

'*Samantha!*' He moved towards her with his quick, lithe tread and caught her arm. 'At least don't turn away from me.'

As usual when he touched her, she started shaking. 'Do you believe her?' she asked recklessly.

'What's happened between you and Rena has nothing to do with it. You won't talk to me, and it's wrong.' An answering tension showed itself in his dark, high-mettled face.

'It's a very tedious story,' she said brittley.

'You're upset.' He put up his elegant hand and touched her cheek.

'In more ways than one.' The feeling she had for him was frightening, nothing easy or relaxed. Perhaps such a passion could break her. 'The Contessa doesn't like me, Nico. It's as simple as that.'

'And you want me to put pressure on her to go?'

'Oh, God!' she sighed, and shook her hair back.

'I asked you a question.'

'And I'm supposed to answer on the count of three?'

'Yes, you will.' His black glance struck her face and the pressure on her arm tightened.

'Really, *force?*' she gave him a strange little smile, more upset than she knew from her confrontation with Rena.

'Don't be childish!' His white teeth snapped together. 'You should be glad to confide in me, but clearly you are not.'

'I suppose *you* tell me everything?' She lifted her

blond head, her sensitive features heightened with emotion. 'How you idolised your wife and found nothing in life when she was gone!'

'Ah!' his black eyes went past her, the dark face brooding yet unyielding. 'So Rena has been talking.'

'Damn it, yes.' Her eyes were fixed on his face with a direct plea for understanding, but he wasn't even looking at her. 'You don't imagine it's enjoyable being told I'm a *nothing*!'

'How old are you?' he asked curtly.

'Obviously not old enough!' Her tone implied that the solution was simple. 'Someone like the Contessa is more your style.'

His reaction came fast, making her nerves shrivel in panic. He swept her into his arms, twisting her long hair back, kissing her with a passion and violence that had the real urge to punish. Her senses had always told her he could be dangerous, especially when the devil in him was let out.

The only movement she seemed capable of was a feeble struggle that infuriated him, for he swung her off her feet and carried her into the same room he had once carried her to before.

The silent physical struggle continued on the bed, with spears of light playing across them from the room beyond. The most alarming part was the anger that burned up in Samantha too, a deadly piece of intent to hurt him as he was hurting her. A primitive war of the sexes. Nico only let her go to strip off her robe and for an instant she was helpless as his hands claimed her breasts.

'I hate you!' she found herself moaning. There was no excuse for his behaviour. Worse, none for her. She, the cool, the calm, the controlled.

'What have I done to you?' he asked harshly. 'I know you better than anyone, better than you know yourself.'

And now her love-hate was clouding with desire, a yielding that became immediately clear to him, for a suppleness invaded her taut body. 'You love me,' he said against her moaning, parted mouth. 'You love me for always!'

She could have saved herself then, but her body needed his desperately. Part of all the misery and confusion was the frustration she had endured.

Her tears were salt on his mouth, but even as he checked himself, she locked her arms around his neck.

'*Love* me. *Do* you love me, Nico?' she whispered urgently.

He pressed his mouth on her temples, her eyes. 'Do you really think I will let you go now?'

'Convince me.' She shivered convulsively and he locked his arms around her.

'You aren't afraid of me?'

'I need you,' she told him with a contraction of the heart.

'Then you have given me your word for ever.' He said it solemnly, like a vow.

After that, little was said, feelings crowded in too greatly. Excitement surged in her veins like wine so her whole body was flushed with it. Mighty indeed was passion, bearing them both along.

She went willingly into an undreamed-of new dimension, of profound pleasure. She was totally without pride or pretence. Nico seemed to control not only her body but her heart and her brain. Even loving him as she did, her senses had not been prepared for such excitement.

Everything she was, she had surrendered up to him, but nothing else mattered. *Nothing*. Except that they were together.

It took her a long time to calm down, and when she did, she found herself folded into his arms, Nico stroking her petal-skinned breast.

'Darling, darling.' She could only make soft, helpless little sounds, thinking she had never really existed.

'I don't want you away from me any longer. I have taken out the licence. We'll get married at once.'

'And what about Rena?' Problems subjugated by passion came rushing back.

'Rena can go home again. I did not ask her.'

'Don't you intend taking her over to the Reef?' She lifted her head briefly from his heart.

'You must know what Rena is,' he said quietly.

'I can't know what you won't tell me.'

'And maybe it is better.' He skeined her fragrant hair around his hand. 'You are a child of light, truly good.'

'Is it because she reminds you of your . . . wife?' Samantha said the last word very softly, very tentatively. 'Is it so very painful?'

'Painful, yes.' He shaped a hand around her head and brought it down on his chest again. 'I don't like to remember my old life.'

'Why, Nico, what happened?' For the first time she thought they could communicate deeply, then in the distance they heard the sound of a car's engine that grew steadily nearer.

Nico left the bed and walked to the window, holding back the sheer curtains. 'It seems we have a visitor.'

'Very likely Rena.' Samantha showed an inclination to laugh. Being Nico's woman had made her strong.

'Who else?' Nico was scowling heavily.

'Well, what shall we do?' Samantha stretched out voluptuously.

'You don't imagine *you're* moving?' He glanced back meaningfully at her gleaming body.

'Are you sure you can stop her searching the house?' She still had the mind to laugh, pitying Rena.

'I don't want you to become involved.' From a pagan Roman god he was Nico again, running a hand over his crisply curling raven hair.

'But I *am* involved.' She sat up swiftly and reached for the robe he had flung over the end of the bed. 'Your sister-in-law's natural inquisitiveness sometimes overcomes her tact.'

'For both our sakes,' he said quietly, 'stay there.'

It wasn't easy, but she did, until she heard the Contessa's voice raised in anger or frenzy, she couldn't tell which. Twenty lessons hadn't equipped her for following rapid-fire volatile Italian from a temperament in which softness was entirely missing.

Resolutely she belted her robe around her, stepped into the nearest pair of slippers and brushed her hair briskly away from her face. Why should Nico have to listen to the Contessa's complaints?

They were standing on the wide verandah and when she switched on the light, the Contessa's tirade faltered and she looked towards Samantha's slender figure outlined against the light.

'Slut!' she cried, in a terrible voice.

Nico's face darkened alarmingly, but Samantha walked towards them with a dignified coolness. 'You're a great one to talk,' she said calmly. 'Why have you come here?'

'And why not?' the Contessa retorted vehemently looking so tigerish many a woman would have cowered back. 'He seeks *you* and spurns my affections? I told you today!'

'Told her what?' Nico took a step closer to his sister-in-law, but she did not retreat.

'That we were lovers. Even when my sister was alive.'

'The words of an adventuress and a liar. You're a ruthless creature, Rena.'

'At my best, never so ruthless as you.' A deep colour spread over the Contessa's cheeks. 'You took Marisa when she was just a child.'

'The same age as myself.' He nodded at her in apparent agreement.

'Of course she adored you. Your devoted little slave.'

'She found no affection in her sister,' Nico challenged gravely. 'I have always believed in my heart you hated her.'

'And so I did!' The Contessa's voice was barely above a whisper, yet it sounded like a shout. 'In our childhood I was nearer to you than anyone, yet it was Marisa who claimed my place. Of course when you had her pregnant you had to come up with marriage. Our families could not have stood for less.'

'It was many years ago,' Nico said wearily. 'I have paid over and over for a single mistake.'

'Yet you seek to make another!' The tremble in the Contessa's voice was only a small indication of her inner fury. 'What drives you towards these innocents?'

'In any case,' Samantha interrupted wretchedly, 'is it any of your business?'

'But you don't understand,' the Contessa's eyes were inky black in a marble face. 'My sister took her own life!'

The terrible statement, the Contessa's face, were like a knife to Samantha's heart. 'Suicide?' her voice broke on the word.

Nico took a step towards her, but she snatched her hands away. 'Please, Nico. I must hear her out.'

'Can't you see that she is lying?'

'She realised,' the Contessa continued exorably, 'that Nico had come back to me. There was no way out for both of us. We were meant for each other from childhood.'

'Then why did he ever leave you?' There was doubt in Samantha's voice.

'Guilt!' the Contessa cried. '*Guilt*. Surely you've heard of it? We were both of us unfaithful—Nico to Marisa, I to my husband. Now both of them have gone.'

'Is it true?' Samantha had to summon up all her strength to ask him.

'Rena has always been my enemy.' There was a terrible remoteness about him, his hooded eyes fixed on that other life. 'I thought, God help me, enough time and pain had gone past. But nothing changes. My wife was killed accidentally.'

'An accomplished rider!' The Contessa cried wildly.

'No more than adequate. I never intervened in the life she chose to lead. The finding was . . . an accident.'

'And you had to pretend to be bereaved.'

'Rena,' he said deliberately, 'you disgust me.'

For an instant all the breath and the fire seemed to be knocked out of her, then the Contessa whirled. She looked around her wildly. Her strong white hand closed over a small sculpture that stood among the plants and as she lifted it to hurl it Samantha, guessing what she had grasped, cried out,

'Nico, look out!'

It wasn't enough to warn him, she had to do something positive. She launched herself bodily at him, not in that moment caring for herself, and the missile that might have thundered harmlessly by him thudded into the side of her temple.

She went down as from a bolt of lightning, and though Nico caught her before she hit the ground whatever control he had imposed on himself was gone.

He looked up at the woman who stood trembling above them and when he spoke his cruelty was as diabolical as her own.

When Samantha regained consciousness, she put up her hand quickly to her aching head, flinching at the pain.

'Samantha!' A man came to the side of her bed, sounding dimly familiar.

'What's happened? What's the matter?' She framed the words slowly, staring into the dark face that swam above her. The eyes were black, startlingly black against polished gold skin.

'It's all right,' he said, taking her hand.

'No.' Her voice was no more than a whisper. 'My head hurts.'

'I'll call the nurse.'

'No.' A spasm crossed her eyes and bandaged forehead. 'Don't leave me.' She thought that she knew him, and a soft melting came to her that made her want to weep. 'Am I in a hospital?'

'Can't you remember?' he said at last, with difficulty.

'Remember what?' Her hand began to shake in a visible sign of distress.

'Everything is all right,' he said soothingly, leaning over her. 'You have had an accident.'

'Oh.' She drew in a long, shuddering breath. 'I know you, don't I? Are you the doctor?'

'Yes, you know me,' he said gently to quiet her. 'You're confused at the moment. You'll soon remember.'

He had the most beautiful voice, black velvet like his eyes. Of course she knew the accent, Italian, but his English was perfect, taught to him by a master. Her face, that had been contracted in pain, relaxed.

'Do you think you could get me a drink of water?' She sounded very young and exhausted.

'Let me ask.'

He went to turn away and she grasped at his sleeve. 'It's all right, I don't want it. Don't go away.'

'I won't. Be still.' He watched her slender body move in agitation under the bedclothes, and he leaned across her and pressed the call button.

Within seconds a nurse appeared. *Sister*, Samantha corrected herself, dwelling on the uniform.

'Thank God, she's awake!' The Sister drew near so she could recognise the caring, compassion. 'Well, Samantha?'

Was that her name? She frowned, trying to remember.

'*Samantha?*' Now the woman leaned over her searching her eyes. She too looked familiar, yet strange.

'She seems to be suffering some confusion.' The

doctor—*was* he?—spoke.

'I'll get doctor immediately,' the Sister said crisply, and hurried away.

'Who *are* you?' Samantha tightened her lips with the pain.

'Don't talk.' He glanced urgently at the outer door.

'I think I'm going to be sick.'

She was, violently, and he held the bowl and steadied her head, taking her slight weight on his shoulder before he settled her back on the pillow again.

'I'm sorry . . . sorry.'

'Hush, now!' He caught at the fingers that clenched themselves around his, his face so austere it was a graven mask.

'Oh dear, dear,' Sister hurried back into the room, distressed and shocked.

'She's been ill.' The man turned his face towards her.

'Doctor's coming immediately.'

Even as she spoke, a tall man came through the door, a stethoscope hanging outside his white coat. He nodded to the younger man and walked straight towards the bed, picking up the patient's hand.

'Do you know who I am, Samantha?'

Under the bandage the girl's brows drew together. 'No.'

'Should you subject her to strain?' A muscle moved along the dark man's cheek.

'Don't worry, I'm not going to ask any more questions,' the doctor said soothingly. 'This degree of concussion can produce a temporary amnesia. 'He loosened his hand gently and tucked the girl's arm neatly by her side. 'I think, Sister, we'll have that injection.'

Sister was already there, looking down at the girl in the bed. In sickness her resemblance to her father was startling, and Ruth McInnes had worked with Doctor Harrington for many years. She made an involuntary little sound of distress and the doctor, who happened to be thinking the same thing, said quietly.

'I have instructions for you, Sister, you might add to the case sheet.'

Sister nodded her assent and as they both moved away from the bed, the girl spoke.

'You mustn't leave me.' Her green, imploring eyes went beyond the doctor to the man who stood in an attitude of waiting by the window.

'By no means!' the doctor said heartily, watching Nico Martinelli with a professional eye. What he had mistaken for a deep reserve, even arrogance, was strain. It would be a relief to all of them when Samantha was out of danger.

When Nico Martinelli reached the bed, the girl's body curved towards him.

'I'll get you a chair, Mr Martinelli,' Sister said, for all the world as though he were Royalty.

He didn't even appear to hear this, his face had the remote beauty of a mask, but as Sister approached he turned and took hold of the chair, taking it from her.

'*Grazie.*'

Sister blushed, taking one more look at him. Mr Martinelli was the handsomest man she had seen in her life. Like someone in a film. A man of secret emotions.

Samantha too was engrossed in him, her expression so appealing it touched Sister's heart. Such a surrendering sweetness when she thought she didn't even know him. Since it had become known they were to be married, the whole town had rejoiced in Samantha's future happiness. Like her father, she was a special favourite of everyone. The old people especially, Doctor Harrington's ex-patients, tended to talk about her for ages; her kindnesses to them and the way she was always so interested in the few little things they had to tell her.

Poor Samantha! She looked very fragile, in the chaste hospital bed. Who would have thought a girl of such grace could take a heavy fall?

In the hours that followed, Samantha's pulse fell steadily and by mid-morning of the next day she was made ready for surgery. At Nico's insistence, a neuro-surgeon of considerable prestige was flown in from the State capital, and if his fee was expected to be astronomical it was unthinkable that she should have less than the best. Bleeding was going on inside the skull, so immediate surgery was absolutely necessary. It seemed like a miracle that John Summerton was available and willing to come.

Not for nothing had he gained his reputation. With a vigil of people waiting in and around the hospital it was later announced that the operation, performed in record time, had been a complete success. The deadly blood-clot had been removed and with her youth and strength the patient should recover soon. Such was the triumph of modern surgery.

It didn't seem to occur to anyone that when Samantha was finally released from hospital she would still be in a state of shock. Fatal creatures were the Martinellis and her memories of the accident, submerged in her unconscious, had come back to her beyond the power to forget.

CHAPTER EIGHT

WHEN Samantha opened her eyes, Nico was sitting alongside her on the redwood recliner, head bent, as though he was examining all the fallen blossoms that scented the air around them.

'Hi!' she said with the uncanny tranquillity that frightened him.

'Hi.' With his lifted head came a smile, which she answered but not with her eyes. 'You look as though you were weeping in your dream.'

'Truly I can't remember.' She did.

'I have been watching your face for an hour.'

'But then you truly love me, don't you, Nico?' She said it with a bitter-sweetness, turning her head restlessly. These days her hair was a golden cap with a fringe to cover the thin scar that extended an inch towards her eyebrow. In time it would fade to a white line, but for now the silky fringe covered it and lent enormous impact to her eyes. Eyes, not like yesterday, luminous and dreaming but possessed of a haunting quality that was intensified by their colour.

He didn't answer, too weary for a fencing match. It was his way now to be very gentle, a guardian instead of a lover for a young wife, yet to look at him one could never guess he was vulnerable. The handsome face, always sombre except for the brief, dazzling smile, had a hard, imperious look to it as though all emotion was under impeccable control. As indeed it was. In the two months since Samantha had come out of hospital, the few weeks since their quiet marriage, he had demanded nothing of her except that she should quickly return to her former state of health.

Her headaches had gone; the scar was fading every day, but the inner wounds remained to trouble her in dreams. Often she awoke, heart pounding and sweating, wondering why she should have to be afflicted with these dreams. In the early days when she lay so weakly, Nico had insisted on being close at hand, but for weeks now she had insisted on closing the door that connected their two suites. The key she had tried to turn, only once, he had taken away, indicating to her from his expression alone that he considered her action beneath his contempt. Her health he watched like a hawk; as for the rest, they lived in a state of almost desperate harmony.

Nico's many business interests were thriving, so it seemed to the town that he had everything a man could possibly want—wealth and all that went with it, a beautiful young wife and, in time, a family. Their marriage, in fact, had softened the whole town's attitude towards virtually being taken over by a stranger and a foreigner at that. Not that the North didn't owe a great debt of gratitude to its Italian community. Over the generations the migrants from Italy had made the North thrive, working the tall green sugar cane and opening up small businesses. Now Nico Martinelli had arrived; a Mangano, Mandelli, Mantegazza, on a grand scale.

A creamy blossom struck Samantha's cheek and she turned her head. 'Sorry, did you say something?'

'I did.' His voice was faintly mocking. 'Antonia and Eliot want to come to dinner. Do you feel up to it?'

She didn't even hesitate. 'Nico, would I ever let you down?'

'Then I'll tell them, shall I?' Otherwise he ignored her.

She lazed on the lounger for an hour or so longer, then took a leisurely swim. She was a trivial commodity around the place anyway. Maria and Bruno were experts at the smooth management of the household, so all there was for her to do was get well and look pretty. The fact that she was very much better made her position start to rankle, but she scarcely thought of it then. Nor did she consider, as she fought out of her depression, that subconsciously she was blaming Nico for everything. Half of everything was unreal and her dreams couldn't be shaken off.

Antonia and Eliot arrived about seven and Samantha walked into the huge, open plan living room, presenting a calm face to them both.

'Ah, Samantha!' These days, for God knows what reason, Antonia had taken to cheek-pecking, a gesture that should have been warm and friendly except that Samantha had to stifle her irritation every time. More—a frisson of revulsion that she

had the sense to realise was not brought forth by
Antonia alone. Marriage and a first pregnancy had
lent Antonia a mellowing maturity, but her resemblance to that nameless someone was unfortunately more marked.

A pity! Samantha thought dispassionately, and
accepted Eliot's honest, caring little homage.

'You look lovely, Sam.' Still holding her hands,
he drew back a little. She had always been slender.
Now she was thin, but the delicacy of her bones lent
that thinness a softening fragility. He had never
thought he would get used to Samantha with short
hair, but it seemed to do something quite heart-
stopping to her face. Perhaps it was the enormous
green eyes or the shining fringe. Either way she
wasn't his Sam any more, but a beautiful, curiously
detached near-stranger.

Over pre-dinner drinks, Antonia chatted away
brightly, carrying the load of the conversation. Her
pregnancy had just been confirmed and she looked
the picture of womanly fulfilment.

Samantha gave her a glance of severe appreciation. At least one of the Martinellis would be blessed
with a son. The thought made her smile grimly to
herself. There was no avoiding life's little ironies.
Antonia was sitting on one of the beautiful white
sofas beside her father, ravishing in her apricot silk
dress that was just a shade deeper than the silk cush-
ion behind her, while her father smiled on her with
a lazy indulgence. Moreover, Antonia could talk
business and wasn't above asking many favours of
her father.

'How many workmen do you think you can allow me, Nico?' she asked cajolingly. She and Eliot had taken possession of their new home, a wedding present from Nico, but Antonia had a good many other requirements. Already plans had been drawn up for a swimming pool, pool house, informal entertainment area, and there was to be a tennis court so Eliot could get in a little necessary exercise at the weekend.

Evidently Eliot had fallen on good times. Married life agreed with him too, Samantha thought. Apart from the fact that he was an expectant father, perhaps to cope with the responsibility, he had put on some weight. It somewhat reduced his boyish look and indisputably gave him a more serious, settled look.

'It's so exciting isn't it, planning one's home?' Antonia looked across suddenly at Samantha, urging her into an answer.

'It's about time I came over.'

'I know.' Antonia gave an uncertain little laugh and blushed. *Antonia*, the alarmingly self-assured! 'Now that you are so much better we are thinking of having a party. I suppose we owe it to everyone. We have so many friends!'

Eliot gave a fond chuckle. 'What a girl for energy! There's never a pause for breath!'

When Maria appeared, beaming, to announce dinner, Eliot came over to help his wife tenderly to her feet and Antonia looked up at him as though he was the most thoughtful, considerate, most desirable man on earth. It gave Samantha the most peculiar feeling that the ritual of married life had escaped her for ever. These days, Nico never touched her if he could help it.

Dinner was superb; Italian style with the concession of Australian wine; one of the delicious pasta dishes Antonia was so fond of, a *tagliatelle alla crema*, followed by *vitello tonnato* and a *zabaglione* to finish.

'Gosh, she really is a marvel!' Eliot ate up enthusiastically. 'But then so's my girl!'

Antonia smiled, even quite modestly, all thoughts of starving herself forever gone. 'You're not hungry, Samantha?' She looked at Samantha's plate.

'Well, no, not actually. . . .' She had been praying no one would notice.

'You must eat, nevertheless.' Nico cast her a brief, daunting glance.

I don't *want* to! she wanted to shriek like a child, but when it came to her health, he was quite capable of spoonfeeding her. She feared him—yes, she did. Obediently she picked up her knife and fork and only then did he return to his own meal.

A certain amount of business was discussed (Eliot was getting himself very nicely off the ground), a little gossip, and Nico, who had a real flair for the amusing anecdote, told a few. All in all, it was quite a pleasant, undemanding evening until Nico put his arm around her when they were standing beside Eliot's car.

She couldn't help it, she went rigid, and though she felt the answering tension in him, he did not remove his arm until their guests were driving away. Then he did so, very pointedly.

'Forgive me, my lady!' he said acidly.

'I'm sorry.'

'So long as you're *sorry*!' Again the brilliant sarcasm.

'I'm tired. I'm going to bed.'

He shrugged elaborately. 'Sleep tranquilly through the night.'

She should have been relieved, except that her eyes filled with tears. They starred the sparkling green and clung to the length of her lashes.

'*Samantha*.'

'No!' She fought free oof his detaining hand. Whatever he was seeking, she couldn't give it. She broke into a run, but before she even reached the pillared house he caught her and held her implacably against further flight.

'Will you at least behave like an adult!'

'So you're tired of your childish wife.'

'But how can you be a *wife*, when you're frantic every second to defend your honour?' he pointed out ironically.

'I can't help it, Nico.' She suddenly put her two hands to her head in protection. 'I can't help it.'

'I don't suppose you can,' he admitted, his voice sombre. 'But think of this. I am treating you as gently as I know how. All I desire is your wellbeing, but you must not even think of recoiling from me in public. For this, I have paid dearly.'

'You want Malabar back?' she returned with some bitterness.

'I am not talking about property.' There was a flash in his black eyes. 'By the same token, you must do something about it. A house like that cannot stand empty.'

'Perhaps I'll give it back to Mother. That's if she ever comes back.'

'Who would have ever thought my enchanting Samantha could have grown so bitter?' Nico sighed deeply and looked over her head. 'It occurred to me that you might like to turn the house into some memorial to your father, a home of some kind. It is very large.'

She gazed up at him with a look of strain. 'But then it wouldn't be mine.'

'You *have* a home,' he said deliberately, 'though you have shown no interest in it in any way.'

'But I'm not well.'

'I have spoken to your doctor.' He put his hand under her chin and held her fretful head. 'You must help yourself now, Samantha.'

She moved her head as though his hand burned her, the scent of jasmine all around them. 'I'm fine as I am.'

'No.' His voice was hard. 'You're full of deep resentments and frustrations. You think you are locked into a loveless marriage, but you are wrong.'

At the very sound of the word love, she got her haunted look. 'Please let me go.'

'Perhaps for a little while. At best, a week. You see Matthews tomorrow. I'm sure he'll confirm what he has already told me. You are quite well enough to be a wife to me in full measure.'

Samantha expected to have her nightmare, but she

didn't. Instead she had an unbelievable dream about Nico and herself, so real that when she awoke she was even shocked at the experience, the way her body, even yet, was in a state of arousal.

In a jittery, bemused state she went down to breakfast, relieved beyond words that Nico had left early. Always a demon for work, he seemed to be under extreme pressure. Maria fusssed over her and hovered anxiously while she made her way through pineapple juice, a puffy bacon omelette and just because Samantha had become very fond of her a brioche Maria had just turned out of the oven. At least she wanted the coffee and Maria made very good coffee indeed.

By ten o'clock she was dressed to go into town for her appointment with Doctor Matthews, a routine check, but one that was looming very largely. How dared Nico discuss her behind her back!

She wasn't kept waiting but ushered in immediately, her heart smiting her as it always did when she came near her father's old rooms. These days there was a partnership going that allowed both doctors more undisturbed hours, and Samantha reflected how her father had always been at the town's beck and call.

Pull yourself together! she told herself angrily. You can't cry here.

Bill Matthews was waiting for her just inside the door. In his early thirties, he was still a bachelor, and Samantha remembered Antonia joking about how eligible he had become. Thinking this, she really looked at him, perhaps for the first time. He had a nice face, not good-looking but full of character. He wasn't very tall and his colouring was sandy, but his skin was golden-brown from the sun.

'Well?' he smiled at her with a little tinge of irony, aware that she had never really seen him except as her father's successor.

'I've run out of tablets.' She felt a little flurried by his blue regard.

'I'll write a prescription.' He smiled again and indicated the chair. 'You look very well.'

'Perhaps I am.'

'That's an odd thing to say.' He saw her seated, then went to answer the telephone, saying quietly that he didn't wish to be interrupted.

When he sat down his brows had drawn together. 'I don't think anyone is going to be able to fill your father's shoes, Samantha. Not in this town. My patients even argue the point with me, telling me what Dr Harrington would have done.'

She shook her head a little regretfully. 'Give them time.'

'That was Mrs Pettigrew ringing the surgery. She's too scared to take the tablets I gave her. She wants the ones the *Doctor* gave her.'

'Just tell her they're the same ones but another colour.'

'Never thought of that.' He laughed gently. 'Nothing wrong with her, of course. Just old age.'

'And living alone. She once told me she used to lie awake at night wondering if someone was going to break in. You know, fears growing bigger by the moment. I think it first happened when those hooligans broke into the Adami farm. They strayed off the highway and picked poor old Joe's place.'

'That must have been before my time.' He pulled out her card and read up on his notes. 'How are the headaches?'

'None.'

'Still having those nightmares?'

'The occasional one.' She didn't want to dramatise anything.

'Your husband has rung,' he said.

'Oh?' Her green eyes went past him to the window. New curtains. She didn't like them.

It was impossible not to notice the change in her face. 'He's very concerned about you, Samantha.'

She coloured slightly. 'I know. I suppose by the time he was finished with you there was nothing he didn't know.'

'He has a right to know,' he said carefully. 'I don't think I've ever seen such devotion. All the time you were in hospital. . . .' He seemed at a loss for adequate enough words.

'Yes, Nico's very good.' It was intended to be a tribute, but it came out very oddly.

'What's wrong, Samantha?' Bill Matthews asked. 'I've sensed something's wrong.'

We could sit here all day and I wouldn't tell you, Samantha thought. Her knowledge of Nico she would share with no one. 'I expect it takes a long time to recover from major surgery,' was all she would say.

'Of course it does.' His eyelids lowered. 'Well, let's get on with this examination.'

There was no need to discard her dress and she didn't want to, for though a definite professional barrier was between them Samantha had become aware of the latent attraction, a kind of undercurrent she had always met before with disinterest.

She waited until after he had taken her blood pressure, then she spoke to him seriously. 'It was my husband's idea that we might turn Malabar into some kind of a home.'

His eyebrows shot up in surprise. 'Really?' he looked at her speculatively. 'What kind of a home?'

'I don't know. It was just an idea. A memorial to my father.'

'Your husband is a very generous man. They're still staggered over at the hospital by his donation.'

'Oh?' She turned on him a look of surprise.

'Didn't you know?' He sat back against the desk.

'I'd like to know now.'

He paused, considering how much to say. 'I believe he gave them fifty thousand dollars. A little token of appreciation for the way they looked after you. Needless to say, they were thrilled. That amount of money can do a lot of good.

Somehow it wasn't even surprising. Samantha knew already that Nico was extremely generous. 'He didn't tell me, but then he never told me either how he sent Aldo Dorelli back to Italy.'

'Ah, yes, the dying mother. He could never have made it on his own.' He took a wide turn around to the front of his desk. 'I can't imagine Malabar as anything else but a private residence.'

'Neither could I before I lost it.' She realised

what she had said and changed tack. 'It's very large, you know, and there's any amount of room for extensions. You mentioned Mrs Pettigrew. I could name a dozen more, old people who still have their health but no family or interests. All of them have a garden. All of them have their own little plots. What about a retirement home? The sort of place they could have company and keep active.'

'*Malabar?*' His expression conveyed that he couldn't think of anywhere less unlikely.

'Why shouldn't a retirement home be beautiful? Have beautiful surroundings? Not only that, I can't leave the garden unattended. It needs loving hands.'

'You're serious, Samantha?' He examined her suddenly ardent face.

'I've only just thought of it now. There are plenty of old people in this district. Such a retirement home would suit them admirably. It wouldn't be in competition with established convalescent homes. The kind of old people I mean are just like Mrs Pettigrew—plenty of life in them yet, but sad and lonely. I've never forgotten her face when Nico offered to drive her home. She lit up like a twenty-year-old.'

'Small wonder!' he said with a cheerful ruefulness. 'I don't think I've ever seen a more striking-looking man in my life.'

Samantha didn't smile back. She looked deeply preoccupied. 'It could mean a great deal of money in conversion, I suppose.'

'Why not discuss it with Nico?' he suggested. 'Basically it was his idea, and he's the man of destiny.'

*

Samantha decided to that night, but he was working later and later in his study. Finally she slipped a peignoir over her satin nightdress and sought him out. The door was closed and she had a momentary vision of his contemptuous face when she had attempted to lock her bedroom door. Nevertheless she found the courage to knock.

'*Favorisca!*'

Come in. From the way he spoke in Italian he obviously expected either Maria or Bruno had knocked.

'May I speak to you, Nico?' She stood just inside the door.

He looked up a little startled, then his expression changed. 'It must be very urgent.'

'Yes.' His eyes were moving all over her and it made her feel weak.

He got up from his chair, not missing her little trembling gesture. 'Sit down, Samantha. You put too much strain on yourself.'

Emotionally she was coming very much to life, and she thought once again of her dream; the way he had taken her. Not with tenderness and passion, but with an overt power and sensuality.

'So, you have fallen in love with my armchair?'

'I'm sorry.' She realised then that she was moving her hand up and down over the smooth leather as though it was skin.

'I don't think you've told me yet how you got on this morning?'

'I'm sure you've already rung?' She lifted her face to him.

'I have.' He looked back at her steadily. 'I think I will take you on a long honeymoon.'

'Please, Nico, be serious!' she begged.

'One can't survive without a little humour.' His beautiful voice was ironic. 'What brings you to my door, *cara*?'

'Would you sit down?' He was so tall, so lean and wide-shouldered he made her throat tighten.

'Certainly.' He bowed. 'Where exactly?'

'Oh, there—it doesn't matter.'

'You don't usually like me so close.'

If he kept it up she'd go crazy! 'I've been thinking about what you said to me,' she said.

'About Malabar?'

Honestly, he was uncanny! 'Yes.' She dipped her shining head, starting to pleat the peach satin of her nightgown. 'Has Dr Matthews spoken to you?'

'He simply can't get past the subject of you.'

'What on earth do you m-mean?' His tone had her stammering.

'I mean you'll be changing your doctor.' He stared directly into her eyes. 'I've had enough of little situations fraught with danger.'

Her face crumpled like a hurt child's. 'I don't know what you're talking about.'

'Very probably not, but I'll deprive you of the opportunity.' His black eyes seemed to be consuming her, moving from her face to her throat to her breasts, the outline of her long slender legs. 'We had better talk of Malabar. You mentioned it to the good doctor?'

'Do you mind?'

'Please don't trouble about me. Of course not.'

Samantha shook her head numbly and bit her lip. 'You sound put out.'

'My beautiful Samantha, I'm keeping a bare toe-hold on sanity.' The humour seemed to be turning to a hard, mocking control.

She slumped down in the armchair and tucked her legs under her. 'All I want to do is tell you what I've been thinking about Malabar.'

'Then tell me,' he said quietly.

'Oh, Nico,' she put out a hand to him instinctively, 'do you think we could turn it into a kind of retirement home? I remember my father—' a rush of tears '—used to worry about all the old people he treated who had no one. I thought it could be a home for people like Mrs Pettigrew and Mr Fenton and even dear old George, old people who are still active and want something to *care* about.'

'I'm listening.' He had her hand.

'The garden needs people who love it. Even if they couldn't work in it, they could sit there and enjoy it.'

'Have you considered the considerable amount of conversion that would have to be done? Extensions, etc.?'

'It would be awfully nice if *you* would.' Her face wasn't tense at all, but warm and eager.

'The Luke Harrington Home for the Aged, is that it?'

Her eyes sparkled with tears.

'All right,' Nico said gently, 'it's done.'

Samantha was not aware that she had slipped out

of the armchair towards him. She had no fear now, only gratitude.

'Thank you, Nico.' Some more exotic accent was creeping into her own voice, part of her earlier dogged determination to master Italian, part an echo of his own.

'When do you start being a wife to me?' He put his hands to her waist, drawing her, unresisting almost down on the armchair.

'*Nico!*' She was staring at him as though hypnotised, but with the old familiar protest at the back of her eyes.

'*Answer me*, Samantha.' He swooped and lifted her across his knees.

'I need more time, Nico. Is it too much to ask?'

'Is it too much to ask you to kiss me?'

I daren't risk it, she thought wretchedly, averting her eyes from his dark face. Because she loved him and because of what he had done to her. Her mind was a turmoil and torn with doubts. At best he was only playing a part, for never, never, never had she captured his heart.

'Don't look so desperate,' he said in such a voice it made her turn her head.

Oh God, why couldn't she just kiss him and get it over?

Her whole being was suddenly flooded with resolution. Most of all because of what he was doing in her father's name. *No!* She lifted a hand to the back of his head, her fingers sinking into his thick hair and with the look of a tragic child offered him her mouth.

'Kiss me,' he said harshly.

She wavered for a moment, but her every instinct told her not to recoil. With her lips closed she set her mouth against his, but as soon as she did so, sensation spread through her body like wildfire. Her closed mouth couldn't contain it, so without her own volition and with no thought of humouring him, her lips parted and sought a response from his own.

It was like a fever and it had never truly died.

Nico's arms, that had been almost rigid on the sides of the chair, closed around her and he twisted her head back into the curve of his shoulder, the dominant partner, kissing her with an elemental hunger and an underlying need to punish. There was nothing of tenderness in that kiss and he kissed her again and again until she was shaking in his arms, the taut nipples of her breasts outlined against the thin satin.

'Tell me you love me.' His hand gripped her bare shoulder, the thumb exploring the bone.

She couldn't breathe a word and he bent his raven head and kissed the hollow in her throat where a tiny nerve was pulsating. 'Sleep with me tonight. I'll ask nothing else of you but to *be* with me.'

'Nico, I can't!' The words ended in a gasp as his hand slid down to catch her breast.

'You can and you will!' With the light behind him his arrogant head was thrown into high relief. 'I only want to hold you in case you have one of your nightmares.'

Her flesh seemed to be burning, torn between repudiation and yielding. There was no question that he desired her because he desired a son, but by now Samantha knew how to protect herself. He wouldn't have his first-born son so easily.

As he held her flushed and trembling body, Maria did knock at the door, calling permission to come in.

'Let me up, Nico, for God's sake,' Samantha groaned.

'So shocking to be found on your husband's knee.' He eyed her appreciatively, flushed skin and glittering eyes, then set her gently on her feet.

Maria came in, her face a study when she saw Samantha.

'*Scusi, scusi,*' she said hurriedly, obviously flustered.

Nico nodded, looking at her goodhumouredly. 'You really ought to put that tray down.'

'But I have nothing for the Signora.' Maria continued on her way to the desk.

'That's all right, Maria,' Samantha spoke with her natural sweetness. 'I'm just going off to bed.'

'Put out my pyjamas, darling,' said Nico.

She knew damned well he didn't even wear pyjamas and the amount of embarrassment she felt was absurd. Of course Maria knew they occupied their own self-contained suite, but as they had an interconnecting door either could walk in or walk out as they liked. Stay for that matter. It would seem incredible to Maria that either could do without the much-needed lovemaking. More—a kind of sin.

Samantha felt unreasonably rattled as though she wanted it both ways at once. She had the light out in her own room, feigning sleep, when Nico appeared at the connecting door. She lay as quietly as she could, despite herself feeling a great lurch of excitement. But his voice when he spoke sounded very ordinary, matter-of-fact.

'Be a good girl and move over. I like the right-hand side of the bed.'

Further thought of feigning sleep was impossible. 'You know as well as I do that you can't come in here.' She switched on her bedside lamp staring up at him.

'Then come into my room,' he said quite amiably. 'If you have visions of being raped, I've been extremely busy these past few days. Now don't keep me waiting while you graciously make up your mind. My room or yours?'

'Just you put something on,' she said, not taken in by the mockery and the casual, elegant stance.

'I think I might manage something quite chic.'

Samantha didn't mean to, but she laughed. It just came out.

'Well?' he shrugged.

'This is terrible!'

'How did we ever happen to get into it?' He smiled at her kindly.

'It was all your idea.'

'So it was.' A flicker of some violent emotion crossed his face. 'Now that we've settled on which bed it's to be, you can go back to sleep.' Lazily he began to unbutton his shirt, wandering for the time being back into his own room.

Sleep came hard to Samantha, but Nico seemed to fall off immediately, his lean powerful back to her. From somewhere he had found a pair of navy silk pyjama trousers, but even for her he wasn't going to overheat himself with the jacket.

She lay on her back for a long time, startlingly rigid, half of her watching the patterns of bright moonlight across the ceiling and floor of her beautiful room, the other half fiercely ready to discourage the slightest advance.

None was forthcoming and it seemed an immense anti-climax. She couldn't bear to look at Nico's outline, inhale his clean, male fragrance, so she turned on her side, presenting to him her own narrow back. She wasn't at all happy to have him there at all, but at least she didn't have to cope with the stunning violence of his lovemaking. Those kisses in the study had her quivering and raw.

Gradually she drifted into a light sleep that deepened towards the early hours of the morning. The moon no longer shone into the room, and it was then her nightmare came upon her. The Contessa was in it, her expression inhuman; Nico, standing tautly, leaning towards her. Samantha knew almost exactly where that third person would be—a ghost, Marisa. She knew them all. She could not endure it and the suffering after. . . .

Her contortions jerked him into consciousness even before she cried out his name.

'No, Nico . . . *no!*'

She started up screaming, the tears pouring down her face, but as he tried to pull her into his arms in her fright and confused state she fought him, raining blows on his chest, as though she imagined herself to be in the grip of a demon.

'Samantha, my heart!' It was necessary to physically overcome her, so he bent her fragile body back on to the bed, looming above her only momentarily until he had the time to switch on the bedside light.

'Oh God!' She was shuddering and fully awake.

'My darling, what *is* it?'

'I can't bear it,' she whispered, still in the vice-like grip of her dream. Teardrops spangled her heavy lashes and she still looked afraid.

Nico too drew a long tortured breath. 'Can't you tell me?'

'She hated me. She tried to kill me.'

'*No!*' He reached down and held her shoulders. 'If you could have seen her afterwards—she suffered terribly. *I* was the one she wanted to destroy. It's all part of the past. Things, even now, I can't speak of. Rena has always loved me, but not in a way that could do either of us any good.'

'She looks so terrible in my dream!' She turned her head along the pillow and gave an involuntary shudder. 'Murderous.'

He put out his hand and brushed her silky fringe off her face. 'My poor baby!'

There was so much tenderness in his voice, she couldn't bear it. Endearments came easily to Nico, she remembered them from her time in the hospital.

'Who else is in your dream?' He sought to quiet her.

'*You.*' The light exaggerated the striking planes

and angles of his face and the skin of his body was dark gold. She touched a hand to the valley between her breasts, trying to calm her agitated heart. 'It's always the same. You, me, the Contessa and one other.'

'Tell me.' His black eyes looked into hers, brilliant in the golden light.

'You know.'

He looked at her searchingly, seeing how terribly her dream had affected her. Her fringe and the silver-gilt hair at her temples was damp and her great green eyes were shadowed with fright. 'Surely you don't dream of my wife?'

'Must you say that?' Her heart was so bruised she thought she couldn't stand it. It was all there in a word—Marisa, my *wife*.

'Couldn't you have told me this before?' he said quietly.

'No.' Samantha turned her head right away so all he could see was the lovely line of her cheek and her throat. 'I know you worshipped her. Why would I remind you?'

'You do not know,' he said harshly.

'And I don't *want* to!' She wanted to scream at him. Have him hold her. *Hold* her. So passionate was her desire, she threw the top sheet back, desperate to run, to hide it all away. Her love for Nico had always been doomed.

She expected him to let her get away, but he seemed equally frantic. He caught her by the shoulders and pulled her back across his knees, his eyes devouring every curve of her body, visible beneath

the palest peach sheen. He had given her everything; tenderness, loyalty, caring, but she had never
yet seen the expression on his face. He looked every
inch a conqueror, his black eyes on fire.

'You will stay here!' he said strongly, watching
the rise and fall of her partly revealed breasts. 'I am
not a demon you have to flee. I won't take you
against your will.'

'*No!*' she said oddly, and started to laugh.

'*Samantha!*' He added something in Italian as
though she was driving him beyond control.

'I thought you wanted a son,' she taunted him
from the depths of her own misery.

'You know very well what I want.' And now it
was too late for both of them. His handsome face
flushed with anger and passion and he turned her on
her back. 'I told you once before to be careful what
you say to me.'

'Yes, lord and master.' She was doing it deliberately, reckless because she was desperate for what
she could not say.

Nico swore beneath his breath and lowered his
head, and if he expected resistance he found none.

Her mouth, her whole body came up to meet
him, softly supple against the lean hardness.

'You're beautiful. God, so beautiful!' The hands
that held her face were trembling. 'I must have you,
Samantha, or I will lose my mind.'

CHAPTER NINE

SAMANTHA heard the door open, but she didn't open her eyes for a few seconds.

'Ah, you're awake!' In Maria's voice there was a curious, heartfelt relief. She was standing half in and half out of the bedroom, her broad cheerful face for once serious.

'What time is it, Maria?' Samantha couldn't sit up because she was naked.

'Past ten o'clock,' Maria explained. 'I said to Bruno, the young Signora is not awake. We were anxious.'

'I'm not surprised!' A smile shaped Samantha's mouth. 'Just a sleep-in, Maria. I'll be out on the terrace in ten minutes.'

'I'll do you an omelette.' Maria quickly took herself to the door. 'You like that. By the way, Signor Martinelli is flying to Sydney today. He told me to tell you he'll be returning on the afternoon plane. Bruno can check the time.'

'Bruno needn't go to meet him,' Samantha called. 'I'll go.'

Maria did the only thing she could do. She smiled. Who could resist a radiant bride!

Because she was feeling so utterly starry-eyed and happy, Samantha rang her friend Gillian and arranged to meet her for lunch in town. She arrived early to give herself an hour or so to shop, then she took herself to the delightful little Italian restaurant beside the river that Gillian had suggested.

'Gosh, you look gorgeous!' exclaimed Gillian, the moment she laid eyes on her friend.

'I know. I know.' Samantha accepted the compliment eagerly, showing Gillian her sparkling face. 'What shall we have? I'm starving!'

'Boy, what I'd give to be in your place!' Gillian grinned meaningfully, and slid into the banquette.

They had a wonderfully relaxing, leisurely lunch—Gillian worked for her father and didn't have to hurry back—and afterwards made plans to see one another at the weekend. Samantha's happiness was infectious and Gillian passed the comment that she had always heard Italians were good lovers.

Not good, Samantha thought. *Superb.* All she could think of was having just such a fantastic experience again tonight. Nico still clung to her, his exquisite lovemaking that made her cheeks flush and her heart pound just to think of it. His body joined to hers. God, she was happy! He couldn't possibly make love to her like that if he didn't love her; the sweet violence, and afterwards to be wrapped in his arms so tenderly. Ecstasy and peace. She couldn't wait for him to come home.

She was moving blissfully towards her car when she saw Antonia come out from the main arcade.

Of course I've got to speak to her, Samantha thought, but she was loath to for fear of the things Antonia might reveal. She *had* to believe Nico loved her. She had accepted it last night and this morning. But still she feared Antonia's dark streak.

Allowing herself no more time to dither, she moved forward, calling Antonia's name.

'Samantha!' Antonia's dazzling smile appeared, and grateful to find her at least friendly, Samantha moved to the younger girl's side.

'Shopping?'

'Some shirts for Eliot. He has terrible taste.'

'Well. . . .' Samantha had to concede it and laughed. 'No one could say the same of you.'

'The fact is, I feel sick.'

'Oh.' It suddenly struck Samantha now that she wasn't smiling, Antonia did look a bit peaked. 'Let's find some place to sit down. Are you going home?'

'I don't think I can drive.'

'Then I think we should pop in and see Dr Melville. He'll give you something to make you feel better.'

'But I saw him the other day,' Antonia said almost apologetically.

'It doesn't matter. What else is a doctor for? If you don't feel well, you must see him. Here,' Samantha held out her hand, 'give me those parcels. I'll run you there in my car.'

Soon after Antonia was ushered into the doctor's rooms, and Samantha sat in the waiting room leafing absently through an ancient magazine. When she had helped Antonia out of the car, the younger girl had clung to her hand like a sick child and Samantha began to worry about the possibility of a miscarriage. One never knew, she had seen the strongest-looking women miscarry, and Antonia for all her abundant energy had obviously not considered the dangers of overdoing it.

Antonia was inside so long, Samantha rose and went to look out of the window. The most beautiful coral tree bloomed alongside, with jewelled lorikeets dipping their heads into the sweet nectar of the blossoms. She and Antonia had never had the slightest empathy, but she was concerned for the girl now. Antonia, sick and trembling and clinging to her hand, was a different person from the cruel little creature she had seemed.

When she turned around, the Sister was looking for her.

'Oh, there you are, Samantha?'

'For Pete's sake, how *is* she?' Samantha had known Molly McAllister all her life.

'All right. She'd been rushing around town all morning and with her blood pressure up she started to feel vague. Doctor has had her rest and he's given her something soothing to drink down. And how are *you*?' Molly's blue eyes were shrewd. 'You look blooming. As far as that goes, sensational. Not in the family way?'

'No, Molly.' Samantha had to smile. 'I think I'll watch other people for a while.'

'That's what they all say!' Molly gave her characteristic guffaw. 'Of course she'll need you to take her home.'

'The car's right outside the door.'

'Good girl.' Molly nodded her curly grey head approvingly. 'You always were super-efficient.'

Not so efficient at handling my own life, Samantha thought wryly. When Antonia came out the door with Dr Melville, Samantha went to her and linked Antonia's arm through her own.

'Rest, is that it?' she asked Dr Melville.

'Indeed it is.' The doctor eyed Antonia with great firmness. 'It doesn't do ever to rush about in the heat, but when one is pregnant——!'

'I won't do it again,' Antonia promised prettily. 'It is asking a lot of you, Samantha, but. . . .'

'Of course I'm taking you home.' Samantha didn't even hesitate. 'Eliot can get someone to collect your car.'

'Oh, thank you.' Rarely had Antonia seemed so ordinary and nice.

Because the sun smote full on the windscreen, Samantha put her gently in the back and as soon as they were underway, turned on the air-conditioning.

'How do you feel now?'

'A little better.' Antonia put her hand to her head, thankful the dizziness had passed. 'I can't understand it, I'm usually so well.'

'It's only early days of your pregnancy,' said Samantha. 'Rushing around will naturally upset you.'

'I was only walking.'

'Fast!'

Antonia took it in good part. 'I wanted to take you on a tour of the house, now I feel I have to lie down.'

'The feeling will pass,' Samantha said soothingly. 'Just put your head back and relax. I'll have you home in no time.'

The house was really something, and Samantha reflected that Eliot could never have aspired to it on his salary. However, Eliot seemed to have no misplaced feelings about accepting a helping hand, so it was all working out rather well.

With Samantha's hand at Antonia's back they walked up the broad flight of stairs and Antonia bade her hunt up the key from a planter of rampant philodendrons. A few minutes more and they were up another flight of stairs to the master bedroom. It was a little dramatic for Samantha's tastes, but the view over the lush hinterland was superb.

'Why don't you get into a robe?' Samantha suggested.

'In the wardrobe.' Antonia gestured and sank gratefully on to the bed. Outside the air glittered, shimmering with heat. No doubt they would have a late-afternoon thunderstorm.

In the end, because Antonia seemed so depleted, Samantha had to help her off and on with her clothes. She seemed, for the first time, very young, and her inability to cope softened Samantha's always tender heart.

'Now what can I get you?' she asked, when Antonia was lying back.

'A cup of tea?' Antonia looked up at her with huge dark eyes. 'I have never liked it before, but these days it's sheer pleasure.'

'Right!' Samantha patted her shoulder. 'We'll have a cup together.'

When Samantha returned in under five minutes, Antonia had dropped off to sleep, and looking down 'at her Samantha thought how truly beautiful she looked. She could never get used to Antonia's beauty. Or Nico's. They were like people a novelist might dream up.

She waited for more than an hour before Antonia stirred and then Antonia had to call her name.

'And what about that cup of tea?' Samantha said teasingly, coming in from the balcony.

'Isn't that funny? I went out like a baby.'

Samantha smiled sympathetically. 'Your colour is much better. Take it slowly, when you sit up.'

Antonia gave her a nervous glance, then smiled when she found her distressing symptoms had passed. 'I thought I was so clever!'

'I can assure you, you are!' While Antonia had been asleep, Samantha had strolled around the house. 'This is a very sophisticated house for a young woman not yet twenty.'

'I am my father's daughter!' Antonia pointed out merrily, then shockingly started to cry.

'Now then!' Samantha was only momentarily flustered from the see-saw. She jumped up and sat down beside Antonia on the bed. 'Surely you're not going to upset yourself crying? Don't, Tonia. *Please* don't.'

'I can't think why you're so good to me.'

'And why not, aren't we family?'

'*Family?*' Antonia repeated, and for a moment said nothing. 'Never will my child know my kind of family life.'

Samantha stared at her, aghast. 'Of course it was a terrible blow to lose your mother.'

'It was.' Antonia got the better of her tears. 'I

can't pretend it didn't hurt me dreadfully, but my mother scarcely knew I existed. She was too busy being the perfect jet-setter to be a mother and a wife. Her whole life was parties and having people stay with us that I used to hate. Nico hated them too—mostly, I think, for my sake. You mightn't think it now, but I wasn't really pretty until I was quite old, about fourteen. My mother thought me very ordinary.'

'Obviously quite erroneously.' Samantha felt stunned.

'Nico used to tell me I was the most beautiful little girl in the world, but Mamma would never agree. I always had Elvira to look after me, my nurse. Nico was so busy keeping everyone rich—the family businesses, you understand. Yet he did everything he could to be a father to me. Nico is perfection.'

'Yes, he is.' Samantha's thoughts were in turmoil.

'Of course they should never have been married in the first place,' Antonia said starkly. 'It was only that they were thrown together in a time of tragedy. Our family home was destroyed in a great flood. My grandfather suffered a massive heart attack and died. Nico saved my mother's life and I suppose out of a tenderness, a need for mutual comforting, I was born.'

'But I thought your parents loved one another deeply?'

'Did you?' Antonia smiled bitterly. 'I liked to think they did, but it was not so. I used to see Nico try to pretend. But I was a woman, even then. I think they never really had anything but me.'

'Oh, Antonia, I'm sorry.' Samantha put her hand on the younger girl's shoulder.

'I've been wanting for a long time to confide in you utterly. I knew at the beginning Nico had found a woman he could love, but I was oh, so *jealous*—a legacy from my mother. She made Nico's life hell with her jealousies. He only had to look at a woman and she thought he was unfaithful. She never saw that his thoughts weren't on women! My grandmother used to say, Mamma never knew Nico at all.' Antonia put her face in her hands, moaning a little hoarsely. 'Of course it was I who sent for Rena, and I implore you to forgive me.'

'Antonia dear, I'm going to get you some tea,' Samantha said hastily, to forestall a flood of tears.

'No, don't go away.' Antonia looked at her with tormented eyes. 'I know what she did to you.'

'It was an accident.'

'No, I know Rena, better than anyone. I thought she was the natural one to drive you and my father apart. After all, she has loved him all her life.'

Samantha could not answer.

'I'll be left with these terrible regrets all my life.' Antonia's beautiful olive skin was almost transparent.

'Whatever you intended, you never meant anything destructive,' Samantha said gently.

'No.' Antonia shook her head sadly. 'I am really very tired.'

'Suppose I ring Eliot?' Samantha suggested.

Antonia nodded, her voice just above a whisper. 'He must never know what I have done.'

'You've got to stop that, Antonia,' Samantha said

in a firm voice. 'You did nothing. Neither were you responsible for your Aunt Rena. She didn't really intend anything destructive either. She simply has a shocking temper.'

Antonia put up a hand as if to fend off any more excuses either for herself or her aunt. 'I would dearly love to be good like you,' she said.

'Then just listen to me this once. We'll make this day a fresh beginning for us all. I love your father and I'm ready to love you as well.' Samantha's face was as serious as Antonia's own.

'Then tell me you forgive me.' Antonia turned to her with pleading dark eyes. 'Tell me you forgive me for all that physical suffering. If we had lost you, it would have broken my father completely. I have always loved him so terribly, yet I sought to deprive him of the one woman he could love. What kind of a daughter am I?'

'Please, Antonia,' Samantha took her trembling hand. 'You're very young after all. You told me yourself your childhood was unhappy, but now you are free to be the kind of woman you want to be. Have a little compassion for yourself. More, think of your baby. You really can't give way to anguish. I won't *let* you.'

'I've never met anyone like you!' Antonia said and flung herself into Samantha's arms.

By the time she had Antonia settled and waited for Eliot to get home, Samantha had just on fifteen minutes to get to the airport and the weather that had looked ominous since mid-afternoon promised a severe storm.

The wind was stronger now and as she took one hand off the wheel to switch on the radio, the car nosed to the right-hand side of the road and she had to put two hands back on the wheel to brace the car along its path.

Damn! As when any storm threatened to strike the traffic was heavier than usual and with the wind buffeting the cars from one side progress was cut back to well under the speed limit. She was going to be late.

The voice on the radio was confirming a severe storm warning, with high winds and hail. People were also being advised to get their cars under cover.

Not at this rate! Samantha made a Herculean effort to get her agitation under control. The car ahead of her had braked abruptly to pick up a hitch-hiker thumbing a lift from the side of the road and if she had not been on the alert she would have run in under its trunk.

The sky was lit now by a peculiar incandescent light, the kind of light she had seen many times before. It meant anything from minor damage to wholesale destruction. She began to pray. Somewhere in that illuminated sky, filled now with screeching birds, an incoming plane was flying. She looked up and with a sudden dryness in her mouth saw an outline through the clouds. A Lear jet. Not Nico's flight.

The radio was still giving concise details about the expected path of the storm. It's on us now, she thought with a mounting degree of apprehension. If the hail came down and she was caught in it, the car could be pitted with holes. Not that she cared about the car; it was Nico's safe return to the ground. The banked-up clouds had taken on the shape of a crouching monster, so realistic that people were looking out the windows of their cars. The car ahead, clearly on a sightseeing tour, had slowed right down, so she gave it a blast that put it farther to the left-hand side of the road and went past it.

By the time she reached the airport, the sun had gone out and great jagged spears of lightning forked through the pearly-black monster. There was little or no cover, and as she looked about her anxiously, a man in a grey uniform waved her into a hangar.

'Gunna be a bad one, miss!'

Samantha could scarcely hear him over the crack of thunder.

'My husband's coming in on the four-thirty flight.'

'Don't worry, love, they'll hold off.' The man smiled at her kindly and nodded up at the sky. 'Looks real weird, don't it?'

'What do *you* make of it?' Samantha was talking to calm herself.

'A crouching lion. No, hold it, that big black steel cat.'

'Thanks for the cover.' Samantha tried to stop worrying and gave him a smile.

'Don't mention it,' he returned breezily. ' wouldn't like to see a smart little car like that peppered with holes.'

Before she reached the terminal building the first giant spatters of rain hit the steaming ground. Then as though they were the heralds, the heavens opened up and she had to fight to hold open the door.

'Here, let me help you.' A curly-headed young man came to her rescue, in the process getting himself wet from the driving rain.

Inside, people were standing around looking anxious, their ears buffeted by the incredible racket on the corrugated iron roof. A young woman held a screaming baby to her breast, cradling its downy little head, and Samantha went to her automatically, producing her car keys with the crystal bauble that the baby promptly stared at, then began to play with.

'Oh, thank you!' The young mother, not used to the tropics, seemed almost speechless with terror, and Samantha sat down beside her, trying to be supportive in the face of her own anxieties. Through the huge floor-to-ceiling windows they could see the incredible bulk of the clouds flashed through with a thousand tints, the great arrows of lightning aimed towards the sea.

'It's frightening, isn't it?' the young woman cried.

'So far, no hail.' Samantha almost blessed herself that hail was so lethal.

Over by the window a group of flower people were in an ecstasy. One of them had dreamed of painting a tropical storm; now it was actually here.

'Anvil cumulus, aren't they?' one with floating hair asked another, of the clouds. It was clear, despite the caterwauling on the roof, that the storm's magnificence was limitless in its appeal.

Samantha too might have found it thrilling, only the loudspeaker had informed them Flight 402 was circling the airport waiting clearance to land. She couldn't even concentrate diligently with her pray-

ers, for the baby, bored with the car keys, had
started bawling again, so she had to produce her
compact which the baby shut and handed back to
her repeatedly to open again.

'You're so good!' the mother said approvingly,
too harassed herself to make the slightest attempt to
distract her child. 'It's all been lovely up until now!'

Samantha nodded and made sounds of sympathy.
Melbourne was a beautiful city, but she wouldn't
care to freeze in the wintertime.

By the time the storm abated, she was feeling more
than a little hysterical, thanking God as she caught
sight of herself in a mirror that she didn't show it.

'Baby seems to have bitten your compact,' the
young mother apologised, handing back the expensive, slightly damaged item.

'That's all right!' Samantha shrugged it off. It was
easy to bite into things when one was terrified.

After forty minutes' delay Flight 402 homed in to
its destination and the passengers disembarked, one
middle-aged lady, only recently persuaded to take
her first flight, weeping incoherently with a young
air hostess consoling her. The storm, apparently,
had flown with them up Capricornia.

Now that the sky was clearing with its usual
amazing rapidity the young mother organised herself efficiently and bade Samantha quite an affectionate farewell. The baby, too, pushed forward its
belligerent little face for a kiss and Samantha bent
her head to brush its temple.

'Let's hope we have a good trip home!' the young
mother said tremulously.

'I know you will.'

No sign of Nico yet. She felt weak at the knees. 'Are they all off?' She glanced at an attendant.

'I think so, miss.'

They both turned to look at the plane and as they did so, a small group came to the door. A woman with two small children, an air hostess, and Nico.

'Oh, good, there's my husband!'

Such a wealth of love and relief was in her voice, the airport attendant grinned at her.

'I guess they'll let you run across the tarmac.'

'Oh, *would* you?' She felt such a prisoner behind the wire fence.

There was Nico helping the children off, and love seemed an inadequate word for what she felt for him. He was her life, her fulfilment, her peace. He was everything she valued.

He loved her.

For the first time Antonia had spoken to her, totally without pretence. Nico loved her and he needed her to restore his own life. It was like waking up to a positive new world. The storm had even washed the world shinier, cleaner, breaking out its rainbow.

A new beginning!

Samantha ran to him with pure, undiluted joy and as he suddenly looked up and saw her, he handed the children gently to their mother and opened up his arms.

'Next time, *next* time,' she said urgently, when she was smothered up against him, 'you'll do the journey by car.'

'Next time,' he said exultantly, 'we'll do the trip together.'

A BOTTICELLI BEAUTY

She's a vision of graceful modesty, a lovely young woman with an air of serenity, a "Botticelli beauty." If you've heard this last phrase and have never studied art history, you may wonder just what it means to be a Botticelli beauty....

The late 1400s in Italy saw a great flowering of art, literature and science that became known as the Renaissance (French for "rebirth"). The art forms of this exciting, creative period celebrated the beauty of human life on earth, thus deviating from an earlier emphasis on matters of religion and the rewards of life after death. Botticelli, an Italian artist noted for his idealized portrayal of women, was one of those who played a part in the Renaissance. Abandoning the rigid style of past centuries, with its stiff, prescribed poses, he painted gentle, natural-looking women against backgrounds of flowers and greenery or ocean foam.

What do Botticelli women look like? They are serene maidens draped in flowing robes or posed gracefully in the nude; their features are delicate, smooth and somewhat rounded, their demeanor shy. A classic example is the *Birth of Venus,* which portrays the Greek goddess of love emerging from the waves.

To be complimented as a Botticelli beauty is an honor indeed, for while modern "looks" come and go, Botticelli women are still revered—five hundred years from the time a farseeing young artist expressed what he perceived to be the epitome of pure femininity.

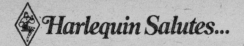

4 FREE Harlequin Romances